Critical Acclaim for Run Away to Glory

Wonderful story. Just have a handkerchief handy to wipe away the tears. I enjoyed reading it. – *Edith Ryder, Proof reader.*

"Vermont is proud to have led the way in banning slavery in 1777, but the struggle continued. This book describes the role that Quakers, free blacks, and abolitionists like William Lloyd Garrison and Frederick Douglass, played in that struggle. It brings to life the stories of Ben Robinson of Randolph, a former slave, and Alexander Twilight, the first black college graduate and legislator in the nation. You'll learn about the 'Factory Girls,' who grew up on Vermont farms and toiled in the cotton mills of Massachusetts, enduring a life, sometimes, no better than that of a slave. 'Run Away to Glory' recounts the struggle for freedom and opportunity and reflects Vermont's key role along that difficult path."

– *Jim Douglas, former Governor of Vermont, 2003-2011.*

"Run Away to Glory" is a work of art. Though fictional, you can envision the story amongst many historical facts. I was fully engaged in the story lines that involved New Bedford and Fairhaven. They touched upon some great local events. Like those involving Manjiro, the first Japanese person to be taught in the US, after being rescued by Captain Whitfield, and a fascinating portrayal of Gypsies in the north end of Fairhaven, MA, (currently called North Fairhaven.) These are just some of the factual events in our Fairhaven/New Bedford area that many do not know about. Additionally, the story brings alive some of the struggles and battles of silent heroes who gave everything, including life, to the work of the Underground Railroad. The story also provides a great insight into the court system in a time of change, the end of the Civil War, the murder of President Lincoln, and the struggles and joys of Helen's awe-inspiring journey throughout an incredible period in American history. Thank you, Elizabeth Palm and George Holt!"

– *Charles K. Murphy, Sr., Past District Governor 2010-2011 of Rotary International and current Selectman, Fairhaven, MA.*

"Run Away to Glory", though cast fictionally is a graphic reminder of the historical significance of a time in American History, that most ignore or tend to forget. It balances the effects of racial indifference and personal strife with those heroically defending the rights of human existence. Its authors have meticulously created a harrowing story of heroism and survival, a must read!"
– *G. Alan Dugard, Author, "When the Wolf Rises" and "Sawadee Buffs, The Final Chapter of the Vietnam War."*

In "Run Away to Glory," Elizabeth Palm and George Holt bring alive the heroism and heartbreak imbedded in a potent moment of American history—the Underground Railroad, as it wended its way through small New England villages. Although this story is a fictional one, its setting in very real places—notably Randolph, Vermont and nearby towns—imparts such authenticity to the tale that it informs us as much as a real history might, while adding a powerful emotional component. The telling is enhanced by the plainspoken voice of the chief narrator, a farm woman married to a devout Quaker who is caught up in the work of the Railroad. Amid the daily chores of a farm wife, Helen finds history thundering into her life in the form of unspeakable cruelties and extravagant kindnesses. As we follow her in her journey, we are deeply moved."
– *M. Dickey Drysdale was for 43 years the owner and publisher of The Herald of Randolph, Vt. His favorite writings are collected in a 2015 book, "Vermont Moments."*

Run Away to Glory

Helen's Story

Elizabeth Palm and George Holt Jr.

This book is a work of historical fiction. Although many names, characters, places and incidents are based on historical fact, others are fictitious. Any resemblance in those cases to actual events, locales or persons—living or dead, is entirely coincidental.

ISBN-13: 978-1503136175
ISBN-10: 1503136175

DEDICATION

Dedicated to Doris Hutchins (née Holt), our oldest sister. Her writing skills and suggestions have been our model to try to duplicate. She has a knack for knowing how to depict characters of the nineteenth century. Abigail was her idea, as she said, "to add some spice to the farm life."

ACKNOWLEDGEMENT

Our sister Edith Ryder (née Holt) deserves special credit for her continuous editing of the many drafts prior to publication. Also deserving credit is our sister Doris Hutchins (née Holt), George's daughter Laura Elizabeth Holt and his daughter-in-law Patty Holt. Many thanks to all for providing many useful editorial comments prior to publication.

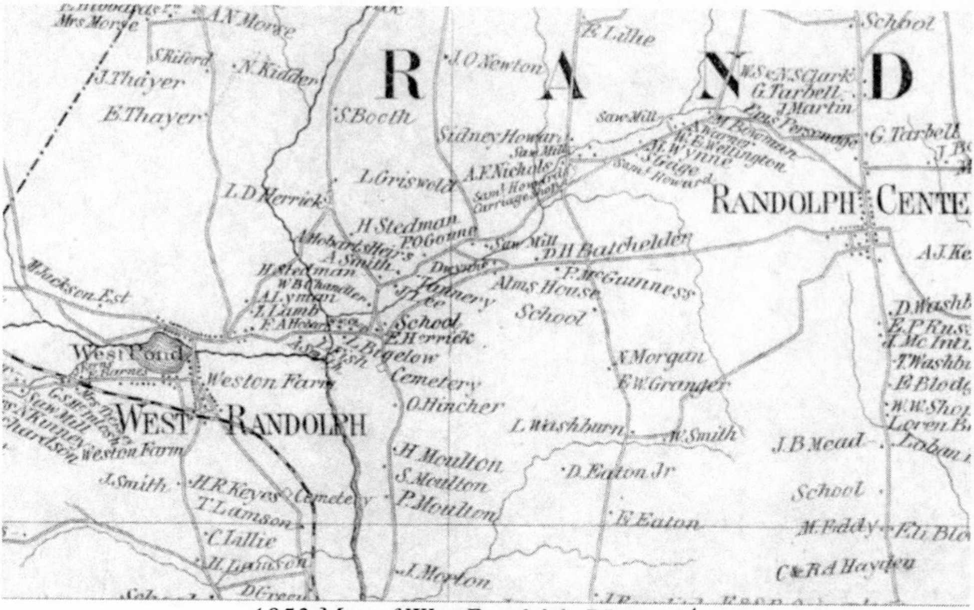

1853 Map of West Randolph, Vermont [1]

1853 Map of Quaker Hill, Braintree, Vermont [1]

Chapter One

March 9th 1851.

West Randolph, Vermont

Joshua was right, the river ice *is* melting. This could mean early spring flooding.

Now who's that fool out walking on the river . . . no . . . the ice cracks, it breaks. He turns and steps back, but too late. He slips and falls through. The current sucks him down, but his arm gets stuck in a jagged crack in the ice. His legs kick out, splashing. Where's his head? Look, it bobs up. Water gushes in his mouth. He gags and coughs as water spills out.

Who's coming? Two men dragging something. Then they stop and turn heel.

"Come back! He needs you!"

Oh, Lord! His head? It's under again. His arm is still caught in the crack. His fingers open, then shut—now open again. And all is still.

I must save him, must try. But my hand, no glove. It's cold and numb. The sky's gone dark. Thick fog drifts in. My face is wet. Here's a warm breeze. But, no sunlight? Can't see, but, try again—look through those trees—that man. His arm still holds him up. Why won't those men come back?

"No, stop pushing. Leave me be. I need to get warm. That poor man, we must go find—."

"Ma, what man? It's me. I'm scared. Why did you scream?"

"Let go my arm. Is that you, Eli? Where are those men? Why did they go?"

"Ma, no one's here. You're talkin' funny. Open your eyes. Are they stuck?"

"No, not stuck, but that man in the river is. Can't you see? And what's all that noise?"

"That banging noise? It's the wind. Something maybe got loose and flew against the door. Are you shaking, like me from the cold? The fire's out, Ma, should I get more wood?"

"No, don't. Stay here. Nothing's wrong. I'm OK. Wait—it's coming clear—."

"But, you yelled. You scared me. I jumped out of bed and Caleb woke up, too. He got scared."

"What's that about Caleb? Is he OK?"

"Yes, cuz I said, 'go back to sleep.'"

"Come here son, morning comes soon enough."

"But, I'm cold, Ma."

"Get under these blankets. We'll light the fire when we wake. Here, I'll rub your hands and arms. Is that better?"

"Yeah, but what happened to you?"

"Nothing, it was only a dream."

He's quiet now, and not trembling. And his breath, the panting, it's slowed down. His eyes close, as his head falls against my arm. Can it be five years since he was born? Time went too fast. Now our days drag on since his Pa's been gone. Let me count, has it been over a fortnight?

"Eli? Where you at? Huh? You hiding with Mama? You got my blanket? I got yours."

"Guess I woke you both. Cal, come, get in bed with me and Eli. That's a good boy. Lay your head on my arm. Close those eyes, good night and God bless."

His eyes, so wide, do not blink, not once. "Mama, you hear them funny noises? Real scary. Maybe . . . a baby wolf? Or a fox, maybe a teeny bear. You go see?"

"No, Cal, it's only the wind whistling through the trees. Settle down, close your eyes. There now, here come the sweet dreams."

I can't sleep. I remember that awful day when Joshua left for Windsor to help runaway slaves. I could not stop him.

I said, "Joshua, you must stay. There's danger out there. Those runaways could turn on you. They are different from you, like night from day."

"Different, you say? Is this really you, Helen? Tell me, are they any less human because men capture them like animals and bring them to our shores? And, how could you know? You've had no contact with them."

"I never wanted them near me. I heard stories and saw pictures. They show what is real. Their hair—it's wild looking. They would scare our boys."

"Yes, I'm afraid after hearing your nonsense, Eli and Cal would be frightened." He shakes his head, then yanks his jacket on. I turn away.

He grabs my arm and says, "Look at me. You never objected in Bethel Gilead, or even now in Randolph, when I alone dealt with them."

"That's because they stayed put in the sheds, and only for one night. Never did they step one foot in our house."

"Helen, they need our help. I hold no fear of them. So, don't worry. Now wish me well." He holds me tight, and I want to scream at him, make him listen. I press my face into his jacket—and my sobs get muffled. He cannot hear me cry.

He pulls away, picks up his two valises and steps out the door.

Sleep, must get to sleep. Wonder about that wind. It's so calm, so peaceful . . . at last.

* * *

Not again. What's shaking the door? The sun's not up yet, and that banging—what a racket. Better go see before it wakes the boys. Light the lantern. Wait, listen again. Is that a kitten, or worse, one from a feral cat? Please, not more wild ones. What's that rapping again?

"Hold on, is anyone out there?"

No answer. Go slow and unlatch. Now peek out. Someone's hunched over. A hood hides the head. It looks to be holding something.

"Who are you? And why are you here so early before dawn? What're you hiding there? Not one of those wild kittens, is it?'

"Well? Can't you answer? I don't receive visits at this hour, much less from a stranger. What is it you want?"

A small hand comes out from under the sleeve and pulls the hood back. It's a colored woman. Her face is so young, like a child.

"Ma'am, I—." Something's moving. What's this? Sticking out—no, don't let it be—not a baby. But it is. Look at that raggedy blanket. That tiny fist clutches at the worn end. It pulls the frayed edge to its mouth. Then spits it out, along with a tiny whimper. This won't do. Coloreds do not come in here—no, never before. My boys will be upset if seeing her. Why must she come here? But, this baby . . . no, the bitter cold won't do.

"Come in, or you'll catch your death of cold.'

"Sit over by the wood stove in the rocker. I'll wrap this afghan around both of you." And, must get some kindling and wood from the porch.

"Ah, that's a good fire. You're thin as a rail, you must be hungry."

"Ma'am, we don't wanna be no bother."

"I'm only heating this stew we had for dinner. And how is your baby doing?" I hope there's no crying again. The boys can't be seeing these two.

"Ma'am. See? My babe, he be under here, an keepin warm."

"That's good. I'm Helen Haskell, what's your name?"

"Daisy Corinda Carrington. Carrington is Massa's name, Daisy Corinda be my momma's name. Folks jess calls me Daisy. An my babe, he Little Tom."

"Come sit at our table. Now, tell me, who sent you?"

"Missus Huckins send me." She must mean Mrs. Hutchins, across the way on Quaker Hill.

"I declare. Without an escort? You're a runaway, aren't you?"

"Yes Ma'am. Missus Huckins, she say, come back tomorrow."

"Fine, now you must eat. This has mutton, potatoes and carrots. Here's three scoops and rolls with sweet butter. Take this spoon."

She dips a roll and sops up the broth, then downs one spoonful after the other. I ladle out two more scoops and it's done with in no time at all.

"Ma'am, I sure glad y'all lets us in. We been runnin, an so cold an hungry."

"You got to the Hutchins' house, all on your own?"

"No. We gets help. An we lucky alla dogs dint smell us. I's prayin t' Lord, an alla sudden, helpin hand come along. Farmer say, 'Go sleep inna barn.' In mornin' we gon' t' go, he say, 'afore law come by.'"

"He must have been on the Underground Railroad helping list?"

"Dunno bout a railroad. But a white preachin man, he gimme sack a food. An, I'se glad he be handin me a big shirt.'

"He say, 'You go on now. Lotta danger lurkin roun here. Bounty hunters an dogs chasin an catchin slaves. We done gon' t' jail if law catches us helpin. Go now. Foller river, an head t' up north.'

"At night, we get t' lookin up t' North Star an we keeps on a run."

"At the end of that river, you knew where to go? You had an escort?"

"Escort? I dunno. But up river a piece, a darkie, he callin out. He say he gon' ridin t' preachin place an I gets t' be ridin in his wagon.'

"He say, 'You go see a Missus Huckins.'

"We gon' roun a lotta trees. An nex time stoppin, he say 'go, high-tail it up hill, it ain't far.'

"An soon I sees Missus Huckins. She run out side door, an she pushin me so fast I be stumblin along."

"My goodness, why? Hope you and Little Tom—you didn't fall did you?"

"No, Ma'am, she done catched me."

"Where did you end up?"

"Missus Huckins done shove me behind her leanin shed."

"What? Why?"

"She say, 'Stay here, cuz Montpelier send visitin men an gon' stay all night.' I wonder, what next?

"Ma'am, it been so cold an windy. An, thinkin on it, makin me shiver now. We gets here last night but no lights an guessin no one hearin me?"

"Must've been when we were abed."

"I hears awful screamin so I gets us under cover down t' your barn an hopin' it be OK?"

"Of course it's OK, and that screaming—someone just had a bad dream. I guess Elly Hutchins and her husband didn't know my husband Joshua was not here. He was the one who tended to guests such as you. Now with him gone, I have no hand in it."

"No, Ma'am. Sorry. I jess done what she say t' do." Tears brim in her eyes before she jerks her head away.

"Now, no need to cry. For one night, you'll stay."

"What? Y'all sayin' I can?"

"Of course. We'll get you back to Mrs. Hutchins tomorrow."

"My baby cryin." She fiddles with him, feeling for his hind side. I find an old but soft dish cloth and rip it in half. This pan of warm water should help. In short time, she's settled him down. He only whimpers every now and then.

"Daisy? Were you alone in that shed for long?"

"No, Miz Huckins come back. She done bring horse an cart. We get under hay but her horse run off so fast we start a roll on out. I gon' hold fast t' my baby—so my feet stick out t' catch on wagon side an we keeps inside."

"What of your baby? Was he hurt?"

"No! My arms wrappin tight an not lettin go. We ridin down her road. An alla sudden, stoppin fast.'

"Come,' she say 'go down cellar at our Meetin House.'"

Her baby's tiny hand sticks out. He whimpers, hiccups, and nestles against her. His tiny mouth moves back and forth.

"Your baby's needing milk, you should feed him."

"Ma'am, my milk don't come no more."

"No wonder it's dried up, look at you, nothing but skin and bones."

"Yessum," she says, and rocks her baby, and hums. I can't hear which tune, but no matter. I need to warm some milk.

"Here, look what I have. Dip this flannel cloth in this milk. Now hold the end of it right over his mouth. Let the milk dribble in. Keep it there till he's had a good taste."

"Ma'am, see? He get the end, but he keep it in his mouth."

"Good, now pry it away, pull it very gently." And she dips it in the milk again.

Just then, two small faces peek from my bedroom door.

"Boys go back to your own bed. Yes, go. If you're wide awake, then play a game or two, but shut your door. I have a guest here and we need to talk. Elisha? You hear me? Do not dare to ask. It's not for your ears, so go. And Caleb, there were no animals out there last night. We just had visitors wanting in from the cold."

They retreat, but Cal tries to hang back till Eli pushes him along. Eli looks over his shoulder right at us. I point to their door. Then with a circled thumb and finger, he gives the OK sign while pushing Cal into their room. The door stops near the final closing. Is it Eli peeking through that crack?

Oh, Lord, how I love that child. My Eli, just like his Pa. And Cal? He's a little imp at times and pesters me to no end. Joshua says he takes more after me, his Ma. Well, maybe so?

Daisy says, "Ma'am? I can do washin."

"No, not for my guests to do. If you're up to it, tell me what happened next at the meeting house."

"Missus Huckins, she come back bringin a blanket t' put roun baby an she gimme a cloak. Bess of all I gets bread an taters. An a bowl a greens. It smellin good, and gets bacon slabs in it. An, yessum, it sho been jess right."

"How did you find your way to my cabin?"

"She say, 'It be Haxell's cabin o'er yonder on Harlow Hill. You go t'night. An a big ole moon, it give y'all light t' see.'"

"What else?"

"Ma'am, she say 'Missus Haxell she gon' feed y'all an keep y'all warm. Come back tomorrow. Gov'ment folk all gone by noontime.'"

"How did you find your way to my cabin?"

"She sayin, 'See o'er yonder, a wood bridge down in valley. Y'all gon' be crossin Ayers brook afore y'all trods up Harlow Hill. Then look up, see Mistuh Haxell's cabin.'"

"And you made it without any mishaps?"

"I made it, but wind blowin a lot. Cuppla times it blowin so fass—hadda walk turnt roun t' keep baby warm. An now it gon' be OK? Here be's a stoppin place?"

"Yes, but only tonight. Now tell me, how did you find food when you ran away?"

"Me an baby, we gets full a luck. We spies people sayin prayers. Far out inna woods. An my big Tom tole me, 'prayin men, God fearin ones, be givin help.'"

"Who's this big Tom?"

"He been Poppa t' my baby. We gon' an runnin away, but my big Tom, he—."

She sobs, and I hand her my handkerchief to wipe her nose.

"That's OK, Daisy, no need to continue."

"No. I be OK now. But I knows he been catched. And bossman, he mean devil. He gon' hurt my Tom."

"You mean he will be whipped?"

"Bossman whip Tom till—no . . . I cain't think on it. Jess prayin he gets healin up, an gets away. He cain't keep gittin dogs afta alla his runnin. We sees a mans gets hissef treed an hungry dogs . . . an, oh I—."

"That's terrible. Can't that man be arrested?"

"No, Ma'am. Who gon' catch a bossman?" What can I say? I know nothing of what goes on. I touch her shoulder. She looks up at me. Now what have I done? Why is her mouth trembling? I need to stop. Ask something else.

"So what happened in the woods?"

"A big man see me, an he yell 'C'mon out!' But, I stay put. He holdin out a pan, an yellin again, 'Stop bein a scaredy cat. C'mon, take yer eatin pan. Go, girl, an filler up.' It been rice, taters an a hunk a bread. An he go t' spoon more on."

"I say, 'Y'all need food fer yer chilluns, an I cain't take it."

"Daisy, you didn't pass up that food?" She stops, leans back and smiles. Then shakes her head.

"He pushen pan at me. An he say, 'See my Bible? It say we gotta feed y'all. An y' knows it ain't right goin agin our Lord.'

"I hears in back a me, 'Hallayluyah.' An he say, 'Amen.' I looks roun seein more folk standin near.'

"He say, 'So, c'mon, c'mon lil momma, eat up.' An he spoon out more. 'Ats good,' he say 'an we gon' keeps y'all safe.'"

"Wonderful, and Daisy you got this far after all. You must be so worn out by now."

Suddenly Daisy sits up straight as a rod, stares at the wall behind me. What does she see, is it something from before? Or is she ailing?

"Daisy, look at me. Are you feeling poorly?" Her head tilts over again. Then she slumps down in the chair. I wait.

Finally she says, "Ma'am, a good sleepin time is all I need. Look at baby Tom. He been sleepin good since his belly gets full. Time t' get on now. Stay put in y'alls barn." She'll not go to the barn. I'll see to that.

"You'll stay in here tonight." She slips off the chair and lies on the floor.

"What are you doing down there?"

"It be's so nice on this rug. You braid it all by yerself? It so soft, an it sho' gon' be a good sleepin place."

"No, don't worry. You can sleep in here tonight, but not on the rug. Under the eaves—I have a straw mattress."

"That be a nice lil room."

"No, you don't go in there. Here, let me drag it out and I'll put it on the carpet. And I'll bring some warm stones to put at the foot of the bed. Do not be alarmed, they are covered in flannel. They'll keep the chill off your feet. Go ahead—get in the bed. Yes, it is OK. I say so. You need to rest. Tomorrow we'll get you back to the Hutchins."

"I s'pose it gon' be OK. Jess hopin no law men gon' be stompin in here."

"Of course not. I am not expecting anyone, no one at all. And my doors will be latched front and back."

"Yessum, an t' morrow I gon' be helpin early on, afore sun's up. An it be makin time fer y'all t' be sleepin in." I will not argue, just let her get some sleep. But she will not be playing the servant here. And not be prolonging her stay.

I check the fire. Flames died down, so I add more wood. The hot embers glow red and new wood catches on. Both boys are sound asleep. The cabin is silent. I peer out my kitchen window. The wind stopped blowing and the moon hangs low in the sky. Hope Cal hears no strange noises. I yawn, my eyes close but I must first scribble out this letter.

Dear Joshua,

You'll never guess who came to our door. It's a young runaway slave girl, with a young baby. It looked to be almost newborn. She was sent over by Mrs. Hutchins. She thought she'd be safer here for the night, because government men were visiting her husband. Of course, she didn't know you were not here. So, because of the cold, I had no other choice but to let her in.

I shall write later about what she told me of her escape and how she arrived at our cabin. For now, it's all too much to keep thinking about.

I must enlist the aid of your brother, Jacob, to get the mother and baby back to the Hutchins'.

We're trying to manage the farm, with the boys trying to help as best they can.

Closing this now, and sending with prayers for your safe return, and hoping to have you home soon,

Your loving wife, Helen

Something's wrong. This paper, what if it got into the wrong hands? It needs to go where it belongs—to feed the fire in the stove.

The letter is gone now, burnt to a crisp. No one will be the wiser, not those who mean to do harm. I worry over him, and it's tempting to write so he'll worry over us and come home. No, I can't do that. Not yet.

Chapter Two

Danger

I must get out from under this warm cover. There's work that will not wait. Sun's almost up. The boys are still abed. Daisy and her baby just need tucking the quilt back over them. Good, they still sleep.

The cows are mooing. They need milking. The windows are steamed up, so it's warm enough for now. My heavy coat will do, with this scarf.

I remember the first time Joshua showed me an early morning view of the sunrise casting shadows across the valley.

He said, "Look Helen, across the valley to the West. The sun's coming up behind us. See, it's casting Harlow Hill's shadow upon Quaker Hill."

And now the warming rays march down, but ever so slow, all in a line.

He told me, "Just watch as the sunlight creeps down from the ridgeline. See how each snow-covered field, once all gray—now one by one they emerge from dark to light. At last, each is framed with tints of pink and purple all along the tree lines."

He had a way with words to warm my heart, no matter how cold it was. I see chimney smoke rising up from farm houses below. Farm wives are up and preparing breakfast for their families. One farmer's already heading out to his fields.

Joshua always gave me a fast salute, saying, "I'll soon be back."

This cold night air will not linger long around here. The sun is clearing the night fog all along Ayer's brook.

Further down the valley a train whistles as it chugs along, pulling into Randolph depot. Never paid much attention to it before Joshua left, but it nags at me now. The second time it took Joshua away, I recall his last words.

He said, "I have to do more."

"The first time you left for escorting duty, you said it would be a week or so. That turned into two weeks."

"Yes, but, I've fixed up things here at the farm, to make it easier on you while I'm gone." He does not realize that it's the day to day chores that wear me out. His brother Jacob helps some, and the boys try to help, best they can.

The barn door is open. Strange, must have been the wind last night.

The cows stop mooing as they see me approach. First, I'll work lard into my hands. As I sit on my stool, I place the bucket under Bessie. Now squeeze, then pull and here's the first dribbles. Good, a steady stream squirts out.

"All right Gracie, you're next. Let me put this pail under you."

That tail swishes back and forth, almost hitting me in the face. A steady stream lets loose and she settles down. Still need to milk the rest and tend to the calves.

Finally, the stalls are mucked and they all have hay. I need to get these milk pails to the Buttery cold room.

Done with that. Now for the chickens.

There's that train whistle again. It's pulling out of the depot. That shrill sound runs chills over me. It dredges up those same memories when Joshua was ready to leave and spoke of that dratted train.

"Folks ride the cars now, Helen, so the Post roads see less traffic. Our routes are much safer to escort runaways between safe houses."

"What of day traveling with your runaways and the big difference in their color, aren't you worrying how to keep them hidden?"

"We can trek through the woods and if tracks are lain nearby then walking will be easier. There won't be so many hills to climb. And we'll go only at night so as not to be seen."

"Why must you go at all? I'll be constantly worrying about what's happening to you. And why must it be you? Why not a man with no family? And, aren't you worrying if bounty hunters catch up with you? I know you are strong Joshua, but you alone will not be able to defend your charges, or yourself."

"Be reasonable, you'll have no cause to be fretting over me. I'll take extra caution guiding these poor souls to freedom."

And that is where we left it. Try as I may, I couldn't argue with him anymore. His mind was made up. Today I must keep my mind on Daisy and her baby and how to get them back over to Quaker Hill.

Here's the Chicken Coop. Get the new laid eggs . . . just a few more steps to go. The hens, they're flapping all over and feathers and dust are flying out the door. What's causing this to-do? The chickens cluck so loud, bumping into each other.

Cough. This coop is full of dust. I'll get done with it and get out of here.

What made them get all stirred up? Hope it's not that same Fisher Cat I spotted last fortnight.

What's that? Up on the hill just past the barn there's an outline of—. It's a horse, but must squint to see it against the sun. It stands free with no rider.

Then behind me—crunch, crunch. Footsteps, so scared, can't move. Something grabs me from behind.

"No, stop! What? Who?"

My heart pounds hard against my chest.

"Can't see. Get that thing off me!"

Smells like an old burlap bag. It's jammed down over my head and shoulders. Kicking out, but can't hit him. Too late, it's stuck all the way down.

"Please un-hand me."

What to do? Clawing at the inside of this bag. Can't grab hold. Is that a rope? It's tight all round my waist. My arms are pinned down. *Agh,* inside this smelly sack—*cough,* so hard to breathe.

"Help me. Let me out." Is it a bounty hunter? Does he know about Daisy?

My knees wobble, I start to fall, "Please, please who dares? Who's catching me up? Put me down. Where are you taking me? Please, please talk to me."

No answer, as footsteps trudge along, breaking through hard packed snow.

Oops, I'm falling, got plopped down on—good, it's only hay? The rope, it's loose. Quick get this sack up and off.

No one's here. What's that? Look around. Hay falls from the loft.

"Who are you?" Are they bounty hunters? Why do they hide?

"Aha, come out, I see you—you're behind that post. Is that you, Jacob? Enough! Get yourself down here, right now!"

Time to teach him a lesson he shan't forget. I cannot keep tabs on the likes of him, never knowing what tomfoolery will come next. Joshua should be here to keep his brother in line. His pranks have gone too far.

He's halfway down the ladder, then jumps and lands. Then somersaults over and over in the hay. He comes right at me, too fast. He bumps me, knocks me over. I'm not hurt, the hay is soft enough.

"Jacob, you scamp. You scared me half to death. Wait'll I tell tale on you. Soon as Joshua comes back he'll fix you. Why did you do that to me?"

Oh, where are my wits? I sometimes forget he cannot hear and never learned to speak. He comes close and hands over a rumpled piece of paper. I wonder, is this word from Joshua?

My hands tremble. But this is in Jacob's handwriting.

> *"Helen, I miss Joshua. Come to dinner this evening? Please bring Caleb and Elisha. Rabbit stew with turnips and cabbage is on my stove. More potatoes can go in, too."*

I force a smile. Jake knows nothing of his brother's work. When Joshua left, I fibbed and said, "He went to lend a hand to some friends."

And, that was not too far from the truth. Joshua deemed it fit, warning me, "The fewer people know about my doings, the better."

But now, Jacob has to know about Daisy. I look at him, catch his eye and I hand sign.

I hold up my first and last fingers to show, "You Devil." His grin disappears.

Then, my thumb and first finger make an O and next a K.

He nods, "OK, yes."

Fingers tight straight up aside my cheek say, "I will."

Then I shake my head, and move my lips very slow, "but not today, tomorrow." I tell him about Daisy.

Time's been wasting so I sign, "Go pick up my basket of eggs. You made me drop them. And feed the chickens. Then, go tether and hay your horse. I will fix breakfast for the boys. Join us if you like."

Jacob's back. He stomps his boots in the mud room. I'm too busy frying eggs, so I motion for him to come near. I speak slowly.

"After breakfast, go to your cabin. Pack a blanket and fur hat. Small for Daisy. By noon, take Daisy and baby to Hutchins' house on Quaker Hill. OK? It's white with green shutters." He nods, and gives the OK sign.

During breakfast Daisy just eats and says not a word. Eli and Cal stare at her and her baby.

"Boys mind your Ps and Qs, and finish your breakfast then help clear the table." They have not seen dark-skinned people before. Just as I was afraid of.

"Missus Helen, what means Ps and Qs?"

"It's an old English expression meaning 'mind your manners.' The boys must learn the right and wrong of it, and how it's not nice to stare at visitors."

Everyone's had their fill at the table and dishes get sided to the sideboard. The kettle steams. I pour hot water in the wash pan. Just then, Jacob sticks the boy's slate board in front of my face. I step back.

Scrawled out in big letters—"Goodbye. Best to keep barn and chicken coop shut tight. You never know what lurks around."

Oh, what a grin, but so innocent. If this water wasn't so hot, I'd dump it on his head—well no, I'd not actually do it. Then he pats me on my back, grabs his jacket and lights out the door for his own cabin.

The boys rush to part the curtains. Uncle Jake rides past the barn on Ole Blue, his Morgan horse. They wave goodbye.

Eli yells out, "See ya, Uncle Jake! I'll bring my spinning top. You can maybe help carve it better? At dinner tomorrow!" Sometimes they forget he can't hear.

Jacob heads home to feed his dogs. He thinks the world of those Beagles. Trained them since birth. Josh says that he somehow talks with them and they understand him. He's seen Jacob train them. Josh told me how he watched him using a few hand motions and later just pats them down.

Josh had said, "Helen, I know lots of people think he is deaf and dumb. Deaf, yes but dumb he is not. Did I ever tell you about the pictures he drew?"

"Yes, but I never saw any."

"Ma would iron out used sheets of white wrapping paper. Then he would lie on the floor and draw beautiful pictures.'

"She was always proud of his drawings. She'd tell people, 'Now, look at these papers. A dog, a bird, and even one of me. Look at my spectacles, and the bun I wear on top of my head. They prove what he lacks in hearing and speaking, he surpasses in other talents.'"

"I did not know he was that talented."

"A crow, for one fleeting moment, landed on our windowsill. Then he drew that bird exactly as he saw it, with only his memory to guide him."

"Where are those pictures, today?"

"Jacob has them. I'm sure he'd show them to you if you asked."

"Daisy, it's time to get you back to the Hutchins'. Jacob will take you back."

"Yessum, but Jacob, he been actin . . . I done been wond'rin, is a cat got his tongue? Why he gon' makin his hands fly round alla time? An y'all do it, too?"

"Yes, we speak by making signs with our hands. Jacob has been deaf since birth and cannot talk. I take it, you never knew any deaf people?"

Daisy shakes her head, and then moves her feet back and forth, across my carpet.

"What is this you've got around your feet? Burlap, is it?"

"Yes Ma'am. My feet, see? Gets fulla sores, cuz shoes fallin t' pieces. I cut pieces a tater sack, an wrap em all round my feet."

"Come here, I'll help you untie that burlap. Now, sit still. I'll be right back."

"Here are some wool socks for you. You can also have my old fur lined boots. No, no, don't give them back. I've got another pair."

"I cain't take em, Missus Helen."

"Shush, you put them on now. I've packed some extra garments for your baby, too. My boys wore them at his age."

"I thank y'all for baby's clothes, an hopes no white folk sees me toten em. Cuz lawman, mebbee he say I been stealin."

"No, Jake will tote them for you. And, Mrs. Hutchins will have a note from me."

Daisy undresses her baby, changes his napkin, and puts Caleb's old clothes on him. The long gown all baby boys wear. And it fits Little Tom just right, I must say.

"Look at you. You'll need to change first before leaving. It appears you might have your milk coming back. Am I right? Look at your dress, the top part. Need to clean up, you are leaking. No more arguing. I'll fix up a wash pan and be sure the boys stay in their room."

She washes up real quick. What's this? She's crying.

"Daisy, what's wrong? I thought you'd be glad for these clothes."

"Yessum, I sure am glad but I'm sad my baby Tom's Pa—he, well, he not here. I sure hopin Bossman's dogs not gon' an catched him. Tom be's my husband after Lil Tom gets born. We went an jumped a broom. All knowed we been joinin up. Bossman an Massa an Mistruss an all family seed us.'

"I been pond'rin on how luck follerin us even after Tom run from me. An how I been mighty glad we done made it here.'

"Y'all diffren from white folk I knowed afore. Oh, land o' mercy yer stew last night sure been good'n tasty. My Momma cooked mighty good stew. But she done gon' to Gloryland, a long time gone by."

"I am so sorry about your mother leaving you. Where is this Gloryland she went to?"

"Y'all calls it Heaven. But in our Gloryland only culluds allowed t' get in." She busies herself with the baby and sings some kind of lullaby. Don't understand any of the words, but the melody is nice.

"What is that you were singing?"

"Our Nana, she sing t' me an alla chillun."

"Very nice. Now, might I ask about this Tom?"

Her mouth closes real tight, and her eyes start blinking without let up.

"I jess misses my Big Tom. Me an Tom, we plannin on runnin away lotta times. So, when baby gets here, we gotta get goin."

"How did you manage to run away?"

"One night, after I washes up supper dishes inna big house—Massa, he drunk. An he been slobberin o'er me. Same's afore Baby Tom done got born."

"Daisy—are you saying—he was taking liberties with you?"

"Takin liberties? I'se gessin so. Yessum. I means he gettin his hands on me, an I tells him 'no' but he cain't listen. Anyways, ole geezer, he layin head on table, snorin, fallin asleep. An I run out, I gon' t' find Big Tom.'

"Tom so mad, he say, 'C'mon, less go, cain't wait no mo. I ain't gon' t' kill ole Massa, but I sure gon' hurt him bad, iffen we stay. We gettin outta here, afore I gets us both a whippin."

"So we slips out back, past our hut t' get Baby Tom from Tom's Nana."

"An poor ole Nana. She cryin, an makin me cry. She done been lookin after alla chillun, an Baby Tom. She quick batches a big hunk a ham.'

"Nana, she say, 'OK, get gon' now.'"

"So Nana wasn't your relative, but Tom's grandmother?"

"She belongin t' Tom. He ain't seed his fam'ly fer lotta time gone by. Some gets sole off. But Nana, she been wet nursin Mistruss lil ones long time ago. So she gets t' stay an can watch cullud chillen alla day long."

"Daisy, stop a bit, won't you? I need a cuppa tea. Would you like some?" She shakes her head. I pour my own.

"I gotta say it now, Ma'am, get it outta my head, OK?"

"Of course, Please tell me."

"We's runnin along a river bank. An we hears dogs a howlin way back inna woods."

"Dogs? So they used dogs to track you?"

"Yessum. An, oh Lordy, I done gets t' shakin. My Tom say, 'Daisy, see here, I picks y'all up an' puts yer feet inna water. It ain't deep. Go cross river t' other side. I stays on my side an keeps alla dogs runnin after me. After crossin river, y'all keeps a runnin. Look for North Star. An, y'all never looks back. Hear me?'

"I grabs his hand an say, 'I cain't go. I cain't leave you,' an I starts cryin."

"How terrible. What did he do?"

"He say, 'Cain't you hear em, cain't you hear alla dogs, runnin an howlin, an gettin close?' He sweatin up a lot, an his hand been slippery. I cain't hold on, but I catch on his shirt tail.'

He say, 'I gotta run now. Let loose a me, gal.'"

"I'd have been terrified, if it was me."

"Yessum, I's jumpin almose outta my skin. I say, 'Don't leave me, Tom. I cain't leggo. I needs you,' He don't pay no mind.'

"He say, 'Now stop, leggo.' Nex, I knows—Big Tom run off on his side a river an I'se crossin over. An, I'se almose fallin, but I jess run."

"And your baby, how did he fare? How could you hold onto him and run, too?"

"Lil Tom? Oh, he safe inside my shawl. Down in front. Nana gets it tied on me, afore we leave. He been jess sleepin, doin OK."

"Thank goodness for that, but what of the dogs?"

"I hears em. It been a lotta howlin, way off inna woods—like a dog gone an treed a coon. I knows my Big Tom been catched. I knows I cain't never see him again. But, I hears him."

"What? You hear him? Are you sure?"

"Yessum, an I hears him now. In my head, an it ain't tellin no lies.'

"My Tom's a good ole singin man. Tom been singin lotta tunes, an reason I got t' likin him. Lovin alla his singin an steppin round camp fires at night."

She stops, then a smile creeps on her face, but disappears as she looks my way.

"Oh, cain't help it. Still lovin him now, an alla his made up songs. I 'member one he sings t' me, an only me."

'Run, run, run, run, Hey Boss Man, whaddaya say?
I been pickin cottin, an pitch-forkin all a yer hay.
Yassuh, Boss Man, I been runnin, alla live long day.
But soon y'all gon' miss me.
Daisy an Baby, an me, we gon' run away.
Yassuh, jess y'all wait an see,
We gon' t' Gloryland, an we gon' be free."[16]

"So Gloryland also means freedom land?"

"Uh huh. Iffin we die or live, we gon' gets free in Gloryland."

"Oh? I see. And what of your Tom?"

"He been bess singin man. He so good, Bossman like Tom t' sing inna fields. An we all gets t' shoutin an prayin, an white folk gets real glad. Figgerin culluds so happy, workin in field an praisin our Lord.'

"Yessum, Tom say we jess like lil singin birds, chirpin away. An, we knows bess how t' keep our backs outta way a whip lashins.'

"Boss, he be clappin, drinkin an stompin, in a hootin ole time. Fiddlin get goin an Big Tom singin away."

"And this was after working all day? Then, having to put on a show for the owner?" How heartless, having parties, and other times, using a whip on them?

"When did you sleep?"

"We allus got restin time, when work get done. An afore party an singin t' white folk."

"Massa, he say to visitin men, 'Look, how all fired happy our darkies are. See, dancin t' beat a band. We been tellin y'all bout it, Senator. Jess look at em, hear em Sheriff? Ain't it so? Gettin treated real good.'"

"How nice, and proper. To keep you all so fit and healthy." Hah, in a pig's eye, it was. No sense throwing cold water on her tale. She feels awful enough losing her Tom.

"So what went on next with Tom?"

"I dunno, dint see him no more. But iffen he in Gloryland, he gon' be singin. Same's he allus tole me."

Run, run, run, run ~
We gon' run away~
Me an Daisy an Baby, too.
Oh, Lord, how bout t'day?
We gon' run, run, I'se sayin.
An ain't gon' stop prayin
Till it be's lass prayin I do. [16]

Noon time and Jacob's back, ready to take Daisy.

I sign, "Daisy will sit behind you. She's to keep that hood covering her face. Strap down this bundle behind her. You hold the baby. He's been fed so he'll be quiet."

Daisy says, "Ma'am, I wanna hold—."

"Don't worry. Your baby will be safe."

I sign to Jake, "Take the backwoods trail. You'll be hidden from view. Stop the horse in the woods. Then go to the house alone. Make sure visitors have left. Then bring Daisy and the baby to the house."

I sign, "God speed, Jacob. Remember, dinner at your cabin tomorrow evening." They ride off. I wonder where Daisy will finally end up?

Chapter Three

Joshua's Calling

I remember the day Joshua told me, of a sudden, about his wanting to leave. He said he had to go. The Lord told him he should. Had to go help the slaves running from their Masters. I wondered if he had some other interest for leaving?

I said, "Joshua, you can't be serious. You'll leave me and your sons? I did not mind you using our home as a safe house. They never came in here. You never bothered me about them. But this is different."

"The work I'd get to do, Helen, think of it, how important it could be."

"You think it more important than being here for us?"

"No, I did not say that. Let me show you. I need, uh, where did I stash those papers?" I should've thrown them in the fire. He's rummaging through my China closet. I wonder if he has letters, not for my eyes, stashed away.

"Josh, stop. You could break one of Ma's best dishes. Try that box over the stove."

"Here it is, take a look. It's William Lloyd Garrison's newspaper, The Liberator."

He pulls my chair out for me. I sit at the table, and begin reading."

"Tell me, what do you think of it?"

"There's nothing here to warrant your leaving." He grabs the paper from me.

"Right over here, see? Garrison shows how the North needs to face up to what's going on both here and in the South. Didn't you see this?"

Josh reads, *"During my recent tour for the purpose of exciting the minds of the people, on the subject of slavery . . . particularly in New England . . . I find contempt more bitter, opposition more active, prejudice more stubborn, and apathy more frozen, than among slave owners themselves."* [2]

"What does that have to do with you wanting to run off?"

"I am not done. See for yourself."

"If I must, but Garrison runs on and on—is this what Garrison uses to convince people? Scaring them? I don't want this, take it. You continue."

Josh reads, "*I determined, at every hazard, to lift up the standard of emancipation in the eyes of the nation, within sight of Bunker Hill and in the birthplace of liberty. That standard is now unfurled; and long may it float . . . till every chain be broken, and every bondman set free!'*

'Let Southern oppressors tremble—let all the enemies of the persecuted blacks tremble . . .'

"I know how I feel and this will not persuade me. Garrison's words are like a man acting the bully. I like words a bit nicer to persuade me."

"He's not a bully, but he is dedicated to the cause. Look at his photo. You can see how determined he is." He lays down the paper. He's waiting. I cannot agree with what he wants to do, so I change the subject and hope we'll be done with it.

"What of the North, why are they to blame?"

"I'll invite our abolitionist leader to come by. He can answer, I'm sure."

Later that night, who might be at the door? None other than the local leader, coming by to help bolster the good cause.

"Helen, be pleased to meet the leader of the Randolph Antislavery Society." A tall, stately man with a slight limp walks in.

I nod to him. "Here, give me your cloak, cane and hat and please come sit at our table."

He said, "I dare not give out my name. We never know when any in our midst might take a mind to getting our Society in trouble."

"What kind of trouble? Joshua, is this so?"

"Well, that big flood wiped out many farmers. And some are desperate. They will not hesitate to turn in anyone, to get cash to feed their families."

"That does not assure me one bit. Surely there are better reasons to leave here? Can you think on it, while I prepare our tea?" I hurry. Must not dawdle. Cannot embarrass my husband. This silver tray with tea and fixings is just right. It should do Joshua proud.

Then I sit down. I must behave as if I am interested.

Joshua asks, "Sir, can you explain to Mrs. Haskell why William Garrison is blaming New England for not being more active in the antislavery movement?"

"You must be referring to his speech that appeared in *The Liberator*. Well, there are people and even religious groups that still hold onto long established prejudices. Especially against people of color. In early Colonial days, slavery was accepted in both North and South. However, in 1777 Vermont became the first state to abolish slavery. And today, Massachusetts and Vermont offer relatively safe havens to runaway slaves."

I say, "Thank you for that explanation."

"If you want to read about the life of a slave, I would recommend a book by Frederick Douglass. About five years ago, he published a narrative about his life. He and Garrison have been very outspoken about the evils of slavery. You are very fortunate to have an anti-slavery library right here in Randolph."

Joshua says, "Yes, we know of Mr. Douglass and I've read most of the anti-slavery books and pamphlets in the library. I've always wondered how Randolph's library came to be."

The leader says, "We can thank Rowland Robinson, the Quaker from Ferrsiburgh. He spent $2,000.00 to stock three libraries. This one in Randolph, the one in Vergennes, and another in Montpelier.[3] Have you had the occasion to read any of those books, Mrs. Haskell?"

"I never got into the whole of Joshua's work. I had my own chores to fill my time. Joshua tended to the runaways. He kept them in our sheds and only for an overnight stay."

The leader continues, "Vermont was very open about airing their abolitionist beliefs. All that has now changed."

"Why is that?" I must appear interested in all these explanations, at least for Joshua's sake.

"After the 1850 Fugitive Slave Act was passed last year, there's much to fear. Vermont passed a law that nullified that Act. However, in our State, the Federal government still tries to assist slave owners. Slave catchers from both North and South can chain runaways and drag them back to their owners."

"Joshua, how can our state go against federal laws? If federal lawmen and our sheriffs are at odds on what to do, then you are in even greater danger."

"It means I will have to be more cautious and I will. Let the leader explain how."

"Some slaves would fight to the death rather than give up their liberty, and be forced back into slavery."

I should not say this, but—. "Sir, you have to be jesting. Now, you're telling me that my husband will be more safe, if he's in the middle of all this?"

Josh says, "He is just explaining how slaves cherish their freedom."

The Leader says, "It would be similar to the ideals of this patriot." He gives me a paper.

"Is life so dear or peace so sweet as to be purchased at the price of chains and slavery? Forbid it, Almighty God! I know not what course others may take, but as for me, give me liberty, or give me death!"
Patrick Henry,
Speech in the Virginia, Convention, March, 1775.

"Yes, I know of Patrick Henry, the Patriot, and his speech. He would die if not free. Being safe is on my mind now. Tell me how my husband can be more cautious?"

"We have routes with coded names and places to learn. No one need know of his whereabouts." This man with no name gives a paper to Joshua.

He says, "Note the stars I've placed by some names. These people, mostly Quakers, like you, are righteous ones and their homes are safe. However, I've crossed through other names. They pay lip service only and are not to be trusted. Take this with the code words and commit it to memory."

Joshua looks it over then shows it to me—a paper with words that make no sense.

He asks, "Would it help if I can secure it on myself? Keep it hidden, of course."

"No, my dear fellow, absolutely not. And, any other writings need to be written with these same codes. Now, do you have any other questions?"

Joshua asks, "If alone, how would they find their way north?"

"They must travel by night, and look for the Big Dipper constellation. Two stars on the cups edge point to the North Star. It's located on the end of the Little Dipper's handle."

"Yes, I know. That's the same as I told them if travelling at night. But, as an escort, how would I be trusted at these safe places?"

"Keep in mind, a letter gives introduction. It assures that you are an agent along the escape route. You will be accepted as a friend. Mentioning the Gospel, or Promised Land, tells of the final destination. A pastor, reverend, or minister, means one sympathetic to the antislavery cause. This letter explains it better. Can I hear you read it, to be sure you understand?"

Joshua reads aloud.

Peacham, Vt., November 2nd, 1849

Dear Friend,

Your nephew, James, has arrived here in my home on this date accompanied by my own agent, the good man entrusted to handle my accounts.

I will be sending him off to you by Friday next, along with that bag of potatoes I had promised.

May the Lord deliver us all from evil. Let the Gospel guide us, and at our end ensure we will have a seat in Heaven, the Promised Land.

Respectfully,
Your friend, Charles Whinstone, Pastor,
Quaker Friends Meeting Place

"Joshua, as you build your network of friends in Windsor, your group must agree on a distinctive pattern of knocks. When you rap on the door of safe houses, the owners will then know you are a friend. When someone asks, 'Who's there?' a good answer would be, 'A friend of a friend.' However, if your fugitive proceeds alone, he should say 'A friend of a friend sent me."

Joshua says, "Thank you, sir. I've been practicing some of the guidance you've just given, in my limited role as an agent. I've been allowing overnight stays and then handing off the runaways to the next safe house. But I'm sure this has been very helpful for Mrs. Haskell. Helen, you must have more questions."

"It's still the one question you've not answered. Why, Joshua, do you, of all others, have to leave? Why not men with no families to worry over them?"

"Helen, I told you I had the call during Meeting Time—."

"And other men do not get called? After this, when you're on the road, you'll have no means to defend yourself, will you? What if you are overpowered and get caught? If bounty hunters are as mean as slave owners, what will stop them from hurting you? And the slaves, will they think of you as a savior? Someone to show them the right path?" He didn't answer. I stand to leave the room.

"Please, dear lady, sit and I shall be done soon." He continues with his story.

"Mrs. Haskell, Joshua had asked if there were any kind owners. Only house slaves might earn a better life with good food a plenty. Yet, they're still not free. I must say that some masters were kind to their slaves. Never-the-less, keeping a human being as a work horse is a sin. Slaves have no rights, beyond what their master grants."

I sip my cold tea in silence, so grateful to be left alone. They continue discussing the routes. Joshua studies the papers, so intent on this adventure. I know it will be difficult to change his mind.

The leader says, "I must be getting on, there's one more stop to make tonight."

Joshua asks, "Would you like something to take, a parcel with food or another drink?"

"Water would be fine. No need of food, though, my wife has packed plenty for me. Yet, the time is indeed late, and I must be going. Might I have my cloak and hat?"

After the leader left, I offer Joshua a drink of hot cider.

Joshua says, "Why can't you understand that more escorts are needed to guide slaves to safe houses?"

"But why must you go?"

"The Elders agree it must be done. It won't be for too long a time, only a fortnight at most."

"Danger will await you, Joshua. Aren't you afraid?

"Helen, it's not what you think. Why do you worry?"

"Without warning, they could turn on you. Look at what that colored preacher from Virginia did. He was called a man of God, but what a devil he was."

"And, who's this devil you're talking about?"

"Wait. Let me think. Yes, Nat Turner was his name. He led that awful uprising against white folk. It was heartless killings of more than fifty white people, with no mercy given." [4]

"Helen, this is Vermont, that was Virginia and it happened twenty years ago. Runaway slaves would know I mean them no harm. We only give help. And, Helen, all Quakers believe as we do, that all men should be free. Now, that ends it."

"Josh, why can't we reason this out? What will I do, here, alone?"

"C'mon, Helen. My brother Jacob can help out. Come here, let's see a smile, and can you give me a hug?"

Of course I do. And I smile. I cannot change him. I know and accept that it is not my decision to make. Worse, I shudder at what might happen if I keep on nagging him. He may not want to come back. Oh, it hurts me to think he puts other people over his own family. But I must let him leave on a good note, and not remember me as a shrew. Besides, he will have enough worries without having to worry about my feelings. I shall do the best I can while he's gone and make do as usual.

He left for Windsor town. That was three weeks ago. He packed two valises. I questioned why he needed two if only staying for a week or so. He had no real answer. That night I lay in bed with the empty space next to me. I prayed that he not be taken away for good.

* * *

I hear a horse outside. It's Jacob, he returns from the Hutchins'. He smiles and gives the "OK" sign.

I sign back., "Five o'clock tomorrow for dinner." He rides on to his cabin.

Years ago, I wrote on his slate, "How do you like living alone with no one to talk to."

"Well,' he wrote on his slate, 'I do not talk like you. Ma taught me. I read her lips. She pointed to them. I watch her talk. Shows me letters. Draws each in my hand. So, I can finger spell. I can show you, OK?"

Jacob showed me every day after that, and finally I learned to sign.

He wrote about his mother speaking of his good and bad days.

His Ma said the learning will come so do not lose hope. I asked about his bad days. He wrote it all out.

"I was six and had temper fit. At school I worry, I am dumb. Boys answer questions fast. I cannot. I could not hear. Could not talk. Girls do not look at me. I am a dunce. After school I run home. Cry all the way. Slam my slate on table. It broke. Ma picks up pieces. I sit, I watch, and turn my back. She turns me around."

"Ma asks me, 'Why did you break it?"'

"I cry. Run to my room. Ma opens door."

"She signs, 'Stay. Do not come out. Not until you know why you broke it."'

"I stay all night. In morning I sit at table. Said I am sorry. I tell her about school. Hate it, and I am not happy."

"She said, 'Be glad you can walk and have a strong back. You have a good mind. Just need to use it more.'

"My mind could not learn. Not fast. I cry in my room."

Jacob's Mother showed me years later the keepsake she had in her souvenir box. It came home one day from his teacher.

It was a blue ribbon. He won it for a bird house he built with pine wood.

It's been a long day and I'm exhausted . . . someone's here, I hear a horse outside. It's Jake. Why did he come back? Thought he'd be getting his dinner fixings all set for tomorrow's dinner.

Jake signs, "I need some more potatoes, OK? Need to make it thick like Ma's stew. And, two onions? It helps making it tasty."

I go get what he wants, and make some hot cocoa. The boys will be wanting some anyway.

He signs, "You look very tired."

I sign, "I had to untangle two sheep that got themselves stuck in barb wire up on the back hill. That just about did me in."

"What happened?"

"There was two feet of packed snow. The fools tried to climb over the fence. They got caught in the wire. Bleating to high heaven, they were. Took some doing, but I got their feet pulled out."

He signs, "Are they OK? And are you OK?"

"They should be fine in a week's time. I'm OK, but my gloves need patching."

He finished his cocoa, and signs, "Bye. And don't get up. You go rest." He doesn't have to tell me, as I am really tired.

The sun is dropping behind the ridgeline of Quaker Hill. It casts long shadows from the trees. They spread into the valley and across the snow filled fields. Its amber glow slowly fades and soon it'll darken the front room. The boys have gone to bed, so I gather up my quill and journal.

There's barely enough light from the fireplace. It just flickers across the pages. Holding one page closer, I squint to see, but it's no use.

I light the oil lamp. The wick starts smoking, making my eyes tear up. Tears fall on the journal. I push the journal aside and turn my head away from the lamp.

It's not the smoke, now, that's bringing on the tears. It's the heartache from deep inside. Try to hold down the sobs. Yet, they keep rising up. Now, they spill out. All of it, it's way too much . . . the hard work, never ending till falling into bed at night. And worrying about Joshua being gone. I'll have a good cry. Grab my handkerchief and be done with it. Must keep the sobs down. Don't wake the boys.

I don't know if I'll survive the rest of the winter. And the start of spring? Maple sugaring time is coming on.

Jake had written on his slate, "Can you tap trees?"

I signed, "I know how to, but need your help. And hauling the filled pails later on? Too many for me to handle."

He wrote, "I can empty them."

"There's also crop planting and sheep shearing. Josh said he would be home for the planting."

"Josh and I can do the shearing. Go sit down. I will list our chores." And he started writing.

I'm too tired to continue writing in my journal. Put it away. Need to stoke the fire again. The boys are quiet, both must be asleep.

My head sinks down in this pillow, so soft. Eyes close, cannot open, too heavy. So peaceful and quiet it is. Snuggle down deeper.

I love Joshua's idea now, when he traded some of his mother's embroidered linens and some of his and Jake's carvings in return for this down filled mattress. It turned out to be a right decision. And, thank heaven, all of the aches, pains, and worries are drifting . . . yes, going . . . away.

Chapter Four

Reminiscing

"Elisha! Caleb! Come here, both of you, help carry this basket of wet clothes. Hang them careful on the rack in front of the hearth."

Both hang their heads, looking down at their feet, as they slowly drag into the kitchen. They pick up the basket, and then half way out of the kitchen, Caleb drops his end and runs off with Elisha right behind—waving a wet shirt.

"Alright, give it here, I'll do it myself.'

"Caleb! Where are you? Cal come out, now. Yes, from under your bed, I see you. Stop dawdling. Help Eli get your warm clothes to wear. And bring your toy basket. Eli, give him a hand. We need to get packed. We'll not be rushing around when it's time to leave for Uncle Jacob's. Do you hear? We can't go if it's dark out."

"Do I gotta, can't he do it alone? Why do I hafta?"

"Because you're the big brother. Tell me, are you going to help?"

"Yeah, guess so."

"Then, you and Cal decide what else to take. Uncle Jacob might show you his ways of carving, and you could try your hand at whittling on something to play music on? Fetch that piece of maple wood lying by the side of the mantel. Jacob has only that pine he used last fall for birdhouses."

Caleb pushes out from under the bed. He says, "Uncle Jake, he gonna make a real nice bird house?"

"Perhaps. Cal? What's in this box. Not another frog, is it?"

"Nah, it's an old one."

"My goodness. Give it here. Eli, take it outside." Cal has a frown on his face.

"Cal, listen, no more frogs in the house. You might ask your Uncle Jacob to carve you a top like Elisha has."

"Yeah. I wanna top. Red, an shiny, an not small, like Elisha got."

"Well maybe. We'll see."

"Elisha, when you're done, grab some apple sauce from the cold room. Uncle Jacob has a taste for apple sauce. Cal, you be sure to help, and Eli, we cannot tote just your favorite blueberry or Cal's blackberry jelly. And see to finding me a cleaned lantern. We might be staying later and probably overnight if it's still snowing out."

Our kitchen is now spotless. All floors are mopped, and fresh linens are on our beds. I daresay, it will be good to come back to a nice clean house, to relax after an outing.

Can't forget my good apron and napkins. Must go look for them.

Ah, here, at the bottom of my linen chest, still folded, never used. They're my best. Ma helped me embroider these, with my H.H. initials. What was I saving them for? Did I think the Governor might come to tea? Sure, in a pig's eye! Well, we'll use them tonight at Jacob's cabin. They'll make for a real nice table setting.

The boys have settled down. There's time left before I get the horse ready to carry our sleigh to Jake's. Now I can pen today's doings in my journal.

I notice a few weeks ago, I wrote, "I hope no harm comes to Joshua. He helps those in need. But he needs watching over, too."

Paging back further, I see where Joshua first got caught up in the abolitionist movement. I must be careful and probably should tear these pages out. They could bring trouble to our home. No. They are too precious. I'll keep them out of the way, under the eaves.

I'm reading where Joshua used our home in Bethel Gilead as a safe house, but I was never involved. He kept them in our shed. Never had to deal with them. Then, living in Randolph, Joshua continues to help fugitives make their way north. He guides or shows them routes to other safe hiding places. He cautioned me to keep quiet about his doings.

"Remember to be heeding me. Don't be blathering to any who don't belong to our family. They could be folks coming from outside Vermont just to snoop around fairs or picnics."

"Of course I wouldn't spread what you do. What's got into you?"

"Well, those Bounty men might be sneaking around. Cash is paid for information. And many Vermonters might be in dire need to feed their families. So, they may not hesitate to help those plantation owners who want their slaves back. So, Helen, it is best that you not be meeting and jawing with neighbors down to the general store."

At that, I could not hold my tongue.

"Such tripe, why Joshua, to think of it, well, my word—when have I wasted time lolly-gagging, like the old snoops at the store?"

Recollecting from earlier entries—days, years passed, and I cannot name one real fighting match we had going. When stuck for agreeing, usually one of us would give in at the end, figuring we'd be wasting time, fussing at each other.

When feeling sad, my Joshua could always give me reason to smile and feel good again. I recalled when I ruminated over sad times in the past. He'd spout off about what I really needed to hear. And, usually with a touch of the poet deep inside him.

While brushing my hair, he'd say, "Your hair is just fine. See Helen, in your looking glass. How sleek it is, and just look, how shiny. And your eyes, my Lord, how they match your hair, they're so alive and sparkling. And how they twinkle at times. Even times when there's not much light in our room." And though he'd get a bit too flowery speaking, I still loved it.

I'd say, "Oh shush up, or you'll be making me vain, the same as Ma always warned, when she said, 'A devil will jump out, when sporting the sin of vanity, if you waste any more time staring in that mirror too long.'"

Today, I see again in the mirror, these high cheek bones. Where did they come from? I am not like my sister Lily at all. Once, I complained to Ma about the difference.

She said "We have aunts on my father's side, living out West, who had looks like you. Now, Lily, with her light skin and blond hair, she comes from my mother's side, looking more like me."

"Yes, but what of Lily, compared to me? She is such an angel, so dainty. And, look at me."

"Well just look at you, Helen. You have a rare beauty not seen in many women, with that jet-black hair, those dark eyes, that ever-pleasant smile. You girls are exactly what I wished each would be. It's not the covering that defines us; it's what lies underneath in our hearts. It's how we treat each other, with never any meanness at all—that is the judgment we shall face at the end. Remember that, and you'll both do well in this life."

"Yes, I suppose so."

When I could not hold back my sad times, Josh was always there to cheer me. He would cup his hand under my chin and get me to look up to the sunny sky. He then would ask me to count those big fluffy clouds lazing around up there, until he saw me smile.

"See, Helen? What's there to cry about? No need for sad tears on such a new day, with never knowing what good things it might bring."

"That's not the Quaker way.' Joshua would say, 'Feeling sorry for yourself, are you?" But, I was not raised in his Quaker ways. I was brought up Methodist, before becoming a Quaker. My Ma never told me not to cry or feel sad if needing to. That is, as long as I didn't make a spectacle of myself and always tried to act like a lady.

Although he could cheer me up, he never showed his own sadness lying deep inside him. I think it stemmed from the time his Pa got took away by the accident. My thinking was right when, much later, he at last told me all about it. I did write it in my journal. I know I did. I'll find it in here if I keep looking . . . yes, here it is.

September 8th 1841:

Joshua related what happened. This is in his own words.

"My Pa took off early one morn with the ox team. He told Ma he was to do some logging in the back ten acres of the farm. Then, about mid-day, Ma looked out the kitchen window and saw Jeff and Pete standing by the barn door, still yoked together. She didn't think much about it, figuring Pa was in the barn fixing stalls and getting ready to de-yoke and bring them in.'

"Much later, Ma looked out again. Jeff and Pete were still standing there with the yoke on. She ran out the door."

"Ma screamed! 'Where's Pa?' I heard her and ran out. Her long dress and shoes weren't meant for the woods. She walked as fast as she could. I caught up.'

"She pointed ahead, yelling, 'Go find him!'"

"I sped toward the back acreage. Took a cross cut and found him. A big maple tree pinned my Pa to the ground. It must have back slipped the cut he made—and crushed his chest. I pushed and pushed against it, tried to roll it off. Tried to lift it, but it wouldn't budge.'

"Pa gasped out, 'Too late, let it be. Too heavy, it's God's Will.'"

"There was such agony on Pa's face. I tried to do something, anything—even dug dirt from under him. Used my bare hands. I knew I'd do it, I'd pull him out from under that blasted tree.'

"Pa whispered, 'No, stop, be a good son, listen. Tell your Ma, God bless.' I moved in close to hear the last, when he said, 'and, help her, Joshua, however, and whenever you can.'

"Pa's mouth stopped moving, his head fell to the side. I waited, but he was so still, not even breathing. I kept on, scratching the dirt, the rotted leaves and sticks, pulled at them, even harder. God was sure to help.'

"I could not even stop when Ma cried out to me, 'Joshua, it's of no use, please get up!'

"I kept on, digging deeper. She tugged at me, almost pulled my shirt off—but I did not hear her. Then she yanked my hair, and I felt that! She pulled me away. I was trembling and then shook so bad that she held onto me for a long time. My fingers were bleeding, but I had no idea, and didn't feel anything. When I stopped shaking, we walked slowly home. The neighbors brought Pa's body back."

"What happened when you got back home that day? Your hands must have been torn up, as you said your fingers were hurting."

"My crying only fully stopped later on in the dark of night when I was in my room by myself. With moonlight shining through my window, I was shocked to see and feel my hands. The pain was oh, so bad. Some of my fingernails had ripped. Yet, I was lucky they hadn't come off. Oh, how they hurt, so much so, that I bit my lip to keep from yelling out. That bite hurt, but it helped put off the agony I felt. My Pa had died. I should've gone with him that morning. Should've been ready, instead of sleeping so late.'

"Later that night, I had to get up, the throbbing in my hands was so bad, and sleep would not come. Figured, maybe I'd get ice from the ice house. It just had to dull the pain."

"Oh, my Lord, Josh, I never knew. That's why you ignored my wave after school. I was so upset, thinking you didn't like me anymore." I move closer to him and rub his back.

"When I got back, Ma was sitting at the kitchen table. I asked her, 'Why did Pa have to go off and not wait for me? If I'd been with him, it wouldn't have happened.'

"Ma didn't know this, but for a long time after Pa's accident, I did not feel the inner light when I went to Meeting. Nor did I want it. It was only after Ma died that I felt His presence again.'

"She said, 'Now hear this, Joshua—it was time for God to take him home and you had no part of that decision. We should remember Pa as hard working and that nothing would hold him back—not bad weather, not even if he was ailing in any way.'"

"He was never sick, was he?"

"Yes, he was, but he never let on, so his boys would not worry. He wanted you and Jacob to have a carefree life, as much as a farmer on this land, our Vermont, could wish. He let nothing hinder him from keeping this roof over our heads and food on the table. Ah yes, a good man he was, since he always placed his family's needs ahead of his own."

"Ma, though I always respected him, and never sassed him, I can't remember his ever holding me tight or smiling just at me. He was always busy, even after suppertime."

"Ma said, 'Yes, Joshua, he was busy, working not only on the farm but fixing things in here.'"

"Did he ever have any pals? I never saw any."

"You mean for after long hours of working, what did he do? Not like some men, going off to the woods, camping out, fishing and hunting with other men friends. No, he loved his home, and puzzles, and figuring out how to make things work, remember? Showing you how to figure out things, getting good solutions. And he had the patience of Job with young Jacob, taking time to show him simple things."

"Yes, Ma, I know about those times. But he never said he cared about us, or anything like that."

"No, I grant you that. He was not one to display his tender heart, nor wear it on his sleeve. Instead he used his actions, not words, to show his love for us."

"Ma, he really cared for Jacob. He let him jump up, so he could catch him when he came in the door."

"Because Jake would run to him while you held back and just watched.'"

I say, "Josh, were you hurt by that?"

"Ah, Helen, what could I say? I was Jake's age once, and my Pa never stood with arms outstretched to me."

I could say nothing to help him forget.

He said, "After the funeral, I was the man of the house, taking over the heavy work. There was no time, no energy left to spend on anything but running the farm. No excuses, I had to head directly home from school to finish up the chores."

I said, "Your mother must have had a hard time."

"Yes, and she put on the appearance of being strong. At first, I tried to lighten her load, but most times, she told me to go study my lessons. When I got old enough to take on more work, I'd see her resting more—well, sometimes."

"That was good, and at least she had you to lean on. And she must have had times when tears would not stop?"

"Oh, no, I never saw her cry. She was a private person, never wanting any pity, but always had to be strong, and not even cry. I don't think she could shed tears. It was the way she was raised, like my Pa, keeping that 'stiff upper lip'—the English way, I was told.'

"Sounds so familiar. My Ma told us to go in our room if we must cry."

"Ah, Helen, not you, too? You were so different from other women I knew."

"Huh? What women? Joshua? You were awful busy, back then. Why do you smile? Oh, stop that, you're just pulling my leg."

His smile quickly gives way and he's serious again.

Joshua said, "The extra work piled on, and I had to head out to the woods to trap or shoot our meat supply. Helen, you might not have the stomach to hear about gutting and skinning."

"Josh, how well I know. I shouldered that task, too. Had to make sure our cold room was stocked up and meats were salted for wintering over."

"Ah, but Helen, many times I wished for another strong back to help me chop all the extra trees to lay up for wood-burning in winter."

"Your Ma told me there was none that had a back stronger than her own son, Joshua."

"When were you talking to my Ma about that?"

"Never you mind, but she did say you were very strong growing up. She said that to test your strength, you would pick up a baby calf onto your shoulders. I told your Ma, 'Well, Mrs. Haskell I could probably do that.' Then she smiled and said 'Yes, my dear, but Josh did this every day, till that cow must have weighed over four hundred pounds.'" [5]

I was flabbergasted and asked, "My Goodness, are you sure? Four hundred? Maybe only three? Tell me, did he hurt himself?"

"No, but the cow looked mighty uncomfortable, laying on top of Joshua's shoulders. It was a sight to behold. That poor cow had such a look wondering how he got up so high? And, Joshua would've kept it up except he heard that townspeople wanted to come out to see him do it."

"Well, true or not?" I asked.

Joshua said, "I didn't want anyone to know about me showing off like that. It's not the Quaker way."

"Quaker way or not, there's more."

"Really?"

"Yes, there is. Your sister, Selena, told me how brave you were. She recalled a time when you both were out riding in the horse and buggy. Two men on horseback rode up and threatened you. They wanted to steal something, your horses, maybe?"

"Yes. I remember that. You sure were all ears with Serena, and you never told me any of this before? How'd you keep it all to yourself?"

"As you know by now, I am not a tell-tale, or gossip monger. It was just before Selena left the farm and went to work in the mills in Massachusetts. Well, anyway, she told how they got off their horses and then tried pulling her off the buggy. You jumped down and it only took two punches from you. Is that right that you knocked one out, just like that?"

"I guess that's what happened."

"That's how she tells it, and then you got in such a rage—said she never saw it in you before. It was when the other man charged at you, and you just picked him up, and with his legs kicking, threw him bodily—right over the buggy. He landed on the other side with a thud. Serena and you wondered if his bones got broken.[5] Joshua is that a true story? Did you really do that?"

"Yes, but I'm not proud of it. I wasn't raised to hurt anyone, no one at all. That's not the Quaker way, not what Pa would've liked, either."

"Come to think of it, the Quaker men probably couldn't have done it like you did, even if thinking it was proper—throwing him so high and right over that buggy."

"Guess I didn't know my own strength. I felt sorry for what I'd done."

"Yes, because Selena said you put those two men in the back of the buggy. Then tied their horses behind and drove all the way to Doc Chambers' office so's he could patch them up."

"It had to be done, couldn't leave them lying about, not knowing how bad off they were."

"Oh, by the way, where is Selena now? She went to the mill, like your sister, Orinda. Where did she go from there? Have you heard much?"

Josh replies, "She sent a post. Said, she left the mill, soon as she found out some of the older workers were coughing a lot. They figured it had to be that stuffy mill with all that cotton dust flying around and no fresh air to be had. So she hightailed it to Gloucester, Massachusetts. A friend told of her own new job up there, working on the docks of a big fishing company. They hired girls to haul fish from boats. In time, she became more seasoned and learned to gut and fillet fish in the big shed."

"Hope she fared better than that cotton mill for wages?"

"It paid her room and board and enough for clothing and other needs. She got extra when a big haul came in."

I say, "Good for her. Was her time out of work her own, and not hindered by company rules?"

"Yes, she had more freedom. She did OK, and caught the eye of a Whaling Captain from a well-to-do-family, right in that city—very presentable—in his early thirties, so not too old."

"She's married? When did you learn of it?"

"Last my Ma heard, they got married in a hurry before he shipped out again. Ma thought, it might have been a 'have to' wedding, so Ma kept it quiet. She asked me not to tell a soul, either."

"Ooops, you just told me. Where are they now?"

"She mentioned they might stay on the Islands, where winter never sets in. Some have the luck that others never seem to get."

"Helen, let me tell you what happened to Ma after Pa died. Once I saw her during her resting times but dared not let her catch me watching. She sat by the window, just staring out at the barn. The saddest look hung on her face.'

"All her smiles were long gone. She took it the hardest at the onset of winter when most harvesting chores were done and she had more time to herself."

"My goodness, Joshua, I wish she could have been happier, but I'm supposing that was not meant for her. How could anyone help her—help replace all that she had and felt for her husband—all the years together?"

Josh said, "I wrote this poem for her. Just hoping to ease the pain."

Memories on Snowflakes [17]

There's a season of the year
When the days grow short
And the wind blows crisp and clear.
It's when the geese have gone
And the harvesting's done
That thoughts from the past appear.

Memories on snowflakes
Drift down from the sky.
Bringing laughter and heartaches
From years gone by.

But this season of the year
When the gray turns white
Is when the mind grows crisp and clear.
Watching the golden sun shine
On snow topped pines
Is when happiness replaces the fear.

It's the time of year
When crystal clear moonlight
Brightens the night ~
Uplifting the heart,
Clearing the sight.

This season of the year ~
When days are short
And nights could be long and unkind ~
Tis the best time of all,
To catch snowflakes that fall,
Bringing loving memories
To dance in the mind.
Joshua Haskell

"It's such a nice poem, Joshua. It must have brought some comfort to her. Your mother was a hard-working woman. She never complained about working the farm after your Pa died, did she?"

"No, she never did, Helen. She got up before dawn—before me, even. Letting me sleep in, while she headed to the fields to tend to the crops—hoeing, weeding, watering, or what all.'

"One time I dragged out of bed, finally, and saw her and uh, it made me ashamed. There she was, even before fixing breakfast, she—well she—."

"What's wrong? Is it painful for you to remember?"

"Ah, Helen, forgive me, I can't help it. There she was, for heaven's sake, mucking out the barn. One of my chores. I had to run and take the shovel from her."

"Was she wanting to take on as much work as possible? Perhaps she was trying to keep her mind off that tragic accident that killed your Pa."

"You think that was all she did? How 'bout her fixing broken boards on the shed, or dragging rails for the fencing. Besides, she picked up heavy boulders to repair breaks in the stone walls round our fields. Of course, when I saw her, I would run over to help. However, she never asked for help. She'd just say, 'Thank you, Josh, you're very kind to lend a hand.'"

"My sisters Orinda and Selena also helped with the work, but Ma had them do mostly housework. She insisted on doing the man's work outside with me and Jacob along to help."

"That poor woman, to have to work like that. Couldn't she hire anyone?"

He shakes his head back and forth and then rests his head in his hands. I hear a faint sobbing. He stands up and goes to the pump for water. Drinks some, splashes it on his face, then dries his hands and face. Delaying, not wanting to talk, I suppose.

He sits back down and continues, "Helen, you asked about hired help? No, we had no cash for that. Did you ever notice her hands? Probably not, since she wore gloves when going to town."

"What was wrong, what happened to them?"

"My Pa had told me, that when he was courting Ma, she had the daintiest looking hands you'd ever see.'

"Then after he passed on, her hands gradually got rough and lined with calluses. Her skin was like leather."

"I wish you could've told me, maybe I could've helped?"

"No, I didn't dare, she wanted no visitors, not then. She said, 'These hands serve me as good as any man's hands. I don't need any paid help.'"

He turned his back, took out his handkerchief and wiped his face, before turning back and grabbing me close to him.

"I'm thinking, Helen, back on that day when I came in from haying the fields and found her lying at the foot of the stairs. She couldn't move.'

"I yelled, 'Ma! What happened?' She could see me, but couldn't talk."

"Yes, I remember. That was the day, she had the stroke. I had gone for salt and sugar at the grocery store. You can't blame yourself for that."

"I know and I don't, but it tugs at my heart when I think about it."

"Well, she could still write. So she could let us know what she needed."

"Just barely, she could only write with her left hand."

"Good enough for her, I imagine? She managed to sign her last Will."

"Where is that Will, Helen?"

"Where it's always been, right here in the family Bible."

I show it to Josh. He reads it.

Last Will and Testament: I hereby bequeath and freely give to my eldest son, Joshua on this second day of July 1846, A.D. all my land, property and other possessions for his sole enjoyment, with a separate ten-acre parcel of land adjoining the afore mentioned acreage for my younger son Jacob's possession under the guardianship of Joshua, as notated in the Land deed, and as affixed below.

Signed, Mary N. Haskell.

Recorded on Twenty-second day of July 1846, A.D.

* * *

Still reading this journal over, anyone could rightly see, from his poems, what Joshua really liked doing. When day's chores got done, he'd light his whale oil lamp and start in writing. He loved penning short stories and poems. He rarely would show them, except to me.

When first he made me privy to his stories and poems, I blurted out what came to mind.

"Josh, they could easily be printed out for others to enjoy. Any newspaper round here should be grateful to get just one of them."

Ah! Here's one of his best. It touches my heart, even now.

Sunlit Flowers
by Joshua Haskell[17]

My love would walk with me,
Through fields of sunlit flowers
And we'd lie 'neath the old oak,
By the side of the hill,
And talk and laugh for hours.

I'd touch her hand . . .
Then she'd rest my head,
Against her breast.
And without speaking,
We'd understand . . .

And experience
An eternity of happiness.

Bright white clouds,
Soon turned to gray,
As stars replaced the blue.
And hushed in the wind,
I'd hear her say,
In soft spoken words . . .
"I love you."

I can always feel Joshua close to me, as I see those lines. Helps, it does, to keep him near, as though he hadn't gone off for such a long time. Instead, it's like he just went down the road a bit.

Chapter Five

Sleigh Ride

That last time we went to dinner at Jacob's I had stomach aches all the next day. Hope this time the rabbit meat is not as hard as leather, like chewing on boiled owl. Maybe he's taken heed to his Ma's recipe book, with bits and scraps of paper shoved in the pages, pointing out the easy fixing ones.

I've harnessed up Jim, our Morgan horse, and as I attach him to the sleigh, I notice his left eye. That infection looks to be worse. Hope he doesn't get blind in that eye. Jim's been a good Morgan horse. Joshua's Pa bought him when he was 15 and now he's going on 31 years. Yet, he's ready to go whenever we need him. Though he's past his prime, he never loses his urge to please. Pat him one more time, rub behind his ears. He loves it.

Finally, ready, with everything set for packing in the sleigh. Caleb and Elisha climb up. They're a little too quick for my liking, as they scramble into the back with heads turned away from me.

"Wait, what are you both up to? Come on, face me, what are you hiding?"

Caleb says, "Didn't do nothin."

I'd be blind as a bat, not to spot Caleb's telltale jelly tracks. A purple mess is smeared over his lips, trailing right up past his nose landing right beneath one eye. Also, Elisha, big as he tries to be, still couldn't rid his face of signs. He's got cracker bits stuck in his teeth. Ah well, so be it. No time for scolding, have to get in front, but first my rag rug needs to be spread on these cold wooden slats. I'm plenty warm enough in my sheepskin coat, and I'll tuck this big wool blanket around the boys to keep them snug.

In the midst of pulling their coverings up to their chins, I grab each one real quick and wipe off their faces with my handkerchief. Then, I jump back down, grab a handful of snow and really do a good job as they squirm like the Dickens. There, all clean, with only a slight red on their faces from the snow. And, without me saying a word.

I climb back on the seat. All set now. "Giddy up."

Caleb and Elisha, not so quiet as before, are now hooting up a storm. They giggle, then laugh before warnings of, "Look out, Ma, here comes another big turn!"

"Yes, you two, hold tight to the sides of the sleigh."

Caleb asks, "Ma, maybe we can cut cross-lots? Maybe go see Pa?"

Elisha answers, "Ain't no way we're gonna find Pa goin' cross-lots. Don't you know he's in Windsor town? That must be a hundred miles from here. Ain't that right Ma?"

"It's not quite that far, but we won't get there, at any rate, not by going cross-lots." Caleb will not be stilled. He misses his Pa.

"Why can't we see Pa? Maybe tomorrow, Ma, why not? Can we, huh, please, Ma?" No time to answer. I must pay heed to seeing our way ahead. Almost there, rounding the next bend, past the lilac bushes that Jacob planted a few years back—not far.

Jim's developed a fine trot and we're moving along at a good pace. As I look back, I can see the snow swirling behind us.

Then, what's that? Coming from the bushes? It darts right out, into the roadway!

"A deer!"

"Whoa!"

Too late, Jim spooks, rears up and bolts to the right. We're sliding along, faster, too fast. The runners slip and turn sideways.

"Whoa! Hold up!"

We go off the road, down the embankment, and slam up against a tree. We get tossed about, helpless. Like rag dolls. Then all is gone, just darkness. A big empty hole.

* * *

"Where, what—my boys? Elisha, Caleb where are you. Talk to me." My back is cold. I can't move. What in the world? Jim? Why so close to me? His hind quarters pin me down. Cannot push him off my chest, it hurts.

My eyes. They won't open. So black, can't see. Smelling something, is it oil? Must be the lantern? How long, where, what happened? Where am I? What's this sticking to my face? Hair, no, it can't be mine. This is so thick. My bonnet is still on. Must be, what? Jim's tail? But, how? Take a big breath, ooh, it hurts, but try to . . . blow it away. Can't reach, can't make it go away.

My side, oh, that pain, hurts like the devil. So still, but the sleigh's on its side. Where . . . where are my boys?

Call out, try to shout, "Ca-leb."

Dear Lord, I hurt, make it stop, cannot breathe. My eyes shut, try again. Louder— "Eli-sha?" I sound like a croaking frog. So tired. Must not sleep—no, no, cannot sleep. Let me up. Let me find them.

Please Lord, get me out of this dark hole. It's so black. Where am I?

My face is wet. I'm shivering. Snow? Yes, falling on me. Soft but so cold. Oh, that black pit, creeping up again, sucking me in, down, down to—it's horrid here, so cold, and the pain—but I sink, and it's going away. But I cannot, my boys, must find them . . . must not stay here—.

How long was I—? Mustn't sleep, stay awake, call out. "Caleb! Elisha! Answer me, please, can you hear? Lord, let me up. Please, I beg. Make Jake come soon, to see what happened."

* * *

Jacob's Cabin:

I'm ready. Where is Helen? Plates, I need put on table. Stew is simmering. Wood stove is hot. Still no sign. Look out window, out there. What moves? It's on the porch?

Open the door. Elisha! He turns his head. Stares at the woods? What's out there? I draw him near. Snow cakes all over, covers his hair. No cap. He grabs my hand. His lips move. Could be, Mmm? Or, Ma? His hand, it shakes. It's all red. Half frozen? He points, where? Down the road? Helen?

Grab my jacket. Scoop up Eli. Run to the barn. No time to saddle. Ride Ole Blue bareback. Bridle him. Hoist Eli up. Sit behind me.

Down the hill, snow, too deep. Slows down Ole Blue. Dear Lord, make Helen be OK.

Eli tugs my sleeve. Points. Under that tree down by the river. A sleigh. Get off Ole Blue. Run. Helen, not moving. Lean down, close. Brush the snow off Helen's face. Her eyes open. She stares. Lips move. See her breath, like mist in the cold air. She's alive. Pushing and shoving—pull her from under Jim. Get blanket, cover her. Put Elisha next to her. Poor old Jim. Real bad off. His head, not setting straight.

"Jacob? Thank God, you've come. And, here's Elisha. I called for Caleb. Heard nothing. Jacob, read my lips, Caleb's out there someplace. Go find him."

Where? I see footprints. Go to river. Not Caleb's footprints. Too big. Red stains—drops? Touch one. Frozen. Hurry, follow them.

Faster, run, help me Lord. Then, I see ahead—on large rock by river. A bundle. Closer. It's Caleb. Snow all over, brush it off. So cold, he is. And, his breath? Yes, it leaves his mouth. He's alive. His forehead, a cut? Watch it, bleeding again. It's OK, just a long scrape. Deer skins wrap round him—that's odd. His clothes, wet, half-frozen. Put my arms under him. He moves, wraps arms round my neck.

Hold him tight. Run back to sleigh. Put him near Helen and Elisha. Cover, under same blanket. Helen's awake, and pulls Caleb in.

Poor Jim, neck—twisted, broken. Dead.

Tomorrow, haul back, Jim. Needs a burying place. But, now, need his reins. Twine together, bind ends tight. Hitch Ole Blue to sleigh. He rights the sleigh, first try. Without my help.

Now, slow and gentle. Lift Helen first, then Caleb. Lay flat in rear of sleigh. Tuck blankets all round, cover faces. Get home to a good fire.

Knots are good and taut on these reins. Jim's harness is good fit for Ole Blue.

All set. What is catching on my jacket? Oh, Elisha tugs at me. Turn, grab him up. Set down. close to me. Elisha touches my face. His hand, so cold. So red it is. Frostbite can hit him. Needs muffler. Mine. Plenty long enough. Wrap hands and neck. I snap these reins.

Helen's cabin, almost there.

Now, stoke the fire. Make them warm.

Helen and boys, all settled. Boys are asleep. Their beds. Helen frowns. Points to her side. Opens her mouth, but it does not move. Not talking? She closes her mouth. Closes her eyes. Doctor Chambers must come.

Helen sleeps. I tip-toe, blow out candles. Now, drag out straw mattress. So tired. I yawn. Sink down in soft mattress.

* * *

Sun out this morning. Clear day. Helen and boys still abed. When awake, they need breakfast. I go milk cows and get eggs.

I am awake. Finally. My hand feels down on the side . . . it hurts. Why, what's wrong?

"Good morning, Jacob. Thank you for letting me sleep."

He writes on Eli's slate. "I see you're still in pain. Can I help?"

I say, "You can fetch Doc Chambers. I'll give you a note."

"OK Helen, I'll saddle up. Go fetch him. You are OK now?"

"Yes, I am. It's painful but I'm OK."

He takes the note, then holds up some deer skins, and signs, "Skins wrapped up Caleb."

"Are you sure?"

"Yes.'

"They are not ours, Jake. They weren't on the sleigh. I don't know where they came from. Toss them in the alcove for now."

He signs, "OK. What can I do, before I go?"

"Yes. A cuppa tea would be nice. And—Agh! my side, that pain—please bring me my journal? I'd like to sit by the window and work on it while you're gone. Oh, and thank you for doing the morning chores?"

"Yes, all done. After I fetch the Doc, I will yoke the oxen. Drag Jim back. Can't leave him by river. Spring thaw, coming soon. Then, I bury him."

"You're right Jacob, and may God bless you for all you've done. Now, be off with you and God speed."

He is out the door in no time flat. Hope he makes it through those large drifts of snow. More got built up last night.

"Ouch!" My side hurts, and all I did was reach for the ink for this quill. Now, look at my scribbling. Need to stop. I'll page back in my journal and read for a while.

I remember when I met Joshua on my very first day at school. How grand he was to look at. He outshone all others, and no one could compare, not a girl or a boy was his equal.

When we set eyes on each other, I knew something locked us together. He was the good friend Ma told me I would make. Though, I'm sure she had not intended a boy. Well, for land's sakes, he was more interesting than any girl.

I recall that morning when he was sitting on our fence, as Ma began walking me part way to school. First, he waved, then stood up and leaped off the rail to gallop up to Ma.

"Hello there, I'm Joshua Haskell, heading on over to school. Can I walk with you, Ma'am?"

Ma said, 'I know you well, young Joshua Haskell, and well do I know your family. Your mother has done a fine job raising you."

"If you have no objection, I could lead Helen to school for you and later see that she gets safely back to your home."

Ma looked at him and then frowned at me, waiting for some explaining to happen. So out came the first thing popping from my head,

"Uh, well, if Ma allows it. OK, Ma, er, uh, well, could I, Ma'am?"

Her jaw dropped open, and she raised her eyebrows in surprise. Perhaps wondering, when did her Helen get so polite—calling her Ma'am and not Ma like I usually do.

Ma tilted her head towards me, and then at Joshua, she smiled and nodded. And, then with no further ado, she headed on back to our cottage.

From that day forward, the last lessons promised the best time of day, signaling soon it would be teacher letting us out—to go explore, run, play, whatever caught our fancy. We dawdled a lot on the way home, till the last minute before racing our hearts out on that last stretch.

We liked games, like flipping aggies into a hole, or 'Peggie'. Josh found an old broom handle and cut off a piece, three to four inches long and sharpened each end to a point. Then he scratched out a small shallow hole.

"See, Helen, we can take turns. First, lay the 'peg' halfway out of the hole. Then whack one of the points with the broom handle, so that peg flies straight up in the air. Then smack it, real good, with the broom handle."

My turn. I swung at it as it came down—hoping to slam it far enough away, to win. Of course, Josh always hit it the farthest.

Later at night, when chores got done, and Ma gave permission, we liked to run off fishing. Then, on the way back, we'd gather up wildflowers or wild cooking greens for both our Ma's. Funny, although Joshua always still addressed Ma as Ma'am, same as he did his own mother, I never got the hang of it.

Ow! The pain is getting to me.

Joshua told me more about his early hardships on the farm.

I asked, "I know you had Jacob, but your sisters, why couldn't they help more?"

He said, "Well, Orinda was much older than me. She left the farm to work in the textile mills down in Lowell, Massachusetts. Her pay, although meager, helped a bit."

"You couldn't get any hired help, not even with Orinda's pay?"

"No, we couldn't stretch it that far. That only left me, Jacob, Ma, and young Selena to care for the farm. Selena could help some but proved too frail for heavy work. Soon as she turned sixteen she also went off to the textile mills. And, then, chores were endless, always waiting."

"You never let on, Josh. We had it hard on our farm too. We had no men at all to help; just Ma and my sister Lily. We had to make it work every day. Either we bartered our goods for cash or sometimes found a willing man to help plow the fields."

"Oh, you did? Which one was it? Did I know him? How old was he?"

I held back my chuckle, but only barely.

"Don't be foolish, of course not. Hmm, you sound jealous? It was a long time ago and I was very young."

I was quick to continue, "To finish what I was saying, what we sold for cash was mostly handiwork, knitted garments, and crocheted pieces. We worked the land for garden offerings, same as other farm folk. Then again, we barely survived lean years when weather was not on our side."

Then he said this, "Helen, you'll make some good man a fine wife someday, with all your skills, and such a good worker you are."

Huh? I thought, What? What's he saying? He's smiling. Oh, he's teasing me? He must be. Or else—.

I went on, "Let's see, where was I? Like your two sisters, my own sister Lily also headed down to Lowell to tend the cotton looms. She was going for mill work when only fifteen. Ma truly thought the work would be light enough for her. Not like mine out on the farm, where I worked by myself or shoulder to shoulder, with hired hands when we could get any. Lily worked in that mill four years, till meeting up with and marrying her husband, Jack."

Joshua asked, "How did your sister Lily take to the mill work?"

"We realized, not from Lily's letters mind you, but it was apparent she just worked herself too hard. She was always trying to be of good cheer when sending a post. We were supposing it was her usual way to try to keep up and be like the older, stronger women. Unfortunately, being too frail, she caught a lung condition."

"Oh, that's awful, what was it, did they find out?"

"The Doctor later said it was coming from all the cotton dust getting stuck in her lungs, and she was told to rest more. When feeling better, and her cheeks began to fill in again, being all rosy and all—nothing could stop her from marrying her Jack. And Jack was so taken with her, showing her off to one and all, you'd have thought he'd won the state fair award for the best-groomed Filly.

Chapter Six

Caspar and Rufus

Five days since Jacob brought us back and my sleep has been fitful ever since. This pain in my ribs and side are bad enough, but the bump and bruises on the side of my head—still are—oh, so tender.

Ah, what a time we've had, but how did Elisha make it to Jake's cabin? The poor lad, he must have been terribly scared and in shock when he went to find Jacob. Well, thank goodness, the cabin was close by. Jacob's window would've been lit up to draw Elisha in. We could've all froze to death by the time Jacob thought to look for us.

Jacob's been staying here for our farm chores. He got that note to Doc Chambers, who came out the next day.

Our doctor said, "Luckily only one rib seems badly bruised. The others are not so bad off. Your insides must be OK, or else you would have bled to death or had a lung punctured if that rib had broken. Mrs. Haskell, there's nothing to do, but let nature heal the ribs. Now heed this, when you go to the outhouse, check on any redness that might get passed. I'll need to know about that, straightaway. Your boys have only superficial cuts and bruises. They'll be OK."

He then offered advice while showing how to tape my ribs.

"See this? I'm applying this poultice with taping plaster but change it often. Try not to cough and don't do any heavy lifting for at least a fortnight. Meanwhile, take this tonic. One teaspoon should do. It will ease the pain."

I took it to the kitchen. One taste, and I dropped the spoon, and gagged. Bitter tasting, it was. Strong, what was in it? 'Laudanum' it said on the bottle and it contained alcohol and opium. How nice, the pain went, and I floated on the ceiling a bit. So, I've only been taking a half portion since then.

Jacob said he gave our doctor two jars of my best Blueberry jam for payment. My mouth dropped open but I kept quiet. Two? Only one, and a smaller jar at that would have sufficed.

Maybe if my eyes stay shut, I can rest. The pain is not as bad now. This wet hand cloth over my eyelids will help. Lying abed and sleeping helps a lot. I am glad Jacob is here to help me. Good, it's all going away. I'm fading, yet it's so cold, my arms are trembling—.

* * *

Wait! I am sitting, what—straight up in bed? What happened? Wide awake now, it's something like that terrible dream. The man crossing the ice, falling through—and two men. Both left. No one to save—but one man came back and stretched his hand out. Did he hold a branch over the man's head? Was that part of my dream?

My hands shake, I touch my face—it's wet from cold sweat. Must get back to sleep. I can't. My eyes are wide open. That dream ruined my sleep. Tell me Lord, is it a nightmare, nothing more? But why and what if—?

Stop wondering. That dream is telling me something. Something dreadful that has, or is about to happen. I need to find out, and right away.

I must go see. Jacob needs to stay here, and tend to the boys.

"Ooh," my side really hurts. And, this poultice—it's come apart. No good at all. Here's the taping plaster, need to fix it up, real tight. My good corset with the whale bones, this one will do me. There, that's better.

Easy does it. Sit down, pull on Joshua's heavy wool leggings. Just get my winter coat on, and now my boots. Need my head scarf, not a bonnet.

Must wake up Jacob. Grab hold of his shoulder, give it a shake.

"Jacob, no time for saying too much." I point to me, my eyes, to the outside, past the door. Make an arc, for "I'm going beyond here."

"Then I'll be back here." I point to the floor, make the OK sign, and point back to myself. Must go now. I leave Jacob to fend for his self and the boys.

Ole Blue's having a time of it, his legs sink in deep snow banks. Snow drifts piled up last night. Some top over the shed and coops.

"Joshua? It's me, Helen! Can you hear?" I hope there's no answer, it's just all in my head.

First, look down by the Tannery on Adams brook. It's narrow there for crossing. No, the bank is too steep and the water's too swift. Better head down past Al Chandler's house and over to our branch of the White river. It's a more likely place—almost the same as in my dream.

Look, down by the river, right over there. Can see how the wind swept some snow off that river ice. Is it hard enough to cross? No. It's way too thin. Look! Way over on the other side! Two men, dragging something like a sled?

"Giddy up, Ole Blue, go—hurry, faster. Good, keep going. Faster, keep it up, faster!"

Pull up. "Whoa, boy."

I yell across the river, "Hallo! You over there?"

They stop. Talk to each other, but I can't hear—their backs are turned.

They hurry—pulling that sled away. I yell, loud as I can.

"No, please? Stop! What's that you're pulling?"

Both halt—the one toting bundles, shifts them to his back. The other one hangs his head, and stares at the snow. He stomps his feet back and forth. Finally, they look my way.

"Ma'am?"

"You are so aggravating. Answer what I need to know!"

Oh, Lord, is that a man in that sled? I'll hold back, be patient, let them answer. One checks the sled. It's nothing more than a make do—made of saplings. He must be tightening the vines that bind the branches. Then, what? They're moving? Sliding the sled along faster. Ole Blue keeps pace on our side of the river.

"Well, I'll be! Don't go!" They pay me no mind. How brazen, ignoring me. Hmm, dark skinned men? Could they be freed men from down south? Having to do with Joshua's work? Then again—could be paid helpers for the slave owners?

I yell, "That man on the branches! Is he, Joshua Haskell?"

They don't answer, and don't miss a step, but hurry faster. Smart Alecs. "Hallo, Joshua? Stop, you must tell me! Is that you?"

The one on the sled turns and waves. Then his hand drops. Why doesn't he yell back? What's he doing? He's propping up that hand with his other one, and—oh my—is that a salute?

"Could it be? Is it you? Joshua! Can you hear?" I know that salute! He did the same each morn, then again, after getting back from the fields.

They stop. I throw off a fast salute. The man on the sled, my Joshua gives out an 'OK' sign. Good, the snow isn't so deep now on my side.

"Giddy up, Ole Blue! Hold on—I'll be right there!"

Big rocks, lay next by next—now I can cross the river.

Jump off Ole Blue, but careful, yet hurry, before the ice moves. It's my Joshua, can't take my eyes off him, while I make my boot land again, good—here's another rock. One more, almost there—!

"Oops!" Missed, but—go, slide on this ice. One man jumps out and grabs my arms before I land almost on top of Joshua. OK, I made it. No harm done.

"Helen, can't believe my eyes—you?" Joshua's voice is weak, and he coughs—now, what's that he's spitting up? Water? He did almost drown, so it's no wonder.

This scares me. "We need to get you back home, real quick."

Joshua says, "We were wondering, *cough*—who that crazed woman might be." Then, of a sudden, his eyes roll back in his head, and his eyes close.

Both men look to me, and one asks, "How 'bout we hoist him on yer horse? It can git home faster." I shake my head and shrug my shoulders.

"Let's wait, see if he comes round soon. I don't know what's best. He might've broken something, and if riding the horse, moving about too much, it might make him worse."

Joshua's eyes open. After a few more coughs, he whispers, "Yes, that fool woman would not let up, with all that yelling."

I try not to laugh. You don't know what this woman can do, especially when taking that tonic beforehand. I needed a few sips, so I could get up on Ole Blue.

I see his face, such a ghastly, almost gray color. Cheeks have deep hollows. His mustache and beard. He had no full beard when he last left home. He's waking again. A crooked grin quivers on his lips, but it slips away. My hand touches his brow.

Joshua says, "Come closer." His lips brush mine. My eyes close. I want to stay in his arms and never leave. I hear a slight cough behind us, and my eyes open. I see the men; they face the other way. One shuffles his feet back and forth. One turns his head, looks off to the woods. They are colored men. I wonder, was he escorting . . . or—.?

Joshua whispers, "Helen, meet Caspar and Rufus. I took a cross-cut—over the river to see you."

"You should have known better.'

"Hello. You kept him from drowning?" They nod.

Joshua asks, "How did you know?"

"A little bird told me." He frowns.

"But seriously, Joshua, you dared walk on that thin ice?" My eyes shut tight, but tears won't stay back.

"Wait, Don't cry." His wet glove brushes under my eyes. He wipes the tears from my cheeks.

"Sorry, Helen, have to—*uh, er, cough*." His hand falls back and his head tilts to the side. No sense talking now.

I tell the men, "We must get him home. He needs to get out of his wet clothes."

We trudge along, looking ahead to the covered bridge

"Look, way on the other side, it's Ole Blue."

I yell, "Hold on, Ole Blue!"

"Can you hear him, Joshua? He's snorting, and stomping, waiting for us." No answer. My Joshua is sound asleep.

We get on the covered bridge, and go slow. Cannot make noise. Yet, no one's around to notice the colored men.

Ole Blue now drags the sled. We're half way home. I turn my head to see Joshua talking but I can't hear. The wind is gusting round us again.

I yell to him. "Best to wait, Joshua, till we get back home. Then, you can tell me about it!"

Finally, we're home. The two men lift Joshua off the sled. Jacob's smile is so big, as he runs out the door. Eli and Cal are right behind.

Elisha calls out "Pa? Ma, you got him? Is he OK? Why's he on that sled?"

Caleb asks, "Pa, how y' doin'?"

The men do not break stride but slowly lumber on.

"Hold on, stop there, don't go up the stairs. Not yet. Boys, Jacob—stop, wait. Let the men carry him into the house. Step aside. Please?" I catch onto Jake's arm, and sign to him.

"Help me, can you tether your horse?"

"Eli, hold the door for your Pa."

Joshua's in bed. I sign to Jacob. "Enough covers, stop piling that big heap of blankets on top of him. The men will be in the shed tonight, so they'll need them. Understand? Good, then, would you help see to their needs?"

He nods, then scoots out the door. Now, lo and behold, he's back to peek over my shoulder.

I sign, "Your help is needed. Soon as we're done; you can go for the doctor."

My side feels like it got stabbed with a knife. But I will not take any more of that laudanum. Can't be sleeping, as yet. I grab Joshua's right arm and start pulling him to the center of the bed.

Josh cries out, "Ow, stop!" And I hold back my own cry of pain.

"Sorry, I'll be more careful."

With a croak in his voice he says, "Just tell me what you are going to do, first, so I won't be surprised. You OK with that?"

"Of course, Josh."

"Now, this torn jacket must come off."

"Ah!" He cries out. His shirt sleeve has dried blood caked on it, and I lift it up carefully, but cannot—it's stuck to his arm.

"Do you feel pain?"

"How can you tell? I just say, ouch, or wince for no reason at all?"

Best to ignore the sarcasm. He's not up to par, not by a long shot.

Have to cut away the fabric, but, there's more blood—yet, it's darker and that's a blessing, because the bleeding has stopped."

Far worse—this blue and purple color at the top of his arm under the big swelling, could there be bleeding underneath it? No need to alarm him till we see what's what.

"Joshua, can you move your hand, now your arm? That's good, right here from your wrist up to your elbow?"

"Is that what you asked? Did I move it enough? It sure hurts, though."

"That was fine, it showed no bones are broken."

What made such a bruise? I look closer—ah, that's a relief.

"Joshua, there's no red streaks darting out from the matted blood."

He doesn't need to hear this, but best of all—there's no yellow pus seeping from under the wound, either.

"Fine, Helen, now I'm so tired—."

"Hold off, wait—I must sign to Jacob."

I wave my hand to catch Jacob's eye. "Look at me. We need a big blanket, and hot soapy water; and then a small pan under his arm. I need to clean his wounds."

I cut off the rest of his shirt to show his whole arm.

Jacob returns and I sign, "First, I'll soak each sore with this hot soapy water. Can you hold his arm up? And this small pan, yes, it goes under. Right there, that's fine. Takes a good washing, see? We can't hurry. Now I'll rinse off."

The pan needs emptying. Motion to Jacob, "Come here. Careful with this dirty water. There's old blood and bits of dirt and what-all in it. Throw that water quite a way from our back yard. OK?"

He nods, and signs, "Be right back."

Not good at this time to ask Joshua, but I wonder if that wound came from that crack in the ice? Joshua's arm is dry now. I've fanned it enough with the clean towel.

"Look, Josh, this poultice has greasy black paste, but will work good."

"It smells, what is it?"

"It's got iodine and will draw out any poison. The sooner it's on the better—so please be still. Just a few more minutes to wrap it, and there, almost done."

Sign to Jacob, again. "Fetch some of that fine linen from my Hope Chest, and bring my medicine box, and mending basket. Yes, the basket's right there. I need scissors."

I'll cut this pillow cloth in long strips, then layer over the bandages, and tie with these thinner strips.

"Thank you for all your help, Jacob. "I ask him to go and get the doctor to come, soon as he can.

Good, done at last. My ribs ache worse, but no matter, I can tend to myself later. Resting is better than that strong tonic.

Joshua's not coughing and his breathing is steady—at last he sleeps. He has no need of my tonic, I suspect. Not if he sleeps good without it.

I have the urge to dance and celebrate, but the pain in my side stops the foolish thinking. My Joshua is home, but I'll wait till we both can dance.

I go to pour a cuppa tea. As I pass by his bed, Joshua mumbles in his sleep. I stop and lean down.

"Have to go, must see her, so cold, oh, how grand, such passion. A fine voice, uhm, oh, oh! No, don't stop. That limb, give it here!"

What? He met a lady and had to see her? What's that about her limb?

Joshua's awake now, telling about his travels.

"Caspar and Rufus needed escorting to Randolph, to meet up with some female relatives. So, I gladly volunteered, *cough.* It gave me the chance to see you and the boys once again.'

"We trekked most of four days. We got to our river. It narrowed, *cough, cough,* but not enough, so stayed alongside of it until just before the West Randolph bridge. Couldn't risk folks seeing us—*cough,* wait, my throat, so dry—I need some water."

"OK, but first another pillow will help you sit up, and here's another to prop up your arm."

"I fixed a good hot drink to help your throat and that cough. Added some lemon and honey, and some cinnamon for taste. Watch it, hold it steady."

"Ah, good. Thank you. Bring a chair over, sit right here by me. Let me see, *uh*—yes, the ice looked strong enough. I asked them to wait. Needed to test out a good path. Made it to the middle. Then stopped when I heard a cracking sound. Too late, there was no turning back. *Argh,* hand me that handkerchief.'

"I tried going on, but hit more cracked ice. Felt it give way. It was breaking up. Right under my boots. I was falling in. That water, so cold—freezing, no use—."

"Wait, Joshua, please—just lie back for now."

He closes his eyes, so I leave to add more wood to the fire.

"Helen, where are you?"

I return to his side.

"Let me go on—*cough, cough.*"

"Joshua, must you speak of it now? That hacking cough sounds worse."

"That drink helped a lot. I can finish. The men went off to find a long tree branch. Held it over me. Tried to catch hold, but I kept sinking. Thought, this is it. Never said a good bye to you or the boys. Then the limb dropped just right. I grabbed it and got pulled out."

"So, that's what happened to your arm?"

"It must've got caught in that ice crack. It sure got butchered up. And, that branch when it missed a few times—you saw where it jabbed me? Should we have Doc Chambers come take a look?"

"Yes. Jake has already left to fetch him."

Usually, my Joshua is not of a mind to have a doctor, not for his aches and pains. But his lungs, and throat, swallowing that freezing water, it could be serious.

He says, "Ah, my throat is still sore. Can I have some more of that drink you made. Once I can talk better, there's so much to tell. So much—"

I filled a pitcher, and left it on his bedside table. Suddenly this odd feeling starts creeping over me. I shiver as goose bumps pop up on my arms. Is it a cold draft from the window? No, it's shut tight. He described my dream. The whole of it. Somehow, I knew of what happened, but how?

Forget it all. Grab my coat. Need a walk to clear my head. There's no moon out, but the stars are shining bright. The sky is so clear, and if Joshua were looking, he'd be sure to comment on it. Same as before, I'm sure he'd point and tell me, "Look, Helen, clear like a crystal, it is. And, there's the big dipper and the little one, too." Looking straight up, I now say, "Lord, you've brought my Joshua back home. I thank you."

Doctor Chambers arrives and gives Josh a good going over.

Now, he says, "Helen, if it had been any other man instead of Joshua, then you would have been burying him instead of nursing him back to health. He's strong as an ox and has a good constitution. Continue caring for the wound on his arm. He should have full recovery over time."

"I am thankful for such good news, Doctor Chambers. And, you traveled here in no time at all. Please accept two of my best blueberry preserves."

"Thank you, Helen. I must be off. I have one more visit tonight."

I hear the boys in the back room. Something hits the floor.

"Uncle Jake, me next? Please? It's mine, Eli, let me?"

"I'm just trying it. Gotta make sure it spins OK."

Caspar and Rufus sit at the table. They had looked in on Joshua, to see how he was coming along. I offer them hot cocoa. It's all gone before I can bring over apple pie. The boys and Jacob need some, too, to hold them till supper. Eli sidles up to me soon as I open the door.

"Ma, Uncle Jacob carved this new top for Caleb. How's Pa doing?"

"He's resting, son. He'll be OK. Why is it you have Cal's top in your hand? Where's yours?"

"I'm testing it for him." Eli hands the shiny red one over to Cal.

Cal pulls on my apron, "Look Ma, see what I got? Uncle Jake made it. Just for me, only me. See? It's special!"

Jacob smiles at the apple pie and cocoa I hand out.

I leave the room but stop to sign.

"Thank you, for taking time with the boys. And, the new top. It's one of your best." A broad smile spreads on his face.

Rufus and Caspar need attention now. "Before retiring for the night, I'll fix up these freestones to warm your bed. I'll set them on back of the stove to keep hot."

They frown, dart their eyes one to the other, and do not reply.

"Don't fear. They won't be too hot. When you're ready for bed, I'll wrap the stones in flannel. You just put them down by your feet under the cover. They'll give off heat aplenty, keeping you warm through the night. And, here, take this quilt and a few afghans, and my sheepskin coat. They'll ward off the cold night air."

"Yessum." Caspar takes the covers.

"Rufus, in this box are some towels, and this bucket to fill at the well. You'll need it for morning time. If it's freezing out there, come in and use the kitchen pump."

Rufus says, "Ma'am, y'all so kind. It jess too much, all we gets—food, an warm covers y'all handin me. Y'all sure knows how to make a body feel t' home."

Caspar adds, "Ma'am, 'bout today down by river side, we sure feelin sorry, us not stoppin, an not answerin."

"Makes no mind now. Joshua explained why. I am beholden, and I'm the one to be sorry, for not thanking you soon as we arrived here. Now, get on with you, get some rest. And, stay put, no need to do anything but laze round a bit. I'll call you in time for a late supper."

Finally, I've time to set a while. Can get out my journal and finish today's writing. The name I'll put on it? "The Haskell Family History."

I'll start off when Joshua first started sheltering runaways, after we married and were living in Bethel Gilead. These were only overnight stays. He continued escorting after we moved to West Randolph. Occasionally he would leave home for one or two days at a time, to take them further north. They needed connections along the 'Underground Railroad.' Of course, not a real railroad, but volunteers loosely joined for when escorts were needed. Many volunteers were freed slaves or other coloreds. Quakers were pushing for equality for all and he was heavily involved in the movement.

Then Joshua felt that he 'had to do more' than just giving mostly an overnight stay. Other safe stations were available but Joshua went to Windsor, Vermont to wait for his assignments. He learned of the Bezaleel

Bridge Home for Runaways. This home had a false closet built on the side of the main chimney. Runaway slaves could hide in it—till moving, and then move on to Hartland Four Corners or Woodstock.[6]

A Conductor, or leader, told Joshua, 'Windsor is now the largest city in Vermont and the fugitives should encounter less problems. Per chance they can walk about more freely in this city. There are many prominent citizens here, more sympathetic to their plight.'

Windsor, Vermont: Joshua heard an abolitionist speech given by a Quaker lady, born in Nantucket, an island off of Cape Cod, Massachusetts. She travels the country giving talks on equality for all.

Joshua wrote in one of his letters.

"Windsor is a quaint old town. How fascinating to be amidst such history. That Old Constitution House, you recall, Helen, from our school books, was the birthplace of the Vermont constitution in 1777."

That was his first trip to Windsor lasting about a week. Since then, he's made two more, each stay becoming longer. Now he'd been gone for three weeks.

I needed him back home, not putting that place over his family, and telling about a great lady who talks a lot.

He's awake now and calls me over, "Helen, you must hear of the woman speaker for the Abolitionists. We were lucky to have a chance to be at a meeting to hear her. Such a fine lady, and such passion in her voice."

Oh, so that explains it. The same lady, it's true, is the one he knew of while in Windsor? She's a speaker for the cause? Who is she? Does she have a beau or a husband? Is she plain. How young is she? And her passion—but is it still meant—? The limb, was it a branch? Too many questions left, but I'll have to let it alone, for now.

He's napping again, so I'll read more of my journal.

May 1st 1847:

Today my sister Lily married Jack Wallingford, a lawyer. She looked so pretty standing next to him and so proud with her head held high. They will now go to live with Jack's mother in an old, but stately, farm house in Fairhaven, Massachusetts. Lily says it is on Charity-Stevens Lane at the end of Bridge Street. When she last visited, she brought me a Fairhaven Book with a good history. Parts of it are now penned in our Family History.

> *From her place, Bridge Street runs West until it crosses the Acushnet River into the Whaling City of New Bedford. The Acushnet empties into Buzzards Bay. On the Fairhaven side, a grand fort guards the Bay's shore.*
>
> *In May of 1775, the first naval battle of the American Revolution took place off this shore, when local commanders captured two British sloops in*

Buzzard's Bay.[7] *Then in 1778 the fort was destroyed when British forces entered the harbor and landed 4,000 men.*

Oh my, when I first read that, I thought Fairhaven wasn't always so quiet a place to live in.

After the War, the citizens petitioned for a new fort. When finally finished, it was called Fort Phoenix, named after the fabled bird, the Phoenix. Though it died, it later sprang up, out of its own ashes, to fly again.

Have to stop reading my journal, and see to Joshua. He's wide awake now. What's he telling? About that same woman? At last I'll get her name. He says she works for woman's suffrage.

"Oh, is that right and you're still impressed by her?"

"I met Lucretia when she spoke at a rally we had in Windsor."

Hmm, calls her by her first name?

"You can tell me about her later. I need to look at your bandages."

"Wait, take it easy, it hurts."

"Looks OK, let me help you out of bed. It's time for supper."

As I lift him, a sharp pain, jabs my side. Can't hold it back. "Ouch!"

"Helen, what's wrong? Set me back down on the bed. Why did you yell out like that?"

"I didn't want to bother you, not yet. But, you might as well know."

"Know what? What's gone on, have you been injured?"

"The boys and I were in the sleigh going to Jacob's cabin. He invited us for dinner. On the way, Jim got spooked by a deer. It jumped in front of our sleigh. Jim bolted. He went off the road. Our sleigh overturned, and threw us all out."

"What? When? Of all things—did anyone get hurt?"

"Poor Jim, he landed almost on top of me. Lucky that he didn't. He was only wedged up against my side, so I could not move."

"Good Lord, Helen, you could have been killed. What happened to the boys?"

"Elisha made it to Jacob's cabin. Jacob came back and pulled me from under Jim. Jim must've broken his neck.'

"Our doctor said Eli doesn't talk about it and perhaps it's best he cannot remember for now. He did act as if he was in a daze when Jake saw him on his porch."

"Where was Caleb, did anything happen to him?"

"I couldn't tell, kept calling for him. Then, Jacob found him up river. He was wrapped in deer skins, lying on a large rock."

"That's curious. And no injuries on him, our little Caleb? Tell me more."

"Just a cut on his head. Footprints and some bloody droppings helped Jacob to find him. Very strange, how and where he was. Perhaps, I thought, a stranger happened by and rescued Cal, but didn't wait to get thanked? Jacob had to get us home. He got Ole Blue to right the sleigh and thank the Lord, made it back to our cabin."

"And, how about you? Where did you get hurt?"

"Our doctor said it was just a few ribs. Only one got badly bruised. Jim almost landed on me, but the snow under me, it helped to ward off his weight. He was wedged right next to me and I could not move. When Jake found me, he had to pull me out from under Jim. Nothing worse, no organs inside were damaged. I use a stiff corset over some taping. At first I put on a good poultice. The doctor told me how to put it on. It'll just take time to heal."

"Helen, why didn't you tell me about this straight away?"

"You had enough to worry about with your own injuries. I did not want you getting upset over me. You'd know soon enough."

"How you've managed with it all, I have no idea. Helen, I'm not so helpless that you must hide your problems, and your own pain. Now let me try by myself to get to the table. Don't try to lift me. Just walk beside me."

"Josh, what about Caspar and Rufus, what plans did you have for them?"

"They'll have to remain with us until I've recovered enough to get them to the next safe house. They can sleep in the shed, but would you mind if they continued to take meals with us?"

"Of course not. They should be our honored guests for pulling you out of the river. Easy now, let me pull this chair out for you."

We all sit at the table, not talking much but busy downing our second helping of Jacob's 'Rabbit Stew'. My sourdough biscuits, with dollops of butter help sop up the last of it. The boys have big grins, and keep looking from their Pa to the two colored men.

No, not just looking, but staring at the men. I give a fast shake of my head with a frown darting right at them. They must not be so rude. Probably curious, wondering about the dark skins. Same as when Daisy was here. Too young, they are, and will take some growing up to understand.

Speaking of grown-ups, I see Caspar and Rufus staring at Jacob. They must have seen a deaf person, I take it. Or, perhaps not. Never saw anyone hand signing before? Jacob's rapid hand signing appears to mesmerize them. Even Joshua's occasional grunt, with a noticeable grimace doesn't get their attention.

When everyone's had their fill, we side the table. The spell is broken.

Josh gets to finish about their trip. Yet I want to know more about the lives of these two colored men, before Joshua helped them.

I ask, "What went on, Caspar, and Rufus—back at the plantation to make you run away?"

Caspar does most of the talking, and I find it curious to learn that Caspar and Rufus are brothers. Caspar being the older and although being a slave, worked as a 'field boss' in charge of sixty-two other Negroes. They came from the Armitage Plantation in southern Maryland.

I ask, "Caspar, your owner must've offered a large reward for your capture? Didn't it take special training to become a boss over your own people? With more eyes on you, how did you ever manage your escape?

"Ma'am, it hurts fo' me to tell it, but Massa ketched dis young un stealin' butter cookies. Mistruss put em on her porch to cool. Massa tole me 'Caspar, y'all take dis boy an gib him ten lashes.' But I cain't do it."

"Oh, I don't blame you, not one bit."

"Yessum, not jess a boy, but he be my chile. So me an Rufus take my boy an we run off."

Josh asks, "Whatever happened to your boy?"

"After fo' days, we lose him. He musta go one way an me an Rufus go 'nudda way. We go back an look, an call 'Jeremiah!, Jeremiah!' But no talkin, no nuddin, all is quiet." Caspar's eyes fill with tears. He lowers his head.

Everyone's so still, not moving at all. Then Joshua speaks up.

"Let us all hold hands and pray for the safety of Caspar's son."

After tucking Joshua in for the night, I head for the boys' room. I best get both talking about the sleigh overturning. Need to know all they remember. Should help to get it off their minds and mine, too.

I sit by the bed and ask, "Are you two still awake? Eli, are you still not sleeping? Are you doing better, after our sleigh got turned over? I mean, any pains, or hurting anywhere? Doctor Chambers said you had no serious injuries"

Their eyes stay shut. Eli scoots way down under the blanket. Cal then follows.

"Is everything OK for both of you? I mean, working right, or are you needing the doctor to check you again, next time he sees Pa?" There's some rustling under the covers.

Elisha inches up in bed, peeks out of his blanket, "My head used to hurt a lot, right here, where the bump is. It's not so bad now. No, don't touch it. Almost forgot, see, my arm here? My elbow? It doesn't hurt, just feels funny."

He shows a small bruise, and I tickle him under his arms. He chuckles.

"Don't worry, looks to be nothing more than what happens when you boys have been rough housing."

Caleb throws off his side of the blanket, and jumps in my lap.

"Ma! Ma! How 'bout me? Look. Here, on the side. My head. It hurt real bad, it did. Is it got blood? Huh, Ma?"

"Yes, I see, and you look as if you're coming along good, but we'll keep an eye on you just the same. Go fetch me a book and I'll read to you."

Thank God, there's nothing much to worry about with either boy. Caleb and Elisha, how we love them.

This story is a good one, "Once upon a time, in the land of giants . . . there was a small boy, who—-." Their eyes are closing.

After the story, I lean closer, and whisper, "Good night, God bless. Guess you're glad your Pa's back? He can tell you boys some good stories, soon's he feels up to it. Now, sleep well."

Elisha barely opens one eye. "Good night, Ma. Here's a hug."

Caleb crawls up to me, but keeps eyes closed, "Night, Ma, love you—my Pa, too." Then scoots under the covers again.

I'm relieved. No real complaints or scary things were told to me. No bad memories are left.

I need to rest a spell, but I must loosen these bones in my corset. What a relief. Don't need any more tonic, I'll sit a spell in my rocker and just close my eyes.

I napped for a time. Our boys are fast asleep, and now I start brooding again. What of that woman, the one by the name of Lucretia? Joshua must tell me about her.

I get up and tip toe to his side. He is awake, wonder how long, but he never called out? He reaches for me. I lean closer, and his hand, although trembling a bit, gently covers my mouth.

"Helen, you look pale. Are you ailing?"

"No, no, well not in that way, this is different. I must talk to you about, well . . . what's been happening and well, I wonder about all you've been doing."

"What have I done, what worries you? Tell me."

"I was wondering what had become of you? You were gone for too long, much too long a time. Where were you? Then you mention this woman Lucretia, the one with passion, the talker . . . well . . . now . . . what was your relation with her?"

He motions for me to sit on the bed by his side.

"Ah Helen, you're looking so tired. Are you that worn out? Should have suspected and come by here much sooner. Too much for you, doing a man's work—though a mighty good job, Jacob said you did."

"Oh, he did, did he? Did he say what he did, and all the help he sometimes did not provide? Why do you talk of him, and not answer me?"

"OK, another time we'll speak of him. I know how childish he can be at times."

"Yes, and I am sorry to think in a mean way about him."

"Helen, are you worrying about things I only *might* have been doing?"

"I did wonder, when you were not here and no word from you."

He strokes my hair and turns my face toward him.

"Look at you. Your eyes always sparkled. Now you've got dark circles under them. Other than the sleigh tipping over, which was terrible of itself, did something else bad happen? Are you ill, and not speaking of it?"

That did it. Can't hold back now. I need a deep breath.

"Did you, Joshua, did you find a, what's called a—."

Find a what? Give me a hint?"

"I will just say it. I will. Did you find a safe harbor?"

He held me close, and I put my face against his chest and kept my eyes closed.

"Harbor? I wasn't out to sea."

"I don't mean a boat in a storm. When I'm alone, I picture you in, yes, the arms of some lady."

"What? A woman? When, where? Who in the—do you think I—no, you can't?"

"No? Not even perhaps one you accidentally met? Not that you looked for her on your own. I need to hear that none of it is true?"

My head stays down, my cheek feels a button on his shirt, and I move the button aside. His heart beats so loud. I must not upset him. He almost drowned. I move away but he draws me back.

"Helen, look up, yes, right at me. I'll not mince words. You'll hear my firm answer. C'mon, look at me. It is a—do you hear me—it's a no. Spelled, with capital letters, N. O."

"Is that all? Nothing else?"

"Do not worry, my darling. The only safe harbor I'll ever have is with you. It's in this house with you and the boys. That's what I live for, nothing more, and nothing less. I am proud to be the father of two wonderful boys. And, first of all, think of it, I am the husband of the most beautiful and compassionate woman I ever met."

Then, that's it, and I am a fool. I must rid my head of all the pictures, the one with him and a . . . oh, no. Lord, take it out of my mind.

Joshua holds me close, and runs his hand through my hair. I almost tingle all over, but, I lay still, and silent on our bed. Cannot get him upset, must remember how sick, how close to drowning he came. I carefully remove his arms, and inch over to my side of the bed. He must have room to get a good rest.

I light another candle. It flickers and throws off shadows against the wall. One looks like a dancing cat. I am mesmerized by the dark figures.

I'm dozing again. Can't keep eyes open.

Next thing I see is the sun peeking through the window. And, Joshua is out of bed, and he's walking? He holds out my school scrapbook. He must be getting a whole lot better.

"Helen, are you getting up? Hope you're feeling better? Take a look and read this one paper again. It's on this page, the one I wrote when first we met."

First grade:
Helen, oh Helen, best of all the girls.
A quick step, a hop, and now grinning.
Please, grant me one a your curls?
Helen, oh Helen with eyes so true.
Am I the one, the lucky one,
The one that'll be winning you? [17/16]

I can see by different ink color, that the rest he's written down at different times.

Helen, my Helen, when we are old
And time grows shorter each day,
Will you be by my side,
Will you still be my bride
With your laughing brown eyes
And your own special way? [17]

The ink is still not dried on this one. He must have just penned it.

Sweet Helen, carry no fear
Remember living in Bethel Gilead
With just ourselves to be worrying over?
The time we looked for the four-leaf clover
In fields rich in buttercups, and a myriad
Of wild flowers unspoiled by the drover.
I loved you then and will love you forever. [17]

What on earth? Tears again? Yes, and they cloud my eyes. Cannot speak, not now. He means it, he loves me, same as always.

Thinking back now, and with mending done, I have time to spare. How good those days were, back before moving to Randolph—when we lived in Bethel Gilead. Joshua again tried his hand at poetry writing. One day he surprised me as I was knitting stockings for presents. He first hemmed and hawed before he handed me a paper.

"Helen, can you be looking at my poem about a dog?"

The Dog

by Joshua Haskell [17]

Four PM, and winter's golden sun
Casts long shadows o'er snowy fields,
And along the barn where swallows run.

From the barn a dog appears,
With matted hair, an obvious stray,
He ambles to our cabin door.
Don't let him in. Scare him away.
"Get", I yell and stomp the floor.
He runs in fear, and is seen no more.

Funny, I've never seen that dog before.
What's he doing at our cabin door?
Where will he go? The snow's so deep.
Was he hurt or hungry?
It's cold. Where will he sleep?

With jacket on, I walk outside,
And follow his tracks toward the barn.
There he's cowering under a log.
With eyes affright, this pitiful dog

Looks at me, just looks at me.

Tucked in my jacket,
I carry him home.
It's much too cold,
To leave him alone.

Five PM, I've fed him bread.
This stray dog, not too old,
Is sleeping now, beside my bed.

"Is it not up to par? I know you have a keen eye for such things."

"This is good, just right for my liking. How on earth can you think upon poems so quick, and still make sense? Would take me ever and a day, and not come out half as good."

Life was good to us back then. That lane in Bethel Gilead we walked along of a summer's day? Have to check my journal for the correct page.

Joshua wrote this piece.

Remember how our old lane in summer had sweet aromas, and how strong they were. You loved the honeysuckle flowers. Then we compared it in autumn when flowers had gone, but trees became ablaze with color. Those precious leaves, all different, all varied markings, no two exactly alike. Some small, some large and some blessed with a subtle coloring. Yet, the best are the truly unique ones; set apart by the brilliance of their hues.

Chapter Seven

Abigail, Betsey and Sally

For the past three days, Joshua's been telling me about a Miss Abigail Folger.

"She's fiercely dedicated to our abolitionist movement and would be coming to Randolph escorting two female slaves."

"I find that quite curious. A woman escort, and not afraid of the danger? How did you chance to meet this young lady? This lady who needs no protection for herself and is eager to partake of long dusty journeys. That's strange. Well, would she be ungainly and just a plain spinster type?"

"She must be about my age and comes from a Scottish family—very prim and proper but not married. She is content, telling family and friends that 'the right man has not yet sought her out' nor is she desperately waiting. Instead, she seeks adventure first."

"Oh? An adventuress, is she? Though, I imagine she's knowing enough to act as a lady? Well, tell me more about this lady friend of yours."

"She'll be traveling with Nathan Anderson a stagecoach driver, a good man and loyal to our cause." Joshua sits back, smiles slightly, waits.

"How'd such a dangerous plan get hatched, to get to our place—quite a distance—and, in a coach? Would they travel at night, not chancing to be seen by day?"

"Do not fret. Nathan has made many trips like this and he's one of our better conductors. Under the stagecoach's back seat, he's built in a hidden area complete with air vents. That area can hold two slaves in complete privacy. I expect they could arrive tomorrow if not today."

* * *

Dusk had just about settled by the time Nathan's coach arrived at our cabin. Nathan's Stagecoach is quite grand looking but I hope, come morning time, folks round here will not take note of it.

We meet and give names and shake hands. Then, Abigail went hollering at the girls, "Both of you, it's time to get out and meet the Haskell's." As they stepped down from the coach, Abigail continued, "See the taller one, that's Betsey. She's eighteen, and Sally is twelve."

I said, "What's wrong with Sally? Why is she crouching behind her sister?"

"She's just shy, and clings like a shadow to her big sister."

Joshua calls inside, "Caspar and Rufus, come and join us."

They step on to the porch. Rufus jumps off in a big leap to the ground. Caspar trails right behind, and both run to see the girls.

"Well, I'll be. Y'all look here Caspar, am I seein' right? Betsey? She sho' gon' git herself all growed up. Thought we'd never see her agin, 'ceptin in Heaven. Uncle Henry an' Aunt Beatriss both be surprised as all get out; iffen they get to see her again. And who this be? Little Sally?"

Caspar joined them. Both hugged Betsey, but Sally stepped back, she was having none of it.

"Betsey, if it dunt beat all, we sure glad y'all gets here."

Betsey tried to get her sister to understand, "It's our big brothers, Sally. Don't y'all remember? Guess you was too young. Caspar was good and he look after us, but Rufus was always in trouble an Old Massa Johnson try t' be poundin sense inna his dumb head. An I ain't lyin, huh, Rufus?"

He shakes his head and frowns . . . but chuckles.

He says, "Betsey, y'all tellin dem tall tales agin."

Betsey grins and continues, "Massa Johnson, he say, 'Lissen up, nigra, y'all don't be running off agin.' But fool headed he was, an he skedaddled anyways, ever chance he get. Each time he get back, he gets a good whippin. Dint stop him, as he had alla dogs after him. When we hear yapping dogs, we guessin it was Rufus out inna woods—back to runnin off again, soon's his back healed up. Well Rufus?"

Rufus chuckles, then coughs. Now he grins, and we all laugh. Rufus grimaces and the laughter stops. He must be recalling the pain from all those whippings. I reach to touch his shoulder and a slight smile reappears as he bows his head. No one speaks.

I ask Betsey, "What about your mother, is she still back on the plantation? And, your father, where is he?"

"We dunno. Never knew him, an she may be dead an gone to Gloryland, but, if she ain't, we gonna find her someday. She been gone away a long time ago."

They all join us at the table and take their pick of the spread that's laid out. There's hot cocoa, and apple and cinnamon pie fresh from the oven. Oh, and apple juice, too, but I suspect milk for the girls is more fitting, especially for the younger one.

Betsey made fast work of her pie, and downed her milk without stopping, then looked over to Caspar.

"Casper, where's your boy, Jeremiah? I ain't seen him yet."

Caspar's mug fell from his hand, but I quick wiped up the spill. His lower lip started to quiver.

"We kinduh got lost inna woods one night, an lost him. We looked an looked till droppin in our tracks. Dogs was far off, howlin away an well, we ain't never see'd him agin. But we will, yes, we will find him agin, jes y'all see if we don't."

Betsey's mouth hung open at first, then she shut it fast as she lunged towards him. She gave him a big hug. Poor Caspar, she looks to be squeezing too tight. Can he breathe? Not in any distress, though, as he says nothing.

Joshua, sensing the unease round the table decides to change the subject.

He asks Nathan. "Tell us about your trip from Windsor to Randolph. Did it go as planned?"

"Where shall I start?"

"Well, right from the beginning, we're anxious to hear all of it."

"OK. It was in the early morning hours, when I pulled my stagecoach up to the stately home of Abigail's parents in Windsor. Then, as I stood watch, she brought out the two slave girls, Sally and Betsey. She placed quilts in the seat compartment and then had them climb in. They were a bit cramped, but nothing was amiss when I replaced the seat cover. Abigail next took her place, and we were off, heading north."

"How many stops did you make along the post road?"

"First stop was White River Junction, a busy town where the White River joins the Connecticut."

Joshua says, "Yes, I'm quite familiar with that town. The factories and sawmills there greatly benefit from the power of all that water."

Nathan continues, "We soon pulled into town, having to cross through it to the higher post road. We intended to make this trip without picking up any passengers. But, leaving the coach stop, a middle aged portly gentleman, all in a dither, with top hat askew, flagged down the coach."

"He yelled, 'Wait, wait!' as he ran, huffing, and puffing, with his few strands of hair flailing in the wind. I had no choice, but to halt the horses.'

"He said, 'My good man, will you be heading in my direction?'

"He probably thought I was the driver of a public coach. Before I could refuse, he started to climb aboard. He said to me, as he peeked inside the coach, 'I am a Banker and would travel as far as the town of Sharon, Vermont.'"

I said, "My goodness, Nathan, that must have presented a problem. What happened next?"

"Well, Helen, this was just the start of a major problem. I'll let Abigail tell about what went on inside the coach, if she's not too embarrassed to relate the tale."

Abigail responds, "Well it was quite embarrassing but I'll continue. I felt uneasy as he proceeded to light a cigar and then stare at me as no gentleman had ever dared before. After the first exhale of that billowing cloud, he leaned closer and whispered right at me. 'Well now, you're a right pretty lass, you are. What's your name and where might you be from?'

"Not wanting to reveal my identity I said, 'Sir, my name is Sally and I've been traveling from Bellows Falls on my way to rejoin my family in Northfield. They shall be waiting there at the stop.'

"That was quick thinking on your part."

"Then he proceeded to rest his hand on my knee. 'My dear, we should become good friends on this trip to better pass the time.' My eyes began to water as the cigar smoke filled the coach. Just then, a sneeze could be heard from under the seat. Straightaway, the man's eyes bored into me, as he demanded an answer."

"What's going on, Missy, and exactly what are you up to?"

"Before I could answer, he shushed me with his gravelly voice."

"No, I know full well what this is about. You can't lie. I will be duty bound to report you to the authorities at the next stop."

"I forced tears in my eyes and began pleading, begging him not to. I said, 'Please Sir, take pity.'

"Then with a gleam in his blood-shot, rummy eyes, he lumbered from his seat, sat down beside me and wedged his bulky stomach up against me.'

"Helen, are the children in bed? They should not hear what follows."

"Yes, they're in their room and the door's closed. Please go on."

"He said, 'Of course, I might reconsider . . . if, *er,* certain accommodations could be made? And, mind you, only to be kept secret between us.'

"I was speechless, as I cowered in the corner of my seat. He pressed his leg against mine—forcing me to crunch myself near to sideways—ending up flattening myself up against the side of the door. And, all the while I held tight the latch so as not to fall out. I was deathly afraid the door would spring open, if I pushed the handle down.'

"I yelled at him, 'Stop it, please, you're hurting me!'

"Next he parted my shawl and fumbled with the buttons on my blouse. Frightened, but gathering my wits, I stopped him, by whispering in his ear. 'No, not here. We must go outside.'

"I called, 'Nathan, stop the coach, please.'

"Then, I helped the banker out the door. We walked, behind the coach and stopped at the edge of an embankment by the river.'

"I turned and kissed him full on the mouth, although I nearly gagged from the taste of tobacco.'

"Then proceeding to unbutton and lower his britches till they were down around his ankles, I looked up to see his big grinning face.'

"I said, 'Now close your eyes.'

"Then I quickly stood and pushed him with all my might down the embankment, watching him tumble, then roll face first, down into the leaves and mud. With his britches around his ankles he couldn't even stand up.'

"I ran back to the stagecoach and climbed on board.'

"I yelled, 'Nathan, drive off and be quick about it.'

"I looked back through the coach's window seeing a very angry gentleman with mud covering him all over, shaking his fist in the air.'

"Couldn't stop laughing as I tossed his top hat outside. Then, I remembered to caution the two girls beneath me.'

"It would be best to muffle your sneezes in the future.'

"Then I heard faint giggling beneath me. Sally and Betsey what were you two giggling about?'

Sally and Betsey start shaking their heads seeming very reluctant to talk. Finally, Betsey opens up.

"I whispered to Sally, 'Bout time Miss Abigail sees what's it like what men folk do. She be's no way same as us. We hafta keep our tongues silent 'bout what white folk done tuh us back at Massa's. But Miss Abigail sure done pull a good trick, gettin him outta our coach. Hah, no mo' man smokin smelly cigar. An we starts gigglin.'

We all had a good laugh at that and then urged Abigail to go on.

Abigail continued her tale.

"I sat up front now with Nathan in the driver's seat. As the coach pulled into Sharon Vermont, I asked Nathan about my biggest concern.'

"Do you think that banker gentleman will report us to the authorities?'

"Nathan said, 'I don't think so. He'd have a lot of explaining to do about his appearance—and why are you calling him a gentleman after what he attempted with you?'

I replied, "Don't know. Just my nature, I guess."

"We were both quiet for a while, listening to the horses' hoof-beats on the post road. Then Nathan started to tell me the story about Joseph Smith and the Mormons. Do you remember what you said, Nathan?"

"Yes, I was telling Abigail how passing through Sharon reminded me of a story I'd heard, having to do with the Mormons."

Joshua said, "If it's about the Smith family that used to live in Tunbridge and Sharon and their son Joseph, I'm somewhat familiar with that family, but go ahead and tell me what you've heard."

"Seems like Joseph Smith Jr., the founder of the Mormon Church, was speculated by people in these parts as being the same Joseph Smith who was born and raised in Sharon on the family farm of Joseph Smith and Lucy Mack."

I said, "What happened to them?"

"Well, Helen, the family moved to western New York when Joseph was a young lad."

"Why did they move?"

"They fell on hard times in Vermont. They had three years of crop failures and a business that went bust. Once in New York, the family began farming again. The part of New York they moved to, at the time, was caught up in a great religious revival experience. They say that's where Joseph saw his visions."

Joshua asked, "How do you know all this, Nathan?"

"Mostly from the New York papers my Uncle reads. He told me of the terrible persecution suffered by Joseph and his followers. Joseph and his brother moved to Illinois and were murdered there about seven years ago."

I said, "That's terrible! What happened to his followers and the Mormon religion?"

Joshua said, "I understand that another Vermonter, Brigham Young who was born in Whitingham, Vermont, became their new leader. He was responsible for moving thousands of Mormons, from Illinois to Utah."

Nathan said, "Thank you, Joshua. That's interesting history."

Nathan continues, "As we passed South Royalton, I remember how my father once told me that South Royalton was actually farther north than Royalton, but he never explained why and for the life of me, I've never been able to understand that riddle. Perhaps you can help me out Joshua. How is that possible?"

"It's hard to convince the locals of this fact, but it's true. The river which normally runs north to south has an "S" curve between the two towns. So even though South Royalton is downstream, it is physically located more north than Royalton."

"Thank you for that explanation, Joshua."

"Please go on. What happened next?"

"Continuing our trip, we took frequent stops to allow Betsey and Sally to climb out from under the coach seat to stretch their legs and to head to the nearest clump of bushes. Yes, near, but far enough away so as not to be seen by others.'

"As the stage coach left the Post Road, we made our way down the hill from Randolph Center. Halfway down, I reined in the team, and called for Abigail to come join me on the driver's seat."

"Why?"

"I told Abigail that she'll probably never see a grander sight in all of Vermont than the sun about to set on Quaker Hill.'

"We both watched. The sun painted the clouds along the horizon a blood red, then the clouds further up soon changed to various hues of orange, pink, and gold. As the streaks grew longer, they stretched out overhead."

"Abigail said, 'Aye 'tis a grand and beautiful sight, and I should like Betsey and Sally to see it also. If that be alright?'

"I agreed, although reluctantly. I said, 'We should not take chances of having them seen.'

"I brought the two girls out of the coach and there they sat on one of the traveling bags, looking at that sky.'

"Then, finally, Betsey let out a long, 'Ooo-ooh.' She nudged her sister, and Sally had a broad smile on her face."

"Tis a good sign for you girls—an omen of things to come. That beautiful sight could mean that one day you are going to be free to look at whatever you want. And never, ever have to hide anymore."

"Betsey said, 'Yassuh, Mister Nathan, we knows—we gon' t' freedom land, oh, I means Gloryland.'

"We'd been dallying too long, so Abigail got the girls back into the coach, before someone might see them."

Joshua stands up. "Great tale, Nathan and Abigail. We're glad you made it here safely. Now, I'm ready for bed. Shoulder's acting up. Goodnight all."

Nathan asks, "Helen, do you mind if I sit on the porch for a short while, and could you join me with perhaps another mug of what you just served? That is, if you would be so kind?"

"Of course, and will you join us Abigail? We can leave the others to catch up on old times, if they wish."

"Helen, not now. I must speak with Joshua. I've wondered how he has been. Is he well."

"He's fit. Still has some pain in his shoulder. As I mentioned earlier, that fall through the ice was an awful thing to go through. It was good that Rufus and Caspar figured out how to get him out."

"I must say, Helen, he was a lucky man to have the two slaves, or I should say, the men to help him."

"Yes, and it's amazing he's here at all, but let him explain it to you. Don't tarry too long. He's tired, and needs his sleep."

I bring Nathan his mug and I settled for a cuppa tea. He's sitting on one of the rockers on the porch.

"Thank you, Helen. It was quite a journey and somewhat tiring, but coming down the hill this afternoon, it was such a sight. You should have seen it with us."

"Nathan, I know the view well, but go on."

"As we started coming down the hill toward West Randolph, I could see the valley extending north to south. All that land, what a blessing it must be.

I saw farm fields filled with corn, wheat, barley, oats, and hay, not to mention the many cows grazing in the fields."

"It's good land, Nathan, and crops can thrive on plentiful water coming from Ayers Brook. All the streams around the brook run right straight into it. Then, the meadows, pastures, and crop lands benefit, filling in with bountiful growth sprouting up all over."

Now, what wound me up to go on like that? Do I rattle on to keep from thinking on what Joshua and Abigail may be discussing? Or doing? Why is she so interested in his health? How close were they back in Windsor? After all, Abigail is not such a plain one at that. Were they spending time, too much time . . . well, no, I must not think of such things. Joshua, even if fit, would never, well, no, never. What? Corn fields, quilts?

"Did you say something, Nathan?"

"Yes, those many fields reminded me of giant patchwork quilts."

"Well, they'll soon be showing full bloom, and gradually running up the slope till reaching the top of Quaker Hill. And, some Merino sheep will pasture along with the cows. Though sheep aren't as plentiful nowadays. They're getting scarce."

"Why is that, Helen? I thought this land was excellent for grazing and didn't you have a thriving sheep business here?"

"Most farmers rid their farms of them, and built up their dairy cows instead. It became cheaper to buy ready-made woolen garments. Farmers found it more costly to feed their sheep, than what they could get for their wool. Many killed off their entire flock just to save money. We managed to keep some, but mostly for the meat."

"Seems like such a shame, not seeing many of those animals in the fields anymore."

"I agree, Nathan. By the way, did you notice the West Randolph church spire? It would have been way off in the distance, and did you hear that clock striking?"

"Aye, Helen, we did. The Church Bells struck the hour as we spotted it. Next, the train's whistle sounded as it pulled into Randolph Depot."

Abigail, appears with her cloak on her arm.

She says, "Nathan and I should retire to the Inn in Randolph. Are you ready to leave, Nathan?"

I say, "Why not stay here for the night?"

"For Heaven's sake, the neighbors might ask questions about our Stagecoach hitched in front."

Nathan says, "I know of a good Stagecoach station and livery stable in downtown Randolph. They can put the coach and horses up for the night."

"Yes, Nathan, let us go, and now is a good time to leave."

She is so forward sounding, too much for a lady, but I must hold my tongue and just say that they should stay.

"Abigail, we have room . . . just—."

"No, Helen, there it is, no, do not insist, though your offer is too kind. It is settled."

She's determined to go. Nathan shrugs his shoulders and turns his head away.

"Nathan, come along. We shall return in the morning to transport the two girls to the next safe house. Perhaps Jacob could accompany us as he knows these parts? Also, I should think that both you and Joshua need time to recover from your injuries."

My, but she is of a bossy nature. She must be well practiced in getting her way.

Nathan jumps up and they both say their goodbyes and start to head out. Then I said, "Wait." and followed them onto the porch.

"When it's daylight, come back. I shall be up early fixing breakfast. There'll be a laying out of warmed up taters, bacon and scrambled up eggs, along with biscuits and special gravy. Don't be shaking your head, now. It's no trouble. I'll put out apple sauce, and there's plenty of cheese, with jellies and jams."

They turned and waved and kept walking to the coach. Abigail now laughing as she looks up at Nathan as they drive off.

So quiet, here in our cabin, as Nathan's horses trot off in the distance. Sally sits over in the corner. She is much lighter skinned than her sister. The firelight dances off her pale cheeks. She looks down at her feet. Then, before she ducks her head again, she looks straight at me—yet, still without a smile on her face. How sad she looks.

Later, when she got bedded down, I covered her with my best quilt. Then as I started to leave the room, she grabbed onto my robe and pulled me back. Well, what is it, was she not warm enough?

"Missus Helen, kin I say somethin?"

"Of course, what is it?"

"Y'all is jes' like my Momma, helpin out, an doin for others. Our Mistruss been the same way, afore getten so mean. The devil hisself must a got inside her, cuz she alla sudden, was hittin and slappin me. Never knowd next time I'd get a whippin from her."

"Why Sally?"

"She was pinchin me till I done want t' holler out. But, cain't, cause she's gonna pinch harder. Most times she done it when no one t' be lookin. She was Mistruss, bossin all us inna house, an I had to do what she say."

"Have you any idea what set her off? What did you do?"

"Wal, my Momma, use t' work inna big house, servin Mistruss, till getten sent away. Maybe Mistruss gets mad at her? Massa, he so nice to Momma, an not mean actin. Missus Helen, Ise shiv'rin jess talkin 'bout my Momma, an ain't knowin where she at."

"Why was she sent away, and why was your Mistress treating you that way. I can't believe that she was so hateful to be pinching you."

"Wal, Ole Massa, he gimme sugar cane treats. Snuck em t' me in his shed. He say, 'Never, ever tell 'bout games we playin, or no mo candy treats. Ye hear? Or y' all gettin sold off at auction. An, he say, 'doncha dare t' be tellin Mistruss.'

"Missus Helen, Massa's games gone on an on. Don't exact know when we git started. He been good t' me, mose times. But he get meaner. Now, my insides been feelin all tore up. An well, you swear t' keep it privy, betwix us?"

"Oh, Sally, yes, I shall seal my lips from this day on."

"Never tole it afore. I bess t' put it away, way outta my head. But, settin inna outhouse, I gets sore. Uh, way down, an bad belly achins makin me git t' bed.

"Sally? What? Are you saying that he . . . oh . . .?" She nods her head.

"Oh, no, how awful. He should be shot."

She cries, letting out sob after sob and sniffing and hiccupping in between. I give her an old but clean towel to wipe her face, whenever she can stop.

What can I say, or do, but cradle her in my arms, pat her back, same as her Ma? I'll hold her till she settles down and her sobbing lets up. Time seems to stop, but no, the ticking clock is louder than ever. Finally, her eyelids drop down. I rub her neck and shoulders. Thank heavens, her breathing is even, and ever so light, and she sleeps at last.

My mind cannot fathom, no, dare not let it linger on evil men and their doings. I ask myself, 'Why are they born? Men and yes, women too are just as bad at times. How can they cause such pain? Worse, yet, who helps the innocent ones? No one? And, who stops such wickedness? There is no law in those southern plantations, or surrounding towns and cities. None to help, so who do they turn to? They do not. They run. They run away.

This extra quilt will keep the cold out if I tuck it up, real close round her shoulders. I'm not of a mind to care if Sally opens her eyes. She'd only see tears running down my cheeks. She needs to know someone does care.

Now in my bed, sleep will not come, not for a long, long time. Sally's words, the pictures they draw up get tossed back and forth to roam around in my head. Would that I could blot them all out.

I'm jolted fast awake as the sun's rays start streaming through the window. Slept too long. The boys are jumping on their bed.

"Stop that, Elisha, and Caleb! Stop that ruckus!"

Time for me to be up and about.

Now that I'm cooking, all these good smells fly through the house, especially eggs and bacon, and butter fried potatoes. Betsey and Sally stand in the doorway, rubbing their eyes. My hand points to the water basin and towel for washing up. Back to the table, standing by me, is Betsey.

She asks, "Missus, cain't we be workin' some?"

"Of course, if you will. I'm delighted for the offer. Three working together will soon get this table set."

Joshua's up and looking a might better. He sits by the window with no shirt on. He can keep an eye out for first sight of Nathan's carriage. This early morning sun, sure helps to warm him up. Wishing that I could do the same. Hmm—his bare chest, I should look away. It shows curves again, and his arms, those muscles—big and strong, almost same as before. Wish we were both fit, and could expect privacy, instead of company.

Oh no, fat just splattered! It hit my arm. Stop daydreaming, pay attention to the bacon before it gets burned. Move that pan. Never mind, get this arm under the pump and keep cold water coming. Don't stop. Good, I can't feel the burn now.

I better pay attention to my cooking, and not what I'd like to cook up with my husband. How silly I sound. It's good no one can tell what's in my mind.

I ask, "Josh, do you think Abigail is being too forward with Nathan?"

"Why do you ask?"

"Well, she seems to admire him so much. Perhaps too much. Why does he have such black curly hair?"

"I must not have mentioned it, but Nathan is a Mulatto. Most people assume he's white, but he had a colored grandmother. She was a former slave."

"That's interesting. I did not know that." But, what of it? Maybe that's why he shuns women like Abigail. Too much to handle, and not for his circumstances.

Joshua yells "I hear them coming. Come look Helen."

I'd better go see what he's pointing at. Horses are trotting, whinnying, getting closer. Then, Nathan shouts, "Hallo there, are we too early?"

As they come into the cabin, Joshua asks Abigail, "Tell me, where shall you deliver the two girls?"

"I had instructions before leaving Windsor to take Betsey and Sally to a Mr. James Hutchins' house in Braintree."

Joshua nods, "Yes, I know Mr. Hutchins. He is a strong supporter of our cause, as Helen well knows. Although not openly advertising as such, he does welcome important abolitionists when they're in Vermont. However, I'm surprised they did not want you to make contact with Lebbeus Edgerton or Daniel Woodward, two of our Underground Railroad agents right here in Randolph." [9]

"I guess they had their reasons. Can you tell me more about Mr. Hutchins?"

Joshua says, "Yes, of course. William Lloyd Garrison, publisher of the antislavery newspaper knows him well. And, Lucy Stone, champion of the women's suffrage movement—both were dinner guests at his house. He and his wife Elly are very kind."

I say, "They were the ones who took in a runaway named Daisy Corinda, and her baby. She stayed the first night with me and the boys."

Josh says, "Sally and Betsey will probably be transported to Montpelier, as that is the next big Underground terminal north of Randolph." [8]

Caspar and Rufus join us for this farewell breakfast. Everything I set on the table is soon disappearing. There'll be none left to even feed Jacob's dogs. He loves them so and I save scraps whenever I can.

Betsey nudged me and nodded over to Sally. Wants me to take a look. Sally cleans every last morsel off her plate, sopping it all up with big slabs of bread.

She then joins her sister in front of the fireplace. Betsey combs out snarled strands on Sally's head, then braids the hair.

I say, "Here, you two, try some of this lavender soap next time you wash up. It's inside this bag, you should have enough to last a while."

Joshua signs to Jake, "Be careful. Watch for dangers, like animals running and scaring the horses."

"OK', Jake signs, 'I will keep a look out."

Nathan tells Joshua, "In two days' time, we'll be heading back bringing Jacob."

"Don't worry. Jacob knows the back roads well. He'll get you there without trouble. I fully expect Mr. Hutchins will invite you all to stay over for the night. He'll have some fine tales to tell and will insist you smoke some of his special store bought tobacco, and take whisky with him. I usually refuse the offers. We Quakers don't use either substance."

Nathan nods, and says, "I would partake of a smoke, but not much liquor. I must ensure my driving will not be held to question later. You should have no concerns for your brother, we will get him back safe and sound."

They are all set, we say our goodbyes. Caspar and Rufus give Betsey a big hug, but Sally stands aside. They both climb aboard the coach, followed by Abigail and Jacob. Nathan, waves his hat, cracks his whip in the air and they trot off down the road.

Chapter Eight

The Request

They've been gone for two days. I hope Sally finds a good family to help her, as well as Betsey. I worry about them. And poor Sally, will she ever grow into a normal young lady? Time will tell, but what a hard life she's had. Lord, keep her safe.

"Joshua, do you intend to contact Lebbeus Edgerton or Daniel Woodward to see if they would be willing to escort Caspar and Rufus, further north?"

"I'm glad you asked that. This morning while they were helping with the chores, I asked them if they were ready to head north. I was surprised at their answer."

Caspar said, "Me an Rufus, we like t' stay on here, iffen it be OK?"

"Why wouldn't they want to continue north?"

"Well, it seems they have not given up hope of someday finding Caspar's son Jeremiah. They figure by going all the way to Canada, they would lose contact with him altogether. Or with anyone who may have found him. That is, if he's still alive."

"What did you say to them?"

"I said I would discuss it with you. You know, we owe these two a lot. I would like to give them a small spread where they could do some crop growing and maybe raise some livestock. What do you say?"

"That will be your decision to make. However, would they agree to continue helping with the chores in exchange for the land you give them. And more importantly, they should be cautioned not to show themselves to strangers."

"I'm sure we can count on them for that."

What's that I hear? Nathan's coach? I peek through the curtain. They are here, and Abigail looks none the worse for wear. How she manages to look fresh as a Daisy is beyond me. Jake and Nathan bring in their satchels.

Abigail enters and I see she's all freshened up. Hmm, is that lavender I smell? I hope the girls kept more of the soap I gave them.

Nathan says, "I'm quite tired, can I have a lie down for a bit?"

"Yes, of course, go use the boy's room. They are outside playing. We'll not disturb you. Joshua is resting in our room"

After he leaves, Abigail says to me, "How manly Nathan is. I've never met anyone like him."

Oh Lord, do I have to hear this?

She goes on. "He presents a grand appearance. I know he's a real man. He fills the air with such energy and he leaves me feeling like a wilted flower. Wonder if he has any interests, any lady friend waiting for him? Have you noticed his curly black hair? No? Well it makes me shiver inside. I'd love to give those locks a twirl." Eee gads, when will this end?

What could I answer? I just nod and stay silent. I cannot say what a twit she is, so vain and selfish. I think her mind was more on the possible romance the trip had to offer, rather than the welfare of her two charges.

"Come Abigail, let's join Jacob and Joshua. They're sitting at the kitchen table."

I wedge my chair next to Joshua. Abigail, instead, scoots herself over to sit on Joshua's other side. Jacob makes room for her. Nathan's awake and joins us.

Josh says, "We're anxious to try out a fine wood game called Chess that Jacob carved. Helen, can you give out the pieces?"

"Of course. Look Abigail, the Queen. It's just right for you, so regal. But I like this one. It has the head of a fine black Morgan stallion."

Abigail grabs for the Queen, but I take it and place it on the board.

"If you capture her, then you may keep her." Abigail does not hear me? She looks over to Nathan, but he's busy patting one of Jake's dogs. It's the female who soon will be a mother. It's almost asleep under my table. I wish we could find another spot for it. One that's safer and away from feet that don't look where they are going. Especially those high buttoned shoes that keep fidgeting, moving closer to the chair next to her.

I ask Joshua, "Tell us, am I right or not? Isn't that the way it's played?"

He nods, and she says, "Helen, could I have a game with you?"

"Of course, let's play." The others look on.

Right off, Abigail took two of my pawns. Perhaps she'd played this quite well before? I'm wondering what next she'll take.

Then she looks at Elisha and demands, "Where's my horse? Come give it back and right now."

Elisha darts off to his room but then comes back to give her the horse. She grabs it from him, without so much as a 'Thank you.' Joshua pats Elisha's head, then lifts him to sit on his lap.

Joshua says, "After Jacob carved these horses, Eli helped polish them. Sometimes he claims them to be his, when he and Cal play soldiers."

I hear a whisper so slight, and it's Eli next to Joshua's ear.

Eli says, "Pa, what happened to Jim? He was so good, did he get dead?"

Abigail perks up, says, "My goodness, who is Jim? Was he from around here? Joshua, do you know his family? Does he have brothers?" Nathan looks my way, and then rolls his eyes at the ceiling.

"Pa, answer me, can't you? Y' know, we went to Uncle Jake's?"

"Yes son, but we'll wait till later and we can talk."

Abigail purses her lips, and is studying our game. She laughs, and pounces on another of my pawns. This is not as much fun as I thought it would be.

Aha, I spy her Queen off by itself. My fine horse rears up to gallop off and is all set to topple her over—but, I hear something outside.

"What's that out there? Josh, look out the window, there's the post rider approaching. What possible news could it be and so late in the day?"

Joshua starts to rise but I say, "No, I'll go, you stay put."

On the porch, I shout, "Hello! Daniel, what did you bring?"

Reigning his steed, he reaches down to his mail pouch, "Just a letter, Helen, but from far away."

I thanked him and he soon turned round to gallop away.

I see it's from Fairhaven, Massachusetts. Must be from sister Lily. She hasn't written in such a long time. My hands tremble as I hold the letter in front of me, not wanting to look at it.

"Oh, Josh, what could it be? How on earth, what could be wrong, what is happening with her?"

"You'll not find out till it gets opened and it won't happen by itself, so give it here."

Joshua reads it. Then with no expression, no frown or even a slight smile, he gives it to me.

"Here, it's only for your eyes."

Dear Helen,

I have been feeling poorly, being very weak and having my chest hurting ever so often, making it worse when I cough. I would be most appreciative if you could travel to Fairhaven and tend to me while I try to rest and get better.

My Jack had recent news of his mother's dire illness of long-standing but this past year it began getting worse. Then one night she just stopped breathing and passed away. He had to leave to arrange for the funeral and shall be gone for two weeks or more. Being the oldest and a lawyer, he had to decide what items would go to each member of his family.

Please come soon if you are able. If not, then I will understand but please pen a return letter in all due haste so that I can try to make other plans.

As ever, your loving sister,

Lily

"Joshua, might I go, is it possible? Should I?"

"Of course, and it's only right and proper. She's all the family you've got left. You should go and tend to her."

"Are you sure about this? How will you manage?"

"My arm's almost healed and there's just the proper tending of Elisha and Caleb we need to address. Rufus and Caspar are already helping with farm chores. Oh, and Jacob is here. Don't worry, we'll manage."

Just then Abigail says, "Helen, I can stay on to help." I shake my head.

"No? Stop shaking your head and do not tell me I cannot. What other choice do you have? You must be leaving without any more delay. Just give me a list of what needs to be done while you're gone."

Nathan pipes up, "Why not go? I'll drive you. I have family in New Bedford, I've not seen in a spell. They'll offer me a stay over."

This is all going too fast, too sudden. And Joshua doesn't seem upset with my going away.

"OK, I'll pack but first let me write out the chores for all of you to do while I'm gone." I must make double sure everyone's time is filled. There'll be no time for dawdling with idle hands causing trouble.

After seeing the list of chores, Jacob signs to me.

"Some chores for Abigail, I can do. Cross these off. Barn work, milk cows. Muck out horse and cow stalls. Outhouse cleaning? Too much to ask of Abigail. I can do those?" Is she so delicate? Why do men get that idea about her?

I sign back, "OK, as you will." But why didn't I get that same help when Joshua wasn't here?

My packing is almost done with, but I'm not anxious for this trip. How I wish Abby was the one to be leaving. She's way too attractive. Her skin, her face, why there's barely a wrinkle and there's no hint of dark circles under her eyes. And, what's really bothering me—she's too well-proportioned to be left here in my stead. No, how silly of me. Joshua would never . . . besides, his health is not yet up to par.

Let's see, do I have everything packed? Mustn't forget my nice apron with the embroidered initials, as I imagine I'll be doing most of the cooking at Lily's house. Hope I've left out my nightgown for tonight. Good, there it is, hanging behind the door and my robe, too.

* * *

Nathan's busy. He's been up before dawn, feeding and hitching up the team. He's planning to take the Post Road most of the way, down past Boston and then the road to New Bedford and finally on over the bridge to Fairhaven.

Abigail's been helping with breakfast and showing me her plans to cook meals. She says she will follow to the letter exactly what's written down in my recipe book.

Making ready to leave. Nathan shakes hands with Joshua and Jacob and with a nod of his head to Abigail, he hefts my steamer trunk up on his shoulder and places it on the coach.

Down the line I go, to give my Goodbyes.

"Smile, Cal. I shan't be long. And, Eli, be good and listen to your Pa. I will miss you both." Then a kiss and a hug for each boy.

Signing to Jacob, "Thank you for all you've done; here let me give you a big hug." He sniffs, and as I move away I see his eyes tear up. I shake Abigail's hand and then on to Josh. "Thank you for letting me go. I'll send you a post as soon as I arrive."

Joshua tries to speak, but his voice breaks. He just grabs me tight and we kiss. No need for words.

Sun's peering through the trees as it comes up over Ridge Road. Nathan is gallant, helping me into the coach, as if I'm such a grand lady. Then we head off into the sunrise. I wave my handkerchief until seeing the last sight of all I've left behind. My homestead disappears in the distance. Then dark thoughts return. I should not have left Abigail there. They could have managed without her. Jake would help; he would do more. I'll put my trust in the Lord. He will keep them safe, and our home will wait for my return. Or else, someone will be answering to me.

The trip to Fairhaven should take about three days according to Nathan. It should be easy traveling.

"But as usual,' he says, 'we cannot expect anything to be easy in this life." I wonder what skeletons are in his closet? He must have some choice ones to be so serious. Does he ever crack a smile?

The weather is just grand. It stays true until just now. It's mid-day. A fog rolls in, and dark clouds cover the sun. The heavy mist turns to a gradual rain until faster and faster it comes down.

We push on through this blasted downpour. There's no let up. We've stopped moving. Nathan cracks his whip high over his horses. We sink down until the carriage wheels are stuck in the mud. We wait inside the coach to stay out of the rain. I am enclosed in this coach with a man, not my husband. What would Joshua say?

Nathan says, "It shall be over soon." Wonderful, wonderful. Keep up the good spirits. This seer of the future, good old Nathan . . . well, his prediction would help me more if he smiled along with it.

The time drags on and the light has gone. Rain keeps on, does not stop throughout the night. My eyes close, now and again, and I must have slept a bit. By early morning the rain stops. The sun peeks out behind the last gray cloud.

Nathan says, "I'll go for help. Wait here." Where else could I go?

I sleep for a while, and then hear men talking. Nathan returns with a farmer.

Nathan raps on the door, and yells, "See what we have here? These two oxen plus the horse team should get us out real fast. We'll soon be rid of this mud pit and back on to solid ground."

And they did just that. He offered the farmer pay for his troubles but the man refused. He said, "No, I'm glad to lend a hand when needed."

The rest of the trip had no more bad luck in store. We did talk a bit about Abigail. I asked Nathan what he thought of her?

He laughed. "Oh? So it's been on your mind, too? Have you wondered at the way she jumped at the chance to stay while you had to leave? I did. Then again, I try not to be so critical of her motives. I doubt if she can help it. She is a bit spoiled. Can you tell? Still, it does not make it right, the way she behaves."

I said, "She acts the role of a flighty woman. Talking endlessly as if not interested in anyone else's thoughts. Perhaps her father gave in to her every whim. My child, if I had a girl, would never be allowed to go off and seek adventures such as she has done. On the road traveling with men? Boys worry us enough, but a girl? She has no boundaries, none to keep her in line."

"Yes, Helen, that describes her. And being such an attractive lady, yes she is, I'll give her that—we can find excuses for her even when she most definitely is in the wrong."

"I know, Nathan, but this is distasteful, this speaking ill about someone not here to defend herself. Although I'm thinking about it all the time, and it still leaves a bitter taste in my mouth, let's say no more. We can hope that one day we may see a change for the better." Nathan smiles, the second time today. He nods and our conversation is over.

* * *

At long last, Nathan's coach is in Fairhaven and we are nearing Lily's homestead.

"Look, Nathan, here's the start of her land. Their crops from last fall have been left in the fields. Weeds have suffocated anything good they tried to grow. I imagine Jack was too busy to notice."

"Doesn't she have children?"

"No. She had twin girls named Bessie and Mary but they died at an early age of diphtheria."

Pulling up at Lily's barn, Nathan tends to the horses. Then he starts walking over to where I'm sitting on the porch.

"Ready to go in?" he asks. I hear a creak, the door opens.

"Lily!" My arms reach out. She falls against me. We hug. I feel her back, the bumps in her spine. How thin she is.

"Lily, what's happening here? Please don't cry. Now, when did you get so ill?" She lets out a long sigh. Her arms reach out.

I rub her cold fingers, till she says, "Ooh, don't Helen. That hurts. Please come in. And bring in this young man. He brought you here?"

"Yes, this is Nathan. He was kind enough to drive me all the way from Randolph."

"That was very kind of you, Nathan. Come in, both of you."

She looks at Nathan, and says, "Have a seat, won't you? I do thank you for bringing my sister."

"You're quite welcome. I have relatives in New Bedford that I've not seen for some time so this trip gives me the opportunity to visit with them."

With her tea cup shaking, Lily asks, "No trouble on the trip?'

"No trouble at all on the way down. Well except for the time the stage got stuck in the mud in Vermont and required an ox team to pull us out."

"Oh my, I'm glad that was all that happened.'

I say, "Yes, I'm happy we got out of it as quick as we did." No sense telling her we spent the night in that coach. No one need know about that and what went on. Nothing, of course, but people would still wonder.

"Helen, you must tell me about Elisha and Caleb and how they've grown." Oh, oh. She starts to fall and I catch her.

"I will, in time, but you need to lie down."

"I'm very tired. Please act in my stead. Be the hostess, won't you?"

"Of course, Lily."

"Why don't you show Nathan around the house. I'll just lie on the couch in the living room for a while. See to that pot on the stove, won't you? It's a stew that's just been made. Help yourselves."

I help her onto the couch and return to the kitchen.

Nathan asks, "Do you think Lily would mind if I had one of these hot rolls? They're warming on the back of the stove."

"Of course not, have one or more. I'll fix us some of this stew."

This stew is just right, and we have roasted potatoes and candied carrots. Must have been a neighbor who dropped it off. Ladle it all out. Nathan must be hungry. He sits down, with a heaping plateful. I have half as much. I cannot think of food right now. Not with Lily looking so sickly.

I start washing the dishes as Nathan brings his plate to the sink.

"Nathan, would you build up that fire where Lily's resting? I'm about done here. I'll go check her bedroom and fix it so she can retire early. Then I'll be joining you."

Nathan's now in the living room looking at the wall over the fireplace. He reaches up and touches the mantel.

"Helen this is a beautiful gun. Jack must have paid a pretty penny for it."

Lily wakens. She looks over to Nathan, and shakes her head.

He asks, "Lily, you don't mind my admiring this gun, do you? It's really a beauty."

"Yes, Nathan, that is something, isn't it? For the life of me, that gun gives me the willies. My husband, Jack, paid handsomely for it. He did make me learn how to load it, and try a shot now and then. Says it's for my protection when he's not here. Still, I don't like having it, and that's just the way I am."

He's busy inspecting the barrel. Finally, he says to Lily, "Your husband knows his guns, I can tell. It's a Revolving Shotgun."

"Be careful Nathan, I must warn you, he always keeps it loaded."

"I'll be careful—just wanted to see who the maker is—ah, here it is. It says 'made by Colt in their Paterson, New Jersey plant.' [10] They're fine gun makers. I'll put it back now."

Nathan rocks in Lily's favorite chair while she finishes a small portion of the stew I gave her. She must be feeling better but her eyelids are drooping, and barely stay open.

"Time to retire, Helen, I've overdone it again."

"Come along, then. I'll help you to bed."

We go slow. One sure step at a time.

Lily lets out a deep breath as soon as she's in bed. Her quilt is on her chair. I cover her with it. Lily's all settled.

"Helen, thank you for coming. You're a dear and I'm so lucky. I don't know who else I could have counted on. There's something I need to tell you—."

"Oh, don't be a silly goose. You should've called on me sooner."

"But your family, they must need you and–. "

"Don't worry, they wanted me to come and tend to you. Now try to sleep."

Something is not right here. I feel that Lily is holding back and is not telling me all.

In the kitchen, Nathan folds his newspaper and sets it aside. Before I can get the kettle boiling again, he's over at the door, reaching for his overcoat.

"Nathan, so soon you're leaving? Would you like a drink or something more to eat? Or I could fix a bundle for you?"

"No, I must take my leave before nightfall. My relatives in New Bedford are not that far from here. But, they go to their beds early. They run a stable business, hiring out coaches. Same as my father does at our home. Thank you for that delicious supper." He puts his muffler and cap on. "Please give my regards to your sister."

"I will, but I should be the one thanking you. Have a safe trip and may God bless you for bringing me here. You are a true gentleman."

After Nathan left, and it was none too soon, I head outside to Lily's outhouse. There it is, over by the barn.

Oh, my goodness, three holes? Each a different size? A small seat, good for children. Yet, I wonder who's so wide to use this last one? What will they think of next? Probably for an unexpected guest? Looks to be carved out of mahogany or a red wood. All so nice and shiny. I must mention this to Joshua. Perhaps he, or Jacob, could make a three-holer like this for our outhouse at the farm.

In the corner, here's a stack of magazines. Good ones, too. They offer some fine things to read about. Here's an Old Farmer's Almanac. Must be expensive keeping those stocked but it's a nice thought, leaving them for guests.

What's this? White napkins, made of fine paper? Must cost a pretty penny. Hmm . . . in our little outhouse back in Vermont we offer old newsprint and be done with it.

Chapter Nine

Joshua and Abigail

Wonder how Helen is faring and if they've arrived at Lily's home? It's been four days. Morning chores are done. I ask Abigail if she'd like to take a walk along the old Indian Trail behind the cabin.

"Oh, Josh, I'd love to. Thank you for inviting me."

As we walk along the trail, I begin to tell Abigail the tale of Running Deer and White Feather. I want to show her what Helen and I found early on.

"There's a rare sight for you to see on this trail, Abigail."

"What might that be?"

"Well, the story goes that two Indians traveled this trail one winter with their newborn son and they became engulfed in a blizzard. When the storm ended and the sun appeared, Running Deer realized his wife, White Feather, was having difficulty traveling through the high drifts and her health was failing."

"What did he do?"

"He sheltered his frail wife and son as best he could at the base of an old Elm tree and then ran off to find help from a neighboring tribe he knew to be close by."

"What tribe were they from?"

"It's not certain but I believe it could have been one of the Abenaki Indian tribes. They are common to this area."

"What happened to Running Deer?"

"Two white hunters readily spied him from their shack just below the top ridge. Amidst chuckling and guffawing, they watched Running Deer darting in and out of spare brush areas, along open stretches of snow covered ground."

"Did they want to help Running Deer?"

"No. Just the opposite. Capturing him was easy. They rode their horses behind him till close enough to lasso him and bring him to the ground.'

"Running Deer found himself locked up at the local jail. He pleaded with his captors, in his limited knowledge of the 'white man's tongue.'

"Release me. Need be free. Take food, water--wife, son."

"His jailors dealt another hand of cards, laughing his pleas away."

"How awful. Didn't they know, or didn't they care that White Feather could be dying out there?"

"The only thing they cared about was that they caught him running away from something and that he could be dangerous.'

"Then on the morning of the second day, Running Deer being half out of his mind, managed to grab hold of the jailor's hand—just as he was ready to give him his meager rations of old moldy bread, slogging around in a tin full of water. Running Deer threw it back in the jailor's face, blinding him for a moment. Then he reached through the bars, clutched the jailor's throat and banged the man's forehead up side the cell door, not once but several times."

"How did he get out of his cell?"

"He grabbed the unconscious man's keys and gun, and made short order of escaping from his cell. Then he swiftly ran away to return to his wife and baby."

"He ran till near exhaustion, but as he approached the old Elm tree, his sharp senses told him something was wrong. The fur wrapped form of White Feather was covered with snow, and he saw no movement."

"What happened to her?"

"He knelt by her side, pushed back the fur wraps and uncovered her face. The worst had happened, and he let out a cry. Such a keening sorrowful wail, echoing through the hills and back, with no thought at all of who might hear. White Feather was dead."

"The baby, too?"

"He heard something, a muffled cry. Pulling back the furs, he saw his son. Still breathing! Alive! The baby's eyes were half open, whilst his tiny hands tugged hungrily at his mother's breast, his lips clenched, still nursing to the last drop."

"How awful. That's so sad."

We arrive at that same Elm tree with its old trunk and branches bent from years gone by. I point out to Abigail a gnarled outgrowth around the bark of the tree. It faintly shows what looked like three faces.

"Look close, Abigail. Although this happening was many years ago, right there you'll make out—this distinct outline of Running Deer, White Feather and her baby. It's etched forever in the bark. This old Elm has become a sacred tree for Indians in these parts and they pay tribute to White Feather, who gave her life to save her son."

Abigail seems spellbound and nearly speechless. She slowly lets her hand touch the gnarled outgrowth and begins lightly tracing the curved gnarls, until a look of wonder comes over her.

"I can tell who they are. How marvelous. Though, the features appear to blend in with the outgrowth. Yet, see where my fingers are? Can you tell if I am right? I can feel each line, each ridge of their faces."

"You are correct, and in the right place. When we first came upon this tree it was Helen that was able to see the faces right off. She had to point out to me the actual features."

"Such a sad tale. My heart goes out to White Feather."

"Do not be sad for her. To this day, she is admired as somewhat of a Saint by this Indian tribe.'

"Now we must return to the farm, as the boys must be famished. I wonder if the Post rider has been by with a letter from Helen?"

* * *

Six days and yet no letter from Helen.

Abigail walks into the living room and says, "Joshua, I'm glad you liked the breakfast I made for you and the boys. I've been thinking. This book I found, hope you don't mind, but it's interesting and I have some questions."

"I see you've got the book on Vermont's history. How far did you read?"

"About half way. Can you tell me what made you get involved in Vermont's anti-slavery movement?"

"First of all, the Haskell family always followed our Quaker teachings of equality for all men and women."

"And, is it true, Vermont was a leader in the abolitionist movement?"

"Well, our State was the first in the Union to outlaw slavery in our constitution."

"When was that?"

"It was way back in 1777.[11]

"Josh, I read that Canada also has no laws against them. It said so in the book." I can tell that she did retain some of what she read.

"Yes, you're right, Canada abolished slavery in 1833. But some runaways remained here in Vermont, hoping to meet up with family and other relatives."

"I see. Thank you for helping me to understand."

"You're entirely welcome. Would you mind seeing to the children now? I had sent them to play earlier."

"I will, but first I'll fix a pot of tea for you." This is a good time to move my chair to the other side of the table, leaving her seat on the far side.

Here she is, again, but has a great deal more than tea on her tray. What a spread we have here. Everything fit for a king. I don't think Helen needs to know of this. She might be peeved that Abigail spends more time in the house with me, than outside helping with the chores and caring for the children. After she sets everything down, she drags her chair closer to me.

"Thank you, Abigail, for this mid-morning meal. Can you give me the book you are reading? Good, this will refresh my memory. As to the tea and all that went with it, I must say you outdo yourself each time. That was just fine, and just what was needed to help give energy for a good walk. You can go with me if you like. Are the children OK?"

"Why, Joshua, I would love to. Yes, the children are fine. Jacob stopped by and will be fixing the hinges on the barn door. Before we leave I'll ask him to tend to the boys. But first can you tell me more of Vermont's part in the movement, the abolitionists?"

Again, she drags her chair even closer, and then, of all things, she puts her hand on my knee . . . what is she doing? I remove her hand. Now I've lost what she just asked.

"Where was I?"

"Sorry Josh. Didn't mean to embarrass you. I was just bracing myself because I felt a little unsteady." I need to hurry along with this.

"Of course, now let's see. Are you familiar with the name Alexander Twilight? Here's a picture of him."

"Oh, I know of him, my Tutor was quite impressed with his doings. Wasn't he the first Negro in the U.S. to graduate from college?"

"He was also a Vermonter, and served in our legislature. Or, for that matter, he was the first Negro in the entire nation to serve in any State legislature."

"How was he able to get a state position, or even get that far?"

"He was not a slave and became a successful and distinguished person because Vermont always considered Negroes as free people. Here, let me read more about him."

She fixes her collar, and starts loosening the top buttons. It is awfully hot in here, yet the day is not that warm. I need to open a window.

"Where was I? Yes, right here. He was also a preacher and a teacher. And look here, see where he built a huge four story granite building in Brownington, Vermont."

She leans close to me—too close—to see where I'm reading.

"He did? Built it all by himself?" She peers closer to my book. I notice her hair has come loose from her cap. It trails on the page I am reading.

"Abigail, sit back in your chair, or move away from me. I must see my book better to continue." Good, she moves back, but now her hair falls down on her shoulders. I must finish this reading soon.

"It served as a dormitory for the Brownington Academy, for which he was Headmaster. He graduated more than 3,000 boys and girls from that school."

"Quite an accomplishment. Where did he get his education?"

"Glad you asked. Randolph is proud of Alexander Twilight because he saved his money and enrolled in the Orange County Grammar School right here in Randolph Center. It's also known as the Randolph Academy."

"Oh my, and to think he could never had gone to any school if he was in the South as a slave."

"You're right. He was originally from Corinth, Vermont. His father was Ichabod Twilight who served during the Revolutionary War. After six years of study, here in Randolph, he managed to accumulate two years at the college level. Then, he left Randolph and entered Middlebury College for an additional two years where he received his bachelor's degree." [12]

She has scooted closer again without my realizing her chair even moving. Now, she grabs the top of my hand and I remove it straightaway, because I have to turn the page.

She says, "You still haven't answered my first question. How did you get caught up in the abolitionist movement?"

"Rowland Robinson of Ferrisburgh was a leader in the Vermont Anti-Slavery Society and in 1837 they had 8,000 members in 80 Chapters. One of those chapters was a Female Abolition Society here in Randolph." Lord, help me get through this. I need to get out for a walk.

"Before my Pa died, Ma was quite active in that group. Many of these societies would gather of an evening to pack boxes of clothes for runaway slaves."

"Your mother was a fine lady to be doing such good works. And she obviously passed that dedication for being so kind on to her son."

"They were also quite principled in their beliefs. They would use maple sugar instead of cane sugar and homespun clothes instead of cotton clothes, because cotton was produced through slave labor. So, seeing the good those women were doing wore off on me and I guess it just seemed natural to follow in their footsteps." [13]

"Thank you, for this learning experience, Joshua. It's enlightening to know how you became such a good man."

I wish she would stop all that flattering talk. It's very uncomfortable and she needn't flutter her eyelashes at me—it is very unnerving.

"Abigail, my arm's feeling better, just a bit weak is all. Can we go for that walk?"

"That would be nice, Joshua. I like taking walks with you. Let me get ready and I'll meet you outside."

She sure takes a lot of time to ready herself just for walking outside. Helen was always out the door before I got my jacket on. She's out now, but why that flowery dress? What is she up to? Did I make a mistake by inviting her to walk with me? Never mind, it's too late now.

"Uh, Abigail, won't you be needing a shawl? It's really damp round here this time of year. Helen has some extra garments for outdoors, perhaps you should borrow one."

"No bother, I'm fine as is. But if I do get chilled, I hope you'll let me borrow your jacket. You're such a fit man, and those muscles must make you quite warm with or without it, I dare say."

What? I wish she would not keep saying things like that.

"Let's get on with it. We'll take the Indian Trail, back of the cabin. That will cross us over Harlow Hill.'

"C'mon, over here, watch your step, a big puddle is waiting. See? Good, you missed it. Must keep an eye out. Don't step on things, such as . . . snakes slithering around. There's something, let me pick this up and see what it is."

"No! You said, slithering? Where? Ooh! Let me grab your arm. Why do you laugh? What's that in your hand? Oh, it's not a snake. It's just a stick. I'm so relieved. But, don't scare me like that. I don't like crawly, slithery things, especially snakes."

"Ah, Abigail, please forgive me. Let's get on with our walk."

"But, Josh you're moving too fast. I can barely keep up with you. Stop for a while."

"Don't fret yourself. I'll wait. Go ahead and pick the lilacs and honeysuckle if you wish. We're almost to Harlow Hill but we've got another hill to cross."

"What, another hill?"

"Yes, it's Hebard Hill and not too far. Here, grab hold of my hand. Let me help you up past these rocks."

"Thank you kindly, just let me wait a bit to catch my breath?"

"Of course. I'll wait. Take your time."

I must not forget, she is not a farm woman and not that sturdy. Abigail is from a big town and rides in a fine carriage. She's more suited to flat ground, with her high buckled, patent leather shoes—too dainty for these parts.

I wish she would stop lifting her dress, checking out if mud is on her heels. Or prickers and burrs on her hem. She should not be showing that part of her limbs.

"Joshua, it's much longer than the walks I went on with the boys. The most we hiked was to Jake's farm."

She hands me part of her bouquet of lilacs and honeysuckle, then grabs my arm to steady herself. I must say, the flowers are smelling quite pleasant.

It reminds me of Helen when . . . but I can't be thinking of that now. I miss her too much as it is.

"You are doing well on this long walk, Abby. But you're looking peaked, here take my jacket. Sit on this stone wall, and we'll wait till you are fit, and able to go on."

"Yes, let's sit, but I won't need your jacket. I'm much too warm as it is. I need to get some of these underskirts off. They hamper my walking, and I'll unbutton my shirtwaist."

Fine with me, I'll look over at the fields, the hills, or something. Just hoping she doesn't take too long a time. Wait, did she say her shirtwaist? She's unbuttoning it? Why? That is not exactly proper, no matter how warm the day. I shall not look, no, not until she is all put together.

"You've come this far, Abigail, are you dressed OK? Be sure to cover up or bees shall be coming around for your flowers and might land on skin that's inviting to them. Can you hear me? Ready yet? It's only a short way more to go. Did you know that Quaker ladies will walk for miles in bare feet in good weather spells? Then, when reaching their destination, they put on their shoes, usually at the Meeting Place or the general store."

"Good for them, but I'll keep my shoes on, thank you. I do believe I'm well rested now, so we can move on."

She turns toward me to get up, and, oh, I'll just look away again—I can't believe my eyes. Her top is unbuttoned down to her waist.

"Abigail, you'd best button up. Bees, and worse, Hornets, they love flowers, too. They all will have a field day if they swarm around here. And you'd have only yourself to blame. Please, fix yourself up."

"Oh, I'm sorry Josh. I hope you didn't see too much. I was just getting cooled off."

I'm beginning to wonder about her. What are her motives? Does she actually plan such things?

"Are you feeling better? Are you ready to forge on?"

"Yes, let's go on."

"We'll be through these fields soon."

"It's been a long trek, but here we are at Randolph Center."

Passing the Congregational Church, we come to the cemetery and I spot a familiar gravestone.

"Come here Abigail. Take a look at this gravestone with the name 'Justin Morgan' carved on it." [12a]

"Who was Justin Morgan? I never heard of that name."

"The stone reads he died in 1798 when he was 51 years old. My Grandpa knew Justin before he died."

"Why was he so important?"

"Mr. Morgan had been our town clerk and music teacher, but my Pa said, Justin Morgan was better known around these parts as the one-time owner of a stallion named Figure. He brought Figure to Vermont from Massachusetts when settling here in Randolph with his family."

She is looking at the flowers, the sky—possibly the vast scenic views, I suspect. She then turns back to me.

"What was so special about that horse, compared to any other?"

"Pa said 'There wasn't a horse anywhere that could beat Figure in a race or a pulling contest.'"

"Oh, and he said that, did he?'

"Sure did, and Pa saw him race in Brookfield. Pa said, 'It was along the Post road and Figure was racing against horses brought in from New York.'

"Pa was at the finish line when he saw—coming round the bend, a beautiful black stallion with flowing mane and tail, with head held high and hoofs a-pounding in the dirt. The rider was doing all he could just to hang on."

"How thrilling. Tell me more."

"Yes, that was Figure, and he crossed the finish line as the other horses just started coming into sight, round the bend.'

"Pa loved to tell that story and said, 'He was a proud horse and it was a grand sight to see.'"

"Hmm, is that so? Joshua, I do declare, how very interesting. You surely know how to spin a good tale."

Her head is now aimed toward the hills past the low fields with all the wild flowers.

"Ah yes, Figure became known as the 'Justin Morgan Horse' and was ridden in a parade one year by President James Monroe. Figure died about 30 years ago. He is buried across that valley."

"Where is that?"

"To the east and beyond the next ridge on a farm in Chelsea." [12b]

Abigail turns, and squeezes my hand. "Oh Joshua, I love your stories. I could listen to you tell them all day."

She smiles, and raises my hand, saying "Wait, just feel this."

She places it almost on—no, not—it can't be. Not on her bodice, and right over her—but no, I shall not touch her. I pull back, yet she won't let go of my hand.

"Joshua, can't you tell? I feel like swooning. My heart is racing so."

I try to loosen her grasp, with my other hand, but have to grab hold of her around the waist as she starts to buckle, and almost falls down.

Yet, she still holds on tight, her nails dig in. Her other hand is quick to join in a tight grip. I let go her waist, and can raise my hand enough to grab her shoulder—.

"Oh, Joshua. Not there, feel here, how my heart beats. I get so excited listening to your fine speaking voice. My head is getting dizzy, oh dear, look at me, I tremble so. I might swoon at any time. Let me lean on you."

I wish she would have a fainting spell, and I could get free.

"I will not, and I don't need to know how your heart beats. Let go of my hand, Abigail. My shoulder is still too tender; I can't move it too good as yet. There, you've finally let go. Now I see my hand is bleeding. Why did you do that? . . . Forget it, it's time to get back home."

I turn and head down the path. She starts yelling.

"What on earth is the matter? I just wanted you to feel my heart beating. I was about to fall down, I was so weak, and needed your help."

Her eyelids flutter, and her eyes roll back in her head. But soon right themselves. Her heart? She doesn't look weak, and whatever is wrong with her eyes and her head?

"Joshua, see, I might still fall—my legs, they feel as if they are almost giving in. That walk was too much. So please keep me steady, hold on to me and do not let go."

"Let's get going, Abigail, time to go home. Getting late and this day is getting cold. Here, take my jacket. Besides, my boy's will be needing their dinner."

Abigail pushes hair strands away from her forehead and a wide smile spreads across her lips.

"Oh, Joshua, not yet. I am so awfully tired. Look at all this dust on me—I'm a frightful wreck from these trails. It'll take some doing to get myself ready for being seen in public."

"Sorry, Abigail, fix yourself up if you will."

"But, well, then—do we have to go right at this instant?"

"Yes, of course but take the time to make yourself presentable."

"Perhaps if you carry me, you can take your jacket back? Then, I'll not need any resting periods?"

No chance of that, even if I was strong enough, "My shoulder still is not up to par. I could not hold your weight. Besides, you'll not need any resting periods. It's downhill all the way back."

We're almost back to home, and no words are being spoken. But, something nags at me. I did not touch her, not where she tried to put my hand. Glad of that, oh, how glad. Wish I had not grabbed her shoulder. I never wanted to touch any other woman, not in any place. But what if someone up there saw us and might tattle on us? Hope not.

I need to get my mind on better subjects. My Helen, did she make it OK? Was I too hasty, allowing her to go that far? No, she had to answer Lily and her needs. Yes, that is so, just as my calling was to help the slaves. I miss Helen. I pray and hope I'll see her soon.

Chapter Ten

Jedediah and Belinda

Lily sits up in bed. Is she waiting for me, perhaps wants to talk? I place this water pitcher on her table.

"Here Lily, take this glass of water. What's that you've got in your hand—a letter?"

"Ah, Thank you, Helen. As you know, Jack is tending to his mother's estate in Boston. His latest post . . . here, you read it."

"Hmm, let's see.

I read, *My dear Lily, I have to extend my stay for at least a month.*

"What? Jack sent this? How odd, doesn't he know of your illness?"

"No. Before he left, there were strange goings on. He acted so quiet and distant. I feared he might have met someone and—.' Her mouth quivers.

She shakes her head, "He may never return, and there are two, yes two, right here—cough."

Let me see, find something to brace her up in bed. Good, here's a pillow.

"Lily, let me raise your head. Is that better?" She nods her head.

"You're not making much sense. Two what? Do you mean people? I see no one else in your home."

"I took in two runaways, after Jack had left. Yet, there's no plan, no route. No safe house to get them to."

"You're telling me, what? No, I cannot believe it, not now, with you sick and all. Not two runaways? You mean fugitive slaves here in this house?"

"Yes, they're in a secret room. You'll have to go down cellar to find it."

"How will I find it"

"In the middle of the cellar you'll see a flat stone in the earth. Look above that and there will be a trap door. Grab the wooden ladder down there, climb up and push on a large square panel. It will open to the safe room."

"Lily, I can't believe what I'm hearing. Are they OK?"

"Yes, of course. They've been allowed out, from time to time, when safe enough. I had no choice but to write you to come. The past few days, I'm too ill to go down cellar. Might not make it back up. It's getting difficult to push up on that trap door to their room."

"What about food and water?"

"They've had water and dried provisions to eat and *uh,* a bucket for sanitary needs. There are no outside openings. Jack built one side against the chimney stones of our fireplace upstairs."

"That should give off good warmth on cold wintry days."

"There's also a small crock stacked full of salt pork."

"That's good, Lily. Salt pork keeps for many days."

"Of course, once settled in, they can use another ladder in their room to come down on their own. They can pump water from the kitchen and wash up as necessary, but only if no windows are left with drapes open."

"How did you get involved with runaways?"

"New Bedford's harbor is known for welcoming runaways. Jack convinced me to offer our home as a safe house. Yes, and it did me good—not being alone, after our twins passed on. Now, the slaves will wait here for a time. Until they head to Vermont and Canada."

It took a while to figure on what next to say.

"Lily, Joshua and I got involved, too."

"You did? You mean with helping slaves? Not you and Joshua, way up in Vermont? You never said—."

"Our oaths to keep silent were solemn ones, we were bound by them. It began when we lived in Bethel Gilead. Joshua would give them an overnight stay. He kept them in our shed. I never had anything to do with them."

"Oh my, Helen, how I longed to discuss our doings many a time. Not with anyone around here. Only with you. If only I'd known."

I replied, "I never dreamed, never thought that you would get involved. I mean, doesn't it beat all? However, we had nothing to compare with the fine offerings you have."

"We could well afford it, as Jack has done well in his law practice. Although, the twins will never be able to share in what we'll leave behind."

"I understand. It was so sad what happened."

"Helen, can you pour me some more water?"

"Here you are, now tell me more about those two in the hidden room."

"It's a man and woman, young ones. The girl's barely seventeen. They're in love and want to marry when reaching Canada. Call themselves—Belinda Beaumont and Jedediah or Jed Beaumont. Not related, it's their Master's surname. I tried to shout through their wall this morning. Then banged on it till Jedediah answered. He yelled that they were OK."

"But, Lily, how did you manage all your farm chores, being as sick as you are?"

"Our neighbor, Mrs. Tellatini, would bring over food once in awhile and her sons helped with the chores. But they never came in the house."

"Is that the colored lady down the road, across from the sand pit?"

"Yes. I see that you still remember her." She lets out a long sigh and closes her eyes.

My poor sister. How much more can be left on her shoulders? And what can I do? I don't need any of this, but . . . she is my sister. Of all things. Please Lord, no more surprises, not today.

"Alright, Lily, now you must rest. Your two guests will be tended to. I'll straightaway have a look. Now don't you be fretting over—well, any of this."

"Remember, they can use the kitchen. Just be sure to lock up and draw the drapes, before you bring them from the safe room."

"I'll be careful. You rest now and do not worry."

I'll take this lantern down cellar. There's the stone and over here is the ladder. Drag it over. Let it rest on the support beam by the trap door. One good shove and that door creaks open. So dark in here. Those two small candles, how can they see? Turn up my lantern, and it gets brighter. There, over in the corner, under a pile of blankets, something's moving. A man looks out from the top cover—his large arms shield the woman's head, resting against his chest.

"Don't be afraid, you over there—do not worry." Best for me to speak softly, so I don't scare them.

"Look at me. Lily's my young sister and I've come to help. C'mon out from under your covers and follow me upstairs. You need food and a good scrubbing. Your clothes also need a good washing and drying."

The woman stands and looks at me.

"You're Belinda, right? Tell Jed, he must leave, too."

Belinda whispers to Jed, yet I catch on to most of it.

"Sure dunno bout her. She ain't lookin or talkin like a fine lady, like Missus Lily. Uh, uh. Missus Lily's sister? Cain't believe it. Where she been livin? Missus Lily, say she done been up north, inna woods?"

Are they willing to trust me—the strange one, who just came from the scary wilds of the north?

Good. They both start to grab up personal items. Misgivings are gone? I suspect they must be needing a good meal and room to stretch.

Can't blame Belinda, thinking of me that way, since I was born and raised in Vermont and married to a farmer. I've not seen such refinement as Lily has. After all, she wedded her la-dee-dah lawyer, coming from his upper crust family. Hold it. I'd better stop ruminating and thinking such mean thoughts. Need to get these two back upstairs to the kitchen.

"Jedediah, can you help close the windows and draw the drapes?"

"Sure, Missus Helen. We allus help Missus Lily. An y'all can call me Jed. Belinda wantin t' know, can she cook up some food? An, how was yer stew?"

"Oh? You made that supper, Belinda? How good it was, and I must thank you. Our driver, said he'd thank the cook if he knew who made such a grand meal."

Belinda says, "Lemme know bout cookin times, what's best times t' be in Kitchen?"

"Nights, when dark I imagine, that's what Lily said. Alright, Jed, would you stoke that kindling in the stove?" He busies himself at the stove, without answering.

"Belinda, can you round up clothes for a good washing?"

"Yessum."

"Good, then Jed, fill this big basin to the brim. Put it to heat on the stove and then when it's hot, put it in this big tub on the floor. When done, here's some clean towels to put around you.'

"Now the hen house is waiting. I must see to fresh eggs. And the cows—I hear them mooing? They'll need milking so I must get on with it."

How did Lily ever manage, even when not so ill? It's beyond me. Didn't Jack leave her with any paid help? Do the neighbors help? I need to ask.

Belinda scurries here and there, tidying up, checking windows. Jed just stands there. He does not discard his long shirt. It's soiled, and is dark gray with buttons long gone from the front. Perhaps my presence keeps him from washing up.

"Jed, I shall leave soon. Later on, I'll make a more filling meal. Unless Belinda wants to be head cook and I can just help her? Belinda, alright with you? Jed, go ahead and undress. I won't be looking your way."

He turns half way toward me, and his smile allows his large white teeth to show. They are straight and quite something to see. He steps nearer, and looks straight at me, and—my Lord! It's a shame to say, but though his muscles and large frame must have fetched a pretty penny at the auction block—his face, the right side, it's—well, appalling. There's a jagged scar, it stretches from below his right eye down to the bottom of his jaw. Wondering, was it earned from his Master, did he also get a lashing or worse?

Belinda is very dark and has a long neck, and such a high forehead. Her cheekbones stand out. Wonder if she came from a ruling family in her homeland? She's quite comely.

"Missus Helen, it gon' be OK, we calls y' Missus Helen, same as Missus Lily?"

"Of course. Or just plain, Helen. Then, how about you?"

"We tells Missus Lily bout gettin wed, jumpin a broom."

"Is it Missus, then?"

"I's savin it, callin me Missus. Culluds ain't 'lowed t' get real weddin. But, we's gon' git t' church soon's we's gon' an settlin in for good. So, cancha jess say Belinda, same's Jed doin?" I nod, and give her a hug.

"Yessum, ats jess fine."

Now a smile appears—oh my, what teeth, how perfect. She must've eaten good meals. Perhaps she was a house servant? Her teeth are healthy, not misshapen. Her big brown eyes are staring right back at me. At least she isn't clinging to Jed. Her sack dress, not shapely at all, almost disguises what should be hidden underneath. We'll have to see about better, more fitting garments for both. She drops her garment, but only after wrapping the towel around her.

I gather up the milk pail and basket for my chores and head out the door. Need to first collect eggs from the chicken coop.

Almost done. Those cows are mooing up a storm as I approach the barn. Three cows. This will take a while. Give em some hay and water. That will keep them while I muck up their mess.

Grab the milk bucket and stool and start milking. It's so quiet here. I shudder since it's so eerie, with no morning sounds; none, except milk squirting in the bucket, and cows munching on their hay. The house door, did I latch it? Should I go back? No need to. Jedediah must know to check the doors.

One cow done and two to go. I settle the stool by the next cow.

"Crack! Bang!" Was that thunder? Reach out, grab for the bucket. Whoa—almost slid off the stool. My arm hits the bucket; it spills all over. Could they, maybe—be—gunshots?

Run—get to the house.

Check, the drapes, still drawn. Wait, listen . . . this door, it's ajar.

"Jedediah, where—?" He's tied to a chair, stark naked.

"What happened?"

He mumbles—a towel is stuck in his mouth. I will keep my eyes straight ahead, cannot look down at him.

"You're OK? Where's Belinda?" He rolls his eyes to the side of the kitchen.

Belinda's legs—they're all I can see, until I get closer. A man lies on her. Work boots, overalls, a bloodied jacket and long scraggly hair. A big, red hole torn through his jacket; he's a bloody mess. Belinda's eyes stare, but not at me.

"Belinda, can you hear me?" Her eyes move back and forth, slowly, and then stop.

She says, "Please, get him offa me."

Her towel, where is it? Oh, it got stripped clean off. It lays under her hand now. Hope this blood, dripping down her arm, is not from her. Must pull this man off. He's heavy, but I get him off.

"Belinda, are you hurt? Did he hurt you?"

"No, Ma'am. Can I . . . please, need Jed . . . I need—."

Jed's struggling but can't get free. I take the towel out of his mouth and drop it in his lap. I grab a kitchen knife and cut him loose.

"OK, Jed, you're not hurt? Only got a scratch on your neck?"

He runs to Belinda, passes by the rocker, and now I see this other man, sprawled across the rocking chair and . . . oh, no. His head is almost blown off, with blood splattered everywhere. Nothing much left, except bits and pieces of bones sticking out and now, I'm seeing jelly-like splatterings stuck on the wall.

Then beyond the rocker, I see Lily sitting on the floor in the doorway; the shotgun in her lap. What's she looking at? I follow her eyes and look up. There's nothing up there, just the ceiling.

"Wake up, what happened? Lily, can you hear me?"

Her mouth droops down on one side. White foam . . . oh, it's spittle. It rolls down one side of her chin. Hands tremble, but she still clutches the shotgun. I wipe her mouth with her night gown. Slowly, ever so slow, I get that gun away from her. Her eyes close.

"Stay awake, talk to me, Lily." She clutches my arm. Looks up at me and tears spill down her cheeks. Where is my handkerchief? No matter, no time to look. My apron, it's handy enough to wipe her face.

"'Helen? Those . . . God awful, terrible men . . . had no right to—."

"Lily, what in Heaven happened?"

"Helen, the door, it wasn't locked. I heard a noise down in the kitchen. Jed, he's yelling, 'No, don't!' So scared I was—I tiptoed down the stairs."

Her eyes open so wide. She whimpers. I hold her to me. I must get her off this floor, but she has to be steady, and not shaking so much.

"Hush, it's all over. You're safe, and Jed and Belinda are OK."

"Oh, my Lord—those two are Bounty hunters. I've seen them before."

"What went on? When did you think to get the gun?"

"I grabbed it. And how heavy it was. Almost dropped it. 'Get out!' I yelled. Belinda started screaming—with that awful heathen on her trying to—and that other Devil had a knife to Jed's throat."

"Wait, take your time."

"I was so afraid he might kill him. Then, he started to run at me. I raised the gun, took aim, and—oh my, how awful. Helen, I did it. I shot him?"

"What about the one on Belinda?"

"He raised up with a pistol in his hand. So scared I was. I pulled the trigger again. Did you see? A hole, so big—I did that? Blood poured out." She pushes herself up but gasps, and slumps down. I raise my arm to cradle her head.

She is breathing better now, not so fast. Hold her close to me, and now help her stand. "C'mon, let's get you to bed."

Now, she's tucked in bed. A cool cloth is on her forehead. How I wish I could lie down with her and have a restful sleep.

"Helen, I may go to Hell."

"No, don't say such a thing."

"It's true, and I'm not sorry. I'd do it again if I had to."

"God will be judging you, Lily, so leave it in His hands. You stay abed. I need to go clean up that mess."

This awful smell. Open windows. So much blood, still draining, and underneath this one, a rag rug. All stained. Wrap it round him. Watch out, his trousers leak, too. Did they drink enough liquor to kill a horse? I wish they'd got sick before running in here. My stomach rumbles, it's about to—. Oh, no, fast, untie my apron, put it round my face, cover my nose.

Need to back away. Open windows. Stick my head out. Ah, good. Feel better. I hear water pumping. Jed fills a pan and washes Belinda, and then he turns her to face me.

He says, "Missus Helen, she gon' be OK. An, look—no cuts, no stabbins."

"Thank the Lord. Take a towel, dry her good. Get another from under the sink, and wrap it round yourself." Both are still naked, and I don't need to keep watching their doings.

"Belinda, tell me did that man hurt you? That blood, it wasn't yours? You know, before, uh, what went on?"

"No Ma'am. Missus Lily puts a load in him."

"Tell me what happened."

"I been washin up, dress soakin in sink—an alla sudden, I hears door slam. Two men. One man w' gun, an nex man w' knife."

"A knife?"

"Yessum, an he both'rin Jed, tyin rope roun chair. An one run t' me, hits my head, push me down. Nex, he gon' an chokin me. I hears other man sayin' 'Gal, if you keeps on screamin, yer nigga gets his neck slit ear t' ear.'"

"You poor thing, it's a wonder you can even talk now."

"Jed, he been here, an I knows he gon' help me. Oh, he cain't talk. He soundin funny. I lay on floor. Cain't move. So heavy, an man . . . he . . . jess movin. I almose get my knee in him. I hears a shot. But he keep on movin. I hears Missus Lily yellin, 'Stop!' An one mo' shot. He stop, an fall on me."

She sobs, until Jed rubs her back. He touches his throat.

"See? Not bad, Lindy Bell, we gon' be OK." I see it's only a knick, and already dry.

"Here are some sheets to wrap round you. Don't look around, keep your eyes off those two on the floor. I'll be busy in here, but I want you to go to the safe room. Once you leave here, don't come back."

Jed asks, "Y'all gon' need us helpin, washin up?"

"No. Stay to your room. Later, if asked, you will know nothing about it. You don't want to be an accessory."

Jed asks, "What is assess . . . oree?"

"It means someone who gets involved after a murder. You won't be blamed because you had no part in the shootings or what happened after. Besides, Lily shot them in self-defense and they broke into her home. That is not what is called murder.

Belinda says, "Missus Helen. Lily saves us. We beholdin t' her and needs t' see her."

"She's sleeping. Tomorrow will be time enough for talking. Try to get some rest." They leave.

I wonder, what would Joshua do? Somehow, whatever went on, he handled everything. Must take my time, figure it out. Step by step.

First find another rug and wrap the other man. Then, I must make it to the barn. It's a struggle, since the carpet keeps falling off this one. Here's some rope, now tie it on tight.

It's been hard, first one, and then the other. Then covering them with burlap feed bags and a layer of hay.

Cleaning the kitchen now. Get it all washed away. Buckets of water, with first mopping and then wringing out mop after rinsing over and over.

Finally—all is back to spotless, the whole kitchen—and I can set for a spell to figure out what's next to be done.

I can't leave those bodies in the barn. Need to get rid of them.

Lily's horse—a fine steed, but I don't know its name. Take time, pat it down, till it nestles its nose against my head. Good, it's ready. Get it harnessed. I tie ropes around both bodies and we start off into the woods.

"C'mon Nellie, or whatever your name is. You're doing a fine job. I bet you've pulled logs much heavier than this." We've made it across the sand pit. I look ahead and there are no lights coming from Mrs. Tellatini's house. Good, all must be abed. Half-moon gives us some light.

Nellie whinnies. "No, what's wrong girl?" Something must have spooked her. Oh, Oh. A light just came on in the Tellatini house. "C'mon Nellie, get over here behind this tree." A door opens. Someone looks out. The door shuts and the light goes out. That was close.

We're now deep in the woods. "Whoa Nellie." Untie the ropes. Drag both bodies off into the bushes. Cover them well with branches and brush. Finally finished. "OK Nellie, let's get you back to the barn."

Back at Lily's and time to relax a bit. It's over and no one will find them. Good riddance to bad rubbish.

Joshua, wishing you were here—what have I got myself into? Why was I so quick to cover up this terrible shooting? Should I have notified the authorities right off? How could we explain this? Would Lily and all of us been arrested for murder? They certainly would have arrested us for violating the Fugitive Slave Act, and Jed and Belinda would have been sent back to their master. No, I did the right thing and God will be my witness.

Chapter Eleven

The Desk

"Lily, look—another letter from Jack. Time to get out of bed—grab my arm, I'll help you walk. We'll have a sit down at this table. Here's your letter. Two cups of tea and a few biscuits with jelly are waiting. Will you have some? I set them out before." She only sips from the tea cup while she peers at her letter.

"Helen, here, you take it. I've read enough."

> *Shall be detained for an indefinite time. There was much paperwork to be done as a will had not been made, and my mother was the last to survive.*
>
> *A great deal of land has to be dispersed between my four brothers and three sisters, and their families. Also, the house and the contents, and whatever monetary accumulation was left would have to be sorted out among us.*

"Helen, you see that? He's settling his family's affairs. I accept that, but does he ask how I am faring? No, he doesn't."

"Just put it out of your head for now. Pay no mind to what Jack may be doing. Here let me wipe those tears from your eyes."

"Helen, with you here, it's almost like having Ma back again."

"We need to get you better. So let's see to your health. You're not looking too fit. Not good at all. I suspect, you'll need more than what my home remedies can provide."

"Jack left patent medicines and cure-alls, but none worked. Our doctor's advice was, 'Time cures all. Meanwhile find a good hobby. Take up needlepoint,' blah, blah, blah."

"Did you try any of what the doctor suggested?"

"What good would it do? I gag at the thought of doing frivolous things, like hobbies. I am tired, and sometimes have no energy to even get up and wash my face. When I first met Jack, I never had bad days. Nowadays, I don't like waking up of a morn. It has been so lonely here these past few years, especially after what happened to the twins. Why should I even get up?"

"You said that all of a sudden you get fevers and at times cough a lot. What else? Any other spells?"

"It's the not knowing. The sickness that comes on without warning. See my hands? They're shaking again."

"Your hands, they're so cold. Let me rub them between my hands. Are they a bit warmer? Raise your arms, and I'll slip this gown over your head—why did you pull your arms down so quick?"

"I had a pain in my chest, and it scared me."

"Is the pain still there?"

"No? Seems to come and go. It's gone now."

She needs more pillows. They'll help soften those areas where she lies too long in one spot. She lets out a sigh, and now she's quiet. What next? I'll make a thin porridge and hope she can keep it down.

She takes a few spoonful's, then moves her head away.

She says, "I'm OK now."

I turn to leave but she grabs my skirt and whispers, "What of Jed and Belinda? We can't have anyone snooping round here."

"What about them? They wash up and take meals in the kitchen; that is, as long as the shades are drawn. At nighttime, they hole up in the safe room, but I must tell you this, Lily. This is no fit way to house guests—not for more than a few days. They've been here much too long. It's time for them to move on. Your home is no longer safe. For them or for you. They must go."

"I suppose you're right, but I can't think about it right now."

"At least tell me who to contact, do you have a name, a way to get an escort for the runaways?"

She starts fishing in her side table.

"Helen? Help, it might be in here."

The top drawer is out too far, and it falls. I pick up the contents. She goes through the papers and hands me one.

"Here's the name; keep it hidden. He will help."

"Good, I'll send him a post in the morning. Of course, I'll use code words. At least those I still remember."

Time to get out of here and get myself settled in my own room. Lily's tucked in for the night. Her eyes are shut, and she hasn't spoken in a while. I'm almost past her doorway, when she calls out.

"Helen?"

"Yes, what is it?"

"Do you think I'll go to Hell for killing those bounty hunters?"

"Don't think on it. You only have to answer to your Maker, and I am sure He understands. Now, get some sleep."

* * *

Three days since that horrible night of the shootings, and that blood all over. I can't free it from my mind. Lily seems no worse for it. She's been having her good days and her bad days. Today is one of her good days. She's in good spirits. She no longer speaks of what went on that night and I won't remind her. I wish I could say the same for myself and just forget that whole night.

At first, Belinda had bouts of wailing but Jedediah held her close, patting her on the back, rubbing her neck, and whispering to her.

Of late, in the evenings, when reading by the fireplace, their singing can be heard. Very faint and coming from behind the wall to the safe room.

On occasion, refrains from *'Go Down Moses,'* and *'Bound For the Promised Land.'* come through.[14] I love to listen. Yet, I sense some sadness in their singing. I wonder how the two are doing after the shootings.

Tonight, we drink mugs of hot cocoa, while we huddle round the fireplace.

Lily says, "Helen, the strangest thing happened not too long ago. You will love this story. Jed and Belinda come closer. You might like to listen."

"Thank you, my dears. Now, one evening this past winter I was reading by the fireplace in my rocker, when I heard a knocking at the door. It was Mrs. Anna Tellatini, a good friend. She's that elderly colored lady, living across the way from here. She had a sad look about her and must've been crying. I brought her in to sit by the fire and asked what was troubling her?'

"She began, 'I was looking out my window and saw in the snow, a chicken that looked half froze to death. So, I brought it into the house and wrapped it in a towel, but it's not movin' much, just blinkin' one eye at me. So, I kept it wrapped up and put it in my stove oven. I thought I'd just start a small wood fire to warm him a little.'

"I said, 'That was kind of you Anna, did that bring him around?'"

"She said, 'No! Good God, I forgets the time and started smelling smoke. I rushed to the oven, but Chicken was pretty well baked by then. So's the family had roast chicken for dinner. But I can't eat any 'cause I still sees that poor bird blinkin' at me. I was too ashamed to tell the children the real story.'"

I can't hold back a giggle, and then notice that Jed and Belinda don't crack a smile and are quiet.

Lily continued, "I tried to keep from smiling as I put my arm around Mrs. Tellatini and said, 'You are one kind lady. You shan't be needing any more fretting or worrying—not since God must be knowing your true intentions for that bird.'"

"My goodness, Lily, that's funny and yet such a sad story." Jed and Belinda say nothing. So, I ask, what do they think?

Jed says, "Eatin dat bird, ain't so bad. But, I's thinkin, best t' kill it first, afore puttin it in t' bake."

Smiles break out on our faces, even Jed's. I am glad Lily thought of that story. She is coughing, so it's time to get her back to her room.

She didn't last long after getting ready for bed. I am back with her chamber pot, and she is fast asleep.

I need to find a good book to read. I see that Jack's library is well stocked with many leather-bound books.

Now, where is Lily keeping her ink well . . . found it, in this desk cubby hole. This is the desk Lily got from Ma. It's such a right fine piece. My Grandpa made it.

Ma said, "He hand built this and it took him through one cold winter on late nights to carve out all the curlicues on the front and sides. Your Grandpa waited till I was old enough to care for it, then with a 'here, take care of it, this is yours,' he gave it to me."

Ma then passed the task of dusting and occasional oiling to me once I was old enough. I never knew my Grandpa, but wished I had. I used to love polishing what he made. I used linseed oil, rubbing those fine crevices with all the ins and outs showing carvings of flowers and birds.

Lily turned up her nose at the polishing task, always found better things to do. When Ma gave it to Lily for a wedding gift, I cried my heart out that same night, as if losing an old friend. Still, as I see it now, it does fit better right here with Jack's family heirlooms.

I was not impressed with Jack when he first met our family.

Ma said, "Oh, but isn't he a fine catch for Lily?" I had my doubts. Store bought flowers he brought and presented to Ma. Then, he took her hand to kiss it. My word, who'd he think he was, the head knight at the round table? Or Prince Charming, more like it.

He announced, "I am so pleased to make your acquaintance, dear lady, as Lily has spoken often of you, and of course her devoted sister, Helen."

Ma nodded, smiled and I just stood silent. Well, he was altogether too haughty and too slick for my liking.

Later after weeks of courting, they arrived together with Lily's cheeks so red I thought he'd taken liberties with her. Here he was asking Ma for Lily's hand in marriage. When he'd left, after getting his request granted of course, I then had my say.

"Ma, you can't believe that man, can you? No one is that fine or perfect."

"Helen, it'll all turn out for the best in the long run. She does care for him, and just think of it, Lily's mill work is done with. Jack is a lawyer from a good family. She'll be taken care of and that's one worry we can put to rest."

What would Ma say now, the way he's been treating Lily?

Hmm, this desk is a bit dusty. Where's the rag and the oil so I can give it a good once over.

Almost finished, but something's stuck way in back behind this drawer, jamming it from opening. If I fish it out, ah, here it comes, and one more pull will do it.

Well, I'll be, it's my old speller and my very first diary.

Lily calls again, "Helen, Helen? Come here if you would?"

I will. Still, I must get back to this desk. It's such a treasure chest. I've yet to see what's been left behind these old drawers.

"Lily, what ails you now?"

"Helen, I confided to you about Jack before, and I'm sorry for adding to your own worries."

"No, don't say that, you're my only sister and we're all that's left in our Nesbitt family. Just tell me, what I can do"

"I thank you for that. As to Jack's behavior lately, it all comes clear to mind. I tried to ignore the signs, I truly did."

"What do you mean? What signs are you talking about?"

"He started gradually going away for longer periods, until he was rarely here at all. I stopped caring how I appeared, and when he did show up—I did not present myself in the best way."

"You? Lily, that's not like you at all. You always were so well turned out, and never let even one hair get out of place. What happened?"

"It was after the funerals when our two baby girls were buried. That's when it began."

"Oh, no, was it that long ago?"

"We were never the same again, not as man and wife should be. He mourned for a while, right along with me. Then when he was ready to go on, I couldn't stop grieving. It bothered him to see me moping round our home."

"Lily, if only you could've sent a post off to me, I'd have come much sooner."

"I must share in the fault finding. My black garments and veil covered me. They shielded me from everyone, long past the normal mourning period. I'd sit on the porch to wait for Jack each evening. He would drive me to the gravesite so I could tell them, 'God bless and rest easy, my loves.' Months went by and I still wanted to go, despite Jack's insistence that I must forget that our girls were gone. He was here, needing me, and I paid him no mind."

"You seem to be getting over the grieving."

"As time went on, I knew he'd had enough. He couldn't abide seeing what I'd become, and that was my own doing."

"What did he do, or say? Did he mistreat you?"

"No, not that, he never raised a hand to me, nor did any cruel or mean words ever come from his lips. Yet, he never offered comfort."

"Oh Lily, I'm so sorry for you."

"Instead he offered excuses for his absences. 'More and more work' he said, 'I'm seeing new clients, must get to the library before it closes,' or 'have to go downtown' or whatever."

"Lily, he's a busy lawyer, after all. Shouldn't his absences be justified."

"One time, there was no Goodbye, just a note on the mantel, 'I must go out of town to check out facts on some legal documents.' He left no endearing term like the usual, 'Love to Lily, from your loving husband'"

Lily stopped and wiped a tear from her cheek. Then continued.

"He's spent enough time gadding about with his so called 'business friends' and he's smelled of strong brew, one time too many. On occasion, a board creaking would wake me, as he snuck upstairs just before sunrise."

"How can you be sure? You don't have one idea about where he was and what he was actually doing. Surely you've imagined more than what appears."

"Imagining? Did I imagine times sniffing cologne on his shirt, or finding that lace hanky, having rouge smearings on it? It was not well hidden, as if he no longer had any care for my feelings. There it was, left sticking out of his back pocket."

"There must be a good explanation. Was not his sister, Marybeth here visiting during that time?"

"Well, yes."

"You say, he'd been drinking heavier after the twins died. Could she have held him close to comfort him and perhaps offered her handkerchief? Could that be the answer? Well, think on it."

Lily stopped talking. She lay back on her pillow and was silent . . . long enough that I could slip from her room. Halfway down the stairs I was, when she called out again. "Helen, please come back."

That desk will have to wait. I hurry back as she might really need me.

She says, "No, my dear, no. What you explained about Marybeth, well that doesn't fit with his behavior."

"Lily, that's enough—it's water under the bridge."

"No, let me have my say. If he'd done better by me—been a better husband—my fears would be groundless. He's had no time for me, yet he spends time, he says, in Boston. What should have taken a few days, settling that Family Will, it's now turned into weeks. No more discussing it, I'm through with him."

"If that's your decision, but shouldn't you wait till your health improves when you've had time to clear your head?"

"I refuse to be silent any longer. I shall confront him, or write him a long letter."

Good, I'll offer to get her some paper. Then, I can spend time, rummaging around that desk.

Lily continues, "He's hiding something, can't you see? I can't sleep and I've no will to get up of a morning. Nothing is important for me, except wanting him with me again, showing he cares. He has no idea how sick I've been. Oh, Helen, many a night I've prayed that this sickness could end it all, so my heart would be set free."

"Oh, stop it. Look at you with all these dramatics, acting as if on a stage. One time you say you're through with him, and then in a moment's notice your mind changes and you want him back. Such nonsense, and another thing . . . I will not pity you, when you dare to mention of ending it all?"

"Pity, when did I ask for your pity? Why, how can you—."

"Now you listen, turn a key to your lips and keep them shut. This is the last time I shall say this, so hear me out. You shall never ever think again of actually ending it all."

"I didn't mean Jack and I would leave each other, well not really."

"I'm not meaning your marriage to Jack. You were hinting about ending your life, were you not? If you ever do, I shall be so angry, your funeral will not have me in attendance. Now take that and digest it well."

She flinched, then gasped and a look of horror crept over her face. Then she slumped down. Her head sank deep into her big, soft pillow. It was quick work to tuck the top of her satin coverlet round her shoulders. Finally, her eyes closed. I stroked her brow—while wishing, praying she'd drift off to a good long sleep. Then I went back to the library.

I have time to scout some more in this desk. There's more I'm pulling out, along with my speller and first diary. It's a packet of letters. Here's one addressed just to me, and of all things—my mother wrote it? Must read it. Hope Lily will not call me again.

To My Dear Daughter, Helen,

Helen, if you ever find this and perhaps I'll be long gone when you do, it's something you should know that I could not bring myself to tell you earlier.

Your real Pa, the one before I married Lily's father, was half Indian. His Christian name was Albert, but he was also known as White Eagle. His mother was a white lady by the name of Anna-Marie St. Pierre who ran a Trading Post. She fell in love with an Indian man, who traded furs at the Post. They were wed in the Indian tradition, and their first born son became your father, the man I married.

Your father, Albert, was from the same tribe as Marjorie, an Indian lady known in these parts for her herbal cures. Your Pa, also knew a lot about potions and other healing recipes.

We could not marry, not openly. At the start of our love for each other, we did have an Indian ceremony. My own Bible presented by my mother, was held by both of us during the ceremony.

He was a kind and caring man, with piercing dark brown eyes and quite knowledgeable of Indian lore. We had a fine, loving relationship and I loved him dearly, the same as he felt about me. But because of old prejudices that still surfaced at the time, we kept it secret and private from the townspeople.

He would not let me suffer any deprivations, and tried to protect me from gossip, or mean-spirited people—especially when learning you were to be born. That's when he decided to leave for a while. Your Grandma agreed with him. She knew how small minded some could be, and so between the two I had no choice but to stay with her. Then, I would mope around hoping to get word that he'd return soon.

After three months, his brother brought me a letter from your father, with his last words. Here it is enclosed in this one from me.

> *For my love, I've come down with the cholera and they tell me it won't be long now. I love you now and forever, and will join with you when our spirits meet again. Wrap your arms round our child when it is born, and give it a blessing for me.*
>
> *Raise him or her in the very same way you were instructed in my ways, to always honor the earth, moon, sun and all creatures as one. And if you choose, let the child know I will always be there, watching over her with guidance in my afterlife.*
>
> *My brother, Running Bear, promised he will look in on you and your family from time to time, but only from afar as he will not intrude on you and yours. He lives in the wild, so I would not expect too much of him.*
>
> *One thing you must promise me. Soon, you should find and accept a good man to care for you. Do not stay all alone as you'll need help with our child.*
>
> *I remain, now and Forever yours, White Eagle (Albert).*

Helen, my life was in turmoil, and all hopes for a happy life had been dashed. My heart told me I'd never meet or marry as good or gentle a man as your Pa was. But you're Grandma made me go on for your sake.

She asked me to consider, "When Helen enrolls in school, think of how she'd bear it if no father could be claimed on her school papers? The children might laugh at her. You know how cruel they can be."

It took much time to finally get myself together, to socialize with anyone. Then, your step-father came into our lives and I was proved wrong. There was one as good as the one I'd lost. Well, almost the same. He had his own good qualities. Yes, it was Stephen Nesbitt, who later became Lily's Pa. He'd been in the Vermont Militia, and he had just come back from his duty.

You must know this about your new Pa, the one who helped to care for you when you were young. He insisted that you be raised as his own, to be known as his daughter and must be treated the same as Lily. It wasn't hard to accomplish, shortly after we were wed.

Please forgive me, for keeping this from you these many years, but it was done with love, and not kept secret to hurt you in any way. You have my permission to tell Lily if you wish. That shall always remain your decision to inform anyone you think should know.

I am now sealing this with love, from your Ma.

I must set for a bit. It's all too much to think on. Now I know where my looks came from. Those dreams and the forebodings I've had—did my Pa have that same gift, knowing of things to come?

Can you hear me, Ma, wherever you are? Stay with me. I wish I could have known my father. I hope he's in Heaven and you've seen each other again? If so, tell him I'm anxious to meet him, when it's my turn to join all of you. What's wrong with me? I speak to the dead, as if they can hear. It's the living I care about. Lily is here and we must get her better.

What an awful thought. Lily wouldn't have been my sister if Ma hadn't got going to attract another man. Mr. Nesbitt, the best father we could hope for. Lily and I loved him. We wept for days when he passed away. It was too soon, but he was a lot older than Ma.

I'll put the letter back, along with this batch of other papers. It's still in a safe place. I wonder if Lily knows. Probably not, besides, with all the cobwebs and dust hanging back there, my letter must have been stuck for ages.

This is all too much. I'm frazzled. I should rest, close my eyes. This afghan . . . so soft. Wrap it around me.

I hear, "Sweet dreams, my girl." Is it Pa, my real Pa? Lord, let me see him, hear his stories. Please come back—don't leave, not yet.

Never mind. My favorite bedtime story was told by Ma, 'The Little Match Girl.' She'd begin, "A man in Denmark, Hans Anderson wrote this. You girls, are you certain you want to hear it again?"

Lily's so young. She sits on my lap in front of the fire.

She whispers, "Mama, tell us?"

Oh, what's this, my nose fills with lavender. Why, that's Ma's own cologne, and it dizzies my head. Are we in bed? And, Ma is right here between us? Lily giggles, and asks, "Mama, c'mon, tell a story."

Slowly I inch myself over, closer and closer. Oh Lord, keep Ma right here? A hand squeezes my shoulder. Lips brush my forehead.

"There was a little girl, so thin from not eating, and she was out selling matches for crusts of bread. She's on a street corner wearing a thin tattered dress. No one stops to buy even one match. Her tiny body shakes from the bitter cold. She lights one match after the other, trying to keep warm."

"But, alas, next morning a few passersby see a small pile of burnt matches. And, next to it, a tiny girl is all curled up—almost covered by the snow. It must keep her warm? But, no one stops, as they continue on their way to their warm homes. The constable is called. He leans over to wake her. But, he knows she does not sleep."

I shiver. Chills take over—that poor thing, but could it be our Lily? No, please, no. Then, where is she? I help pull her from Ma's other side and she snuggles up to me. Finally, her warm little body is so calm. I stop my shaking.

Then, it all drifts away, yet I still see the Match girl in the snow.

Chapter Twelve

David Hatcher

I managed to send a post to Joshua about my mother's letter. He will be surprised but perhaps he might have always wondered about the difference between Lily and me. My black hair and darker complexion compared to Lily's blond hair and light skin. I wonder? Anyhow, I hope he can join me here soon.

Summer will be fast approaching. I've not yet received a response from my post to the local Leader, that contact Lily knew of. However, it's only been a few days. Perhaps I worry too much.

I peek through the window curtain to see what a day we'll have. It looks as if rain won't start, not yet. What's this? There's a man coming up the walkway. He's all spruced up and official looking. He stands by the front door knocking away to beat the band.

"Coming. I hear you. Just don't let that knocker fall off, the way you're banging away on it."

What neighbors could be in such a hurry, so rude? I can't have Lily disturbed and certainly not for an uninvited guest. Could that be the contact we were waiting for? Or worse could it be a lawman? Just in case, I'll ask questions. He must identify himself. I'll open this door just a bit. I'll let him think I'm the maid.

"Who is it? Are you a friend of Mr. and Mrs. Wallingford?"

"I am Dr. David Hatcher, a friend of Reverend Billingsly. He asked that I pick up two mutual friends on my way to Vermont."

"Mrs. Wallingford is not receiving guests today. And most certainly she cannot see strangers from out of town."

"My dear lady, my home is right here in Fairhaven. Please hear me out. It's my annual trip to procure a supply of gourds for seasonal decorations. My church welcomes the gifts and the Reverend said your lady might like some on my return?"

Is he serious? What's this talk about gourds?

"Miss, in my hand is my letter of introduction." I understand there is an urgency here. I was told that there should be no delays. Am I correct or do I have the wrong address?"

"Hold on, give it here. I must be sure your reverend friend gave you the correct information."

The code words in his letter show me that he is indeed one of us.

"Come in Mr. Hatcher. My name is Helen. I'm Lily's sister. Are you really a doctor?"

"Yes, I am, and you are not really the maid, I take it. Please call me David." He has a nice gentle look about him and his smile appears to be genuine, not reeking of sarcasm in any way.

"Come with me into the kitchen. I'll introduce you to our guests."

Here they are at the table, "Jedediah and Belinda, I'm presenting Dr. David Hatcher. He is a friend to help us in our need and will aid you on your way to the next safe house."

Both jumped up at once and nodded. Belinda sat back down but Jed just stood there. His eyes bored into me, not knowing what to do.

David said, "Sit down, sit down, my good man. It's good to make your acquaintance."

"Please join us at table, David, and let me provide some offerings. Here's our pot of tea to begin with."

"Just a cup of tea will do. Yet it all looks so good, perhaps one of those rolls, with a tad bit of that Blueberry jam."

"Of course, here you are. Now tell me how you, being a doctor, came to be involved in the anti-slavery movement?"

"I needed a change of pace from my medical position, though I do love being a doctor. Helping with the Underground Railroad was something new to me and it started off as a diversion. It was a relief from my normal practice. More importantly the runaways sometimes are in need of doctoring."

"Well, you may have bitten off more than you can chew, coming here. There's something important, and I'm glad you're a doctor. You may have to do double duty."

"I am well qualified and more so for doctoring than escorting. But go on, please continue. You said there was something important. Tell me what it is. I am at your service."

"My sister Lily, the lady of this house, is very ill. She needs a doctor to attend to her. I felt it necessary to get these two runaways on their way before fetching one.'

"Jed, for Goodness' sake, please stop drumming your fingers on the table.'

"Now, to get back to—where was I? Yes, you must understand my position, having to care for the two runaways, in my sister's stead. We can't, or rather she won't think of having a strange doctor here, or of going to a hospital. Not till she's sure the runaways won't be apprehended."

"Yes, yes of course. Where is your sister? I will give her a once over right now. But first, tell me what you think is ailing her."

"Lily has taken to her bed since she's been ill. That's why she asked me to come from Vermont to care for her.'

I lower my voice so she can't hear. "You'll notice her yellowed skin and her being like a skeleton in places, yet puffy in others. Also, she can't keep much down when eating. Yet, I'm more concerned about this hacking cough she has."

"Those are not good signs. We must find the cause of the cough."

"She worked in a cotton mill, could that be a good reason?"

"Perhaps."

"Let me take you to her, but let me check first. She may be indisposed."

"Lily, you may have heard us talking downstairs. Good news, a conductor who is also a doctor has arrived. He's agreed to examine you. Are you OK with that?"

"Of course, but could you get me a nice night gown and fix my hair?" I did as she asks. Then I place a clean sheet over her. It's time to call for David to come on up.

He enters the room, and she shuts her eyes, but keeps one half open.

He holds her hand till she opens both eyes.

"Do you mind if I check you over? Your sister is right here."

"Lily, this doctor is also the answer to your letter. He's going to help escort Jed and Belinda to the north. His name is David Hatcher."

"Pleased to meet you Dr. Hatcher. Do what you will."

"First, we check her head, then the eyes, to see if they follow my finger when it moves. Now open your mouth and yes, go ahead Lily, say it."

She said, "Ah."

Now let's have a look in these ears. Good, there's no potatoes growing in them."

Lily pulled her head away.

"Sorry, Lily, I forgot, but that usually gets a chuckle out of my young patients."

He then felt under the sheets as Lily looked up to the ceiling. He was quick, checking her stomach, thumping on her chest, but ever so gently. He tapped her knees, her elbows, wrists, and listened, through the bell, to her chest sounds. No time was wasted in talk, not till he was done.

"Well, Mrs. Wallingford, I mean Lily. Both of you, please take note. Lily, your skin is extremely dry, and your upper arms have flabby skin, see it hanging loose?"

Lily is listening, and her mouth is shut tight; but her eyes are wide, bigger than they ever were since I arrived. I shall ask the questions, if she won't.

"Look, why are some parts of her arms not the same?"

"Yes, Lily's forearms are just the opposite, and are all puffed up. Yet, Lily, can you feel? Here are your ribs—very prominent, almost sticking through."

Lily starts coughing and wheezing.

"Lily, we must ask David, how can we help correct this?" Lily nods her head at him, waiting for an answer.

"Take more fluids, water, any liquids you can tolerate. If they don't stay down on the first try, then load up on crackers or dry biscuits. That should line your stomach and not cause upheavals."

"Yes, I shall try. Thank you. We will, or rather Helen will keep on top of it all."

He asks, "Is there anything else you're worried over?"

"Well, is rest good? Sleeping helps, though I am still tired all the time."

"Yes, rest all you can but try to walk a bit when you feel up to it. You should not worry. We'll find out how best to help you. Meanwhile get more sun, as much as possible. It will help lighten that yellow cast to your skin. Come Helen, let's move her bed nearer to the window."

We moved chairs and furniture out of the way. Soon we had her bed all set by the window and she asked, "Please crack it open a bit?"

David says, "Ah yes, the fresh air should help with your breathing. Keep a warm shawl over your shoulders to fend off the cold air. Helen, can you see now that her breathing is getting better?" No, I don't see it, but I say nothing. She coughs again, and again, with wheezing in between.

David grabbed up his medical bag and says "Lily, I'll take my leave. I'll check back in the morning to see about tending to your two guests."

He told me, after leaving her room, "You've managed the fever and you must know how best to get it down. She most likely has contracted a disease. I don't know of any definite diagnosis, so we won't mention any of this to her, until we are sure. Then again, her lungs are not good. Listening through the bell, I detected constant wheezing sounds, and that cough appears to be of long standing. How old is your sister?"

"She's twenty-three."

"That's hard to believe. She has the look of a woman twice that age. You said she had worked some years in a cotton mill? That may be worth noting. Possibly her liver has damage and can't handle what she eats and drinks. That jaundiced or yellow skin is a warning sign, along with vomiting most liquids. The sun will help do away with that yellow skin pallor. It won't cure her, but won't hurt, either. Just, let her know, she is not to stay too long a time in sunlight. Might cause sunburn."

"Yes, I will."

"Her skin being dry and bloated, is not a good sign. And the fever from the sweating and then the chills—her body is trying to fight off what caused the damage. Hospital tests would give the answer. We'll need arrangements made to take her in."

"She won't like that, not at all. Do you think it best?"

"This is too serious to ignore. You'll have to convince her."

"Yes, certainly I shall do that. Thank you for looking in on my sister"

"No bother, none at all. As I said before, being a doctor is what I do best—much better than presenting codes to a mysterious lady standing behind a door."

I covered my mouth, yet "Hah!" just went and slipped out. It's what Joshua teases me about. Calling it a hearty horse laugh. I was relieved when David joined me with a chuckle.

Before entering the Living room, David made me stop to listen to him.

"I need to take some measurements, Helen. The two runaways need proper garments to travel with me. I'll see to providing them with decent clothes of good quality—they are in trunks stored in my home.

"How will you be traveling with the two? What did you have in mind?"

"This may seem bold but we'll be out in the open and I'll pretend both are my free domestic servants. They must be dressed in proper attire and suitable for a gentleman of my stature."

"I see what you're intending. That's very bold. Do you think it will work?"

"What do bounty hunters look for when pursuing escaped slaves? The clothes they wear is what gives them away."

I reply, "Can't have them looking like ragamuffins, now, can we? Yes, that frock of Belinda's, it is totally unbecoming. It has the look of old potato sacks. Jed's old shirt and long baggy pants make him look like . . . well, what he is—an escaped slave. So, you'll fix him up proper, with white shirt, black jacket, trousers and tie? I can help trim his hair to keep it closer to his head."

"Yes, we'll even fit him out with a top hat. Belinda can wear a scarf or kerchief . . . perhaps a nice bonnet."

"Forgive my grin but I can just picture Jed in a black top hat setting on top of his head. Just don't go so far as to get him a white wig."

With that we both chuckled. I hoped the two couldn't hear.

"Now Helen, what would you propose for Belinda?"

"Well she could wear a long dress, run through with lines of pink ribbons and lace trimming. A matching lace trim on gloves and a fancy shawl having pink rose buds at the ends would also be nice."

He nods all the while. Does he think me serious? It might just work. If they're out in the open—who would suspect any skullduggery was going on.

"Good choices for both, let's bring them in here."

Fetching Jed and Belinda from the kitchen, I say, "Please be still now, the doctor must take your measurements. You may call him Mister David."

Jed says, "Missus Helen, what Mistuh David doin? An touchin Belinda, an feelin her feet?"

"He's going to fit both of you with shoes and new clothes."

Belinda asks, "Missuz Helen, why we goin? Why we hafta be fancied up?"

David says, "Helen, let me answer. See here, what do you think we might be planning? You'll need new wearing apparel for where you're going."

Jed says, "Y'all gon' be cartin us on t' auction blocks. I jess knows it."

He has to stop this carrying on like this.

"No, Jed, that's not true! Listen to me. Stop imagining the worse. We only want to help."

"How y'all helpin' us? My Massa—he allus get us fancy duds. We knows y'all gon' hire us out, same's he allus did."

"No Jed, I said we are not like that. Belinda, can't you tell him?"

"Ma'am, ah cain't tell Jed. Shoot, y'all done tricked us. Y'all say, we gon' git free? Funny way a doin it."

"Don't worry, the good doctor works with us. He will get you to the next safe house."

Jed responds, "Wal, y'all tellin it true? An Missus Lily, too, she knowed? Anyways, wal, Belinda? It gone be OK?"

Belinda looks at both of us, "Missus Helen, Mistuh David, OK, we gettin new clothes? An I'se gettin a new dress?"

David replies, "Yes, yes. Tell me, have either of you been branded at any time? You must hold still, Jed, so I can get these exact fittings, and lengths."

"Yassuh." Jed showed his forearm with the 'JB' brand raised on his skin. Belinda hung back, till Jed grabbed onto her arm, pulling her close to him. Her mark has an H added.

"Belinda, why is there also an 'H'?"

"It meanin house nigra, owned by Massah an' Mistruss, an spose tuh get special food. Can even take leavins off table. Mebbe iffen ah was plainer, Massah lemme alone. Am I right, Jed?"

"Lindy Bell, why you talk like dat. Massa ain't here now. We's bein ready tuh git freed. So, better hush on up."

David let them go on a bit. Chatting away back and forth. They now appear much calmer. Then he warned both on how to act and to keep their sleeves down at all times, no matter how hot it might be.

"I can't have you rolling up your sleeves to show your arms while we're traveling."

He takes me aside and lowers his voice. "Helen, I'm taking a big risk with these two. They have an independent streak about them. What can you tell me about their background? Shall we send them to the safe room so we can talk in private?"

"No need, we can discuss it in front of them. There are no secrets here."

Jed relates why they ran from the South Carolina plantation. His speech is halting and his words sometimes trail off altogether.

He asks me, "Missus Helen, can yuh tell Mr. David? Missus Lily musta been tellin you 'bout it, dint she?"

"Yes, of course." No wonder he wants to forget. They were terrible times. Belinda's eyes are cast down to the floor—her lips are pursed together so tight. Well, she won't be saying much, either.

"David, it was a miracle how they survived on a ship taking them North."

"What ship was this?"

"Both were stowaways aboard a New England Schooner. This particular anchoring was a scheduled landing stop in Charleston, South Carolina for cotton to be shipped to the New Bedford textile mills. First let me tell you about their life on the plantation and why they ran away."

"Yes, please go on."

"John Beaumont, their Master, had them slaving, six days a week, from early dawn till dusk. At times on Sundays, each could be hired out for day labor even though this was the one day that most slaves looked forward to, as it was their day of rest.'

"Jed and Belinda were hearty workers and more presentable than most. They always gave their best efforts and hoped to become another master's house slaves. Both were in demand to work in the homes of their master's friends on calling days. So, their Sundays got taken up more and more."

"Did they get any payment for their labors?"

"Hmm, well if they did it was very little. It was their owners who got the pay from hiring them out. If they had gotten actual wages, they would have run off a lot sooner."

David is now inspecting Jed's arms.

"How did you get all these scars?"

"Massa's boss man been whippin' me. I gets more on my back."

He takes his shirt off.

"David, look—raised scars, like large crosses. He can thank that hate-filled Master of his."

"Yes, quite horrific."

David turns to Belinda. "Young lady, tell me of your work as a house maid. Your Mistress . . . how did she treat you? Or your Master, did he ever deal out harsh punishment?" Belinda hung her head.

Jed replies, "The Mistruss she good, she take a likin t' my Belinda. Some days she learnt Belinda ABC letters. Belinda tryin' real hard t' learn readin. But Massa John, he one mean man. He tole Mistruss, 'stop learnin Nigras. Nigras spose t' be workin, not settin aroun.' Times he gon' been whuppin Belinda for no good reason. An, Belinda tole me, 'Massa sure been evil man. Devil ownin his soul.'"

"Is that right, Belinda?"

"Yes sir. He be's touchin me, pattin my hind end, an I skip along fast outta his way. I gets busy washin dishes. An dint see ole Massa sneakin roun corner. Afore I knows it, I feels a hand . . . slidin up my leg."

"Oh my, how could he? Sorry for interrupting. Continue."

"Dunno, he jess dun it. I jumps back, droppin big dish. He run out an next I sees Mistruss. She bringin broom t' me, an I jess standin, not movin, an she bendin down pickin up pieces, sayin 'Step back, watch yer feet.'"

I ask, "Your Mistress actually was doing your work? Do you think she saw what went on?"

"Dunno, Missus Helen, but she dint stop Massa from whippin me, cuz I'se breakin big ole plate.'

"Nex morn, Mistruss sittin on my bed, puttin lard on my lashins. I open one eye, wantin t' stay sleepin, but it hurtin so bad. Mistruss say, 'Here' an she handin me funny looking pants.'

"She say, 'We call em bloomers. Alla drafty ole rooms is needin heavy cottin on yer legs. C' mon, Belinda, y'all gon' wear em—so put em on.'" Belinda sits down, folds her hands in her lap, looks to Jed and rolls her eyes.

"Mistuh David, afta Belinda, she be cryin an she tellin me bout Massa—I'se thinkin, bess we gets out. We be's hearin all bout culluds runnin t' go up north. Songs we singin, an whis'prins at night, sayin bess way t' go."

"Oh, and what ways were they? They were told as secrets, of course?"

"We hearin bout signs t' look for, lookin up—findin Big Dipper. It be's pointin t' north star. So gon' run—soons Belinda gets healin all done. An we been hearin Massa thinkin on sellin me . . . so we cain't wait. We's knowin how t' allus gon' be *Crossin Jordin.* Rivers git us way up t' north. An walkin in water, it makin dogs cain't smell good. I start in t' plannin—gotta go, an gon' run far."

He grabs Belinda round her waist and pulls her closer to him.

"These signs, did they help guide you?" Jed nods and then grins.

He says, "Me an my Lindy Bell, we allus plannin t' run. But affer she get bad whippin, I cudda kilt Massa. We hadda run, an if Gloryland be's so cold—we stick close, keepin warm. We gon' run far, but we go by boat, landin inna good place t' be livin an raisin chillun."

"Why did you decide to go by boat?"

"Ole Massa's head boy, he say boats in Charleston go to New Bedford an culluds like me, workin on fishin boats, gettin' coins for work."

I say, "They left the plantation in the dead of night. It took three days to reach Charleston. There, they hid out in alleyways. Reward postings were tacked up and Jed pulled one off. He showed Lily when they first got to her house. Here it is."

"Luck was with them next morning. It was a Sunday and seamen were either sleeping off the night before or attending church services nearby. Jed figured it was a good chance to sneak aboard the ship."

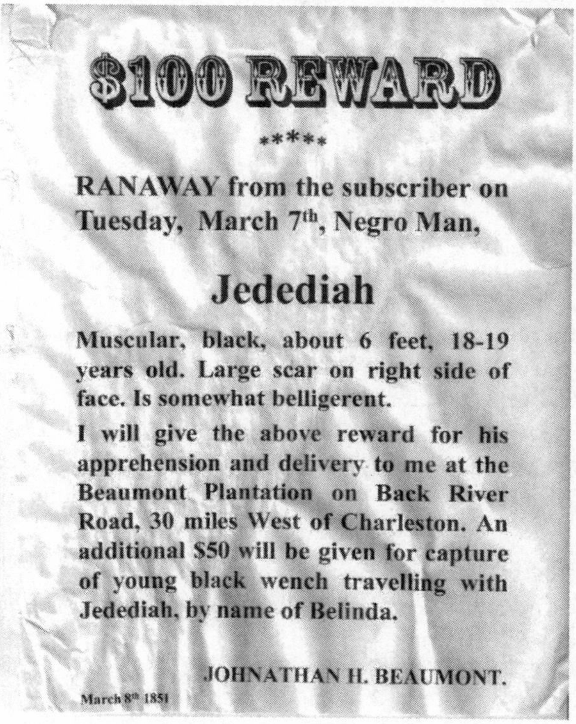

$100 REWARD

*****

RANAWAY from the subscriber on Tuesday, March 7th, Negro Man,

Jedediah

Muscular, black, about 6 feet, 18-19 years old. Large scar on right side of face. Is somewhat belligerent.

I will give the above reward for his apprehension and delivery to me at the Beaumont Plantation on Back River Road, 30 miles West of Charleston. An additional $50 will be given for capture of young black wench travelling with Jedediah, by name of Belinda.

JOHNATHAN H. BEAUMONT.

March 8th 1851

"Would you like to continue, Jed?" Jed then began telling about their voyage. Or started to, then stopped and left the room. He came back with a glass of water.

"I'm sorry, David but Jed might not want to go on with this part. Lily told me they hid down in the hold of that ship, while sailing north to New Bedford. They were fairly well concealed, as they hid between large cotton bales. However, rats were all over, and they had all they could do, trying to keep their feet off the floor. When moving about, they jumped fast to keep out of the rats' way and not step in their leavings. This left them exhausted with no time for any sound sleep."

Jed says, "Yassuh. I'se seed em skitterin roun, an I keeps my feet up high, cuz I seein teeth been chompin— big as Lion teeth."

David smiles. "Jed, I imagine, being so afraid . . . you did think they were that big?" Jed's eyes open wide, and a slight grin appears. It shows off his scar, how deep it is. That old mark won't stay put when he smiles.

I say, "Jed and Belinda got to feeling ill, smelling burlap and tar, mixed with the smell of dead fish. After four days, they nearly died from thirst. Belinda and Jed do you want to tell more?"

Belinda says, "Yessum, Jed gon' lookin t' fetch water. An—aw, c' mon, Jed. Y'all good fer tellin tales, an bettren me."

Jed says, "I waits till dark an sneakin on deck. Crawlin cuz I cain't walk good. Jess bout to reach water barrel—an alla sudden, I gets t' feelin . . . who grabbin my arm? I turns roun t' see it be a workin mate. I'se shakin, cuz I gon' getta lashin, a cat-tail. I knows it. An I gotta git away. I'se scootin off, crawlin. But he catchin on t' me."

David asks, "What did he say to you?"

"He say 'c'mere. Doncha gets t' fearin me. I'se cullud, but I'se a free man. Here, take my water jug.' An, he say, 'wait doncha move, jess hole on.' He gets back an gimme salt pork."

I say, "Wouldn't he get in trouble for doing that?"

"Afore he leave, he say, 'Y'all bess t' stay offa deck. Doncha git my Cap'n afta me fer lettin y' all stay. An doncha take no mind, I sees y' all later w' more water an fish, OK?'" Jed looks to me and nods. He sits at the table and folds his arms.

"I can finish if Jed likes, or if Belinda needs to carry on to tell us something." She looks down. Then, walks over to Jed and stands behind him.

"Ok. But you two, let me know if I leave out anything from what Lily told me.' They both nod their heads.

"The rolling of the ship and the stench kept them sick and looking ghastly to each other. It lasted all the way to New Bedford. Yet, Jed took pride in knowing this time the ship was of his own choosing. At least he was not chained, nor confined as when he got shipped from his homeland in Africa."

Jed stands and says, "We been outta sea gon' onna week, an we's hearing rain pourin down. Big waves crashin on deck an pushin an rockin ship worsen afore. We gets sicker an wantin t' jump oer board. Comin from Africa I sees men jumpin t' die inna sea. But, no, I say to Lindy Bell, 'we betteren at.' So we prayin moren more. Afta a day, an inna morning, it stoppin, an we's gets done fer alla rockin."

David says, "Jed, oh, my word! It sounds like you went through a gale. What an ordeal. And, Belinda, you survived that?" Belinda just nods.

I say, "Yes of course, David. Now hear what happened to them when they first arrived in port after ten days at sea. Cape Verdeans in New Bedford, the men working on the docks—gave food and bed but not much more. It was only a coupla-three days before they had to move on."

David says, "I know of the Cape Verdean people. As dock men, they were afraid of outsiders taking their jobs. New Bedford whaling ships made regular trips to the Cape Verde Islands off Africa, just to pick up those willing to work in the whaling industry. This was dangerous work and wages were low, but many volunteered. Sorry for interrupting, please continue."

"Well, after Lily got word of the two runaways and their sad plight, she brought both to her home. Then Lily took sick and there was no chance of going any farther north. So, it was best to stay put right here and keep them out of sight. At least till better plans could be made."

David moves close to Jed and shakes his hand.

"Jed, you've both been through too much as it is. I will assure you now, we will certainly carry on for Lily. And will guarantee you get good care on your next stop, too. Mark my word!"

"So, David, you *do* have a plan in mind?"

"I've given this some thought and I believe this is the best course to be taking. We'll start out by avoiding the Post roads heading north. They've come under closer scrutiny of late. So I plan to transport Jed and Belinda by booking passage for the three of us on a Steamship from New Bedford to New York. Then, we can continue on up the Hudson River until we reach Albany NY. Fulton's steamships are very safe vessels and most comfortable."

I see both have such a scared look on their faces. They are deathly afraid of water. Their voyage North left them with a horror of any further ship traveling—even if they'll not be stuck in the bottom of a boat. Nevertheless, David continues with his grand plan.

"We'll then take the canal route on a smaller vessel until we reach Lake Champlain. At Crown Point in New York there is a good docking place. We can ferry over to Vermont from there. Then we should be able to proceed to Randolph."

"David, as an option you could proceed north on the road to Ferrisburgh and seek out Rokeby House."

"What place is that?"

"Joshua, told me it's a safe location on the underground railroad. It's run by a Quaker named Rowland Robinson."

"Ok, we'll hook up with the Post and Stage Roads to continue on to Ferrisburgh. I shan't worry once we reach Vermont, as I suspect the authorities will be few and far between."

"How can you not be worrying? Jed and Belinda look as if they are horror struck, about that voyage on the ship. Can you convince them it is safe and unlike the voyage from South Carolina?"

"Steam boats are very safe and the trip up the Hudson river and into Lake Champlain will bring calm waters.'

"My affairs are in order. I just need to gather up the clothes for Jed and Belinda, so I should be back, day after tomorrow. I'll take my leave now."

"Thank you for coming David, we are ever so grateful. Take care and God be with you."

* * *

I am at the window, sitting and rocking, waiting for David. I'm starting to doze with the warm sun on my face. Pictures from the past start to flood my mind . . . First, snow falls on me, and then, the picture changes. Too warm in here, now sitting by my fireside in Vermont. Lily is so small, cuddling in my lap, smiling up at me. Then she's gone, along with flickering flames from our fire. I look for her in our room, and out the window. She's not there.

Now she's grown up and I see three horsemen with long overcoats out by her barn. Then that picture fades.

Now I see a boat. Oh no, it's sinking. People drowning, children screaming, towering waves rush down on them, no one saves them. No one is there.

I try to move but cannot. Then, here come those horsemen, racing, right at me, shouting, "Look what we found!" Wait! Why are they here? They knock me off, what is it, the boat? No! I've slid off my chair. Oh, Lord, this hard floor—what a jolt! My back hurts. My eyes open now, so get up, look around. Take my time. Wipe my brow, it's cold and clammy, but I'm wide awake. What in the world was that all about—that dream, what was the meaning of it? A boat and horses and . . . I am too tired. Must forget dreams such as this. They cannot bode any good.

Who is it? Rapping at the front door? Knocking at this early hour?

It's David. Oh Lord. I'm not fit for company. Not dressed. And no shoes, or even slippers on my feet.

I yell, "Jed, go open the door for Doctor Hatcher."

"David is that you, I'm in the library."

My clothes are rumpled and my messy hair is not pinned up. Think . . . what can I do, where to hide? Run, pull out the drapery. Now, hold it close, and turn round till it's covered back over me. Hurry. Now, he cannot see anything, nothing from top to toe. I am sure. Calm down.

"Come in, David. You are in the hall? I must finish checking these drapery linings. They must be replaced before winter sets in."

"Can I help?"

"No, I'm almost done. Did you bring the garments for Belinda and Jed—what they'll need for the trip? But first, pour yourself a cuppa tea in the kitchen. I'll join you after I fetch my sewing basket from upstairs. We'll need it for their alterations."

His footsteps fade away to the kitchen. I tiptoe past the kitchen, and then scoot up the stairs to my room. A quick cold water wash does me good. But, hurry, fast, make it doubly quick.

Ah, here's a clean garment. On the way out, I pass by the mirror. Eee gads, my hair, it's all mussed up. Strands stick out, every which way. Must stop, pin back this mess.

Good, looks more presentable now. Then, I shall walk, not rush downstairs. And, slowly pace, as I enter . . . to join David in the kitchen.

David, where is he? Oh, over on his knees, trying to fit a shirt sleeve on Jed—who just stands, feet wide apart, with arms folded. So ram rod straight, and so defiant he is, I know he's not wanting to hear any more about ship passages. Belinda stands in the corner waiting her turn.

"Well, David, hello again."

David removes pins from his mouth.

"Sorry for coming at such an early hour, but time is of the essence.'

"Helen, I've more to do, but what do you say about Jed's fine clothes?"

"Why, they look fine thus far and very fitting."

He says, "By the way, when you order the linings for the draperies, be sure to add six inches or more. And might be a good idea to get more for the drapery hems, too."

"Why?"

"They need to reach the floor to keep all drafts out." Oh goodness. He must have seen my feet. He looks up at me and smiles.

Now it's Belinda's turn.

"Belinda, come here, and do hold still while the good doctor fixes that garment. Try not to move."

He starts placing pins. Then Belinda jumps to the side. "Ow!" The pin sticks in her waist coat, and a ruffle unravels as other pins fall out.

David does not get upset. He just sighs and says, "This dress came from my mother's rummage box in my attic. It belonged to her. She was also an expert seamstress, working at home. I watched her fitting and helped when needed. Now, please, let's try it one more time."

Lily has come to join us. She's now sitting in her rocker.

Belinda's still pouting, and her hands grab at the corset hooks and laces.

David says, "I am sorry, Belinda. I've told you both, we must hurry. We'll need to sew these clothes and leave soon to board the steamboat at the New Bedford pier."

Belinda jumps back, and holds onto Jed.

At mention of a steamboat, that ghastly dream I just had, came back. I yell, "No! You must not plan on going by boat!"

Lily says, "Helen, what's wrong with you? David has already arranged the boat trip."

"I didn't mean to shout, but both of you, it cannot come to pass. I've had this strange feeling something dreadful will happen to that steamboat."

David asks, "What are you talking about?"

"I can't explain, except when my husband nearly drowned, all water trips of any kind just scare the daylights out of me. Also, Jed and Belinda are unwilling to get on a boat. Doesn't that settle it?"

I take Lily's hand, and note how cold and dry it is.

"Lily we need to talk in the living room."

"Please excuse me, David. I did not mean to sound like a tyrant of any sort. But can you think on another plan, something without a hint of salt air? We need Jed willing to trust us. And I need to get rid of my own demons. I'm just hating the thought of any drowning, whether reasonable thinking or not."

In the living room, I find Lily, looking a bit peaked. I rub her hands between mine, and feel some warmth spreading back in.

"Lily, shall we tell David about the bounty hunters?"

"Do you think he can be trusted?"

"As your doctor and helping with the runaways, already he's taken vows for secrecy. I'll tell him all of it, what actually went on, if you agree?"

"Yes, we should. It would be terribly unfair not knowing of our doings. Will you explain it to him?"

"Of course, first, I must tell of the dream last night. So awful it was, all those people drowning in a storm."

"That is reason enough. I'm getting a little weak now, so I'm back to bed. Go talk to David about these matters."

As she was about to leave she turned and asked, "Helen, lend me an ear. My Jack and I have nothing left to hold us together, I do not want to stay on here."

"No, Lily, you can't mean it. Do you? You actually don't want Jack as your husband?"

"I fear I've lost him to someone else. I just can't stay in this house any longer."

"Lily, in my dream I also saw three horsemen with long overcoats come out of the mist and ride up to your barn."

"Well, that sheds a new light on it all. Let's see what other plans we can conjure up to get out of here. David must figure out some land travel for us."

"Yes, and the sooner the better for all of us. Lily, let me go talk to David. He has to understand what went on here. Please go back to bed."

Belinda was busy gathering her not so welcome new outfits. I offer to help alter them. Even with a change of plans they may still need these new outfits. She packs her two meager garments, along with the new ones. Why not? They are more comfortable.

I hear Jed talking in the hallway. David strides in with him. At David's direction, Jed turns round and round to provide a full view. He beams, and his pride is the same as a Peacock strutting its feathers.

"Well, Jed, so you let David finish his alterations. Good for you. You now have the look of a free citizen. Yes, you are quite believable."

Now that David and I are alone I begin to tell him what happened on the night when those bounty hunters broke in, but got only as far as the shootings before he stopped me.

"No, that's enough—do not say another word. I am here to help, nothing more nor less."

"Thank you, David. I just knew when first seeing how you tended to Lily and the way you treated Jed and Belinda, that you were a man of caliber, a man to be trusted."

"This was never going to be just a hobby, or something to take as a lark. At present, I can combine both my vocation and my mission. Lily is in need of a doctor as well as the two runaways needing help."

"Thank you, I knew you'd understand."

"I also understand your concern about travelling by water. We'll have to make a change in plans. However, our first priority now is to leave Lily's house, until this current situation resolves itself."

Just then, Lily appeared and said, "I heard you both talking and David, you have every reason to back out of this arrangement. It was not fair for you to be brought into this without full knowledge of what had happened here."

"No, Lily, say no more, I will commit to help all I can. First, we must realize that those two men have probably been reported as missing so they will be watching the post roads very closely. If it was known by their friends where they were going that day, then the authorities could very well be coming to this very house. Thus, we shall need a hiding place. We should leave today and go to my home by Fort Phoenix, and there we can make further plans."

Lily said, "Yes, that makes a great deal of sense."

"Ladies, my carriage can hold all of us and it has room for your steamer trunks. Now let's get busy and prepare to leave."

We cannot leave telltale signs behind. I bid David, "Please take a last look around. Suspicious eyes cannot find the slightest hint of a passageway leading to a hidden room. The water buckets, food—anything in the shelves used for their larder—all must be removed. Stowed back in the proper place in the house."

David patted me on the back and said, "I've already double checked. Lily had Jed and Belinda help out, too. Do not worry."

After the dust covering sheets were placed on the furniture, there was one last thing Lily needed to do.

She told me, "I must leave this letter for Jack."

Jack, I am leaving you. I trust your judgment and fairness to distribute our possessions and belongings, knowing what I hold dear, and I, in turn, will grant you whatever you like to have for your own keeping. At this time, I must go away for a long rest to recuperate from the poor health I've been experiencing.

Our neighbor, Mrs. Tellatini and her sons have agreed to tend to the animals until you return. Please give her something, and make it a generous offer, for her trouble.

In my present state of mind and body, I believe a divorce would be exactly the right course for us both. Please see to those proceedings, also. Sometime in the future, if it is meant to be, perhaps we might see each other again, as I must be close to our girls, and where they now lay. But present circumstances now force me to acknowledge a reunion would be most unlikely.
As ever, Lily.

No time to discuss anything more. We're ready to depart, and I take one last look around.

"Lily, look outside. There's a grand sight to behold."

Arm in arm, Belinda and Jed are waiting, all dressed up in their grand outfits. Jed grins like the cat that swallowed the canary. They clutch tight to their bags. They are ready to go and are way ahead of us.

Lily had me lock the last door and we're on our way to David's house.

Chapter Thirteen

Fort Phoenix

"David, have we arrived?"

"Yes, this is it. I border the Acushnet River close to Fort Phoenix. Let me help you and Lily get down from the carriage."

"What a nice home this is. Lily, look at those blue and white Pansies hanging from the porch columns."

"David, why are those birds circling round the roof top, and some are landing on a platform up there.?"

He says, "The Gulls rest on what we call a Widow's Walk."

"Why would a widow go to it—so high on the roof?"

"That is where the wives of sea-going men took to waiting—wanting to spot their husband's ship returning from the sea."

Lily asks David, "May we walk about?"

"Of course. Would you like to join us, Jed, or go in the house?"

Both shake their heads and walk to the porch.

David says, "Go on in. The key is in the flower pot near the door. Take whatever you like in the kitchen. Check the cupboards. They are well stocked." Belinda finds the key.

"Do not worry, you two, make yourself at home. We shall be in soon."

We walk closer to the shore and Lily rests on a bench by a small shed.

David points to a lighthouse and says, "That lighthouse is the guardian. It stands guard for all seafarers."

He continues, "Listen. Hear it? That Fog Horn out there?"

My eyes scan the water as I listen, and wait. At first a slight sound and then followed by a low rumbling sound. No, it's a deeper moan, slowly growing fainter while it echoes and bounces across the waves.

The wind is picking up now, bringing a colder breeze and I feel somewhat chilled. Is there something odd going on? What's in the air? A quick shudder takes over. I wonder, did this same draft hit David and Lily as well? Yet no one complains. It's just a change of weather, I guess.

The sky starts to darken and it becomes quiet. Too quiet.

I say, "David, Lily, listen. Can you hear that sound far off? That's thunder. When we were kids we would pretend it was an angry, growling fairy-tale giant dragging heavy chains along the skies."

Lily nods in agreement.

"David says, "Look at how the water has suddenly become calm with no big waves or white caps, not even a ripple."

"David, is this normal? That big heavy cloud, spreading and combining so fast into one large gray sheet."

"Yes, it's tenting us over, shutting out sunlight, and covering us in a blanket of damp, chilly air."

I'm sporting goose bumps, same as when an omen urges me to take care. The feelings I had since very young, but never wanting to let on . . . figuring others would think me daft.

Then a giant white spike splits the skies followed by thunder bursting down. The ground shakes. A lightning bolt pierces the edge of the New Bedford shoreline. Thunder claps sound far off.

"David? What on earth—why are those Gulls flying in, and circling . . . are they looking for a spot to land? Where did they come from?"

"It's their nature to get home from wherever they are flying, especially if a storm is brewing in the ocean."

"Come, we need to get in the house. Looks like a bad storm or something worse is coming our way."

In the house, he hurries to close windows in the Parlor and Library.

Then, he goes from one window to the next, closing heavy wooden shutters. I go to help, and ask, "Shall we keep one open? We need to peer outside."

"Thank you, we need to finish up fast. I'll leave this one in the front hall open. Can you see the fog? It's getting heavier, as that dank air rolls in."

"Yes, and the sky's much darker. Do you hear wings flapping and that screeching by the seagulls? Should they not take cover? Why all that flying about?"

"Neighbors hereabouts know that when massive flocks of seagulls circle overhead, they better take heed as to what could come next. This is nature's warning. It usually comes ahead of any man-made alarms. Villagers here take heed and never disregard such warnings."

Seagulls squawk louder and louder, and then, fast dip down, to light on David's picket fence.

I yell to David, "Is danger still coming, or getting worse? Is it going to pass on soon?"

A sudden fury of rain pelts down, it hits the roof hard and fast, as winds howl and drum against the shutters. David runs to bar the forgotten front door. A good slam, and the big bolt gets pushed over to drop down, keeping it shut tight.

I ask Lily, "Where are our charges, the two we're supposed to be helping?"

"They are in the sitting room, and both are holding tight to each other."

Jed leans close to Belinda. "Lordy, Lordy, Mistuh David sure's not tellin us 'bout what's happenin."

David hearing this says, "Didn't you ever have one, Jed? You lived near water in your homeland. It's a Gale out over the water. Once on land, it turns into a hurricane That's when flooding and high winds do great damage to anything not bolted down."

I almost could figure as much and Lily must've guessed it by now.

He continues, "This tide is just right to do some serious flooding. We need to fill pails with fresh water and pack up food."

Crash! Bang! Out of nowhere—no hint of what's next as light streams in, crackling, zigzagging—lighting up the whole livid sky. More lightning streaks follow, darting from heavy moving gray clouds. One jolting flash hits an old oak, splitting its trunk in two. Then that fierce wind twists and tears off one half. It slams across the roof of a shed nearby.

Trees bend and threaten to uproot. High winds whip back and forth, then grab up light machinery tossing them about like toy wagons. Rain starts pouring in, filling up window wells. Can't plug them with towels soon enough.

David yells, "Hurry, get on up to the second floor."

Lily yells out, "Jedediah and Belinda? Where are they? Are they all right? Helen, can you find them?"

How can she disregard her own ill health and be able to think of others at a time like this?

"I'll look for them but first we need to get you upstairs."

Just as we start climbing the stairs Lily slumps like a rag doll, more limp than before. Carry her? Try, but my arms cannot bear her load. Hoist her up onto my back—there that does it. I lumber on up to the second floor.

Stop for a bit, and rest at top landing. I can wait to prop Lily up better when David is here. Where is he?

David is talking to the two downstairs.

"For heaven's sake, where are you?"

Jed's voice rings out, "Here we be," as he and Belinda walk out of the parlor.

I yell, "Hurry, Jed, I need help getting Lily to bed. She's on the floor at the top of the landing."

He runs to the top of the stairs and speaks softly to Lily when he reaches her.

"Got real scared, Missus Lily. We hears awful crashing noise, an I been thinkin, mebbe roof come crashin down." He picks her up and carries her.

Her eyes open. "Don't worry, Jed. It will be alright."

Laying his hand on her shoulder and looking into her eyes, he says, "Missus Lily, how y'all doin? Belinda and me . . . well we thank y'all for savin' our lives. We sure be-holdin to y'all. Here, lemme put y'all in y' bed. OK?"

With Belinda helping, Lily is now tucked in good under the covers.

Lily is tired, but smiling, and beckons Jed to come and get closer. She whispers, "God bless you and make sure to take care of Belinda."

Jed and Belinda got settled in fast. First, taking their bedding to the last room at the far end of the upstairs hall. David cautioned them to move away from any windows, as he said, "The wind might break the glass."

David looks to be worrying. He has shown how he takes care of problems, but now his forehead has deep lines that knit together. He bids me to join him at the hall landing, then motions for us to go downstairs.

"I shouldn't be taxing your strength with added burdens, but I need you to assist me when the worst of this passes."

"How can I help?'

"The tide is coming up higher than usual compared to past storms. It's already flooded by the porch, and if it rises further it will come under the front door. One reason I had everyone scoot on up to the second floor was so they would not see this and be more panicked than ever. This house is old. There could be dry rot in beams holding the floor up, not to mention my concern for cracks in the clapboards outside. Down cellar, it's only hard packed slate stones with a dirt floor."

"Are you saying your house is almost falling apart? Do we have to leave?"

"No, no, that's not what I meant. It's just to be prepared. If that rain pelting our rooftop loosens shingles . . . well, we'd have to possibly move out completely. For now, we can only wait. Sleep will help to pass the night faster." Sure thing. Just go to sleep and do not worry. I can do that. Like in a Pig's eye I can!

Everything's buttoned up and secure. David managed to crack open one small window in the front hall but the sheets of rain barred any view to be had. We are in the front hallway with the big drawing table and comfortable chairs. My head is filled with worries. What next, what to do? Too anxious and I can't think of going upstairs as yet to sleep. No, how could I?

"David, what are we to do? Can't we do something? Anything, except just sit here and wait for the water to flood over the floor?"

"For now, that is all we can do. We must keep our composure, at least for the other's sakes. It's rather senseless to muddle over stopping nature from going its course. Time will pass quickly if we get to our beds. Remember, we also have the attic for higher ground."

I take his advice. We quietly go upstairs.

First, we check on Lily. While making her comfortable, we hear Jed's worrying coming to light again. He's not as careful as before. Doesn't keep his voice low enough so just Belinda can be privy to what he says. Hope Lily in her fitful sleep cannot hear.

"Belinda, hear me, we's not goin' no further, no sir, I say, no sir-ee."

"Why, Jed, what y'all talkin 'bout? What we gonna do?"

"Mebbe it been our Lord callin? Sendin light an alla noise. He wants us t' steal away. We can be doin it near here, in New Bedford."

"Why you talkin so foolish?"

"Remember ole Massa's head boy? He say afore we runs off, about mens workin cross de river in New Bedford. Mens like me, workin on fishin boats an getting' coins for work."

"Jed, don't you go scarin me. You seen alla horses and wagons onna bridge. De drivers be carryin white folks. Darkies, we gets scooped up an we be right back onna plantation."

"We stay free, long's we keep hid and mind our manners."

"How's it gon' happen? What's a cullud man gon' do, how y'all gon' t' get work, if keepin hid? You gon' wear a blanket over your fool head?"

"Don't say no. You're my own Lindy Bell, you knows we gon' fit in. An bounty hunters ain't gon' pick us out. Lotsa culluds livin inna big ole whalin port."

"Maybe, Jed, but I can't know. I can't think on it, leave me be."

"You gotta know, Lindy Bell. It can work. Maybe I hire out to sea. Sailors, whalin men, some light and some dark skins too. Makes no never mind to bosses. We all gets paid, long's we work hard onna boats. Best of all, no chains. We gon' be free!"

"But after you goes away on boat an comes back? I knows you, Jedediah, you don't keeps yo' big head duckin down. Your grin an white teeth shows you off an you gets catched up for sure."

"Doncha be frettin."

"Ya, you goes on boat an I stay. An what's it I be doin?"

"Maybe rich ladies want sewin an washin done. You say, Missus, I'se a freed slave, my man he done gon' fishin out t' sea, an' I needs work. I be doin alla cleanin so's y'all be so happy. I can be fixin real good, some Tea Times too. I can do y'alls washin an' scrubbin steps onna porch."

"White folk won't believe me. I sure t' be laffin afore I sound like a fool cullud slave. Y' knows I talk better'n alla culluds usin dummy plantation talk."

"Well, you gotta smile at white ladies. If her ole man poppin eyes at you, doncha be actin up. You gotta look away, act like a uppity freed woman, an, you gon' be fine."

"You say we can be actin free, an not hidin, an sneakin round no more? An not talkin so funny, makin white folk think we's so stupid?"

"It's what we gonna do, Lindy Bell. Maybe we get us some land? A farm, and raise some young 'uns, all our own."

"I'll think on it. You say chillen, our own? An we gets em freed, too?"

"Right, we do it for them. Uh, how 'bout we git started now?"

" Jed, no, oh you . . . no, don't tickle me."

David grabs my hand, shakes his head and whispers, "Come, time to move on but we'll need to have a talk later with those two about the dangers in their plan. You notice how they can use good English when no white folk are listening? They are skilled at acting."

"Yes, I heard, but we can't let on we heard, though we do need to talk to both of them."

Suddenly it is very quiet outside. I go to rise up but he stops me, "Not now, later when the storm clears. Nothing more can be done until it all calms down. High tidal waters will gradually recede, but it's only half way done. Now is the lull, or eye of the storm . . . the middle of it when everything is so quiet. Still got the worse part, or back side, the tail end, to snap right along. We should all try to get some rest meanwhile."

I would love to, but wish my heart would slow down. Thank Heavens, Lily fell off to slumber, a deeper sleep now, with her breaths coming out more even.

* * *

It's morning time and I'm still abed. Not much rest did I get but I'm covered under this big quilt and laying on this very plump and soft feather bed. All is still, so quiet, wondering . . . has the storm ended? The rain's not making a racket on the roof.

Then, loud voices startle me. I can see out the window, rowers out there in boats. They're shouting back and forth.

I head to the back door, downstairs. David already has it wide open to show clear across the river and out to the Bay. The storm has gone.

He says, "High tide's slowly ebbing away leaving only a faint lapping of waves."

I ask, "Is it over, I hope?"

"Yes, but I need to head out to check for damage. Do you want to join me?".

I grab my cloak and bonnet. No time to waste. Need to return before Lily wakens. Belinda is already into morning chores. Says she will keep an eye out for Lily until we get back.

High tide has surely gone down, and I mutter, 'good riddance'.

David points out, "See, in the tide's wake, nothing but litter—floating pieces of houses, and livestock . . . unlucky ones—should've been kept out of harm's way."

Then he covers my face with his scarf. I can barely see.

"Why?" I ask. Then, *ugh*—such a putrid smell. Dead fish? What else?

"Keep the scarf over your mouth and nose. This smell is too heavy, and blots out the usual salt laden beach odors." I do as I'm told.

"So sorry, Helen, but these are sights not fit for your eyes. Just keep walking along side of me for a while. Some poor sheep of my neighbor's got caught in high tide. The raging waters drew them on down, only to surface and get caught up in jagged rocks. They are in their last resting place now and nature, and the tides will soon take over."

I grab his arm tighter. I do not want to look, anywhere, or smell anything worse.

"Helen, let's walk down to the Wilson's cottage. Must let them know where their flock can be found. I can look to their other animals while there."

We picked up our pace, while holding my breath till the stench had cleared.

David pointed out Mrs. Wilson, and we hurried to her. She was standing in front of their barn. Her eyes were all red and her wadded up handkerchief was scrunched up in her fist. Poor thing, she was bent over, consoling a young boy on the ground. He was sprawled out, pounding his fists into the muddied ground.

David asked, "What's wrong with Henry?"

The son sits up, lets out a gasp, and says, "Me and my dog Laddie, we were trying to round up the sheep and baby calves. They ran off, all over. Laddie tried rounding them. He ran ahead but the wind blew too hard. I called and called after him but Laddie never came back."

David stood Henry up and put his arm around the lad's shoulders.

"Now Henry, take your time. Laddie did his best and in due time when the waters go down, per chance we'll find him on high ground."

"Mrs. Wilson, get Henry taken care of. A good hot cider drink will help. He can busy himself and stop this ruminating."

He takes Mrs. Wilson aside and says, "Phyllis, we saw some dead sheep earlier that could have belonged to you. Time for your family to wait and have faith that it all will turn out alright in the end. I'll check on your other animals."

"Your animals, that had not been out to pasture, were all penned in. They are all doing well. All are hale and hearty."

Mr. Wilson arrived, thanked David, and told the boy, "I looked all over for Laddie, but I need to feed the animals. Don't fret, I promise to look again."

They settled Henry down, and we helped to tidy up their home. We left and hurried down the pathway.

David said, "Nothing more to be done, not here, not today."

I ask, "What is that—it's left high and dry on the beach?"

"Yes. It's a large fishing boat—first drug down to the deep. Then huge waves and the rising tide spit it back on shore. That wharf could not keep all the empty craft anchored in. Many were claimed by the pounding waves."

"Are those fishermen out to the docks again? Why so soon?"

"They're loading the few boats that survived. They are weary and not as boisterous as usual. But that's their living. They must continue preparations, and work to go out to sea again."

"David, look to where I'm pointing. Floating suitcases, steamer trunks, and clothing. Hope there's nothing more. What, does that mean? Oh, no. Could it be?"

He hugs me close. I almost draw away, thinking. Oh, oh . . . what is this? I get that suspicion out of my head. His actions are natural, and only as a doctor with healing, comforting ways.

"Yes, Helen, I see. It's not for me to fathom the sense of it all. What's done is done, and cannot help any poor souls who didn't last out the storm. What's come back, that's all that's left."

"You and the others living here, you take it all so lightly? Can't anything be done to stop such tragedies?"

"Nature can't be made to go away. We are used to seeing floating debris like this. It's called flotsam and jetsam. Flotsam is debris from a shipwreck or accident. Jetsam is debris deliberately thrown overboard by a crew of a ship in distress, most often to lighten the ship's load."

"Why live so close to the water?"

"I guess we just love the sea. The good, as well as the bad it brings--it's all part of the bargain." I want to get home. I've had enough . . . oh, I wish he'd walk faster. No, not this fast. Where's he going?

He yells, "Stay put.! More might float in later—coming from boats."

I cannot wait. I must see what he is doing.

He says, "I need to pull this body up to higher ground."

"I can rightly tell that big storm had easy pickings but forgive me if I refuse to understand the workings of nature."

Then a loud barking noise carries over the waters to where we stand. Turning, I can see a dog splashing out there. It draws near to shore. We wait, we watch . . . until seeing . . . could it be?

David smiles. "It's Henry's dog."

It shakes off seaweed and foam, then trots off towards the Wilson's. We hurry on.

"Go in the house, Helen. I need to notify the authorities about that body. When I get back, we'll need to speak with Jed and Belinda about their plan to go to New Bedford." I clean the sand from my boots and go in.

David returns, "They've been notified. I had to fill out some paperwork, but they've already sent out a team to recover that pour soul's body."

"Let me get you some tea, I've asked Jed and Belinda to wait for us in the Parlor.'

"Jed had asked if we would drop them off in New Bedford. I said they would need people to offer housing, and a means to live."

"So, you did warn them?"

"Yes, but it's not that simple."

"Come on then, let's get this over with."

They sit on the sofa, waiting.

David begins, "You two will need to have a good community, well insulated from the other neighborhoods. It must be free of busy bodies and any willing to turn you in for extra money." Jed looks all around, everywhere but at David.

"Jed, how can you expect to mingle out in the open? The Cape Verdeans are of lighter skin—their ancestry is both African and Portuguese. In comparison, you will stand out more."

"Aw, Mistuh David, cain't y'all be knowin how tis . . . we jess—."

"Of course, I do not know how you intend to live in this world. So, hear me out. You two are too much of a contrast to the ones sporting much lighter skins. How do you hide when among them? Perhaps going out to sea might help. No one cares what color hands casts the net or harpoons the whale. But, on land you'd be under constant danger from bounty hunters."

Jed looks at me. I shake my head and say, "Sorry, Jed, running off to New Bedford is too dangerous."

Belinda moves nearer to him, throws her arm round his neck. Her face hides against his chest. She sobs quietly.

I say "Think on this, if you will. If anyone hears you talking like that deep plantation talk, folks will say 'They're not one of us.'"

Jed is starting to look uncomfortable.

"Mister Hatcher knows, as he lives here. You can cover over the branding on your arms, but that will draw questions, especially in the heat of summer. Jed, you cannot hide your arm and hands when working, can you? How will you explain that scar on your face? Also, the sound of your voice with that heavy plantation talk will give you away. No. We need to get you moving north with the help of escorts."

Jed responds, "How we gon' know escorts be our friends?"

"On the way to Vermont and on to Canada, many escorts are freed blacks, as well as Quakers, like my husband Joshua. He helped slaves run to freedom." Jed says nothing and will not look at me.

"Heaven forbid if anyone sees branding marks, the ones your dreadful Master burned on your arms. You'd both be herded right back to him by the law, or most likely a bounty hunter wanting his pay."

I ask, "Do you realize that those two men who broke into Lily's house, were bounty hunters? They lived in New Bedford."

Jed grabs Belinda's hand, and they head to the kitchen. At the doorway, Belinda turns.

She says, "Now, we gon' finish cleanin up." We cannot hear them talking.

Then, Jed sticks his head out of the kitchen doorway.

He says, "Yessum, Missus Helen, an Mistuh David. Belinda an me, we's not gon' be runnin away. We's sure gon' stay an we gon' plant our feet ahind Missus Helen an follow her trail." They scoot off to finish kitchen chores.

I lower my voice, "They can rest easy, and must remember they are no longer slaves—not up here in the north."

"That settles that, and now Helen, I must consider Lily's well-being. As a doctor, her care requires treatment and prolonged rest in a hospital. Unfortunately, that's not an option, now."

"I agree, but what shall we do? We not only have Lily to look after, but we have Jed and Belinda to keep hidden."

"Do you know a quiet place where all could stay. Where Lily could have some peace, until it's safe to be on the move again?"

"Lily told me last evening of a place called Ginny-town. It's in a remote area, away from the locals." [15]

"Is it far from here?"

"No, it's up river in the north end of Fairhaven. It's not a separate town. It's just a place where Gypsies camp during spring and summer."

"I've never heard of the place."

"Not too many people know about it, according to Lily. She said it's partly sandy with tall grass and some rock cliffs all round. Not good for farming so local folk usually pose no objection when Gypsies stay there."

"That sounds to be ideal. How did she find it, this place called Gypsy Town?"

"No, it's Ginny-town. Lily's husband Jack told Lily about these camp grounds. In his work as a lawyer, he helped the leader, Salavino.'

"Salavino was accused of stealing a horse off a neighbor, but Jack, who is a lawyer, saved Sal from going to jail. The neighbor told police that they both had an agreement—his horse for Sal's baskets and fish, but he claimed that he never got the barrel of fish nor the baskets. Turns out, they found in his barn a dozen baskets, along with a wooden barrel filled with smoked fish. That was everything Sal had traded for that same horse. So the Judge threw the case out of court."

"Helen, do you think this Sal, as head of the Gypsies, might return a favor to Jack's wife? Lily could get plenty of rest, and get on her feet again. Let's hope he's also willing to hide you, along with Jed and Belinda?"

"Lily said the Gypsies can be friendly, as Jack found out. Yet, they're very clannish, sticking to their own kin and campmates. She went with Jack, one time, on a visit and said it would be an ideal place. No neighbors or others sticking their noses in. Their campground would be well hidden from the Police."

"That sounds good for all of you and I am for it. We'll head on out to Ginny-town tomorrow. Tell the others, won't you? Now, can you help me clear the mess from the outside? The front and back yards took a big hit from the winds. We've got work to do. I'll ask Jed to give us a hand."

"I'd like Belinda to stay put in the house, in case Lily needs anything."

"Good idea. I have to nail back all those shutter hinges that broke loose. Would you also ask Jed to check the cellar for any water damage?"

It didn't take any time at all before Jed got back. He only could see from the steps halfway down as the cellar was still flooded.

"Missus Helen, cannin jars, some done broke. But up on shelf, all gon' be OK. Trunks still floatin, an hafta wait till water gone by."

By the end of the day, we all were all so tuckered out, we went off to bed early. David shut down the house; he was pinching candle wicks and latching shutters. I slipped in a "Good night,' as I headed upstairs. Lily was tended by Belinda today and is fast asleep, for a welcome change.

* * *

It's first light. So quiet, but must get up. I smell bacon sizzling in the fry pan. Belinda must be fixing breakfast. Lily's not up yet. She can rest till we're set to go to Ginny-town. Jed's now up and sits at the table. Belinda fills his plate with some fried potatoes and eggs.

"Good morning, Jed." He nods, finishes chewing, then says, "Hi."

David comes in, and says, "I've been out feeding the horses and hitching them to the carriage. They're a good team and raring to go."

"Are you ready for breakfast, David? Belinda has been cooking breakfast for us. She seems to enjoy it."

"Yes, I'm quite hungry, but I need to find something first."

He walks to his desk and picks up a large sheet of paper.

"What is that you have in your hand?"

"It's an 1853 map of the Acushnet River, Fairhaven, and New Bedford."

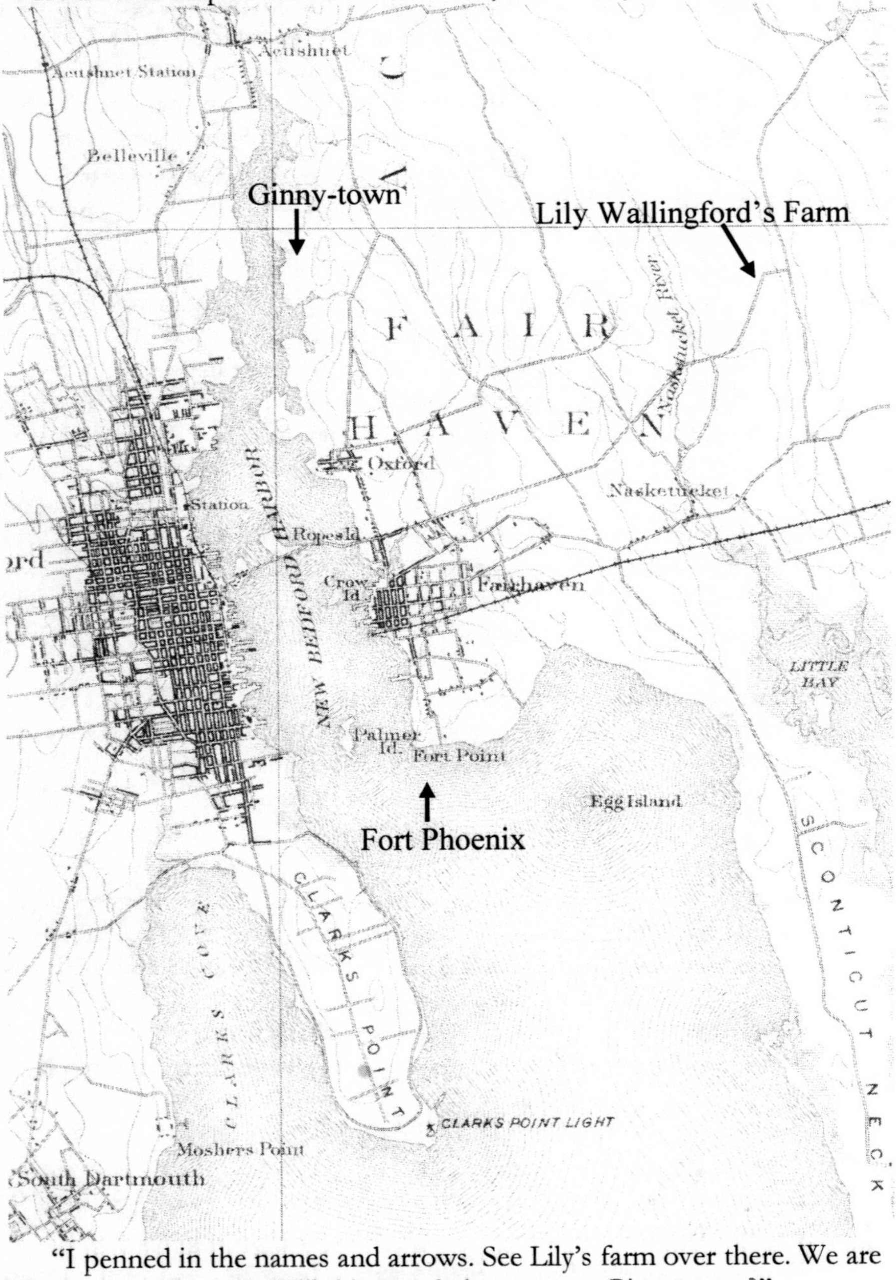

"I penned in the names and arrows. See Lily's farm over there. We are here by Fort Phoenix. Will this map help get us to Ginny-town?"

"Of course, along with Lily's directions once we get there."

Belinda dishes out more fried potatoes and eggs. Then two crispy pieces of bacon go on top. I shake my head. My stomach turns over.

"Belinda, no, I don't want my share—put it on the other plates. Some of these rolls will do me fine."

Belinda offers raspberry jam to spread. No, oh goodness, no. It's so red. I breathe in and out. Take one good, deep breath. Must now hold my hand over my mouth. That awful night, the smell . . . when that bloody mess—. Hurry to the pump. Splash cold water on my face. Belinda keeps her head down, keeps on with her cooking. But holds a towel up for me to take.

"Excuse me, David. I need to sit down for a spell."

"Are you ill?"

"My stomach's a bit queasy—that frying . . . it set off thinking of Lily's the other night. But, this cuppa tea is enough with some rolls. I'll go sit in the Parlor."

"OK, I'll see how you're doing after I check the horses one more time."

Ah, yes, this hot tea did me good, along with this peaceful room.

I see an embroidered piece up over the fireplace. Says something about fishermen.

The quiet is broken by footsteps in the hall. David's back from checking the horses. He hangs his hat and cloak on the coat rack, then straightens his tie in the mirror. He wipes his spectacles with his handkerchief.

He's a bit old but still a fairly handsome man. Not fair like my Joshua, nor as big and striking. Although, he's nice as can be and surely, he'd make the proper woman a fine catch. Wonder why he never got led to the altar?

He says, "You look to be feeling better, that's good. I see you've noticed my mother's handiwork. She finished it just before she died."

"Oh, I didn't realize and I'm so sorry to hear of her passing. Would you like to tell me about her?"

"Well she went suddenly with no warning. She was sitting in her chair right here when I found her in the morning. It was a peaceful passing, though quite a shock to me."

"I imagine it would be. Now this framed embroidery. Is it about fishing? Did she stitch all of it?"

"Yes. It reflects her idea of living by the water with the smell of salt air; seeing seagulls gliding in the breeze; and the fishing boats going out to sea. They both loved this house. He had it built, with the Widow's Walk added later."

I nodded.

"She was always hoping that special man, my father, would return. He never returned. He was lost at sea."

"Oh! I'm sorry, David." I cannot add anything to that and will not try.

"That's OK, I thank you for asking. I rarely speak of them, since most days my practice and patients keep me busy, so I'm glad of the chance to reminisce."

"What of your brothers or sisters? Are they living nearby?"

"No, my parents were never fortunate to have more children. And so, they gave me many indulgences, in fact, too many. My father retired from the Navy. Then, he had his own fishing boat, when he could have taken it easy. Yet, he worked to pay for my medical education.'

"Now let's see about that embroidery, let me read it for you."

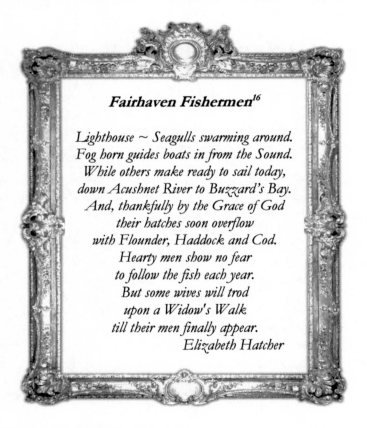

Fairhaven Fishermen[16]

Lighthouse ~ Seagulls swarming around.
Fog horn guides boats in from the Sound.
While others make ready to sail today,
down Acushnet River to Buzzard's Bay.
And, thankfully by the Grace of God
their hatches soon overflow
with Flounder, Haddock and Cod.
Hearty men show no fear
to follow the fish each year.
But some wives will trod
upon a Widow's Walk
till their men finally appear.
Elizabeth Hatcher

"Your mother was quite talented."

"You see; my father was Captain Jeremiah Hatcher. There is a longer tale to be told but it was kept in her trunk."

"Could I see it, if it's not too much—?"

"It's not a problem. I'll go fetch it from the attic."

"Pardon me David but I must see what Jed and Belinda are doing. Perhaps they could come and listen?"

"By all means, invite them in. Oh, and would you all have a cuppa tea and fix one for me."

"Sorry to keep you waiting so long. I had to dig deep past the old scrap books and albums. But first let me show you this photograph. It's the lighthouse she was going to use as part of the embroidery on the wall."

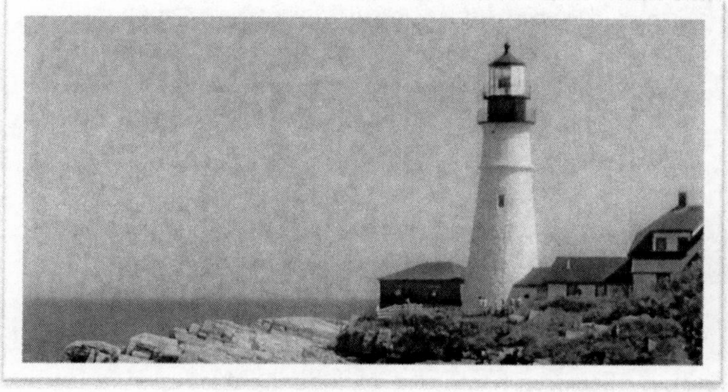

"That's nice. Would she have also included seagulls, circling around?"

"Yes, I believe that was her intent. Now let me show you my father's last log book from his boat. It's yellowed and the parchment is so delicate and near to brittle, so thin the pages are . . . perhaps I should read it?"

"Yes, would you?"

Captain's Log [16]

July 2nd, 1823

The men unload their catch by the light of the moon,
since the weary sun lay down beyond the sea.
Ah, I think, what a boon—as that empty hatch
deserves reward, bar none. So, I shout, "A job well done!
And ye shall see, ye'll get your share in the bounty."

July 3rd, 1823

"Aye, aye sir. The boat's almost all clean.
Yet, with the rising sun, other boats did relay,
'more fish were seen just past the Bay,'
but they'll soon be gone, since needing to spawn."
"Now, Mate, another time will do,
because we must bide by oncoming weather, too."
But, all in tandem, the men ask to 'cast off again.'
And so, I see my ever-hearty crew can easily skim through
cat's-paws of rippling waves—nudged by a southern breeze—

to promise much calmer seas.
And, it's down the Acushnet we go, to the start of Buzzards Bay.

July 4th, 1823
Once in the ocean, strong winds do push us on.
And, again our nets overflow.
"Now, Mate, tis best to batten the hatches,
we've got our fill, and need no more
swabbing tonight—as we've now come upon
this old whaler's delight."
"Aye, aye, Sir, and men, ye heard him.
Go and stow away every last bucket.
Here's the Isle of Nantucket, where rocks abound—
with danger so deep, we must go around."
"Sir, look heaven ward, 'tis such a foreboding sky!"
"Aye, my Mate, it's way on high—where heavy clouds, far worst,
rumble on, and seek to burst!
While lightning does surround that big one, and it splits,
letting rain crash on down."
I allow that Gale's fury is yet to come.
My Mate does ask, "Is it time to
break out the rum—to keep the men on the go?"
I nod, and yell, "Aye, aye!"
Then, give order to "heave ho.' yet, tasting
heavy salt in the air, while our boat goes nowhere."
"Ah, Mate, do ye recall how one poor boat sank?
'T was oft the Starboard bow—over there in Georges Bank."

July 5th, 1823
"Captain, now see what's happening.
That northern wind whips the sails again—
and the churning sea? Bashing the side
and rising higher than before.
Oh no! Here's one—we cannot ride!
We cannot take much more."
Ahoy,' I call out, 'Grab hold!" Yet, now the boat lists~
"Ah, Mate, it's a gonna. It can't do naught but heel-to!"
I yell, "Look at me, lads, can ye see?
Go grab the Dory and secure the oars, any way to make do!
We've naught to do, but weather it till it's passed."
The Bosun says, "Cap'n, one's got loose,

it's floating, now gone, pulled from the stern.
With only one—can we secure a safe return?"
Crack!
"Hear that, Bosun? The mast it's tilting, and won't last."
Answer me, where are you? My Mate, where do ye be?
Ah, no . . . ye did not—and where's my men?
Gone? All lost to the sea? But, who's calling again?"
"Cook? Try to crawl. If ye stand, ye can fall.
Come close, here I be. C' mon man, hurry!
That's it, hang to—almost got you!"
"Here, hold tight—this chest, aye, grab the rope handles."
"Watch that boom, and our deck, it's awash with the sea!"

Cook cries out: "Now I see. Oh, my Cap'n,
why'd ye go and give it to me?
But, I thank ye kindly. Reach out, please, your hand— no,
'tis not your fate. Lord, don't let it be too late?
But, my Cap'n, he shoves me.
'Don't, oh Lord,' I say. Can't you save—."
Yet, that horrendous wave, it took him away.

"Helen, see here, the last few entries must've been placed by the Cook. It's penned by a different hand. At any rate, that tale ends."

"How sad. Tell me, whatever happened, did anyone get saved . . . anyone at all?" It appears he does not want to answer my question.

"See how my mother, her name was Elizabeth by the way . . . how she matted and framed some of the pictures, the boats and light houses."

"Forgive me, Helen, my spectacles need cleaning."

Jed speaks up. "Mister David, your father, he the Captain? What did he . . . uh, where is he . . .?"

David says, "Wait, Jedediah, you'll learn in time. I must take a moment to compose myself. These lenses—so dirty, misting over for some reason. Something's in my eye? *Cough.*'

"I shall continue now. Well, more than a few fortnights passed when, as I mentioned, a package appeared at our door. T'was from the cook and he told how it all came to pass. Allow me to read it."

Madam: I was the cook, and here is our Log. Might I unfold the history of what I know? The Captain grabbed hold of my shirt as I slid down, over the deck, when a big wave tried to carry me off. He made me grab the rope handles of his sea chest. He must have somehow managed to drag it out of his cabin.

Then he let go my hand, and pushed me but I tried to reach for him. Yet a big wave took him away. And, while floating with the Captain's sea chest, I found the other Dory to crawl into, though it was without oars.

I knew not how much time had passed, until later, as I drifted in the Dory to some land, which lay not far away. The Captain's Log was in the chest, enclosed in an oilskin wrapping. So it let no water in. When back on land, I took the liberty to finish penning this tale.

The Captain was prone to put his entries in verse. I tried to follow the same, but must admit, I am not a poet, not by a long shot. This Log had your address listed, and so—I now submit it to you.

Respectfully
Jacque LeBeau
Cook, The Phoenix Maiden

I ask David, "Did she ever hear from the cook again?"

"No, she did not."

"David, what a fine tribute that was.'

"That walk on the roof top, called the Widow's walk, did you ever try to fix it? When we arrived, it looked like it was falling down."

"She did not want it reminding her of that horrid time. The walk was never set foot on again. It was left to rot in the salt air and the mist driven winds. She also kept the ship's log locked away since it told her what she already knew and needed no painful reminders."

"Hmm, I wonder . . . did she not think you might like to read it someday?"

"No, just the opposite; she wanted my future to be rid of sad memories. But, I cherished reading his log. Those were the last bit of any personal papers I had left of my father."

Enough questions for the poor man, we must let him alone. He needs some privacy. He heads for the stairs. I'll check on him later when Lily needs attention.

Chapter Fourteen

Manjiro and Cinque

What's that I hear? Where are they? Belinda? Jed? Must be pumping water. Jed's got the pump spilling out water, while Belinda hums a tune. Good, Jed is smiling, a real smile, finally. Perhaps they have their minds off that terrible night at Lily's for a bit, but I find it hard to stop picturing it. Those drunken fools breaking in and what they almost did, if not for Lily.

If only we can get away from this town—cross my fingers and just hope no one finds their bodies, such hateful ones. I must remember, the mothers of those two young men. They must be heartbroken. I read where Demon rum and other spirits can turn good men into monsters. It can, in the bat of an eye, leave ruin in its wake. Those poor mothers who did no wrong, they will be the ones to suffer now.

Lily's calling. Must get upstairs.

"Helen, come here." she says in a faint whisper. "I need some water." I pour water for her and freshen up her bed linens, plump up her pillow and wipe her face with a cool cloth. She falls back to sleep.

I go to the drawing room to sit and ponder. Where do we go from here?

David tells me that he's put the horses back in the barn.

"Why? I ask.

"Neighbors told me there are still too many trees blocking the roads. Not good for traveling this early in the morning."

I agree. "Probably best to wait. Lily needs all the rest she can get."

I ask David, "How did your mother manage to live in this fine house, just on her own wages?"

"She swore that I would never go to sea, wanting me to just concentrate on my studies. She did all she could with the savings my father left her. Along with her volunteer work, she mustered good wages as part time teacher and seamstress. With all of it, she managed to get me through Medical school.'

"That's enough of my own tales, would you like to hear more of the history of Fairhaven and the Whaling business?"

"Yes, go on. I love hearing about this town."

"We have time, while waiting for the roads to clear and seeing that Lily's still resting. Let me see, where shall I begin . . ."

Reading from some old papers he starts.

"Many do not realize this but in the year 1838, just thirteen years ago, Fairhaven was ranked as the second largest whaling port in America. Twenty-four vessels sailed from town during the course of that year.' [18]

"David, that's amazing."

"However, Fairhaven and New Bedford have had more than their fair share of tragedies—mainly from losing men at sea. There have also been some brave heroic rescues.'

"Please go on."

"One, in particular, took place about ten years ago, when Bill Whitfield, Captain of a Whaling ship, rescued five shipwrecked Japanese fishermen from an Island off the coast of Japan. One of them, a young lad of only 14 years, by the name of Manjiro or John Mung as he came to be called, was brought back to Fairhaven by Captain Whitfield.' [19]

"Helen, you being from Vermont might not have heard the name of this young lad but I'm sure Lily's husband Jack had seen John about town from time to time.'

"I don't know, but I'll ask Lily when she joins us."

"According to recent newspaper accounts . . . here, I've found some.' [18]

"In 1841 Mung, a peasant boy from a fishing village, and four companions were shipwrecked by a winter storm off the southern coast of Japan. The fishermen drifted until they landed on an uninhabited volcanic island in the Pacific Ocean.' [20]

"After many months of near starvation, they were rescued by Captain Whitfield of the whaling schooner *John Howland.* As noted in the ships log on Sunday, June 27th;

> *...The isle in sight. At 1 PM sent in 2 boats to see if there was any turtle, found five poor distressed people on the isle, took them off, could not understand anything from them more than that they were hungry...'*

"Because Japan feared colonialism and Christianity, they often put to death Japanese who had contact with foreigners, the Captain dropped off Mung's companions at Honolulu in the Sandwich Islands. However, the Captain was impressed with the intelligence and resourcefulness of the young John Mung and convinced him to go back to Fairhaven with him." [21]

"David, you say he was only 14 years old. Can his age be right? He would be so young."

"Indeed, he was. However, the *John Howland* remained at sea until 1843, harpooning Sperm whales and converting their blubber to oil. It was not unusual for whaling ships to remain at sea for two, three, or even four years until they had their complement of whale oil stored in wooden barrels. So, John was 16 by the time the *John Howland* made it back to port.'

"In Fairhaven, Mung first attended a one room, stone school house on Bread and Cheese Lane at Poverty Point."

"David, why was it called Poverty Point? Did poor people live there?"

"Its real name was Oxford Village and it was once the business and shipbuilding center for many years. At least 15 great ships were built in the yards at the Point and whalers set out directly from Oxford. However, when the New Bedford - Fairhaven bridge was built in 1790, transport to the open sea was cut off plunging the area into economic collapse. That's how it got its name Poverty Point.' [22]

"Please go on. What happened to this Japanese lad?"

"John later attended a smaller school on Sconticut Neck where the captain built a new home for his new bride.' [21]

"One day the Whitfield's and John Mung were attending church. After the service, a spokesman for the Elders said that they were all pleased by seeing the young boy attending services. But he suggested that in the future it might be well to have the Japanese boy take a place in the section set aside for Negroes.' [21]

That's terrible. What did Captain Whitfield do?"

"He was a man of sterling character who was held in high esteem within the community. So, he promptly made financial arrangements to acquire a new family pew at another church in town.' [21]

This troubled me, "David, why wouldn't the Captain have left that Church long before, if they were keeping Negroes segregated."

"You raise a good point. Remember, as Garrison, the Abolitionist, pointed out in his newspaper, many people and even Churches in the North had mixed feelings about slavery and did not want to 'rock the boat', so to speak."

"Why didn't he leave earlier?"

"He may not have approved of what his Church was doing and this incident could have been the 'straw that broke the camel's back.'"

"Good for him. Please continue."

"John became a normal lad, like any other in Fairhaven. At one time he had a liking for a certain classmate and gave her a May Basket with a note attached.'

'T is in the chilly night
a basket you've got hung.
Get up, strike a light
And see me run
But no take chase me.' [21]

"That was when he was younger. Here's a photograph of him when he was much older."

Lily must be awake. I hear her slowly coming downstairs.

"Good morning, Lily. Did you get any sleep last night? David's been telling me about John Mung. Did you ever meet him?"

"I did manage to doze off a few times. As to John Mung, well no, I did not. However, Jack knew of him before we married. He'd seen him once or twice, said he seemed like a nice young man."

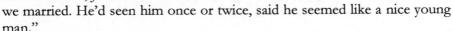

"Was there anything else that Jack might have remembered?"

"Yes, he said that John attended the Bartlett School of Mathematics and Navigation on Spring Street here in Fairhaven. This was before Jack went on to Law School. John was known to be a quick learner. That is all I remember. Oh wait, yes, there was a story told by some friends in town."

"Tell us but rest a bit first, then take your time."

"I feel better, Helen, truly I do. Do not fret. Let me begin.'

"Seems that John was visited by some young ladies, while at his 'adopted' Aunt Millie's house. One of them, Mary Ann, had an embroidered Rooster on cardboard with her and had propped it up on the mantel shelf.'

"Late in the evening, after talking and joking together, Aunt Millie told John to be off to bed as she wanted him to rise early in the morning. As John left the room he pointed to the rooster and indicated he would rise when Mary Ann's rooster crows.[21] They all had a good laugh."

I piped up, "My goodness, Lily, do you recall any more?"

"That's all I remember.'

"David, I've been listening to you from upstairs. You have a wealth of knowledge about Fairhaven and the whaling industry. I'm enjoying it. Please continue."

"I'd be glad to. John left Fairhaven in 1847 to head back to sea on a whaling ship called *The Franklin.* We learned later that Mung became a full-fledged whaleman, as well as a professional barrel maker, which would have stood him in good stead aboard any ship. Barrels had to be taken apart to save space and then re-built at sea, as needed, to be filled with whale oil.'

"Some recent newspaper accounts say he was off to California to prospect for gold but we don't know where he is today. I've heard folks say that his real name was Manjiro Nakahama. He's also known to have been the first Japanese to ever set foot on American soil."

"David, you have such a keen mind to recollect those sea stories. Times were indeed terrible for those sailors back then. Yet, what about hardships suffered by slaves while at sea?"

"From all accounts we know of, the slaves were not in the same 'boat' so to speak. None knew where they'd end up, or if they even stood a chance to make it to land, being chained in irons by ungodly, evil men.'

"Now that you mention it, there was a very interesting account of one of those slave ships. It happened about 12 years ago. Let me see if I can find those newspaper accounts."

"Ah! Yes, here they are. It was not far from here. This newspaper states that a vessel was discovered at anchor on the high seas, by the United States ship, *The Washington.* It was a half mile off of Long Island, New York. Some of the Negroes were on shore at the time but they were brought back on board the slave ship *L'Amistad.*"

"Are you telling me that these Negroes had their own ship?"

"No. Let me continue. The vessel, with a total of forty-nine Negroes and other persons on board, was brought into port in Connecticut. They were completely bewildered and none spoke English or any language that could, at least, be understood' [23]

"That must have been quite confusing."

"Here's what I found out about where they came from and what subsequently became of them. I've saved many of the newspaper and magazine accounts of their story:"[19]

"A slave ship, the *Tecora,* was built in the 1800s. It was large, fast and maneuverable so it could avoid British patrols. English laws had been passed outlawing transport of slaves across the Atlantic." [24]

"So, that's the story that plantation owners would rather not tell about?"

"Money was the driving force to cloud their conscience. They preferred to think of the slaves as merely cargo being transported for profit." David stops his reciting and turns around to see Jed and Belinda in the doorway.

"Can we come in?"

"David says, "Of course, come sit down."

He smiles, rattles his paper and says, "Ahem, I shall continue if my audience is ready?'

"In 1839 a group of Africans were kidnapped from Mendiland and got transported to Lomboko, the African slave port. A Portuguese slave trader purchased about 500 of the Africans and forced them to board the *Tecora.* It headed to Havana, Cuba."

"How could they survive such a trip?"

"Many did not survive due to illness, starvation, or severe lashings. That whip could rip open a back and cause too much loss of blood."

"How terrible."

"If any slaves showed signs of a disease, for example like small pox, they were thrown overboard, alive." Belinda jumps up, and shouts out!

"I'se glad we's not gon' on no mo' boats."

I say, "Do not worry, we will travel by land from now on. Please continue, David."

"First, tell us this, Belinda, were you brought over on a slave ship?"

"No sir, I'se plantation born. Jed come on big slave ship. But we come t' New Bedford on smelly ole cotton boat."

Jed asks, "Mistuh David, why slaves needa land in dark? How can a man see? He be shuff'lin 'long in chains?"

"Because importing new slaves into Spanish-controlled Cuba was illegal. So the slave traders smuggled them ashore at night in small boats. They landed in a small inlet a few miles from Havana. Once on land, the slaves were placed in a barracoon."

"David, a barracoon? Never heard that word before."

"It was a series of barracks or huts, well-guarded of course. It was where slaves were temporarily housed and fed. It was simply a 'slave pen where they were kept, until picked up for further shipment.'"

Jed says, "I 'member place lak barracoon in Mendiland."

"How awful! Rounded up and penned in like cattle."

"That's true, but in Cuba, under Spanish law, the Africans were technically free. However, they got classified as native Cuban-born slaves. That way they could be separated and sold." I must say something, I can't be still about the whole of it.

"How conniving, how evil to think of . . . how could they do that to human beings? I'm sorry for interrupting. Tell me, what happened to them?"

"Two Spanish plantation owners, bought 53 of the surviving Africans. There were 49 men, a boy and three girls. Ruiz and Montes packed their cargo and slaves on board the schooner *La Amistad* and set sail for their plantation at Port Principe, Cuba."

"Here it's reported in the New York Morning Herald that on the fifth day out, the Negroes rose on the captain and crew and got possession of the vessel. They killed the captain and his mulatto cook. The cabin boy was saved. Two white sailors escaped in the schooner's boat. The lives of Jose Ruiz and Pedro Montez, the owners of the slaves, were also saved. But in the scuffle and fight, Montez got two or three severe cuts."

"No. How could they do that? I mean, chained and with no weapons?"

"Somehow the slaves got loose from their shackles. The blacks then told Montez to steer for the coast of Africa. He contrived, however, to sail north and run the vessel on to this coast. That's when the slaves were taken and imprisoned.' [25]

"Queen Isabella, of Spain, claimed that the vessel, cargo, and slaves, were the property of Spanish subjects. She insisted it was the duty of the United States to return them."

"Those poor souls, they had no say? I heard from Joshua, only a bit of that revolt but not the ending. I wouldn't blame them, trying to free themselves. I might have done the same, even knowing it's not right to kill for any reason."

"Through an interpreter, the Negroes, especially Cinque, their leader, denied that they were slaves. They stated that they were native born Africans; born free and still of right, ought to be free, and not slaves."

Jed says, "Cinque, he been brave man. He fight back t' be free. Mebbee soon's I get chance, I gon' fight to be free. I 'member place call by Mendiland an be's like my own village." I hope he doesn't plan a revolt against the wrong people, the ones trying to help him. No, how absurd to think that.

"Jed, you'll soon be free, once we get you both further north, to where it is safe. David, how did this end?"

"The District Court in Connecticut, ruled that the Negroes were not slaves but free men. They rejected the Spanish claim and decreed that the Negroes should be delivered to the President of the United States to be transported to Africa. Needless to say, the Africans were ecstatic."

David continued, "However, President Van Buren appealed the decision to the Supreme Court."

"That can't be true, our very own President? Why would he do such a thing?"

"He thought the ship, cargo and Negroes should be returned to Spain. His motivations? No one really knows. It could have been to appease Spain. Others thought it was for his own purpose . . . that maybe he'd gain support from the southern states for his upcoming re-election."

"A man who is our President, and yet not caring for right over wrong?"

"Luckily, but only after much persuasion, John Quincy Adams our Ex-President came to the fore. He was in his seventies but delivered an eight-hour argument before the Supreme Court on behalf of the Negroes."

"He was a good man. I am glad for the Negroes to have at least one of our Presidents stand up for them"

"Yes, and at one point he stated, 'The moment you come to the Declaration of Independence that every man has a right to life and liberty, an inalienable right, then this case is decided. I ask nothing more in behalf of these unfortunate men than this Declaration.'"

"On March 9th 1841 the Supreme Court announced its decision. Justice Story, speaking for the Court said that the Negroes were 'kidnapped Africans, who by the laws of Spain itself were entitled to their freedom.' They were not criminals: the 'ultimate right of human beings in extreme cases is to apply force against ruinous injustice.' The Africans could stay or they could return to Africa."

"How wonderful that it had a good ending, and they could choose."

"On the day of the Court's decision, John Quincy Adams penned a letter to Lewis Tappan—an ardent Abolitionist fighting hard to free slaves.'

"He wrote, 'The captives are free! Thanks, in the name of humanity and justice, to you.'"

"How did they get back to Africa?"

"Well, that's another story. You see, although they were set free, they had no money to return to Africa on their own. So many families in Farmington, Connecticut took them in. One African girl by the name of Ka-ne, was placed in Charlotte Cowles home. The Cowles family had long helped runaway slaves navigate the Underground Railroad."

"How were they treated in Farmington?"

"Very well, I understand. Charlotte wrote her brother that *'our little African. Ka-ne is the one that lives with us. Ta-me is at Dr. Porter's, and the other one at Uncle Timothy's. I never saw anything like their affection and generosity. Their wealth is not very great, but they always find something to give each other. So they go on all the time, seeming to find no pleasure in keeping, but all in giving.'"* [26]

"Enough for now. We've spent the good part of the day with these stories. We'll rest for a while longer to give more time for the roads to be cleared. Helen, we must get Lily back to bed. Look at how she has dozed off."

"I'll take her up. Will you see to Jedediah and Belinda? They must be ready when we're set to depart for Ginny-town."

Can't stop thinking about what I heard. Recalling the plight of those Negroes aboard the slave ship. Why would they mutiny? How could they get the strength? Still . . . if they possibly could, then why not? If it were me, could I live in slavery? No, I know I would not and could not. It makes me wonder and admire those that cherish freedom so much that they are willing to die for it. It makes me think of how I almost turned Daisy away from our door that night.

Chapter Fifteen

Maria and Salavino

We're on the road heading to the Gypsy camp in Ginny-town. David often stops his carriage as he and Jed try to clear the way of debris and tree branches in our way. Some roads are impassable and we're forced to turn around to find another way.

David says, "We need to get back on the cobblestones."

Now on Main Street, the going is better. Approaching Oxford Village, we take a slight detour and end up on North Street.

David says, "This used to be called Bread and Cheese Lane. Do you remember me telling you about the little stone school house where John Mung attended? That's what you see up ahead. It is small, but built to last. The house where Captain Whitfield used to live is only two blocks from here on Cherry Street.'

"OK, we're back on Main St. We'll be passing by the new cemetery on the left. Oh, oh, I see carriages are stopped on the roadway. There are some in muddy holes. We'll have to sit and wait while the ones up front try to move on."

"Jed, why are you fidgeting? Is something wrong?"

"Goin' by cemeteries, be's bad omens follerin us." Belinda nods her head in agreement.

David says "There is nothing to be afraid of. Riverside Cemetery is like a nice Park, with flowering bushes, trees and rolling hills."

I lean close to whisper "Please, not too loud, Lily might want to visit the gravestone of her twin daughters."

"Alright. While we wait, I'll give you some more history."

"Warren Delano bought this land for the cemetery about four years ago. His ancestor, Phillip De La Noye was one of the first colonists. That was long before the name got shortened.' [27]

"Do you know what the Indians called Fairhaven?"

"No I didn't." At this time, I wish he would just figure on knowing how to get moving. Jed is squirming in his seat, does not like being this close to the cemetery.

"The village of Fairhaven was called Sconticut by the natives. It signified their summer place."

"No, David, I did not know that, but would like to hear more sometime."

Our carriage has managed to move up a bit. Other young men give us a hand when their own wagons are freed up. I can see the sign now, it's called The Riverside . . . but a big overturned tree blocks the sign and the entry way. Belinda is up on the seat and spells out, then tries to pronounce that sign. Lily sits straight up, and yanks at my sleeve.

She says, "Oh, Helen, I've not been in to visit, since Jack had the girls moved from the Old Burial Ground."

"Someday you'll be able to visit them again, and I will go with you."

"Thank you, Helen. And your shoulder is so nice to lean on."

Jed jumps down when a lad asks for help to lift a big tree. They try, time and again—but cannot get that big trunk to budge. If Joshua were here, I wager he'd have it up and out of there in short time.

David removes his hat and top coat, and hands me his spectacles before he jumps down. I hope he does not hurt himself. Then, I am amazed at his show of strength. The three of them get the tree moved enough to get by and we move on.

We pass a smaller cemetery on the right.

Lily says, "That's the Wood Side Cemetery, so it's not too much further. You'll see a lane off to the left."

"OK, I see it." Turning left, we head down a hill toward the river.

"Jed, can you walk ahead, see if it's safe enough for us to manage it."

Jed runs down the hill and at the bottom, he waves to us and makes a motion to come ahead.

David asks, "Where is Ginny-town, Lily?"

"There's two homesteads at the end of this lane. The Tripp families live there. Go past them, to the river."

The horses are at a slow pace. David keeps yelling, "Whoa!" Then on the third stop, he explains, "This is the end of the path. Look at those pink and white beach roses spread all over.'

"Everyone stay put. I'll go on ahead to make sure we're welcome. That is, if I can find my way in."

Ah, here comes David. He's got a woman by his side. She's in a long gray skirt. This woman matches David's strides. A crimson and yellow blouse covers her front. Starting from her shoulders, the sleeves flare out into a big ruffle and covers her wrists. Jumping up on the side of the carriage, she grabs my hand, and shakes it. Then she turns round to Lily.

"You are Lily? Jack Wallingford's wife? I am Maria, wife of Salavino. We are Romani clan and old families lived in Romania. Sal very busy—cleans up beach after storm."

David says, "Maria you must meet Helen, and this is Jedediah and Belinda."

"Hola, you all welcome, now Doctor come, please? Follow me."

"My preference is to use David, not Doctor, as my name. Now, my question is, do we leave the carriage here in the lane?"

Maria points down to the river. "No, bring carriage, we have pathway, but cannot see it. I will show." We're on our way.

I say, "Maria, who's that up ahead, holding a long knife."

Maria chuckles and says, "That's my Sal, a good man. Yes, my man, no one better."

Sal calls out, "Maria, la mia bella moglie celeste principessa."

I have no idea what he just said. Coming closer, this big bulky man, he is something to see—and is more like a Pirate we read about in books. He sports a mustache but it curls up at the sides. Stray locks of black hair hang from under a red bandanna. His skin is a golden brown, and not as light as Maria's.

He says, "Please forgive, hadda cleana beach. Many fish washin in, anna high tide bringa boards broken offa boats inna bigga storm. Ona beach, no good, alla splinters stickin outa sand—nada good, Bambino feet geta bad hurt."

Maria says, "Sal. It is Jack's wife. A fine looking lady; like picture Jack show us. She wed Jack Wallingford, a good lawyer, our compadre."

Sal runs to Lily and shouts, "Benvenuti!" He, tries to hug her, but she draws back.

"Ah, I see, I ama so sorry.' He slaps his face. 'See, I slapa for you my face. My manners, my speakin nada so good, forgive a please?"

Lily's mouth almost keeps a smile on her face and then Maria chuckles and I laugh.

"Whatsamatta for her? She feela bad? Maria? We must keepa Jacka wife tranquillo, si?"

I say to Maria, "Lily is not feeling well and we try to make her days more pleasant, not less so. I am so curious, what did he call you before?"

"My name he give to me 'bella moglie celeste principessa' it mean 'beautiful wife heavenly princess.' Sal very smart, he try always to stay on my good side."

Then she whispers to me, "You say Lily not good? She sick? Sal and Jack, many times down in taverns, they meet. Now he no see Jack for long, long time."

When we reach the camp, Sal looks up at David and asks, "You hear alla news? Many a boat lost inna big storm."

"No. I had no time to buy a newspaper. What happened?"

"I go an see New Bedford after storm. Five fishin boats, an none, nada one coma back from sea. Alla lost. Many cryin wives an chilren, waitin ina Seamen's Bethel over ona Johnny Cake Hill. All prayin an beggin God, bring em home. Ah, so sad."

He goes on. "Wait, more bad news! A big steamboat, it sink! Come from New Bedford, an heada to New York. Get stuck ina storm between Cutty Hunk an what's a name?"

Maria says, "Block Island."

"Yes, Blocka Island. Close by, coma boat but not a big ana fasta one. It go too slow, an you guess it . . . it see big boat starta sink, an alla people go down, screamin. No luck, to save a people. Terrible, terrible, too late—all go down wida boat."

"Here you look, see a newspaper, Maria read to me this mornin."

David reads the rest aloud from the newspaper.

"It says here, 'It was blowing a monstrous gale at the time,' and, it's all true, the horrible disaster with all the rest of it."

Then, looking up at me, he nods and sends a silent, 'Thank you.' He no longer doubts the warning I gave after my dream, not now.

I can smell a strong odor on Sal. I step back and cough.

Maria says, "Garlic, yes, is what you smell? You no like? We wear round our neck to ward off coughing spells. Good to chew, help throat not get sore."

She gives some leaves to Sal and suggests that he chew those leaves.

Then she says, "Here you try, chew spearmint."

I tried a few sprigs and found it quite refreshing.

Out of range of Lily's hearing, I tell Sal, "Jack and Lily are not getting along. She is coming to Vermont with me. But no one should know of our destination. You surely understand?"

Sal said, "Si, si. Such a shame. Jack—he help me plenny a time, he's a gooda man."

We are famished, with nothing to eat since early morn. Sal told us to sit round the fire pit. He said, "Hai voglia di mangiare qualcosa con noi? What? You no answer? Oh, prego. Maria, you ask?"

Maria says, "Do you want to eat something with us?"

I ask, "Where is it?"

Sal asks, "You wanna Clam a Bake? We begin make a four hours ago. We got a plenty."

Maria says, "Supper's our big meal. We sit, eat, talk, sing, be happy together." Children play games. They bring trays of food.

"Maria, this is so good. The husks are still on, but the corn inside, it's so sweet. What's this, wrapped in paper? It's from that same big pit—the one with all the rocks round it. Is that how it's cooked, but how?"

"Fish, it is baked in layers. The sausage we make easy."

"This must cost you a pretty penny?"

"Fish we catch, and sand gives clams, and river gives up other food from ocean. We trade for what we need. You like? Good. Sal can show tomorrow how he bakes and how rocks get hot. We get lots of seaweed; put over rocks, so steam comes out."

"Yes, I'd like to see that. Ooh, these clams; they're so small and tender. What? There's more?"

"Try this Clam Chowder, we make with cow's milk, onion and cut up potato, too. See? Plenty clams and bits of fish, and crab meat, we get much fish, crabs, and sometimes an eel, when boys catch."

Jedediah and Belinda have heaping plates. Must be enjoying the feast.

I am so full. I cannot put another morsel in my mouth.

"Maria, what smells so good? Well look at that. It's a tomato stew and mmm, it's brimming with greens. Well, I might take a . . . no that's too much. Make it just a wee bit of a taste."

Good lord! I've never seen Lily have such an appetite. She's resting now with a pleasant smile on her face.

Sal walks over, "You like a food?"

"Yes, I did. Do Gypsies always eat this well.?"

Sal winces, and says, "Yes, we cook a good a food, but please a no say we a Gypsies. We a Romani people. We no like a be called a Gypsy." [27a]

"Oh, I'm sorry Sal. I did not know that."

"It's a alla OK. We alla be amicos, now."

David asks to take a walk with me and Jed and Belinda. He puts his arms round them, drawing them close.

He says, "Don't you be worrying, you'll soon be able to follow your own path. While here, just do as Miss Helen says and you'll be fine. I only need time to make plans and have a good, safe route we can all travel on."

Then going to see Sal, he shakes his hand and says, "Sal, Lily is sick, but I think this camp and the fresh air along with the sun will do her good."

Maria overhears and says, "We take good care of Jack's Lily. Romani herbs and medicines will be good help for her."

David responds, "Thank you Maria. Sal, you're both good people and very kind for taking Lily and the rest of them in. I'll be back soon to check on them."

His carriage is ready. His horses are already groomed by Sal's boys. They won't accept coins for their work. They smile, saying "No, no" and look to their father. David tries to put the coins in Sal's hand.

"Nada, put coins away. You no hafta pay. Glad you bringa Jack's wife. You no worry; we take a good care of alla you amicos."

Then with one last look at us, David turns the carriage round and heads back down the path.

Then altogether our shouts ring out.

"See you nex a time, soon you get a back!"

"Come back when you can!"

Jed yells real loud, "Mistuh David, ah purely am grateful t' y'all!"

Belinda whispers, "Missus Helen—whats it y'all calls it? A cossit? An whale bones? They hurt awful bad."

"Come with me; let's go in the Vardo. No one will see you in this covered wagon, and I will take it off for you. You won't be needing it here in camp."

* * *

Two days are gone, and here's David, returning to see about Lily.

"Well Helen, after one look at her, I can see her health has improved a bit. But she's not yet fit enough for traveling. How is her appetite?"

"I wish she would eat more, but she doesn't seem interested in food. Of late she has a deep melancholy look about her. Did I mention to you, that she had two young twins that died of diphtheria?"

"No, but that could contribute to her illness. Oft times, melancholia creates loss of appetite."

"Well, her husband not being by her side, and that terrible event at the farm must constantly be playing on her mind."

"But she appears fairly normal, today. Look at her smiling."

"Yes, I know. Some days she does better, but the next sick spell can overtake her in a snap, before she can blink an eye."

"Then I see we'll have to bide our time. I trust that you and Jed and Belinda are making do each day, and it's not too hard on you?"

"No. Not hard at all. Every day there's something new to learn—much more than we expected. Sal says he'll be making ready for the Carnival. It's coming soon. He said we mustn't worry as this camp keeps us well hidden and Jack won't know we're here. We had let Sal believe that's the reason why Lily left, due to problems with Jack."

"Well, let's hope you all are still taking precautions, and not accidentally bringing attention to any of you. I'll check back from time to time, but send a message if you need me. You have my address."

Before he leaves, I hand him a letter I wrote for Joshua. He reads it.

Joshua, you must try to come and help us. Lily would do much better in Vermont, and so we are wanting to go back home. Pastor here at Lily's Meeting House, requested we take two friends with us, and has given us his blessing for the trip. He also requested that you should be with us to escort us back at this time. As you know, many bridges need crossing heading back north. Lily's Jack, is away on business, attending as agent for his family. Looking to see you as soon as you can make it here.

Yours, and ever your loving wife, Helen.

"I see you've included those special codes in the letter. Do you really think Joshua, coming from that great distance, will be able to help?"

"I would hope so. He's had a lot of experience helping runaways and we certainly need all the help we can get. Mostly I'll need him for moral support. I gain strength when he's with me."

"OK, I'll post your letter today, with my return address."

Then he was off again.

Salavino, or Sal, is so good as a host. He doesn't mind answering my questions about his Romani ways and he doesn't mind me writing this down in my journal. When he's too busy, I watch and listen to how happy and how content the others seem to be. They never worry about what the weather may bring but instead let each cloud roll in, to drop rain or just float on by.

I ask, "How can you be so calm? You never complain about mishaps, big or small and never raise your voice in anger."

"Ha, ha! I do raise a my voice when I'm a happy! An why waste a time a gettin mad? Life is beautiful an we need enjoy it all, no matta what."

"When boy be good, Father, he tell boy, come, ir de pesca."

"Marie, what is that, 'er, uh, pesca?'"

"Oh, sorry, forget. Means, how you say? Go fishing. He tell boy, jump up, he carry on shoulders, they catch mucho pesca."

What a big day it was, learning Romani ways from Maria and Sal. Now, I must close this journal. Got to check on Lily to see if I can get her up for some food. She needs to be fit for traveling. David said it must be soon.

She's awake. But looking closer, I know it won't be for long.

"Helen, no, not today. I can barely walk. Just let me rest for now?"

"Whatever you say. I've heard Carnival Time is coming. Salavino makes the camp ground ready for it and neighbors will be setting up along the shore of the Acushnet River. You might feel well enough to join in by then."

* * *

Today, there's no new questions for Sal and Maria. Just need to explain old answers.

"Sal, can you tell me more about how your family manages to get along so well? Even when life cannot give you what you want or need?"

"My people, our children—not wanta for nothin. Nada. Most a what we want we gotta right here—deep inside. Nothin outside can fill it up, only we gotta do it.'

"We love life an alla livin things around us. We no worry if soma body gonna like us or not. We get a plenty good happy feelins right here.' He spreads out his fingers and thumps his hand on his chest. "An whata we need coins for? We make alla what we need."

"Please, can you wait while I fill my quill with ink? I don't want to miss a word of what you say."

"OK. I go slow. Si, startin from a inside, deep in our hearts, we got alla we need. Some days, it fills up, like it gonna bust a wide open. But, no matta, we give it away."

"Then what happens, don't you have an empty hole left?"

"Nada, no. What we give, it come a back, like tides in a river, never fail. What goes out, always come in again."

"Oh, I see, I think. Now, how do you get fish?"

"OK, OK. Good. I tell. We row a Dory down a river to Fairhaven an a New Bedford fishin wharfs. We row between a pier an a big a fishin boat. When fishin boat swings a big net full a fish onto dock, many fish fall in a water."

"Then what happens? How do the fish come out?"

"We pick fish out a water an put in a Dory, till Dory almost full.[28] An fishamen donna care, they give a 'thumbs up.' An we row back to Ginny-town. Then all join in, guttin a fish, smokin a fish, bein a sure to savin livers—an gotta squeeze oil out a each a one."

"Sal, what's this about those boys who don't live here?"

"I see boys, mean boys, hurtin poor things. I chase away, but boys come a back. I think maybe I tell alla fathers.'

"What are they doing to be mean?"

"Boys make a fun catchin Seagulls. They tyin bit a fish on long a piece a twine, an go hide in a bushes. Gull swoopa down, an swallow fish. Gull fly off, but boys holdin end a twine. What boys think? Flyin a kite? An a poor thing, it goes roun in circles, stretchin it's neck. Boys, laffin, an a laffin, an Gull soon come a back, an throw up a fish an a fly off."

"How cruel, how mean. You must report them—or tell David, he will."

"I donna wanna trouble. These boys also catcha Fiddler Crabs a funny way. They tie a string aroun large a claw an a drag it. I no tell a fathers, maybe I hafta keep my big a mouth a shut, after all."

"Good, we don't want constables snooping around here."

Salavino wiped his eyes with his bandanna before going on.

"Boys know to respect alla living things. Just catcha fish, ana crabs, ana lobster. Take home to Mama, to cook. We catch only to eat."

"We Romani people learn a sayins our Papas handa down to us, an Granda Papas, too. All get respect. Fathers teach a son to pay mind, hear good from heart an nada lissen to bad ina head. Maria take family to church, boys ana girls, sing 'All things a bright ana beautiful. Ana God love em all.'"

"Sal, Joshua has always taught our boys the same way. Yes, my boys respect all of nature, everything in it and what it gives us."

Maria, Sal's wife, mentioned, "Oil from Cod fish livers, only for special medicine." I'm hoping she gives a recipe later. Then, it's getting added to my home remedying box.

I'm fascinated watching two boys catch blue crabs. Tying fish heads to twine lines, they throw them out into the shallow parts of the river. One by one. They wait. Then they slowly pull in the lines, and crabs start to walk in while biting at the fish heads. Now, close enough to shore, they scoop the crabs up using small nets on a long handle.[29]

One falls out of the net and the smaller boy runs in the water to catch it.

"Ouch!" He screams, as he flings the crab up in the air—with a piece of skin from his finger lodged in the crab's claw. The older boy first laughs, but then runs over to comfort the little one.

Early one morn, I went along side Maria and some other Romani women to pick dandelions. They boil and eat dandelion leaves and also use them fresh in salads with olive oil and wine vinegar. [30]

Maria's now showing Lily how to make dandelion wine.

"Go, Lily, you try. Take yellow buds from dandelions."

Later, Maria gave a taste of wine already made.

Lily really enjoys it but I tell Maria, "That's enough, I don't want Lily to start walking crooked." We all laugh at this.

"Lily, remember how we gathered wild greens back in Vermont. Ma showed us how to gather herbs and flowers when we were knee high to her apron strings."

"Yes, Helen, I can see it in my mind's eye. I know you can, too."

"I liked it best, Lily, when scouting around for cooking greens. Ma picked out ones good for eating. Remember that first time when we spied a whole bunch and hauled them home, but they were just weeds?"

"Yes, and we sure got to know the weeds after that, and fast enough, didn't we?"

"Oh, yes. She'd say, 'See the difference in leaves, know what to look for next time. These being lamb's quarters and over there, cowslips. And almost with the same flavor, fiddleheads.'

"Some funny names but right tasty. We just had to learn to cook them with proper seasoning."

Next day, I took Jed and Belinda with me for a walk and found Sal to ask him about his travels.

"Good a mornin Helen an a Good a mornin' Jed an Belinda. Come a sit."

"Good morning, Sal. Do you have some time to talk for a while? I was wondering, do your people stay in Ginny-town all year?"

"No, nada, in warm part a year we visit local fairs all around New England. We sell smoke a fish, wine, an a medicine like a cod-liver oil an many a basket."

"Do you get money?"

"Some a coins an a we like a gold chains, an many rings."

"Where do you go in winter?"

"Romani people go south an nex a spring, we come a back. Folks no say, 'Hey! You a Gypsy man, you go away.' They say, 'No problem, we like a carnival.'"

"Now, I must go check, see how much a help Maria need. Plenny work for cookin tonight."

"Mistuh Sal, Belinda an me, we's gon' to see Maria an help. Is it OK?"

"A course a Jed, c'mon along."

Chapter Sixteen

Anticipation

It's been five days. I am awake before sunrise. Joshua might arrive today. I need my shawl to ward off the cold. I step out of the wagon. The fog is creeping in off the river. Something breaks the silence. A horse whinnies and snorts. It comes closer . . . then fades away. Only a horse and wagon—my heart sinks.

Wait, is that a man walking? I see him clearer, now. He's waving. Could that be Joshua? Yes, it is. That's my Joshua!

I start running. My feet barely touch the grass. I leap up, and jump into his arms. I can't hear a thing, except my heart beating. His arms fold around me, tighter and tighter. He slowly lets me slide out of his arms, but my knees are weak and my legs give in. He scoops me up and turns back to the camp. What? He stops, parts the tall grass and pushes through.

"Joshua, where are you taking me?"

"We'll stop and rest for a while."

No one is nearby. Birds rise up, flap their wings and fly away. We are alone.

The sun's now higher in the sky. It looks to be a warm day for our Carnival. Joshua brushes the hair from my brow, and I smile. He stands up and looks around, then picks up his hat. Some pins came loose from my bun. I find them, and get them back in. Oh, no, I ran off without my morning cap.

"Josh, how are the boys? I can't wait to see them again."

"They're fine. They're in good health, but they miss you something terrible. I've missed you too, my Indian maiden."

"Oh, you got my letter, about who my real Pa was?"

"Yes, I did. It was kind of sad that he died before you were born. I can see where you got your hair and your eyes. White Eagle must have been very handsome."

"Now I realize why I look nothing like Lily. But that's in the past, long ago. Do you know why we came to this camp? You'll never believe what happened."

"Tell me, don't beat around the bush."

"Lily shot two men. They were slave catchers. They broke in."

"Are you saying she shot and killed them? Our Lily? You're right, I can't believe it. And she was also harboring runaways, the two friends you mentioned in your letter?"

"Yes. Then I had to clean up the mess. Had to get rid of the bodies." I shake a bit, and he holds me close.

"Where? How?"

"In the woods. Her horse dragged them."

"Oh, Lord, what next? You're still trembling."

"I must know, what you think of it all? I couldn't put that in my letter. Was it wrong, what I did?"

"Was Lily too sick to handle any of this?"

"Yes, and I was so worried that the law would be hunting us down. Lily would get taken away. The slaves would get hauled off back to their owner. I needed, so badly, to talk to you, Josh . . . I'm so glad you're here."

"Lily can't be faulted. If she hadn't been so sick, she wouldn't have let you get into it. She may have offered herself up to the law."

"Was I wrong in not reporting it? The two escaped slaves are here with us at the camp. But, Josh, those poor mothers. They lost their sons and have no way to find them."

"As I see it, Lily defended her home and anyone in it. You did what you had to do . . . took care of your sister, who is too sick for any jail, and you shielded the runaways."

"You really think I did the right thing?"

"Nothing can change what's happened. The Lord will be the final Judge. We'd best give it up to Him and leave it in his hands."

Ah yes, I will do just that. I smell meat cooking, must be bacon. I am starved, and can't wait.

"Look, the Gypsy ladies. They're starting breakfast."

Maria, calls out, "Is this your husband? Joshua, right? Nice to see you. Come, you two, you want hot water and tea leaves? Good, take these tin cups, and wrap leaves in cloth. Be careful, so hot. Now, Helen, hold your hands out. Here, take some fried sugar cakes and bacon. It's good, no?"

This cake is so good, and one more . . . just what I need. I see Joshua gobbles his down before I start eating. We head over to the big rocks.

"Helen, I had no time to eat before leaving Randolph. I'm hungry." I give him the rest of my sugar cakes, and most of the bacon. I sit and pour the tea. Maria was right, it is too hot.

"Joshua, how did you manage to get here?"

"I took the new railroad line from Randolph to New Bedford, changing trains a few times on the way down. I went to Dr. Hatcher's office. He was not in, but he left a note with directions to get here."

"Where did you get the money for the trains?"

"Sold some items off the farm, borrowed some of Jacob's savings and the rest came as a loan from the Elders. I wanted enough to get us safely back home."

"I'm so glad you're here. You must meet Jed and Belinda. They help me look after Lily."

"What do these Gypsies know about what happened at Lily's house?"

"Sal and Maria knew we needed cover—."

"Who is this Sal you just mentioned?"

"His full name is Salavino, and he heads the Gypsies. You'll meet him. However, they don't like to be called Gypsies. They are Romani people. Anyway, Lily told Sal that Jed and Belinda needed a safe place. He knows nothing about the shootings."

"That's good."

"Josh, let's go see what Maria needs and what we can do to help her with her cooking."

Maria's children are helping, best they can, but most just play around her.

She says, "Sal helps carnival workers. He meets you later."

Joshua says, "That's good. Meanwhile, what can we do to help?"

"Can you find more firewood?"

"Look, Joshua, here comes Jed and Belinda. Let's take Jed with us and Belinda can help Maria with the cooking." I see Joshua staring at Jed's face.

I take Josh aside, "That scar—he does not talk about it. Maybe, to you, he'll let on what happened . . . but he wouldn't answer Lily or me when we asked about it."

Here on the river's edge, we pick up driftwood. Jed gets more than an armful. Pieces spill out.

He says, "I gets me good firewood and good pieces. Sal tole me, I can be's carvin on em nice pieces. Good t' sell."

"Time to take a rest,' I say. 'Go ahead, sit a spell, while I even out the loads. Some of your finer pieces I can carry."

Joshua says, "Jedediah, you must be a brave man, coming to a strange country, lasting through all of it. Think of it, what a hardship, getting captured and living through it. Can you tell me about your days as a slave?"

Jed hesitates for a moment . . . and then it all comes spilling out.

"In my country, I gets onna boat wanting t' be fishin man, goin to America. My people, we live onna coast, an have heavy rains givin poor crops. I needs t' work for coins so's I can help feed my people." He stops, looks at his feet. Then, stares at the river.

"Go on, what did you do?"

"Nex I hears all bout sailin mans come t 'port handin out silver trinkets, an rum. At first rum burnin my tongue but I likes it, an I's dancin all night. I sees sailor mans runnin round, havin good life. Mebbee I gone t' sea an join up on fishin boat. So I signs my X on paper. Ah, I been dumb, gon' an trustin mans I dint know afore."

I'll not talk. I'll just let Joshua hear his tale.

He says, "Don't be too hard on yourself. How could you have known?"

"I tries t' fergit about it, but cain't. Cuz we's on ship an goin out to sea. Mans gon' an push me down a hole. Maybe findin a bed? But we's endin up in bottom of ship—an, wond'rin, how can it be's our workin place? How we's gon' go catchin fish?"

Then, tears fill Jed's eyes.

"Here, Jed, take my handkerchief."

"Massa Josh, we's never seein sun agin. Men put irons round my neck an feet. I gets smacken on down, but I gets up. Nex, dis man whippin my back till I yellin an caint stop."

"Why did he do that? What did he say?"

"He say, 'No boy, you quitcher whining. Gon' fix dis nigguh boy. What y'all lookin at? Iffen y'all don't shut yer faces up, I gon be whippin an pourin vinegar on y'all, an, it'll larn yuh.'"

"No, did he ever do that? Vinegar, wouldn't that hurt?"

"Sure, an I doin like he tellin me. But, he say, 'You ain't a man, you like a animal, livin inna jungle. Ah shee-it, you dumb donkeys, don't none a yah know no better den believin dem stories—alla riches in far off lands. I swears, y'all sure needs lessons t' learn yuh.'" Jed keeps talking so fast and can't seem to stop now.

"An, Mistuh Haxell, I caint—." Joshua reaches for Jed's hand. He holds it tight, and Jed stops all the sputtering. I can see Jed is too excited, and too worked up.

After a while, Joshua says, "That was terrible. Are you feeling any better?"

"Yeah. I gon' go an get it out now. He gimme me a big whip crack, an blood run out. Nex, he pourin on vinegar. Oh Lordy, it been hurtin awful bad all night."

"I've heard similar tales. Jed, don't finish if it hurts you to recall it. I wondered, though, you had nothing to ease the pain?"

"No, an I cain't cry out, or I get whippin agin. Dint make no never mine. I get lashin fer doin sumpin, or doin nuttin."

"What did they feed you?"

"We gets food alla sailors knowed ain't fit eatin. Like ole rotted meats hangin since sailin."

"Did it make you sick?"

"Sure did, but food gets better afore landin in America."

"Why's that?"

"Big boss want us lookin fit an strong. He gets gold an supplies tradin us at slave auction.'

"We cain't be workin as fishin man, we be nuttin but slavin mans. Wanna go back home, but cain't. I be shamed to show my face. People knowin what a fool I bin, believin alla lies. Nah, no good, cain't never go back."

"I just hope that a much better life is in store for you. Sometime, I'd like to talk more with you. I've wondered, about that scar on your face. Would that be OK?" Jed puts his hand to his scar, but does not answer.

I speak up, "We best get this wood back to camp."

Jed nods and says, "Sure. An, Missus Hellun, gimme yer wood. Aint right y'all carryin it." He's not back on the plantation where white women don't do work like this. I won't argue, though, I'm glad he told of the pain he suffered. Hope it helps— getting it out. It's no good letting it fester inside.

Here's the camp, Maria is outside. She waves, then the men take the wood to the fire.

I say, "Josh, Come with me to the shore line. I want to show you something'

"See these bubbles rising from the wet sand? Clams are under there."

I dig with a stick. "Look, Josh. Here comes a whole slew!"

"Clams? So that's how they get them. Look over here. What's on these rocks, what are they called?"

"The Romani call them periwinkles. The children love to boil these small ones and then pick out the insides with a pin and eat them." [31]

"Ugh, can't imagine how they'd taste. Do you know?"

"Quite good actually. I closed my eyes once and tried one. Maria says that in Europe, larger ones are favored by the wealthy. Their cooks call them escargot."

"That's a funny name. Well, I won't be eating any, so let's head back to camp. Look, who's that man? He's coming to see us?"

"That's David, our doctor. He's been helping to care for Lily and he's also an agent, like you, supporting the underground railroad."

"So, he's the one who left the note with directions on how to get here."

I say, "Good morning, David. Why so early? Do you have a patient nearby?"

"No, just Lily. There's no one else in these parts I have to see. Hello, you must be Joshua. Helen's told me about you and it is all good."

Here comes Sal. He stops to wash his hands and face in the big bucket. Next, he joins us as he shakes his head to get the water off his hair.

David says, "Hello, Sal, I stopped by early because we need to discuss the best route to get all your guests out of here safely and the sooner the better, wouldn't you say?"

Sal grabs Joshua's arm. He whispers to him. Joshua nods. Then Sal says, "OK David, but why not a stay over? Joshua need a rest. He must get a sleep first and the ladies need a time to pack. Well, wadda you say?"

Before David can answer, Josh says, "Yes, I agree. We need time to plan our route out of here."

I nod in agreement.

Joshua says, "Consider this plan. Before I left Randolph, I was told that one of the Society Friends, living nearby, might offer the loan of a private coach. He also has a map of safe houses further north. David, your time has already been taken up enough. You need not come, unless you want to go along part way."

David says, "But, Josh, I'd planned to stop in Middleborough at James Hawthorne's home. He's been a freed colored man for a long time, and he surely would put Jedediah and Belinda up. We could settle them at his place before you, Helen and Lily continue on to Randolph. You could take the train out from Middleborough, go through Taunton and then on to Vermont. How's that for a plan?"

I speak up, "Joshua, David, my head is swimming around. Can we please stop for a bit? Why so many plans and changes. Let's take time to think about it. There's no rush."

They turn to me, then Sal stomps his feet back and forth and coughs quite loud.

David looks at him. "Sal? What is it, you have something to add?"

"Why sure, alla you plans is a good ways to go an I gotta good idea too. I can take alla you to Middleborough."

My goodness, that's something we never dared to ask.

Sal pats Joshua's back. He says, "Carnival gonna be packing up after tomorrow night. Neighbor men round here, they help. Then we can a go. Is that good for alla you? Well?"

David asks, "How will you do it?"

"My Romani Vardo. This wagon gonna be a good place for you, got a top on, an a cover. What more you want?"

My dear Sal, I shall miss him in days to come.

Chapter Seventeen

Carnival coming

"Lily, just think, it's a grand time ahead. The Carnival is coming."

"Helen, my legs are so weak."

"If feeling poorly, we will bring you back. Come with me and I'll see what Maria has for us to wear."

Maria says, "Come Helen, we go see our finery. We fit you and Lily."

Maria and I duck under the curtain in back of the wagon. Maria hands me two sets of garments. One for Lily.

I help Lily into the Vardo, and Maria starts dressing us.

"Lily, I've never seen such wide billowing sleeves. OK good, now we'll pull up this long skirt. Here's a fancy net shawl, with sparkly stones and ribbons." Lily smiles.

"Maria, may I wear that large strand of beads." She dangles them round my neck. Then Maria wraps a silver chain around my waist.

My buttons and shoe clasps are fastened. Just in time to surprise Joshua and David. Sal went to round them up along with the children.

Now here's our audience. I see Maria first when we push the curtain aside. She smiles and nods, then claps. We make our grand entrance as my arm wraps around Lily's waist.

I yell out, "Holay!" The children laugh and clap. I look at Josh and David. They say not one word.

I say, "We heard some who live nearby love costumes. We can never be recognized, am I not right? We won't draw attention, will we?"

Joshua says, "Oh? What can I say? It's so different, never saw you like this. You both, I say—if that is your costume, well, then—so be it. I mean you are dressing for the occasion, I suppose."

David's eyes are glassed over. He quickly covers his mouth as he coughs.

I ask Joshua, "Please, quick, take a look at David. Is he choking?" We run to David's side.

"David, let me help! Tell me, why can't you speak?" I slap his back.

"What's wrong? Josh, take his tie off!"

What's this? David lets out a deep sigh. His hands fall to his side. Good, he finally got his wind back, and he grins. Tears roll off his cheeks.

Then I hear Joshua laughing.

I turn around. "No, not you too? You think we should be laughed at? Well, I'll whack both of you with this shoe."

"Whoa, hold on, Helen. Give me a minute . . . *cough*. You two ladies are—my word! Such a . . . well . . . yes, you are a fine sight to behold."

David chimes in, "Forgive me ladies, it just took me by surprise. Most Romani ladies do not have their hair in upsweeps or buns. Nor do they wear high-topped shoes. Also, their hands are usually bare, to show off painted finger tips and bracelets. Not covered with white gloves."

"I agree.' says Joshua 'But, you ladies do look quite alluring."

Maria says, "Joshua, you try Romani clothes from Sal. I show Helen and Lily, how to darken eyebrows. We use burnt stick. Then I make Lily's skin dark with Walnut paste."

Each stroke of Walnut stain darkens that once pale face. For a brown lady, Lily is quite nice looking. I help Lily down from the Vardo.

"My word! Joshua is that you?" He is spiffed up in Sal's clothes. A big red bandanna covers his nose and mouth.

"Joshua, you look so grand. But, what are you? A cowboy or a mysterious Romani man?"

"A Romani man, of course."

"I like that white shirt with billowing sleeves. And those long black boots. Yes, you'll pass for a Romani man."

We find Lily by the campfire, lying back in a big chair. Maria cuts watermelon pieces. Lily reaches for one smaller piece. Here comes Sal with a small bottle of grape juice. I pour her some and I take a sip. It's a sweet taste, but it's more than juice.

Now Lily says, "Helen, I'm staying here. I enjoy watching the children. They have so much energy, laughing and running about. Can you pour me a little more before you go?"

"You don't want to come along?"

"No, you two be off. I may join you later if Maria wants to escort me. Don't worry, no one will know me in this outfit."

"My word, Joshua, what a perking up she's had."

"Yes, and let's hope it continues."

Belinda and Jed dance round the fire wearing Indian costumes.

Joshua asks, "Was it Jed's idea, those feathered head dressings and masks?"

"Yes. Belinda also sewed up burlap sacks for the costumes."

"Josh says, "With all that jumping around and hollering, I'd best warn him. No sense being too good of a dancer. He might draw a crowd over. I'll go talk to him."

"Hello, Jedediah and Belinda. That's quite a dance. Can I talk to you for a moment?"

"Sure, Mistuh Josh."

"Remember, many are here for the carnival. You don't want people asking, 'Who are those dancers?'"

"You right, Mistuh Josh, we gon' stop. Asides, we gon' try alla foods put out."

"Good. Here's a few coins for you. Those masks should hide your faces well. Especially yours Jed, with that large scar you have. Can you tell me about it?"

"Sure, Mistuh Josh. I want freedom, but get catched alla time. Bossman say, 'OK nigra, y'all need a knife t' remindin y'all. It gon' slow yer runnin down.'"

"Why would he do that?"

"Wal, he say, 'Iffen ya'll runs away agin, I give reward for catchin slave showin scar on face.' An it be why we's hiden on ship. An no one sees my scar."

"That cut must have hurt bad. Why did you keep running away?"

"Yassuh, Mistuh Josh, I run for freedom, an iffen I die, I be in Gloryland. Y'all be knowin, I gon' be a free man in Glory."

With that they run off, hand in hand. Josh hurries me along, and we're going downhill, not steep but heading down to the river.

"Josh, look at those women over by the water. What are they doing? Let's go see."

"They light small candles, and place them onto pieces of birch bark. Now, they cast them off to float in the river. Look downstream, Helen—so many points of light in the darkness—same as stars in the sky."

"David told me about that custom. They remember their men. The husbands, fathers, brothers, and sons, all those lost to the sea."

Each woman is covered in a long black garment, perhaps a mourning dress? Shawls of lace cover their heads. They kneel, kiss their prayer beads, as lights float out to sea.

I shiver at the thought of their men, gone forever.

Joshua hugs me closer as we walk over to this table. It's laden with crafts. Small ships and jewelry of a sort. Must be what the seamen make, when out to sea.

"Joshua, what is this?" The man behind the table holds something up.

"Whaling men made the engravings."

Joshua takes it, and asks, "How is it done?"

"With a steady hand and a pocket knife or a large sail maker's needle. A picture gets etched on whalebones or the ivory teeth of a whale."

"Must have taken a long time?"

"It had to, but they had long stretches at sea to make these. After etching they would fill in with a mixture of whale oil and soot. Sometimes gun powder was used."

"Really? What's it called?" Joshua asked.

"Scrimshaw. It's a nautical term, it means 'wasted time.' That was the time they waited before they sighted whales."

"Josh, let's buy some pieces for the boys."

"Yes, but just a few. Remember, I had to borrow money to come here."

"You're right. I like the ship for Cal, and the whale etching for Eli."

Josh pays the man and we move on.

"Look, that clown over there. Joshua, turn your head. See, he bends down over a wood box—what's he doing? Wait, I see. Dolls dance and bounce up and down."

"I do see. Let's get closer. It's a Puppet Show? Heard tell only big cities had them." We watch for a bit. But having the puppets hit each other on the head? And people laugh at those antics? That's not right.

I ask, "Can you hear singing? Is it coming from that tent? Let's go see?"

A poster outside the tent tells it all.

Fortune Teller[16]

Madame X sees beyond in all ways
through her séance and crystal ball.
Only she can tell all.
Yes, all events of coming days
of your happy home.
So, make haste, come inside,
where spirits roam.
Yet, for you they do not hide.
You'll see what lies ahead.
Hurry now, do not wait,
for you will learn
of good days, as I said.
But, only if you dare
not to hesitate.

I walk fast, take a quick peek but stop after a few steps inside. On a shelf looking up at me, is a doll. She sits in a white silk-lined box. It's so real and just so beautiful. When I was young. I wished for one just like her. But we learned how to make clothespin dolls, instead.

"Come here and look at this doll, Joshua."

"Eek!" A black cat jumps away. Did he step on it?

"See this? It's in a fine gown of red satin. Maybe it came from a Romani woman? See the fine stitching that holds the pearls on the sleeves."

Joshua draws me to him, "Do you believe in fortune telling? They tell only good news, else no one would ever come back." He's probably right but the lady beckons me. Joshua hands her a few coins, then he goes outside.

Madam X leads me to the next room. It's dark in here. I wish Josh had come with me.

She lights candles. They flicker on a round table. She starts swaying back and forth, dancing around the table. What's that humming? It's all one long . . . is it called a chanting? Her hands fly round and round over her head. Then she sits.

Such awful sounding words—are they groans? They spill from her mouth. Could not be an actual spirit, could it? If it is, it must be in pain.

The voice fades away and her eyes open. She gazes into a large glass ball. She looks at me, then turns my hand to show my palm. One finger drags along the crease. It almost tickles, but her finger nail is so sharp.

She says, "Some lines are short, but look, these are very long. They show your life will be very long. Only good days lay ahead. Yes, many, many prosperous days. What a happy future in store for you."

I asked. "In your crystal ball, do you see any danger for me?"

She gazed for a long time—then looked up, shook her head. Next, a small boy appears and snuffs out the candles.

A pair of bright green eyes glow in the dark. Oh, no. I start trembling. Where is Joshua?

'Meow!"

I am relieved. It's only her cat. She picks it up and ducks behind the curtain.

It's over. No warnings of sheriffs or strange men out looking for me. Yet, it was a good show. I liked the dancing, but that groaning? It was too much, and she didn't need all that smoke from the incense.

Outside, the misty air smells of fish and seaweed. Maybe it blows in from the river. I clutch my shawl closer round my neck. Where is Joshua? Here he is. "Helen, come along, stay close behind me. That dancing crowd is too rowdy. Sal said he had rules against guzzling strong drink here. But, did you see the bottles they swig on? They are not just water."

"Where are we off to now?"

"I saw something earlier. Wait, there they are—."

"I see how pretty the ladies are in their costumes."

"No, not the dancers. I mean those two watching from the other side, dressed as Indians, completely disguised."

"Yes, it's Jed and Belinda, but we can't give it away that we know them."

"I agree. Look at the fiddlers playing and how Romani men and women are in step. So smart they are, as they glide along to the music."

"Now they circle the concertina players and the music is much faster. They step and twirl over and over as the women give one last high kick when the music stops." Coins are tossed at the boy holding the hat and they're off to the next crowd.

Joshua says, "Oh, oh. We may have a problem. Can you see that group of young men surrounding Jed and Belinda? Looks like they are up to no good. They've probably been drinking. Stay here and I'll go over and talk to them."

"No, I'll go with you . . . Josh, look . . . one of them is grabbing at Belinda's long dress, and Jed is trying to push him away."

Josh let's go my hand, grabs an axe handle setting on a wooden barrel, and starts running over to them. I yell, "Be careful, Josh."

Josh grabs the one, pulling on Belinda's dress, by the scuff of his neck and says, "What are you young men up to? No good, it looks to me."

"Mister, these two aren't Indians. They're Niggers. Look how black this woman's legs are."

"Let go of her dress and stand back. All of you."

"Mister, if you're looking for a fight. There's five of us and only one of you."

They start to approach Josh. He steps in front of them and says, "You're wrong. There's three of us, and this axe handle. It does a good job of cracking skulls and breaking knees. Now who wants to be first?"

They back away, and as Josh starts walking toward them, they turn and run.

I hold Belinda as Jed goes over to thank Josh.

Josh says, "There's no need to worry. They did not pull off your face masks. But, there could be more danger here. We should get you back to camp."

"Thank you, Mistuh Josh. I be getting ready to smash my fist in dat man's face, iffen dey harm Lindy Bell."

"No, you did the right thing by keeping still."

We waited until both had found the path back to camp.

I say, "That was close. It was probably a mistake to have them come to the carnival. I'm proud of the way you handled that."

Josh says, "I agree, their safety should always come first. We may be having a grand time at this carnival, but we can't lose sight of our primary duty for protecting these two. We can't let down our guard. Now let's forget that scene and come along, we still have a carnival to see."

My Joshua. How strong he is and how safe I feel when he holds my hand.

"Helen, look. A whole pig roasting on a spit. Here, try this pork, it's got some kind of tomato sauce on it. Watch it though, juices are running from it. Have a bite but be careful. You don't want it to drip on your finery. Too late, here let me wipe it off for you."

"Oh, no you don't. I'll tend to it. Mustn't let others see the big Romani man trying to touch my bosom, now can we?' He steps back, lowers his hat more to the front of his head, and looks shyly back at me.

"Hmm, it is good, come back here Joshua, look at this. All kinds of pan-fried fish, crabs and sausages. Here's what's called linguica. This man said he's Portuguese and makes sausage to sell. I tasted one. Here, want to try it?"

"I never had so many good aromas tempting me. I'm stuffed to the gills.

"Hear that man yelling, the man with the big top hat and funny clothes, what is he yelling about? Let's see what this fellow has to say. By the looks of it, I don't believe he has what we need to see."

We near the Side Show to see the man who'd done all that yelling.

He now calls out, "Come see the freaks!" 32

The Side Show[16]

See the wonders from seven seas,
It's all true, I tell no lies.
Come inside, and before your eyes,
You'll see all kinds of oddities,
They come from all over our land,
Yet out there, where you stand,
That show is always free.
Why not believe me—see under this flap,
it's only pennies, if you please.
So c'mon in! You're sure to clap
your hands at our rarities.
"Come here, over here, get a look,
Don't worry. You won't get took.
Just come over here, come see!
Oh, you Sir? You heard me—
you say—yes? And, loud and clear?

Then, hurry, hurry, get over here!

"Josh, what a shame it is, parading those unfortunate people about on that platform. Whatever can the owners of this show be thinking, to be so callous, so insulting?"

"I imagine it must earn them a living they could not get anywhere else."

"Poor souls, though misshapen, it is so unfair for people to gawk at them, and call them awful names. They are born that way through no fault of their own."

Joshua digs in his pocket, takes out a small coin and whispers, "Let us leave a donation but we shan't make cruel sport of them." Tossing it into the hat next to the ticket man, we then walk off.

Passing by the end of the platform, we see the Fat Lady propped up, and setting in a big wheelbarrow.

Then as we walk away a high, tiny voice, calls, "Wait!"

We turn. She lifts up her arm then edges it past her wide belly, slowly, ever so slow. Her elbow lands in her other hand where it stays propped up. Next, she rolls her chubby fingers to her painted mouth, then holds a kiss in her hand. Making contact with our eyes she blows it our way. Finally, winking, she utters a soft, barely heard, "God bless you both."

Joshua, holds my hand, protecting me, and vows not to let me get lost again. Now we're walking along an overgrown pathway along this stretch of rocks. This is way past the Carnival goings on. We are alone.

He mumbles, "The crowd can't be interested in anything out here. Perhaps, might be a good place, uh, what do you say? It does offer a bit of privacy. More than back at the Caravan, right?"

We slowly traipse past the rocks. There's a big Elm tree, off the side of this small cliff—its branches hang low, with a gentle swaying up and down, beckoning, waiting to gather us in.

"Joshua, I wonder if we can stop and rest a bit? Well, can you hear me?"

His heavy breath warms the back of my neck, as he leans his head down, and closer. For too long a time he gives no reply. Until he moves in front of me, and takes my hand in his.

"This way, follow me. Watch it, there's some prickly bushes here."

"Wait, Josh, is this what we need? Here's a nice bed of cushiony plants."

"Yes, nice and with no prickers, no thorns, none at all."

***

Next morning, Joshua nudges my shoulder. I wake up and wonder, why is he not talking?

He whispers, "Don't talk. Be quiet, so no one can hear. My arms are itching something fierce. Cannot stop this scratching. Do you think there are fleas in here?"

"Fleas? I've not seen any. Let me take a look at your arms." He bares his arms and holds them out.

"Oh my, there's dried blood here. Looks as if you dug up your skin with scratching. There's fresh bleeding behind your elbow."

"Where?"

"Right past your elbow, where it's hard to see."

Then, he turns his back side to me, and drops his trousers.

"What happened there? Let me check the door so no one tries to get in. I see you can't move too good?"

"Well, it's itching real bad down there. Can't figure out why."

"Wait, now. Don't drop your drawers. I'll believe you. David needs to come by today. If he does you should ask him to take a look."

He gradually pulls his trousers on, and we go outside. Joshua takes one careful step at a time, and makes it to the fire pit. We wait for boiling water for tea. He cannot sit, but does not want anyone to suspect what's wrong. He leans close to me and I smile for the both of us as if everything is just fine.

Joshua whispers, "Do you think it could be fleas, or some bad infection?"

"There's David now. Go ask him."

Joshua stumbles and I grab his arm to hold him up.

"Wait, just wave, call him over, Josh."

"David, I'm glad you came, can I see you in the Wagon?"

I get me a tin cup for my tea, and a plate for these rolls, with a good dollop of honey. Ah, good. Apples are in them and just hot off the fire. How this lady can bake such tasty food with only a covered pan, is beyond me.

I see David helping Joshua down the steps. David smiles and takes his leave—with not even a good morning from him? Strange.

Joshua lowers his voice when I reach him, "Come, we'll go behind the wagon. Just go extra slow, OK?"

"Well?' I ask. 'What is it?"

"Can you believe it? David is positive I've been off in some bushes with a Romani woman and of course, you knew nothing of my doings."

"Oh, he did, did he? What in the world is he talking about? Have you?' I hold back a laugh. 'Well, did you do, what he said?"

"Yes, of course. He said we must keep it from my wife. Something about how he understood how difficult it must be, *ahem* without a woman for such a long time."

"Goodness, how could he think of such things? I doubt if any Romani lady would do such a thing. Not the ones I've seen."

"David told me to be prudent and not tell anyone, since no other harm was done. Meaning I did not catch a disease. He said, perhaps you should be checked, too?"

"What? He did not suggest such a thing! You're pulling my leg?"

"Watch out Helen, don't yell. Someone might hear. I just threw that in, about you getting examined. He says what I have is contagious."

"Stop fooling, what is wrong with you and why do you have a rash?"

"I've got a good case of Poison Ivy, and I should not scratch at all."

"Really? What can you do now?"

"He said, make up a paste to put on. It will help, especially when I can't scratch certain places."

"What paste is that?"

"Oatmeal it works good for skin itching. David gave me some, he got from Maria. She didn't question why he wanted it. We can make it easy enough, just mix with warm water. Let's do it now."

We go to the reeds for privacy. I hold the pan of water—with the oats blending in, to make a good paste. Joshua lathers it all over. I help with places on his arms and legs. He takes care of the private areas. So, I keep my face turned the other way.

"You can turn back round, I am done. I have my drawers on, too."

Then, the hardest part, I help get his trousers back on, but very carefully.

Later in the day, Joshua's face looks frozen with his mouth drawn in, and shut tight. His eyes can only squint at me. He must be in pain."

"What's the matter?"

"I need to get a pan and some water fast, to wash off the oatmeal paste. Where we put it on—well, it dried up too hard, and it hurts like the devil."

"OK, why don't you go to the same place as before, and I'll bring a pan of water to you."

He walks at a snail's pace, and probably would crawl if he could get on his hands and knees. He makes it to the reeds, and I take water to him.

"Here, I've got enough, don't you think? Now, let me help you."

"I can do it, give it here. Wait by the campfire, OK?"

Here he comes out of the reeds. He's walking easier, still balancing side to side, trying to stay upright.

Much later, after sundown, as we gather round the camp fire, Joshua tells me he is tired of standing all the time. But he fidgets while sitting.

Sal asks, "Josh, you nadda more walkin like a duck. You feelin' mucha better?"

It's all I can do to hold in a laugh, as Josh responds, "All is fine and I'm feeling more up to par, just needed a good rest."

Joshua then relates to Sal and David what happened to Jed and Belinda at the carnival.

"Sal, you have been very kind to care for us in your camp but it would be dangerous for us to stay here any longer. No telling what those young men may be thinking. They may want to even the score from last night. How about the rest of you? We can head out in the morning. If no one has any objections."

We all nod in agreement and then confirm David's plan to take Jed and Belinda to Middleborough, where Mr. Hawthorne's safe house is located.

We then retire for the evening.

Chapter Eighteen

James Hawthorne

We are going now, but Maria will stay behind. She says "I help Carnival people make plans to leave."

Sal's eyes are wet as he blows his nose into his big red bandanna. Maria gives me a quick hug and a kiss on both cheeks; and then it's David's turn.

One by one she goes down the line kissing everyone goodbye.

Children come from behind the wagon, giggling behind their hands, till I wave them closer.

"Hurry, we are leaving and we must say Good bye."

Then, they run to hug me.

Jedediah holds out wooden tops he's been carving. The children look up at Sal, first. Then they take the tops with a soft, "Thank you."

"Joshua, where is your handkerchief? My eyes . . . oh, thank you." Tears brim up then drip down. My head pushes against his chest.

"This camp—such good people, good friends. They are like family now."

"Yes, Helen, and the youngsters remind me of our boys and I yearn to get back to them. Now get a grip on yourself; let's see those tears dry up."

Sal jumps down, grabs my arm and tells Joshua, "Never you a mind. Whatsa matter for you, for alla you? Donna be worryin. Go ahead an give a good cry. What you think God give a you alla tears for? You gonna miss stayin here? If you don't a cry, I think you no like us no more. An can't wait to go." Then I cried some more but I did feel a whole lot better.

Sal grabs a new bandanna from Maria's hand and ties it round his head. He says "C'mon jump up and get a youselfs all in. Gotta get a goin."

Then cracking a whip over his horses we're off, leaving the camp. Nothing but dust covers our tracks till we get to better pathways.

Sal's singing a merry tune, something like, "travelin a road, gonna go on a bigga trip, gonna go backa home. Val da ree, val da ry! Hey, you like a my song? I make up a lotta words."

Joshua let me sleep, until Sal shouted, "You all need a stop? Hold on, I find a one." He went down a small lane, off the road. "Here's plenny a bush, this a good for alla you."

Finally, here we are. Joshua asks David, "Is this really our destination? Is this Middleborough? Where is the house?"

David says, "It's quite hidden from view."

Sal says "Nice, you see? An lotta trees. Quiet, an justa right for keepin a nosey people out."

Joshua says, "Here's what looks to be a pathway. David, come with me to the house. Everyone stay here until our friend, Mr. Hawthorne meets us. We need to show him we've escorted 'friends' from Fairhaven."

Here comes Josh and David with an elderly colored man. He sports a gray beard but sadly, has a noticeable limp. He sticks his hand out and welcomes Jedediah. Then turns to Belinda.

"You are a welcome addition, too, my lady."

Now he leads me with Joshua and David following—we're on a tree lined path to his home. It's a large stone house. And all around are white birch trees. They shade a well-maintained lawn.

We enter through the front door. At first look, I can see this home should certainly do them till they can get further north. He leads us to the back into a library filled with books. I feel the leather cover of one.

He says, "Wait." He pushes on one wall panel—it rotates and opens to a large area.

"These two rooms are hidden from the rest of the house. This kitchen area has running water and a stove for cooking—."

Joshua says, "Excuse me Mr. Hawthorne but David had mentioned that you were a former slave. And the original owner left you this home?"

"That's true but it was many years ago—and please call me Jim. You see, when I escaped it was well before the Fugitive Slave Act was passed. And, before what is now referred to as the underground railroad. I arrived at William Hawthorne's house mostly on my own. I worked for him for many years until he passed away and left this property to me in his will."

Joshua says, "Tell me about your fine library. I ask because I have always loved books, and learned so much through them. Your speech is such, that well, pardon me if I might sound a bit forward—but you speak perfect English."

"Thank you. Mr. Hawthorne, whose name I have taken, was my mentor. I spent many hours in his library, under his tutelage. I've read nearly every book in the library we just came through."

I say, "Might I ask, if you were ever married?"

"Yes, but my wife passed away during childbirth."

"I'm sorry to hear that."

"Our son, the one she gave birth to, is living in Vermont and is very active in helping escaped slaves to freedom. I'm very proud of him. And sometime he does drop by. Our two new guests will meet him soon."

""That's good of you. I'm sure they will be pleased."

"Now I shall show you what these two rooms have to offer. You'll note that there are no windows except for those two large skylights in the roof above. So, there is complete privacy. The back room is the bedroom."

He points to the left of the skylights and says, "That opening up there leads to the top of the barn loft attached to the back of this house. Now follow me."

He leads us to the right side of the kitchen and down a flight of stairs.

"Keep your heads low and you may have to bend a bit. This tunnel is very dark. Wait until I light my lantern."

David asks, "Where are you taking us?"

"Do not fret, David, we're almost there."

Jedediah and Belinda hang back. They clutch at each other's hands. I shake my head and motion for them to hurry along. I see a light at the end of the tunnel. We walk out onto a green area beside a brook.

I ask, "The water runs, so is it a good place to wash?"

"Ah, yes. In warm weather, it is used for bathing and washing clothes. It is completely hidden from view.'

He looks at Jed and Belinda, "You'll have to be careful not to make much noise out here." They smile now. At last I believe they are more relaxed.

"OK, let us all go back to the library. Watch your head again as we go through the tunnel."

We sit round a table in the library. Mr. Hawthorne brings us tea and biscuits. My goodness, what a gracious man he is.

Josh says, "Mr. Hawthorne or rather Jim, seeing that you're so well educated, have you ever thought of writing a book about your experiences? I mean, not only during your life as a slave—but your current involvement with the underground railroad?"

"I've thought about it. I've always admired Frederick Douglass and I've read his book the 'Narrative of the Life of Frederick Douglass, an American Slave.' However, I doubt if I could be more eloquent than he, in portraying the evils of slavery."

Joshua says, "I imagine you'd add a good bit to the history of those days."

"I suppose I'd be able to contribute to the narrative. There are very few of us who could tell the real story of what it is like to be a slave."

"Why is that, Jim?"

"Almost all slaves are unable to read and write because their masters prohibit them. They do not want them to learn about the outside world."

David says, "I heard there were laws forbidding anyone to teach slaves how to read."

"Yes, they should only know about working on a plantation and to understand their role in that life. Slaves must accept being subservient to their master. Most are born into that environment and know no other life."

I say, "But if they are severely beaten, a slave would want to run."

"Yes, and some do, but many accept the punishment. It's as if they feel that they are to blame and hope to get back in the good graces of their master. They know of no other way of life."

David says, "Jim, what a shame, how this all plays out. Hope to God it all ends soon, and every man and woman can be free."

"That's another reason why I could not contemplate writing of my days, not now—not for a long time would I. No, it would be too risky, while too many still need our help. We must maintain our secrecy."

Jed says, "I gets lotta tales t' tell bout why we runs away. No suh, aint gon' go back. Belinda ain't gon' let no man—." Belinda tugs at his arm.

"Sorry, Lindy Bell. I gotta say, I jess hadda git out, cuz I gon' be hurtin ole Masta if I stayin. Yessuh, no nex times he gon' git t' whippin my Lindy Bell—he allus actin mean as a ole Devil pushin his whip."

Now where did Jim go? He never said a word.

"Joshua? Did Jim say . . . oh, here he is."

"I have some photos, I'd like to show you. These plantation slaves are dressed in their Sunday best. Their master shows off his slaves, as if one big happy family. But, do you see any smiles on their faces?" [32.a]

Jed picks up two of the photos and says, "No man lookin happy."

Belinda says, "I cain't see em smile, cuz I ain't lookin t' put smilin faces on my fam'ly. I jess hopin any still roun dint get beaten, cuz a me."

I say, "Jedediah. You and Belinda are two of the lucky ones to run away from that life. Let's hope the Lord guides you to the North for freedom ever after."

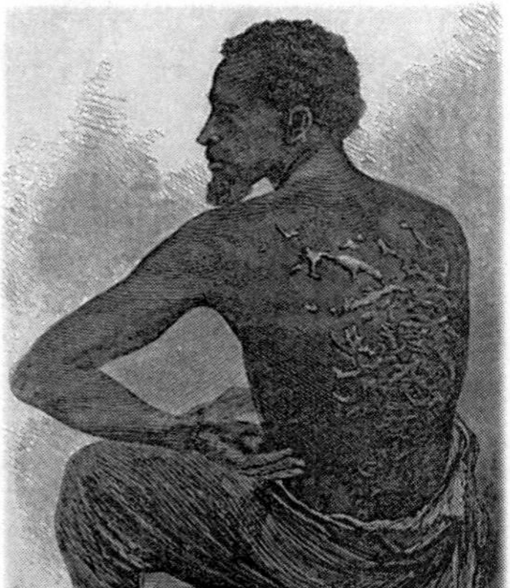

Jim says, "For those managing to escape? They'll carry the story of their captivity on their backs. Take a look at this picture from a newspaper." [32.a]

I ask, "Those are horrible scars, what caused them?"

"A Cat-O-Nine-Tails was commonly used. A whip with several smaller ends to it. But in this case, he might have suffered a severe beating with a whip."

I say, "Jed has similar scars on his back." Jed turns his face.

"I'm sorry Jed. I should not have mentioned that." Belinda goes over to him and puts her arm around his shoulders. I hurry to Jed and hold his hands in mine.

Joshua says, "Jim, you say because many slaves have been kept illiterate, that they cannot write about their life on the plantation?"

"Yes, that's my point. Even if they do get set free, many stories will be lost forever. Some could last through telling from one generation to the other. But there will rarely be a written record."

Joshua says, "How sad, but perhaps we can help spread their stories in some way?" I wonder if Josh means printing out the tales once he has his own print shop?"

Jim says, "Here, you can take these pictures if you'd like. Just do not say where they came from."

I say, "Thank you for taking in Jed and Belinda. Now we should not be overstaying our welcome."

Joshua, says "Yes, we should now take our leave."

Jim says, "Wait, I won't be long."

In no time, here he is again.

"Mrs. Haskell, please take this bag of biscuits for your sister and Mr. Salavino. They've been very patient waiting this long. Jedediah and Belinda, it's time for you to go with them to say your final goodbyes. I'll await your return."

Joshua leads and we follow. I am so relieved to know about this place, with this nice man who will be harboring his guests. Yes—guests are what he calls them.

"Lily, you'll be pleased to hear this. Best of all, it has more than one room, and an underground tunnel leads to a brook. It'll be so easy for washing clothes and bathing. Here Lily and you too Sal—take these biscuits as a gift from Mr. Hawthorne. He is such a nice gentleman."

David shakes Jedediah's hand and gives Belinda a hug.

Jed says, "Thank you, Mistuh David and thank you Mistuh Josh. We beholden to you."

They grab their belongings, and I hug both.

Lily beckons them to get closer. She whispers, "Jed, Belinda, be careful. Per chance when danger is all past, we can meet again?"

"Sure, Missus Lily, I tells a ridin man t' take a lettuh t' Mistuh Sal, mebbe? An mebbe he gon' take us t' see y'all?"

He holds Lily's hands in both of his, and says, "Thank you, Missus Lily." Belinda says, "Jed been learnin t' talk real good, caint y'all tell?" She puts her hand on Lily's shoulder and gives her a kiss on the forehead.

Jed grins then clutches Belinda's hand to hurry off. Before rounding the house, they stop— look back and wave.

At the train station, Sal says, "You come a back any time you wanna place to rest. In Sal's Vardo, you always gonna be safe."

Finally, Sal waves his hat in the air, and tells his horses to "Giddy up."

I hear that steam whistle, it steadily blows, as the clickety-clacking gets faster—till the rocking motions put Lily to sleep in my arms. So peaceful she looks, but her skin has red spots on her wrists. I gently push her sleeve back and can see her elbow. It, too, has a red area on the bony part.

I fish through my satchel. Found this paper I got from David before we left Ginny-town. Later, I'll put it in my journal.

Dear Helen,

We have no cure; just help her be peaceful, suffering as little as possible. Use these potions specially made for her. When she cannot get out of bed on her own, keep her turned every few hours. Her skin is too weak and like parchment—we cannot allow any sores building up. Just let nature take its course. God will step in, one way or another.

We doctors are only men and can never predict what the future may bring. Another thing, it appears that Maria gave her some grape juice Sal had made. It seems to have aged a bit, and has a calming effect. Let her have it, since it cannot hurt at this point. It should help lessen her pain. She is against strong drink. No matter, just do not tell her what it really is.

Your friend, David Hatcher

Hope David can get word to Lily's husband, Jack, on how bad off Lily's been doing. Be good if he can find time away from his important business and his taverns. The Lord only knows why he needs to get himself fortified with whiskey. He should get a good jolt from above and come to see her.

How I fell fast asleep, I don't know. I did so want to enjoy my first train ride. Now that I'm awake all the familiar hills and farmlands slowly pass on by. They tug at my heart and the train needs to go faster and faster. Soon, I will be with my boys again.

God bless you, Jedediah and Belinda, wherever you land up.

Chapter Nineteen

Abigail's Dinner

The whistle blows, steam hisses from the boiler and the train pulls into Randolph depot.

Joshua nudges me. "We're here. It's time to come full awake."

"Oh, but I have been. How could I sleep knowing I'll see the boys soon? Joshua, do you think the boys have had good care?"

"I'm sure Jacob and Abigail have managed in my absence but the boys were quite saddened by your leaving. They'll be glad to see you."

Joshua jumps off the train first. He helps me off and then Lily. Joshua leaves while we wait by the luggage. Lily sits on the big trunk.

Is that one of the Elders with a wagon? Yes, Joshua is riding with him. Leave it to Joshua, he always finds a way.

The wagon ride was bumpy but it wasn't such a long ride—in fact, the best I've had, yes, very enjoyable—especially since I'll soon see the boys. We're almost at the cabin and there in the field, I see Rufus and Caspar.

I ask Joshua, "Have we time to stop and say a quick hello?"

"Don't see why not; they've become almost like family since working their own plot out here."

He asks the Elder to pull up. Joshua waves his hat, yelling for the men to "Come over!"

"Caspar, Rufus please meet my sister from Fairhaven. This is Lily."

Rufus takes his hat off, then, says, "Please t' meet ye, Ma'am."

Caspar doffs his cap, "Same here, Ma'am."

Then looking at me and Joshua, he says, "An, glad t' see y'all back, safe an sound. Bess git on in an see dem chillun; dey sure been missin y'all. Elisha allus been askin, 'yuh seen my Ma an Pa comin down de trail t' day?' An Cal been sayin, 'Ma's comin home, ya know.'"

Rufus joins in, "An Caleb sure been makin us laff, as he pulls dat toy waggon all over; yessuh, he been stuffin his frogs an turtles in it. Den, aksin fer help tuh fine em cuz he been loosin em haff de time."

I said, "That warms my heart, how you two look out for our boys, and such patience you have. But, we have to hurry home. We shall get together soon. Please come for supper whenever you can?"

Caspar says, "That be nice an we's sure can. Thank ye, Ma'am."

Getting closer to the cabin, Lily says, "Who is that looking through the window? That blond hair, such a tow head. Can it be Elisha? He's looking like Joshua more and more. Look how he's grown since last I laid eyes on him."

Abigail runs out the door. Behind her comes Elisha and Caleb.

Elisha calls out, "Ma! I seen you and you brung Aunt Lily?"

What a sight for sore eyes, these two boys.

Joshua says to me, "Time to let our friend, the Elder, get back to his farm."

He thanks him and says, "Of course if ever needing a good turn, just call on me, OK?"

I clamber down from the wagon and they jump at me, both at the same time. My arms stretch out as I gather them in. Then all four of us are giving and taking a whole bunch of hugs and kisses.

Here's Jacob coming from the barn, bringing milk buckets. He stops short, sets down the milk and then runs up to Joshua, throwing his arms round his brother's neck, hugging and patting him on the back.

We settle in. Josh and Jake takes the boys to the barn for the chores. Abigail hovers around me. Why is she acting so eager to talk?

"First days, Helen, I was so busy. There was no time for resting at all. You must be made of iron. I tried to follow the list you left but soon fell short. I had no way to keep up with it all. And carrying milk buckets? Just one of them proved too heavy for me. My hands hurt so bad, and my fingernails were so awful to look at.'

"When I got to the hen house, oh my goodness. I never realized how far down the hill it was. Jacob was such a big help, though. He took over my outside chores."

Oh, my Lord, Josh was here, and he let her get away with that?"

Joshua enters the house and she talks softer now . . . her voice is not so much of a whine. No, it's more like a kitten purring.

Look at her bustling around. What is she up to? Can't put my finger on it, but . . . she's busying herself, wearing my best apron. Now I understand. She sidles in with a tray of my best mugs. She's offers tea or coffee to Joshua. Coffee? Time to step in, I do believe.

"Abigail there's no need. I'm here now so you can be my guest again."

Abigail says, "I can manage. Just sit in your rocking chair and I shall prepare our meal." And who am I, just a guest?

Now she straightens the table, clearing it off, before covering it in my best lace table cloth. What's this? Lighting the candles? It's not dark yet. Where'd she find my silver candle sticks?

She says, "Would you like your deerskin slippers, Josh, the ones we found before you left to go to Fairhaven?" If she dares to put those slippers on him, I'll pull her hair out. Yes, I will.

Josh says, "Do not bother yourself, Abigail, I can manage just fine. Helen is here now to take care of my needs. Truth be told, I can do for myself on most things."

Well, bully for him at last to speak his mind. Once again, I'm controlling my temper. Inside my head, Ma's voice is sounding off, telling me "Do not speak at all, if you cannot think of a nice thing to be said." But my tongue hurts from biting it so much.

So, I say, "Well, Abigail, we are certainly beholden to you for agreeing to stay on here while I was gone. We wish to thank you for minding the children while Joshua came to fetch me and Lily."

* * *

I've noticed in the past two days that Abigail has taken to wearing rouge and lip paint. Friends frown on acting the fancy lady. She's been wearing those finer go-to-Meeting, Sunday clothes. But, she doesn't go to Meetings. She stays in the cabin, except on occasion she'll venture outside. Especially if she sees Joshua out there doing chores.

Joshua said, "Don't let her bother you. That's just Abigail for you."

Time for me to speak up. "Goodness gracious, Abigail you must miss your family back in Windsor. Will you be leaving soon?"

"Soon? Why do you ask? You are my family now and I'm really enjoying my stay here. You both need me more than ever with all your ailments."

That's it! Josh and I have to talk.

I take him aside. I say, "She really must go, don't you agree?"

"Yes. She's been putting on some strange airs around me. I'm sure you've noticed?"

"I'd have to be blind not to. She's started this fluttering of her eyelids. Is she trying to get your attention?"

"Yes, it's made me uncomfortable. How do we convince her it's time to go?"

"Leave it to me."

"Oh, Abigail, come here, will you? Maria, the wife of the Gypsy leader, Sal . . . she gave me recipes. Take a gander at these greens. All fit for a King, and best eaten in their natural state."

"Let me see. Move your hand. Is this . . . aren't these weeds? Helen, those are just dandelions. I can't believe—."

"But, the dark green ones are tasty. We'll add a bit of oil and vinegar. For the flowers, I'll steep in boiling water for a minute with a dash of sugar." She goes to the back room and shuts the door.

I call out, "Abigail? I need you. Come with me to my garden? Put your cloak on, it is a bit chilly."

Ah, just what I need. I reach down to gather them up. I hand her a few.

She fast snatches her hand away, and jumps back. "What? No! Get them away!" I pick them up again, poor things. They just need a good wiping with my apron. They aren't slippery now.

"See? So big and healthy. In France, they are a delicacy. Come now, stop shaking. You'll not be worried, if you know the name. It's Es-Cargo. Only the upper classes can afford to eat them."

"They're ugly. No matter what you say. They are nothing but snails. Don't give them to me."

"Abigail, settle down, you've no idea how this will all come together. Now we need gather our chestnuts. They must be fresh as can be, with no cooking. Another of Joshua's favorites."

"No, they must be bitter, I'm sure."

"Maria said 'Don't put them to the fire, as heat destroys their goodness.'"

"Joshua can have my share, I do not believe I want any."

"That's your choice, Abigail. I will gather them later. Come along, we've lots to prepare."

Joshua's nose is stuck in a book. She walks ahead, and I look back. He winks at me.

She turns back, grabs my arm. "I must ask, Helen, do you really need my help? I was already cooking a big stew. Can't your new recipe wait?"

"It won't go to waste, that stew will keep. Yet, from now on we shall eat much better. As they say, an apple a day keeps the doctor away, and this new food will keep worries from our door."

I bring a snail from my pocket. "See, how grand he is? We must hurry as they need be devoured as fresh as can be. Again, no cooking for these fellows." Her hand covers her mouth.

"Maria said to hurry the snails along with the chestnuts. They must get to the table soon as the dandelions get to a plate."

Joshua nods and lays down his book. He says, "Sounds delicious, and I will need a good share. I've read on them just now. Snails are not cooked. Like raw oysters—it's really the best way to eat them."

Abigail steps back, goes to sit down. She must not realize there's no chair behind her. I hold her steady and walk her to the table, pull out a chair. I hear strange sounds. Is she gulping or is it gagging?

"Take this, Abigail, it should help when the stomach feels queasy. Sal and the others save this from the Cod fish they catch. Here, take a spoonful."

She gulps it down, then turns and walks to the hallway. Now she winces, and I hear a, yes, it's a burp. She's back at the table. Sitting. Silence surrounds us, and I love it.

Joshua comes up behind me, and says, "I'm famished. Is our grand meal almost ready?"

What's this? Abigail covers her mouth, pushes her chair back and stands. She holds onto the table. I go to help her, but she rushes to the door.

She turns and says, "Helen. I must go outdoors for . . . uh, some private matters."

While she's gone, I grab a basket. Must round up more snails. I hurry to our Chestnut tree. Oh no, it's way too soon. None are on the ground. Walnuts will have to do—so I must run. Here's plenty in our storage shed. I can't wait to get this meal all spread out, waiting for the arrival of the Queen.

Joshua asks, "Helen, have you noticed? Abigail has not returned from her private time as yet. Should you go find her? Or shall I?"

"Neither of us. It would be embarrassing, I should think."

Everything is all set out and here comes Abigail. I wait, but she does not sit at the table. She stares at all the healthy food I prepared. Then puts her hand over her mouth and backs away. She's off again. I take it she is heading to the private place.

I wish she'd stay in here, and stop all the running back and forth. Dark is coming on and supper hour is near over. Cal calls from his room, "Why can't we eat?"

The back door opens, and look what the cat dragged in.

She looks rather pale. "Helen, I think I should leave today. I must have an allergy—perhaps the feathers and dust from the hen house? Also, my dear father is worried about my absence. He has wanted me to return to relieve his mind."

I shake my head, as I cannot get in a word. I let her finish.

"Ask Jacob if he wants the stew I made. It's ready on the stove. He always loved it. Well, will that be good for you, my departure at this time?"

"Do you have to . . . must you? We shall dearly miss you, but if it's meant to be, then so be it."

Joshua is in his chair. I didn't hear him come in. He smiles at me and nods at her. Then he throws a few hand signs my way. I chuckle but stop short. Abigail has never seen or wanted to understood hand signing, I am sure. I suspect she just wrote out her orders of the day for Jake.

"Can I help you pack? Also, I can bundle up some of this feast for you?" She shakes her head and goes to her room.

Joshua whispers, "Well done, Helen."

When her belongings are ready, Joshua flags down the post delivery man. Ah, good, he drives his coach today. The rider says he'll drive her to the train station, and hauls her steamer trunk up to set beside him.

Joshua carries Cal out and they stand with me. Cal is chewing on a cookie. This one time I shall not scold him. Eli waves one time, then ducks back into our cabin. Cal scrambles out of his Pa's arms, and trails after his big brother. Rufus and Caspar did not come in from the fields. Where's Jacob? Probably finishing all of Abigail's chores.

Joshua chuckles, then says, "That's done with. Will you tend to the grand feast still setting on the table, or shall I? Where should I dump it?"

"It can't be fit anywhere but the slops for the pig sty. But please put the snails back in my garden, will you?"

Everyone's left me alone on my porch and I relish the moment.

Abigail is in the mail coach. And thankfully she'll get delivered to her rightful home. There it goes. It rounds the last bend in the road. Finally, it's gone at last.

How beautiful this day is. How utterly charming the clouds look. Some on the horizon are quite dark. We shall have a grand downpour. The fresh water will help wash away any lingering stale air.

"Joshua, Elisha, Caleb! Fetch Aunt Lily and come to supper. Has anyone seen Jacob—never mind—I'll put some aside for him. Come to the table. Smell this wonderful stew. Abigail made it for us."

Not a peep out of Lily since supper. I must look in on her.

She's resting but so still, not moving as much. Look closer, check her breathing. Good, it's in and out—at a slow pace, but quite even. I can take this empty glass and wash it—the one that held her grape juice.

David had said, "Fine, let her have it whenever she asks. It will help get her through each day."

Chapter Twenty

Facing Reality

Spring in Vermont is one of the best times of the year. We are outside today, and Lily is sitting under the big maple tree. She wears a light shawl. The boys play in the lower field. They whoop it up, racing back and forth with broomsticks between their legs.

David sends posts to Lily about once a week, if not sooner. He tries to help her think ahead.

She says, "Helen, I hope this sickness goes away soon. If not, I hope I go peacefully at the end."

"Oh no, Lily don't say that. It just takes some good Vermont air and sunny days to help you."

Joshua is just as worried as I am but I'm thinking he has to show his strength more and cannot let on with the exact way he feels.

Out of Lily's hearing he says, "Remember, David's last letter said he had asked the advice of doctors in Boston. All of them agree this sickness is common among mill workers."

"Tell me if we can hope?"

"He said that they had suspicions that the breathing problems stemmed from poor ventilation in the cotton mills. Cotton fibers most likely got inhaled, and long exposure did a lot of damage.'

"David also noted that the yellow tinge to her skin, the needing to sleep, taking frequent naps; it all fits what he believed was her undoing."

"Are you certain that David said there was no cure."

Josh continues, "Remember, David said we should just keep her going as long as we can, giving the same love and attention he knows she is getting."

***

Spring has turned fast to summer. Sweet smelling honeysuckle is hanging in the air, making it nice to be catching a whiff in the early morning breezes.

Joshua's arm has completely healed. Lily has good days and then again, bad days follow right behind. The boys have been acting like boys do with their usual ways, whooping it up and having a grand time. I'm so glad to be home again with things getting to be the same as always.

Jacob seems happy, but at times I can see a mournful look to his eyes. He's been taking to waiting every day for the post to arrive, when before he never showed much interest in any mail coming in.

I'm just wondering if Abigail and Jacob might have been getting a bit too close? No, what a thought to be holding. Even Abigail would hold back and know better.

Joshua's finding time to write more of his poems which he loves to do. I love to read them as he's always wanting me to be the first to look at any. Joshua's writings are good for Lily, too. They help get her mind off her sickness. Still, I must own up to it, she's not getting better. I sense it's only these warm summer days that's helping. Though she's now smiling, I fear she won't be lasting through to winter.

On warm days we go down to Ayer's brook. In our basket is plenty of dried up bread. We set ourselves down on the cool grass. I take off our boots and run blades of grass through our toes. Same as we both did when young girls. We made rings and necklaces of long straw pieces. The boys call out for the ducks to come, but they only cower across the brook.

I find a long blade of grass and stretch it between my thumbs. Make sure it's taut, then I take a deep breath to blow into it. What a sound! Just like a honking of a duck.

One gets too close and Cal chases it back to the brook. But more keep circling round us.

Eli stands in front of Lily.

He yells, "Shoo, get away! Come back another day! Hey, Ma, it rhymes. Am I a poet like Pa?" I am laughing so hard I cannot answer. And Lily? She has a wisp of a smile.

A swarm of butterflies land on the clover. When we looked for wild flowers for Ma, we always ran to catch them. But now? Of course, Lily cannot try to run. And it's been a while since she walked on her own.

Lily's not been eating much and I cannot see any meat sticking to her bones. Some fever comes and goes. Now her forehead is hot. I dip this facecloth in the brook. And hurry to hold it to her brow.

I'm so glad we agreed with David that we shan't let any doctor do any of the new practices on her. I would not want to get plunged into a cold bath or a brook. And, I will not let anyone do that to Lily. Or that ghastly bloodletting some doctors advise? No, and David agreed.

Morning chores are done. The mid-day meal is finished. I'm wondering what next to do. Joshua comes in. He's alone, after taking the boys to Meeting Hall.

"Joshua? Is that you? I meant to mention a dream I had last night. It was so odd. I dreamt of a woman, with light hair, in a field. It was a field of golden barley but nothing more could I see."

"Strange. Did you not recognize her?"

"No, but my dreams are usually that way, as if I am supposed to figure them out. I'd just as soon forget about it."

"C'mon Helen, our boys are going to be staying there for a bit. They'll be learning their church lessons. Then there's a picnic in the back, with the Elders and their wives in attendance. So take off your apron, grab a shawl—and let's be off. How's that sound, just the two of us?"

"Don't bother asking me twice. Yes, a long time, too long since we took some time together."

Hand in hand we start towards the Indian trail. Next, we're breaking into a run. If only we were kids again with not a thing to worry about. Now we slow down and take deep breaths. The warm summer breezes bring honeysuckle and lilac smells to float all around us.

"Ah, Helen, does this bring back sweet memories? You know—the same as when we first married?"

"Yes, and without a care to bother us we would run through the tall grasses till our breaths gave out and then—just like now, we'd collapse on the ground."

* * *

We leave the tall grass and first Joshua brushes the hay seeds from my arms and the back of my neck. Then I return the favor. My turn takes a bit longer since he has more seeds clinging to him. Well, the last of the poison ivy left Joshua quite a while ago and with no telltale signs.

"Helen, here's the old elm tree bearing the likenesses of Running Dear, White Feather and their baby."

"It's been some time since we've been this way."

Joshua says; "Well, I brought Abigail here one time. Told her about that Indian legend."

"When was that?"

"While you were at Lily's home."

"Why are you just now telling me this—was that your secret with her? Why she felt so cozy, and did not hide her feelings when I was present?"

"Of course not, Helen, just calm yourself. We took walks when chores were done. Only to regain my strength till my arm healed. She was a good companion."

A good companion—was she? I bite my lip and say no more.

Now we're halfway along the Indian trail and we come to a clearing. Joshua grabs my arm and makes me stop. He points across the meadow. It's Jacob sitting on a log in the shade of a big maple tree.

Josh says, "Don't make a sound or a sudden movement. We'll let him be."

"There is such a sad, melancholy look about him."

Josh whispers, "Let's go back, we'll take a cross cut. Watch it, don't step on the dead branches. Walk behind me. Make sure he does not see us—and he cannot know we've seen him."

We hurry and in no time, we're back to our land.

"Joshua, I don't like what I saw in Jacob's eyes. I've never seen him so upset, as if something is tormenting him. Had you noticed changes in him? I mean after Abigail left. I've been meaning to ask you."

"Yes, but nothing like this. He's keeping something inside and it should be let out, before it breaks out of him the wrong way. Aye, Helen. I've seen changes in Jacob. I've tried to whittle it out of him but Jacob can be stubborn, making him as clumsy in his thinking as a pig on ice. He just won't sign or write anything to me. His mind locks up so tight and there's no way to get any answers out of him."

"Joshua, in the past, Jacob's been telling me confidences he dares not share with others. If you agree, I shall go to his cabin this evening. I can take some preserves, Apple sauce—and of course Apple jelly, the two that he favors."

Joshua thinks on it and then nods his head. He sighs first before answering. "Yes, it just might work at that. At least you could give it a try."

That evening Joshua stays with the boys while I walk over to Jacob's cabin. A long walk, but the air feels good.

Approaching his cabin, I can see no light from his windows. No lanterns glowing, not even a candle light to brighten away the darkness.

He could be out to the barn, tending the cows and sheep. As I step up on the porch, I can now hear him moving about. He must know I'm out here. What's taking him so long to open the door? I wait.

At long last he bids me come in but doesn't look at me. Instead, he scurries around to light his lantern and attempts to start a fire in the fireplace.

Clothes lay in a heap on the floor. Scraps of food litter the table and dishes need washing. His stove is all greasy with bits of food stuck on top.

Jacob then sits next to me at the table and cracks a smile but it does not last. He grabs an old rag near his trash bin, wets it at the pump and tries to wipe down the table.

I sign to him, "Jacob, sit right here and be still."

I side the table, put on a kettle of water for dishes and then start cleaning his place. His dogs need more food and water. I hand their dishes to Jake to fill up.

Finally, it's all finished. The cleaning is done and well enough for now.

I sign to him, "Why have you been acting so strange lately?"

Jacob, signs, "Do not worry, I shall be alright. It is just a small fever."

Signing back, "Jacob, you're such a fib teller. I shall not leave till you tell me what's been ailing you. C'mon look up, right at me. We've been close for a long time, same as one of my own family and of course Joshua wants to help you, too. But we cannot help unless we know what bothers you. Tell me, Jacob, please?"

Jacob went to a cupboard. He scrambled in it for a bit, before he found his pencil and paper. Then he signs, "Not to look till I finish."

Might as well put the kettle back on the stove and make both of us a cuppa tea. I set rolls with apple jelly beside him. His eyes brighten up some and then at last he smiles weakly and hands me what he wrote.

Helen, I am such the fool. While you and Joshua been gone, Abigail was good friend. We took walks. She wrote to me at night. Wrote, how nice I look. How strong and how she liked me. Wanted me as best friend. Forever.

Abby is so beautiful. Most women folk never want much to do with me. Not for dancing. Not at Church functions. They never sat by me at picnics. Abby was lonely.

I put arms round her. Tried to comfort. Then she kissed me. Right on my lips. Not on cheek. I fell in love with her. My beautiful Abigail. Only woman to look at me and want to stay with me.

He barely finished the biscuits, but scraped the last of the jelly from the jar. I continue to read what he wrote.

Then, at night we cuddle under one blanket. One thing led to another. Each night we laughed, played games, and now she has gone. My heart aches so much. Only she can make me happy. But she left. And no goodbye. No goodbye for me.

Poor Jacob. Abigail went too far, flirting and sashaying round and all. In Jacobs words, what Abigail did shows what she was. Not a friend, not even a neighbor would do the same as Abigail.

I am a fool. I wanted to marry. I wanted children. Same as Joshua. Ma said I was as good as any man.

I stop reading and sign to him.

"Jacob, you are just as good as any other man and better than most. You must never doubt that for one moment. I read what you wrote about your Ma saying that when you got older you could marry, too. She was right. You are dependable most times and try to follow the golden rule. 'Do unto others as you would have them do unto you.' And you always give help when needed."

He signs back, "I am not that good am I? Don't try to make me happy by saying things not true."

"Jake, you know I do not lie. I know you, same as your Ma must've known. You would never hurt a living thing. Certainly, not another human being. You are without a temper and love children. We see it when you play with Caleb and Elisha. You'd be a wonderful husband to the nice lady you surely will meet some day."

He continues signing, "My insides are churning round. Am I sick? My stomach cannot think of food. My head is stuffed up. Cannot stop thinking about Abby. The pain will not stop—will not go away. How can you and Joshua help me?"

Oh Lord. How cruel, to lead him on as she did. Has she no feelings for others? Did she have no church teachings that sunk in when she was little, to help guide her later on?

I stick my head close to his; let him see my mouth moving to understand what I say.

"Jacob, you should be feeling lucky and should not be grieving over this. You must believe that it is her loss not yours. She was not taking time to really know you. It's her bad luck and not yours. Do not be worrying one whit longer. She was not good enough by far. She did not deserve such a man as you, Jacob. I trust that Joshua will figure on a plan, what best to do. You can set your mind at ease."

I give Jacob a hug and sign again to him. "I know what pain you're having, and can rightly feel it. We shall stand by you and see you through to better days. You come to dinner at our place tomorrow. Joshua and the boys will be very glad to see you."

Jacob sat still for the longest time, looking at the flames in his fireplace. Then he turns to me and nods OK.

It's dark, and no moon to guide me, but swinging one of Jacob's Lanterns, I can slowly trod through, or round, anything I might trip over. I can easily find my way back to our cabin.

Joshua opens the door before I have a chance to grab on to the latch. Before taking off my cloak, I hand over Jacob's writings.

He spreads the papers on the table.

When Joshua finishes, he pulls out a chair at the kitchen table and says, "Please sit with me, Helen."

"Well, what do you make of it?"

"I see he's been calling her Abby and their relationship was more than just friends. Ah, poor Jacob, I had no idea how much she meant to him.'

"Helen, I've been very lucky."

"Oh? What do you mean?"

"I never knew the hurt that Jake must be feeling. After all, I didn't end up with a woman like her."

"Joshua, I'm just glad to be rid of her."

"I have the same thoughts about her character but we must be careful with what we say to Jacob. In his case, 'Love is truly blind'. He has set her on a pedestal and naught what we say would make a difference."

"I've seen that she thinks only about what she wants and with no room in her heart to consider another's feelings. I heard what happened with Nathan. She described the details, at least her version. She was so taken with him; said he had such great attraction."

"Yes, Helen, and Nathan told of her being so forward with other men; tales he'd heard of but did not want them repeated. But never did I once think she'd set her sights on Jacob"

I ask, "What can we do?"

"I'll think on it, but I know we must not knock Abigail off that pedestal just yet. We must go slow and be careful with Jacob. So sit with me this evening and we'll put our thoughts on paper—then we'll be ready for Jacob when he comes by tomorrow"

***

Mid-day and Jacob's here. He has his carving tools with him, and holds up a small wagon. He signs, "Get Eli and Cal? We can fix wheels."

I must finish sweeping up inside. Wait, such a commotion? I peek outside . . . it's only giggling and laughing. Jake swings each one round. Rough housing again. Now he holds Eli's arm and leg, spins him and dips him up and down. Over and over.

Eli laughs, then yells, "Stop! Dizzy! Put me down!"

Cal rolls on the lawn, then sits up and says "No, keep swinging him. Looks funny." Time to make cocoa and bring out some cookies.

I start cooking our meal. Bacon grease gets poured in the frying pan and when the fat sizzles I let the fish drop in. Jacob's coming in and looking at the stove. He signs, "Is there enough to go 'round?"

"Of course, and for extras to go round again. You go sit at the table. Joshua's there. He wants to talk with you."

Joshua starts by talking about the weather and then asking about his health. Then he signs about a place where schooling for deaf people can be had. It's down on the island of Nantucket and it was what that Lucretia lady told him about.

Jacob understands but he's not looking any different. He just has those same worrying and frowning looks on his face.

Joshua continues signing, "You could, at least, go with us to visit to see if it would be fitting for you. We could stay on for a bit, if you wanted to go around the Island to meet people. There are all kinds of activities, dancing, game playing, fishing trips and trips to the mainland."

Jacob signs, "Perhaps good idea. Or maybe a school near to here would be good?" He might be taking an interest in Joshua's suggestion? Then, Joshua gives the paper we both worked on last night. Jacob starts to read.

Jacob, always remember this. Having a broken heart for whatever reason can be a pain so unbearable, it seems as if it will never stop. It can hurt just as bad or even worse than a real wound. But that pain will only last for a certain length of time. Same as dark clouds go away, when getting pushed aside by sunshine. So, it takes time to heal any wound. But putting happy memories inside to crowd out the place of the bad ones, will heal the hurt just that much sooner.

The pain you now feel can be like having a hornet stinging you in your side and try as you may, you cannot remove its stinger. The pain will not let up. It will hurt like the dickens if you do not remove the stinger. Until you take it out, you will not be rid of it once and for all.'

Jacob's nodding his head, he stops and coughs.

I sign, "What is it? Are you coming down with a bad coughing spell?"

He shakes his head, "No," and continues reading.

After a time with better things happening, you will start to forget the sting and then the pain will go away for good.

What you feel now shall all be in the past and sooner than you think. You can be filling up places in your heart you never thought could be filled again. Meanwhile, you must talk about it. Let the pain come up. Get it out. Let us know how you feel. Don't let the hurt stay inside.

Gradually you'll have only good remembrances to think upon.

For a long time, he did not answer. He just wanted to sit a while. So he did and leaned back in his chair and looked up at the ceiling rafters.

At last he gave a sign, "Yes, I do understand."

Then he signed, "Thank you Helen and Joshua for advice and offer to take me to Nantucket to see lady and her school. After thinking on it I give my answer this way. I have farm here with chores needing to be done.'

"Cannot stand more than one broken heart. If I be leaving you and the boys, the getting well time may never happen. So I stay in Randolph at my own place. Then I work hard to heal my wound. And pull out that stinger."

Have we managed to heal his wound? Only time will tell.

Chapter Twenty-one

The Flower Fades

The sun is shining. Not a trace of dark clouds in the heavens, nor any that threaten to appear from far off.

Lily asks, "Can I go outside?"

We wrap her up warm in my best quilt. Today, she'll try out the new chair Joshua and Jacob made special for her. They fixed it so the back can lower into a bed whenever she wants it that way.

"Joshua, turn her sideways to keep her legs from hitting the doorway on the way out." As if he would not think of it. I must think before I speak sometimes.

He replies, "OK, and can you bring those chair cushions with one pillow for her head?"

"Yes, and my special old quilt needs to be waiting on her chair. I'll hurry on ahead."

I sprinkle lavender water—Ma's favorite—on this covering as he sets her down in her favorite place under the old maple tree.

How curious, Joshua with not a hint of warning is trotting back to the cabin.

"Where are you going?"

"Don't worry, I need to fetch something from the house."

No time for wondering. Lily's legs need covering better. I'll tuck her in all the way up to her chin. Can she smell the wonderful scent of lavender? A smile crosses her lips, so perhaps she does.

That was fast. Here's Joshua coming back and he's holding a package. That's strange. I didn't hear the Post Rider today. How did it get here?

"Lily, Helen, look."

I see, but Lily is fast asleep, "Joshua, when did you get that package?"

"Don't worry, it's for her. Will she sleep very long?"

"Lily, can you hear me? It's Helen. Wake up. Here's a package for you."

She stirs a bit, but does not open her eyes. Maybe she's dreaming of long ago.

"Joshua, see if you can get her to understand."

"Yes, Lily, listen to me. The post rider said his station master told him this package started out at the New Bedford station before landing at ours."

Lily's eyes start to open. "Here's a printed note, Lily, see? It's sticking out. Who could've written it?"

Her hand moves out and grasps it as she squints her eyes and then finally whispers, "Helen . . . please? Can . . . you?"

I read, *"To my dear Lily, please accept this token of my lasting love."*

She lets out a soft cry. I stop and hold her in my arms and let Joshua read the rest of it.

"Ok, I shall continue reading it."

> *"I wanted to bring this gift but cannot make the trip. I have been detained due to my own ill health. Do not be concerned as I am not. The doctor said I just need a good long rest. As we both knew, there were too many business concerns amidst my mother's recent death. Then there was the funeral and all that transpired later."*

Lily pronounces her words slow and very faint. Leaning closer we can hear, "Jack . . . Oh, yes . . . My Jack."

Joshua continues reading.

> *"I have been at a good place to recuperate. I am not suffering any dire illness. Soon I should be up and about and then able to pay you a visit. Until then do not fret over me, as only my dear love's wellbeing is uppermost in my mind.'*
>
> *'This gift was one of many shown to me by my friend. That well-meaning, good hearted soul, Salavino. He thought you might like one of them. It was in the strictest confidence that he informed me how you happened to stay in his camp. I swore my silence. I never betray any trust, especially any concerning you, so my lips are sealed.'*

Lily pushes on her elbows, tries to sit up, until Joshua braces her back with the pillow. She asks, "Where is it? May I . . . Helen, please."

Joshua puts it in her hand. She looks at it and puts it under her blanket holding it close. As she settles back down, Joshua reads on.

> *'When I saw this doll with the exquisite, silken gown, well, it reminded me of the delicate, beautiful lady that I've known, as well as having had the good fortune to wed.'*

"Last and most important, I am writing to say, no judge on earth can tear our marriage asunder. We were joined together under God's eyes and for all eternity and so, I remain, your loving husband, Jack."

My eyes are wet now, so I use the end of my apron to wipe them.

Lily says, "My love . . . my Jack . . . did not . . . forget."

Joshua takes his handkerchief to wipe the tears off her cheeks. He smiles and looks very pleased. Someday, I might tell him how Jack is almost as good a writer as he is.

I nod at him and mouth a thank you. I must remember to never chide him for giving away a doll I admired. Was it kept for a surprise gift at birthday time?

* * *

Days grow short. Lily has no energy, no will to keep awake—at least not for long.

She says, "No, leave me be. I must be done with it." She clutches that doll. Won't let go of it, even when I try to wash her hands. When sleeping for a spell, I slip it out of her grasp, but must replace it before she opens her eyes.

Last night she moaned, then said, "Jack . . . please come here."

Try as I may, Lily cannot eat or drink much of anything. An offer of grape juice only gets a few sips past her mouth. Like as not, it soon pushes back up. A wet cloth is kept handy to dampen her cracked lips. Her chest barely moves—each breath hardly fills her lungs.

Joshua is here to help keep the vigil. I value having him near. It helps me to get through this.

I say, "Look, how painful it must be. With each breath—how she labors to push it back out. Please, Lord give her a rest, a time to get some strength."

Joshua holds me tight to him, and I hear him sniffing. He clears his throat, and stops. We try not to cry in her room, to shield her from our sadness. She must not be afraid, cannot suspect—.

He says, "Her eyes—are half open; yet, they only stare."

I ask, "Lily, can you see me, can you hear?" Her eyes roll back, before closing again. Joshua brushes her hair back from her forehead before putting a wet cloth over it. Then fixes her pillow, and all without her stirring one bit.

He walks to the door and says, "Helen, come out to the hall with me. This is just for your ears."

On the other side of Lily's door, he says, "I was getting some hope yesterday as she looked towards us every chance she could."

"Oh? You saw that, too? Is it a good sign, perhaps—?"

"No, not good. She is so weary. Must be tired of it all.' Joshua lowers his voice so I can barely hear. 'Have you seen—when she mouths a few words? Do you understand her?"

"You've heard it too? The dreadful thing she's wanted me to do?"

"Yes, Helen, and it's too much to ask of anyone. Do not let it bother you."

"Well, I'm at my wit's end. The worrying of what to do. Just this morning, she again pleaded with me. She clung to me with those little bony fingers, begging, 'Please, let me go. I need—.' I walked out of the room. I could not hear any more."

"Helen, I know it's to be expected when hope is gone, and pain won't go away. Did you notice when she does sleep for a short time, that doll stays clutched in her arms?"

"Yes, of course I see that doll, and she won't let me take it. She has strength from I know not where, but she won't let go."

"I've tried myself, and can't pry it loose. Maybe she's just stubborn, same as the other Haskell girl has always been."

I grin, then wipe it off my face. It's no time for it. Still, he does make me smile. He knows how to calm me in the midst of it all.

* * *

It's morning time. "Joshua, wake up. I am getting upset now, and cannot ignore what I saw last night."

"Is this why you sit straight up at the end of our bed, wringing your hands?"

"It startled me so, that I jumped right out of my sleep. It was that same dream about that woman in the field. You recall. I told you before?"

"Thought you forgot all about that?"

"I had, and finally pushed it from my head. Yet, this dream, she's back again, and so stubborn—she will not stay out of my sleep."

"Now what did she do?"

"She was frolicking about in a field of barley and time and again would bend over for a flower. At least that's what I thought. But no, when straightening back up—she had a net, trying to catch a butterfly. . . but they always got free."

"What? Is that all? What did she look like?"

"I seem to remember she was wearing a blue dress with a black cape and long black apron and of course a morning cap."

"Don't worry, Helen, 'twas just a dream. Nothing more."

The sun is with us again. It looks as if, at least for one day and night, Lily has rested. Her lips are still so dry and reddened since she's chewed on them, again.

She writes on her tablet, but just a few lines, "Helen, Joshua . . . take me to the glen. Must go now, please?"

This time we hurry, knowing it is not for a picnic or the usual lazy day just passing the time away. How I wish it could be months far in the future and not right now.

Joshua calls out, "Are you ready yet? Here, while I hold her up, help stick that blanket under." I wrap a blanket round her and we quickly head on out. Let the sun stick around, Lily needs the warm rays and maybe she'll hear a bird sing.

We are here. I sit under the maple tree and my arms reach out for Joshua as he gently hands her over.

He whispers, "Helen, can you see the smile, as it crests on her lips?" Then her head leans over and slowly sinks down to rest on my bodice.

She grows so light in my arms. Her body is not as stiff as before and her face is relaxed, free of the deep frowning marks that marked her pain. The birds are singing.

"Lily, can you hear the birds?" No response.

"Lily can you hear me? Oh no, Lily answer me. Josh, she's not moving." Here comes a breath. It's long and heavy, then it stops. Joshua sits closer as the one last breath leaves her. A butterfly lights on her shoulder and just sits there, never moving.

Then my Lily is so still and she—no, is she—oh Lily don't leave us. Joshua puts his arm round my shoulders. The butterfly lifts off, lightly, circles upward, then flies away.

I kiss her forehead, and whisper, "God be with you. Be at peace. I know God has set you free. You'll be in His care forever."

My tears spill over and a big lump in my throat won't go away but I must talk.

"Joshua, just look at her, she's my young sister. I never wanted anything bad to happen to her. She would never hurt anyone, not deliberately for no reason. Why did it all have to happen, that horrid night when she had to grab that gun. I hope the good Lord will let her in now, where she belongs."

Joshua says nothing. He just stares at me with his eyes clouded over by tears. He bends over and gently picks her up. I wrap the blanket over her legs and arms.

Joshua coughs and says, "Come, follow me back to the house. We'll make Lily all set for her journey."

Back in our cabin, I help clean her up, making her ready for the last goodbyes at our Meeting House. Lily wanted to be admitted to the Friends

Society. It was not a hard thing to do, not like some churches and their requirements for membership. All she needed was to say "Yes, I will allow the Lord in to commune with Him at opportune times, and that way He can show me the way to His everlasting peace."

Joshua says, "Don't fret about where Lily is going. Our Lord will see to having her where she deserves to be. He forgives us all, and never would have a change of mind in taking her in. Besides, we know that He is already within each and every one of us. So of course, He understands all that Lily went through."

"Josh, she was only twenty-four. Now look at her lying there."

"I know, that's the sad part."

Later, when finished making her suitable; I dressed her in her white morning dress, the one with lavender and pink ribbons running through the cuffs and ending with small bows. Her few curls are tucked into her cap and I fib a bit, but say, "You are looking so pretty, just like before you left for the job in the mills." Where is her doll? Oh, I see; it's tucked under her arm where only she knows it will be forever. Joshua must have been in here at one time—of that, I am sure.

My back aches and I stretch a bit before leaning back in my rocker. On the table is the last of the grape juice. Joshua offers it to me.

"Thank you but just a few sips will do. That is all I need. Somehow, knowing Lily is not in pain anymore—a great weight has lifted from my shoulders."

What's that he's writing about, I wonder?

He shows me, and when I've done reading it, he asks "Do you think it will be fit to read during the funeral ceremony?"

"If Lily's looking down upon us—she will love it as much as I do. Yes, you must read your words aloud for all to hear."

Joshua is my fortress; the one I depend on to always be there for me. He is the head of our family, though he often mentions that I am the heart and soul that holds us all together. He didn't come from a fine upstanding, wealthy family like Lily's husband Jack, with his being a lawyer and all. No, he is plain and simple, just like me.

She's finally at rest in the front room and we go to see her again. Have to make certain that nothing was left undone, as she lies on the sofa.

"There now, she looks so pretty. Josh, it reminds me of that morning many years past, when only fifteen, she dressed up in her finest and got ready to leave on her grand adventure. She was so proud to become a factory girl in that mill in Lowell, Massachusetts. I remember, there was a light breeze blowing through her tresses and a smile on her face as she climbed aboard the coach with three other girls and headed south. I still have her letters. They're here in the cabinet. I was just looking at them yesterday."

"May I see them?"

"Josh, could you read them aloud for me. This … is the first one she posted.[33] Will you start with this one?"

Dear Ma and Pa and Dearest Sister Helen *18 July 1843*

The work thus far has kept me busy. The supervisor had me trained on a power loom that makes cotton cloth for bed sheets and such. We begin work each day at five in the morning and finish work at seven in the evening with two thirty minute breaks for lunch and supper. We live in the factory boarding house. Our room has ten girls and we sleep two to a bed. I'm the youngest of our group and the supervisor told me to say I was sixteen. Factory rules don't allow anyone younger to work the loom machines.

We work six days a week but have Sunday off. All girls must attend Church on Sunday and the factory gives education classes and speaker programs for us to attend 'to improve upon our education and social awareness.' Dormitory doors are locked each night at ten o'clock.

You needn't worry about me running out and galivanting around, since I am asleep well before ten.

After taking out for room and board my first week's paycheck was two dollars which I enclose herewith.

God bless you all.
Your ever loving daughter and sister, Lily.

Joshua said, "Sounds like my own sister when she was working in one of those mills."

"Yes, and knowing what we know now, we should have held her back. Here, I'll read part of this one she sent, it was addressed just to me."

… over the years, we factory girls are required to do more and more with the same or less pay. Quotas must be met and we are required to attend two or more looms at a time. But don't mention a word of this to Ma. She needs what I can send her and I will endure. At least, for as long as I can.

"Here's what Lily wrote in one of her last letters from the factory."[33]

Dear Ma and Pa and Dear Helen *3 August 1847*

Oft times I grow weary. Now I'm nineteen and the constant thirteen hour days of tending three looms causes aching legs and back.[33.a] *Tis true I've gained a good education from Factory provided lessons, but of late all I can do of an evening is rest my weary body; and I pray for a good night's sleep.*

I start to wonder how my condition compares to the slave who tends the southern cotton crops—the same crops that feed these factories in Lowell. The whip keeps the slaves in bondage, and the law gives their owners rights to do as they will with them. We are not that bad off, with no physical punishments, not like the poor slaves . . . but necessity keeps us factory girls bound to our current conditions. Where else could we earn any pay?

We work and produce nearly the same quotas as the men and yet receive only one half to one third the wages. Some girls think they are free to leave and seek better employment at other mills. But, if they leave, they find themselves on a black list where no other mill will hire them.

The cost of room and board has increased but our wages have not. Now I clear one dollar and fifty cents a week. So now I'll be sending home only three dollars every two weeks.

The factory air was hot and stifling today, and I've taken on a cough that won't go away. Oh, how I long for the clean fresh air back in Vermont and to lie in a field of buttercups and look up at the clear blue sky with fleecy clouds floating by. I long to be free again. Do you remember those days, Helen?

God bless to all. Your ever loving daughter and sister

Here's a post script, something I've been meaning to tell you about. I've met the company lawyer at the Mill, and he appears to have taken a liking to me. I will write more when I know more.

Lily

Joshua thinks for a while and then says, "You know, there seems to be something similar about what Lily went through in her mill working days and what Jed and Belinda struggled through in their life on the plantation. As a young girl, she ran off to be free of farm chores and hopefully find a new life in the mills. She was proud to be able to send money home to your family. Then after years of long hours, and little real pay—working in dreadful and unhealthful factories to ruin her health, we come full circle to today's event. Her last wish was to be done with all the pain and heartache. Today was her time, her soul is set free."

I fold Lily's letters and put them away.

* * *

"Well, Joshua, we must make ready to give our final farewell to Lily. Can you help get the boys dressed in their best garments?"

"Yes, I will. I've already hitched up our horse and carriage."

We are all together, and people from far and wide have come for this funeral. We do have such good people in Vermont. Somehow, they know when they are needed, when at other times they usually stick to their own business.

The Friends meeting is now announced by the Elder.

"We are Meeting for Worship in Thanksgiving for the Grace of God, as shown in the life of our Friend, Lily Wallingford."

No one felt moved to speak at the meeting. Lily was a recent convert to the Society of Friends and others attending today are not familiar with Quaker meetings.

At the graveside, Joshua starts out with a fine, deep voice. Best of all, it's filled with such caring and love.

Time Stands Still[17]

In Memory of Lily Wallingford
September 9th 1852

By this brook in the glen,
Where flowers blossom free
Where the sun parts the elms,
And cascades o'er the lea.

We gather in this field,
And almost become intoxicated,
By the scent of wild flowers,
Wafting in the Autumn breeze.

With Lily, we remember picking blades of grass,
With diamond drops of dew.
It enraptured and enchanted us . . .
Now thoughts turn back to you.
To you, Dear Lily.

While we search for the four leaf clover,
You run to catch a butterfly,
Monarchs, grand and noble.
In fields of gold they lie.

Now time stands still,
As clouds traverse the sky.
White,
Ever changing,
Rearranging ...
In fields of blue they lie.

Then shades of gray,
Will turn to night.
And the nearness,
Of that far-off light,
From the evening star,
Will make us reach,
In hopes to grasp,
Lily,
From afar.

Beautiful Lily,
You were one of the best.
You left too soon
For your eternal rest.
But at least,
If not at last,
You'll find peace.
And we'll hold fast
To those pleasant memories
of you, our own dear Lily.

Farewell sweet Lily,
May God hold and protect you,
till we meet again.

I give Joshua a silent 'Thank you.' Then take off my gloves, grab two handfuls of dirt and toss it on Lily's Pine box. I will not think of it, ever again, how it's laying six feet down—under dirt. Joshua does the same and others follow. I thank each one for coming.

* * *

I awake with a start.

Joshua asks, "What's wrong Helen?"

"Look at me. I'm too warm, and my arms and hands, they tremble. That same woman . . . she was in that field of barley."

"Who? And when did you see her?"

"Just now. She wouldn't come back."

"You were sleeping. No one is here."

"Oh. It's that dream again, that's where she haunts me. This time she started to turn, but stopped and kept walking. She pointed ahead. A bright light, it blinded me. Help me get this blanket off. It's too hot."

"Was that all?"

"No. Just before she disappeared, she turned and said, 'I must go. My girls are waiting.' I could not call . . . Josh, was she heading to—perhaps the gates . . . and was it Lily?"

"In your mind, at least, that was your sister. She showed her pain had gone. She must be finally free."

"Do you think she's with her twins?"

"Yes, no doubt. And she is now happy and wants you to be as well."

"Thank you, darling. I'll sleep easy now. Goodnight."

"Come here, lie in my arms. Goodnight, Helen."

Chapter Twenty-two

A Quaker Christmas

It's Christmas season again. With only a fortnight left, I remind Joshua what Aunt Millie said. Last month she visited us and raved about the shops in Burlington. Already they were displaying fancy gifts.

She said, "People are happy. The children have fun counting the days, and everyone's excited over it all. The shop windows show gifts and decorations for trees. They even remind people how Santa Claus will be coming in his sleigh pulled by reindeer." [34]

What does he say about it? He settles into his easy chair and grabs his book on George Fox, the Friend's founder.[35] I wait, but Joshua reads, ignoring me.

"Josh, have you any different thoughts about Christmas?"

He puts the book aside and says, "I agree that times are changing, but not enough to forego our Quaker teachings."

"Why do you say that?"

"Gifts, and a tree? How does it celebrate our Lord? Both are not the Quaker way. If we don't spend that day giving the poor some food and clothing, then we are amiss in our duty."

"But we always give to the poor, what we can afford."

"Listen to this. Our founder, Mr. Fox—he just reinforced what we've been taught. It says so in his journal. He says we need not follow teachings that don't show us the inner light—one that is only shown by God."

"Josh, you well know I had followed other religious ways, growing up in my Nesbitt family, and sometimes I long for those old traditions."

"But, Helen you know it's against . . . and the boys, do they get taught what you believe?"

"No, I committed to follow you, but I thought you knew, I don't think God is inside of me. He might speak to me, but not as my inner light."

"I knew that when we married, and never expected you to vow to follow every tenet. I did hope you'd eventually come to see how true it is, if going to enough meetings."

"No, he cannot be right here, knowing all that I think and do. It is too scary to think on. I want Him up in heaven, not so close."

Finally, Joshua stands up, and his book slides to the floor. He picks it up and smiles. Then, gets his jacket.

"I'm heading out for wood."

He returns in time to keep the fire from going out.

He says, "What's he got to do with it?"

"Who? Did a visitor come by when you got the wood?"

"I'm talking about that big fat man with that smelly old pipe."

"Who's that? Did one of the Elders come by?"

"No, stop it now, your Aunt mentioned Santa Clause, remember? I've seen pictures showing a pipe sticking out of his long beard. I've seen the newspapers. And flying through the sky? Who could believe such tripe?"

I will not laugh. He is so serious.

I say, "Of course, people do not really believe that. He's just a jolly figure patterned after a saint who gave to the poor. Saint Nicholas, I believe it was. He represents the spirit of giving."

"Still, we do not need any rituals from any church or their special holidays. Or songs, little jingles really, written to entice us to do right and spend coins we don't have. We can, on our own, forsake selfish thoughts or evil ways. For Quakers and our beliefs, it's always been that way."

"Yes, I know, but what of the boys? Some friends and neighbors have a grand time on holidays."

"I don't know, Helen. What of the Elders, and other Friends frowning on those new ways? I'm still not convinced. Just wait a bit, and let me think on it. You know, Thanksgiving is the day our government says we should give thanks. Why do we need another holiday?"

"I think, we need a happy day for children when they are young."

He looks for his book; the one I returned to the shelf. I give the book to him, but will not leave the room.

"Joshua, look at me, please? Christmas day is meant for giving presents, and--."

He turns the page.

"Joshua, are you listening? Each child sees how nice it is to please, and can, if just for that time—forget his own selfish needs." He puts the book on the table.

He says, "I guess learning to leave behind any selfish ways is good. Do you think, if we make a small celebration, we could treat it like any other day of giving thanks?"

"Are you saying you agree?"

"Do I agree? Those shopkeepers, the ones your Aunt Millie tells of, the way they advertise the day to get people to buy gifts? No, I am not agreeing on that."

"You are so right. Gifts can come from our own two hands, not store bought goods."

I stop talking. He again starts reading George Fox's good book.

This is maddening. I wish he would talk.

"OK Helen, we can do it. Let Jacob and the boys know—as long as only hand crafted presents are given out. As for the tree, a small one from our own woods will do quite well."

I won't ask about decorations for it. That will come about in time. He and Jake can take the boys to pick out a nice tree. I can't believe he said what he did, but he did say it and I'm so glad.

* * *

Finally it's here, and counting the days made it drag on so much longer. Christmas. The boys are up early this morning, and peek into the wrappings. I catch them and shake my head. Time to prepare our meal. Right now, the Goose needs cleaning. I'll scrape out this extra fat. Now chop some onions and celery and mix it in with bread crumbs. Stuff it into the Goose and into the oven it goes. What next? I'll make ready some cold sliced up ham. Now, this looks good, some smoked tongue. I've also time to fricassee up some chicken.

How pretty our tree is. Jake helped Eli fashion a tin star. They punched holes with a nail and it shines real nice.

Josh gives the OK—and the boys grab for presents, strewing paper wrappings all over. Here's one I hand to Jake. It's a scarf with old burlap dyed red for the big bow and with J.H. stitched on the ends.

Our boys open up presents from their Pa and Uncle Jake. Then I notice that Joshua's left the room.

I best get these wrappings picked up. I step over new games, and tops, along with a big wagon for Eli and a small wagon for Cal.

Eli rips the wrappings from both their mittens and woolen caps.

Cal says, "Oh good, mittens. Eli, see what I got? I gotta try 'em on."

Jake's standing in front of me. He grins, holds something behind him till I sign, "Is it for me?" He shakes his head and grins again, but I grab for it.

"Such a nice board, and maple wood, with my initials carved in. Thank you, Jacob. It's what I hoped for." His face will break if that grin gets any bigger.

The boys gave cards with verses. What a big to do when they presented them—with a big bow from the waist at the end. Did Joshua have them practice reciting those till they were just right? I won't let on that their Pa helped.

Oatmeal and sugar cookies hang from the tree. Yesterday we all pitched in to finish them. Pieces of nuts spell out each name. Popcorn garlands got strung last night, and almost look like snow. The smell of the tree mixes with the fragrance of the evergreen boughs on the mantel.

Jacob's acting the same, just clowning around.

Then Joshua returns and who does he have with him? Rufus and Caspar? My goodness, I never thought to invite them. I am so glad Joshua brought them, but what's that he's carrying? A burlap bag, and with something sticking out, wrapped in old newspapers.

Joshua invites them to take a seat. He says, "I saw them all dressed up in their Sunday best and wondered what was going on. I'll let Rufus explain."

Rufus says, "Did y'all know, Sally an Betsey comin t' dinner t' day? Our Auntie bringin em but jess one day. So we's gon' git back soon."

"Where are they staying?"

Josh answers, "Rufus told me they are staying the week with the Hutchins in Braintree. James Hutchins had fetched them from Hinesburgh. The girls are living in a hillside farming community, just outside of Hinesburgh. Free blacks have been living there for many years. Betsy said there is a farm there, run by Almira and William Langley and it is used as a safe place for those escaping slavery." [36, 36.a]

I say, "Well that is really good news, I'm so happy for those two."

Rufus says, "We's wantin t' say God's sure lookin out for alla Haskells, cuz we knows yer home filled w' good'n plenty grace galore."

Caspar says, "An t' day, it be God's day, so we bess be sayin 'Amen."

I offer a cuppa tea and they sit with Joshua near the hearth. He's talking men's talk, about their farming and penning animals during winter. They know that a barn is best and might have plans to build one.

I recall Joshua mentioned that both men had taken to church going. And more often than most others. Perhaps preaching might be in store one of these days?

Rufus stands up and says, "An I say, Amen t' y'all." He hands out candy canes to Eli and Cal. Then, they head for the door.

"Wait, Caspar. It'll take just a bit." I won't let them leave empty handed. They wait by the door.

"Here's an apple pie, and some jars of green beans, winter squash and pickled beets to take home. I've wrapped them so the jars won't break."

Joshua says, "You must promise to bring your guests by when they are ready to take their leave." Good idea, and I shall wrap additional jars for the girls to take back.

I say, "Yes, please bring them by, and Merry Christmas to both of you."

Quiet now abounds, and I must find out, what's in this package?" I have it half unwrapped and I see—.

"Oh my!" It's my special gift. I pull Josh closer so no one can hear.

"Thank you. It's so fine, and you made it for three. The small hole will come in handy, since the boys won't have to balance over that old seat anymore."

Time to finish preparing our meal.

"Joshua, can you fetch fresh milk and cream from the cold room, and ask Jake to help cut up the carrots and turnips? Wait, don't forget . . . bring in our winter squash. I put them down in the root cellar." Almost forgot, but Josh reminds me. He'll get some light cream. He likes to add the finishing touch.

Next, here's Joshua's favorite, carrots and turnips. Mash both together. Can't forget salsify root with that delicious oyster-like flavor. For the salad? Jakes' hovering over me. He can help.

I sign, "Can you add these small onions? They've been boiled and cooled off now. Then can you chop up this celery root?"

He's finished and I sign, "You did a good job." I add pickled beet slices, crushed walnuts and a slight amount of maple syrup for taste. As Ma used to ask at her holidays, 'Have we made enough for an army yet?'

"Josh, can you place some pitchers of sweet cider on the table? Along with some bowls of apple sauce? Also, have Jake grab a load of knives and forks, and some big spoons for the soup. Ask the boys to help. Eli can fetch the napkins to help set the table. Can we find something for Cal to do?"

Let's see my list, is it all checked off? For dessert, I've baked mince pies and of course we'll have jelly and jam sandwiches, nuts and . . . what else? Can't forget my special plum pudding.

The goose has been cooking long enough. The oven door is open and it smells so good. Joshua comes up behind me and wraps his arms round me.

"Helen, my nose tells me our 'goose is cooked.'" I laugh.

"Sorry, I didn't mean to be funny, but the goose . . . it must be done?"

"Ah, yes, it's time. Have them come to the table."

Josh calls everyone in to sit. He asks each to pray but, only in silence.

He says, "Wait for the Lord to enter if He chooses." God never talks to me that way and I am not disappointed.

Then, Joshua thanks the Lord for all His blessings including our food. Finally, he passes the goose platter. I ask for the gravy boat and put big helpings on each plate.

I walk round the table and check if anything more needs to be put out.

I ask, "Does anyone want anything else from these plates? There's more than enough for seconds."

Now, I'm all set and will sit myself down. Yet, I hear something. Is it outside?"

"Listen, Joshua can you hear that noise? Is someone out there?"

He says, "I'll go check."

"Oh, no, stay there. I haven't started on my plate as yet. I'll go." Can't see through this door curtain. I pull it aside.

"Joshua, there are two men down by the fence. They're tethering their horse and wagon. One of them is Sheriff Larson.'

"Joshua, is it bad news?"

He puts his arm around me and draws me close. He whispers to me.

"I've no idea but hoping they're not rounding up runaways. Surely they wouldn't be in cahoots with federal agents. There's my cousin Jimmy. He's wearing his uniform."

A loud knock on the door makes me jump back. Joshua steps in front of me to open it.

They enter. They remove their gloves and the Sheriff reaches into the pocket under his long coat. Cousin Jimmy blows his hot breath into his hands then rubs them to keep his fingers warm.

Joshua says, "Sheriff, what is it? Come in. You need not stand out in the cold air. Not today of all days."

Larson speaks up, "Pardon, Joshua, but it's Helen we're needing to see. Me and my deputy come here on official business. It's not a social calling."

He unfurls a crumpled paper and hands it over, saying, "Uh, how can I put it but straight out as there's no sense beating round the bush. We have this warrant, Helen, it's for your arrest."

I ask, "What on earth, what does that mean? Are you sure this is for me? And, on Christmas Day?" Then, I remember the boys.

I ask the men. "Please follow us to the Front room."

Joshua asks "Now, Sheriff, please, can't this all wait? Whatever it is? Can't you come back another day?"

The Sheriff shakes his head back and forth. He, then, reaches in his back pocket and digs out his shackles.

We're in the Front Room now. I close the door.

I say, "Please have a seat. If you like I can fix a plate from our table. You can eat in here at our study table. No? Then, perhaps some hot cider? Joshua, can you fetch those drinks?"

Then I whisper to Josh, "Please help get the cider mugs and perhaps a dash of hard cider will do? Use our good mugs and then wait till I find out more. It must be some mistake."

"Cousin Helen,' Jimmy says in a low voice, 'we know it's a bad time and all but we have to do our duty and—."

The Sheriff interrupts Jimmy. "The Warrant requires you to be arrested for murder and a violation of the Fugitive Slave act. This comes from a request of the Massachusetts Gov'nor to our Vermont Gov'nor. They're asking our Gov'nor to extradite you to Massachusetts. Says you murdered two men in Fairhaven, Massachusetts—about two years ago. Can that be right, Mrs. Haskell?"

I cannot speak . . . oh Joshua, hurry on back with those mugs. You need to be here. My head is swimming round.

Jimmy says, "Stand up please and you must put your hands together." The door creaks part way open. Jimmy's irons clang in front of me. Joshua swings the door wide and it hits the wall. Jimmy drops the irons. Joshua slams the mugs down on the side table, they almost fall off. He hurries, gets between Jimmy and the Sheriff and pushes me behind him.

"No, you are wrong, my Helen killed no one. It must be someone else and what is it you have there? What is on that paper? Who lied and told such stories?"

I grab Joshua's arm. His other hand runs his fingers through his hair. I hand sign to be silent. He removes my hand and walks back and forth.

Please Lord, help him hold his temper in.

"No, Joshua, come here. It's no use. Sheriff Larson is only doing his duty. It will be OK. God will stand by me and the truth will come out. Besides we must be quiet and calm down. We cannot upset our boys or Jacob."

I'm amazed at what I just said. Usually it's Joshua with the good sense and the level head.

Joshua finally stops pacing. He gets close and hugs me tight.

He says, "For Heaven's sake, can't you leave her unbound? Jimmy, why did you not let us know ahead of time? You waited till now, this day of all days? After working all morning preparing and cooking, she hasn't even had time to sit down and enjoy her holiday meal."

Sheriff Larson mulls it over. He strokes his chin. Takes more sips of cider and finishes the mug.

"Would you like another mug?"

"No, I've had enough. Well, first of all, it's not up to your cousin to decide. That's my job. We act right off and have to. Can't wait—not when something like this comes by special post rider. But being as your wife is not about to run off, it might be all right to leave off the shackles for now. She'll need to pack a few things, so we have no quarrel with waiting."

I'm able to get a few things packed, with Jimmy watching my every move, except for taking bites from his oatmeal raisin cookies. Josh brought them along on the same tray with the mugs. I could've dashed out the back door—but that's only a fleeting thought.

The Sheriff says, "Mrs. Haskell you can also finish eating if you like."

But my appetite has disappeared. Joshua packs a basket meal for me to take along.

Joshua then offers each man a big slice of mince pie with sweet whipped cream to top it off. He's a crafty one, my Joshua—it can't hurt to keep on their good side.

The Sheriff says, "No, we've had our fill, but thank you kindly."

Joshua says, "I shall see to the boys. They should be in their room with Jacob." It's all too quiet. I ask to check on them myself. The door is almost closed, but I can see enough.

Jake is playing soldiers with Caleb. Eli piles his presents in his new wagon—the one Jake surprised him with.

The Sheriff coughs again so I hurry back. I ask Joshua "Can you get me a warmer coat? One that's not so threadbare or needs more patching."

The Sheriff says, "Go along with him, Mrs. Haskell. Make sure you have what you need. You won't have anyone at the jail running errands for you. And we're sure to be expecting more cold weather coming along. Jimmy stay here while I get the wagon ready."

"Joshua? Help me on with my cloak?" What's he doing now? Packing warm blankets? Then, what on earth? He fishes through my wardrobe for my shawl and more day gowns.

I tell him "Not too much. I do intend to get back here soon. Joshua, please come closer? Will you come see me if you can? I will send word where they've locked me up, and if you can visit. Just remember why they are taking me. Lily's memory is dear to my heart, and yours, too."

"Helen, wait. How can you not be worried like me? I am livid, so upset. I could go knock them out."

"Please, don't talk so loud. We must make sure the ones in the other room cannot hear. Can't you control the bad feelings? Our boys don't need you to get carted off to jail, too.'

"Josh, please tell the boys some other story, one you can surely make up that would sound reasonable. It won't be a lie, just treat it as a fairy tale you're so good at telling."

He nods, and holds me and I want to stay in his arms forever. I shut my eyes tight—our sons will not see me crying when they take me away. I feel a soft kiss to my forehead.

Cal and Eli have not let out a peep. They are too quiet in their room. Now their door opens and they come over to me. I bend down, give each a hug. They wrap their arms tight round my neck.

"Don't worry, just ask Pa, and he will explain later. I shall be back soon, but, remember each night—I will be with you in your prayers. When Pa puts you to bed, and wraps his arms round you for a good night kiss, think of those arms as coming from me, too. Will you do that?"

Caleb says, "Don't go. Ma, please don't go." One sob comes out, and then another; now he can't stop the flood. There's nothing I can do except wipe his tears away. I try to keep my own from falling. My heart is heavy—but I will not cry.

Eli won't let go, and keeps hugging me. Joshua holds tight to Cal and then grabs up Eli.

"Please, be good, and know that God blesses and takes care of you both, each day and all day long—the same as he cares for all of us."

Then, I sign to Jake, "Bless you, Jacob, you are the best uncle for these two. We are so lucky to have you in our family."

Our Sheriff comes back in. He stands at the door, waiting.

He says, "Make ready to leave now."

Poor Eli and Cal—they're white as ghosts, with eyes so big—I hope they can get to sleep tonight. Jimmy holds onto my arm and leads out the door. Eli calls out, "Ma, no, don't leave; not today, not again! Pa, make them men go away!" I turn my head far as I can. I wish I didn't have to see such carrying on . . . my poor sons. If only I could carry their pain away with me.

Our Sheriff steps towards me, but looks to Joshua as he jangles his keys. Joshua carries our boys to their bedroom.

Sheriff Larson puts the irons around my wrists.

Jimmy says, "Sorry, but I can help you up into the wagon."

We are ready to go, but the good Sheriff gets down and fishes something out of the back trunk. He holds it out to me.

"Here's a blanket. Cover your hands, and keep 'em resting on your lap."

Please Lord, take care of my family, my boys and Jacob, too. I must write to Joshua when I arrive. Must let him know I am OK and not to be worrying. He is taking this very hard.

Chapter Twenty-three

Easing the Pain

Helen had to go. I could not stop her leaving, and the boys cried themselves to sleep. I need to do something with them to take their minds off the events of yesterday.

"Caleb! Elisha! Time to get up. I've cooked us some eggs and pork fat."

Caleb shuffles into the kitchen first.

He asks, "Pa, when will Ma come home?"

"Do not worry, she'll be back soon."

Then, Elisha drags in, rubbing the sleep from his eyes.

"Pa, something bad has happened? I saw the Sheriff put those chains on Ma. What's she done wrong? You've got to tell us."

"I will son, in due time."

Stomping his foot on the floor, Elisha yells, "No, Pa, you have to tell us now! Where did they take Ma?"

"Come here, both of you. Sit at the table, start your breakfast and I'll explain,"

They both sit and start eating.

"You see, when your Ma was visiting Aunt Lily in Fairhaven, two men broke into Aunt Lily's house and were killed. The Police think your Ma had something to do with that."

Caleb says, "Pa, Ma would never kill anyone."

"Yes, I know son and I'm sure the truth will be known that your Ma did not—could not, kill anyone."

Elisha responds, "Well, who killed those men?"

"That's something that I'm sure the authorities will find out, but for now just take comfort in knowing that your Ma did not do it. Now finish your breakfast. Then I'm going to take you snowshoeing. We'll tend to the animals when we get back."

"Where we going, Pa."

"We'll head on up along the Indian trail."

With the sun rising and casting a golden glow on freshly fallen snow, the two kids and I strap on old, catgut woven, Maplewood snowshoes.

"Are your bindings tight?"

Eli answers, "Yes, Pa. We're ready to go. Caleb! Stop your pushing. You can go first if you like."

Caleb heads for the Indian trail which starts in back of our cabin. Winding uphill a ways, it bends off to the right onto the old Deer trail. Following Deer tracks, we spot some scat and come upon a hollow in the snow.

Eli says, "Looks like a large buck spent the night here."

Breathing heavy and steady now, we continue to wind our way uphill, Elisha humming to himself and Caleb talking excitedly. Making good time we intercept another trail and follow it across Harlow Hill. Accompanied by the sound of dogs barking, we cross the road and press on toward Hebard Hill.

"Caleb and Eli, we'll stop here and rest for a while."

I take some milk from a bottle in my knapsack and the three of us drink as the bottle is passed around.

"Ok, let's continue on. The trail is level here and the going should be easy."

Eli takes the lead and is setting a good pace. The stillness of the surrounding woods is only interrupted by the sound of our breathing and the crunching of snow underfoot.

Eli motions for us to stop. "Caleb, Pa, can you hear that?" We listen and hear the faint hoof beats of horses pulling carriages off in the distance.

"We're close to Randolph Center, so that may be folks visiting relatives and exchanging presents . . . Eli, why are you crying? Come here."

"Pa, they took Ma away, before she could even sit down with us for Christmas dinner. Why did they do that?"

"They had to. Your Ma was unable to eat because of what was happening."

"I hate Cousin Jimmy and the Sheriff."

Caleb, says, "Me too."

"Boys, the Sheriff and Jimmy were doing their lawful duty, and it pained me something terrible to see your Ma taken away like that. But your Ma would want us to be strong and if she were here she'd say not to use words like hate. Here, Eli, take my handkerchief and dry those tears."

"Yes, Pa."

"Well, my legs feel strong and we could trek a few more miles, but the animals need tending so it's time to head back."

Approaching Harlow Hill, Caleb takes the lead. He's backtracking along the tracks we made uphill and both boys are doing well. I slip and slide a bit coming down the hill—drawing laughter from the children. Yet, the boy's snowshoes almost glide along the surface of the snow and they make it down the trail just fine.

Helen would smile noticing the boys are dry but my britches are wet in back from the fall. What am I thinking? She's not here and she won't be at the cabin to open the door for us.

As we approach the cabin, I know this has been a good trek. One to remember. At least one to take their mind off the horrible events of yesterday. Still, the pain I feel in my own heart is still there.

* * *

"What's keeping Helen from writing? Sheriff told me that she had been delivered to New Bedford and was locked up in the county jail. Has something happened in that jail? It's been too many days. I'd better get word soon or might have to travel down there.

What's that out there? Could it be? Yes, it's the post rider. I run to meet him. He hands something over and I blurt out, "Oh, good, finally! Thank you kindly, my good man, you've made my day."

It's here at last. As I walk back to the cabin I cannot stop myself, I must know. Hastily I rip it open and begin to read.

Dear Joshua,

I pray this letter finds you and the boys in good health. My health is fine. I'm in jail in the New Bedford County Court House. My case goes to the Grand Jury. That is, to see if I should go on to a regular jury trial. The Police asked me to sign a confession, but I said, "No, I did nothing wrong." I'll send a post to you when I hear of more details.

Lily's husband, Jack came by to visit. The Police had questioned him but he was in Boston at the time of the killings. He knew of Lily's passing, but only learned the date after her funeral.

He said, "I rued the days I could not be there for her. But was glad to learn she had you caring for her at the end." He wants Lily reburied in Fairhaven, beside their two daughters at Riverside cemetery. Of course, it's his right, as her legal husband. I believe, if we could ask her, she would now prefer to be back beside her twins, her only children.

During his visit, the air was laden with the smell of peppermint leaves. I wonder, does he think chewing the mint conceals the alcohol on his breath? I did not complain or mention it to him. It was good that I held my tongue. As he left my cell, he did say, "I shall look in on you from time to time."

Visiting is allowed, but you have little time to be coming to see me. There are books to read and knitting to keep me busy. The Matron, she's such a love. She's brought in yarn for my knitting. Says she gets the extra woolen goods from a lady friend, a mill worker.

I am saddened that I was unable to meet with Betsey and Sally before I was taken away. I'm concerned about Sally. And duly hope that she learns to speak up more when in company. Perhaps, since she did talk to me a bit, I might get to see her to continue a friendship. That is, if I get out of here in the end. Were you able to give them the jars of green beans, winter squash and pickled beets that I had set aside for them?

I had the strangest dream about Jacob. He had papers clutched in one hand and his other hand was behind his back, as if hiding something. He had that same strange look about him when we came upon him that day in the clearing. Maybe it means nothing but would you check on him and let me know how he is?

I want to be home with all of you. My goodness, how I miss our home, more than I ever expected. But, enough of that, and do not tell our boys how sorry I feel for myself. I am doing much better as days go by. Now, time to close. Sending all my love to all of you, and especially to you, my dear husband.

Always, with love, Helen.

"Hallelujah!" Helen's doing fine. I will be sure to satisfy her concern about Jacob right off. She has me worrying, so I must go look in on him without fail.

As I pull up to his cabin my horse starts in whinnying and then snorting. It senses something is amiss. Hurry, if anything happens to him or whatever is going on, I can't be too late.

His door is ajar. It's cold in here. No fire is lit to warm his kitchen. Check all the rooms. He's not here.

"Jacob! Where in the hell are you? Look at this place, it's a mess."

Barn doors are open. Horses are resting. One looks over at me, then lays his head back down. Jake had sense enough to water and feed them, along with tending the cows and chickens.

Ah, there in the back of the barn, I see him. He sits on a bale of hay, with his dogs at his side. As I run toward him, I know he sees me but he's staring beyond me as if I'm not there. I stop and see his cheeks are tear stained.

Grabbing his shoulders, I give him a good shake till his eyes meet mine. Careful, better think on it. Hope he's not come to harm nor hurt in any way. He's way too thin and weak looking. It's my fault. Should've come by more often.

I sign to him, "You, Jake? No, don't close your eyes. Keep them open. Look at me. Now, tell me what's wrong?"

He does not answer. He's holding tight to a stack of envelopes. A tear falls, then more line his cheeks. He slowly loosens his grip on the crumpled-up mess. Each envelope falls through his fingers and scatters at my feet. I pick them up and read the address on the front. First one, then another, until every last one shows Miss Abigail Folger's name. All of them are unopened with a large printed note on each, spelling, 'Return to Sender.'

Oh, oh, watch it. What's he doing? What's that he's hiding behind him? I grab his arm real quick but see that it's only a rope. Catching hold of it, I pull the rest of it from behind him. It's a noose with a knot tied to the end.

"Jacob! no, not you." I wrap my arms around him and hold him tight. He pushes against me and tries to squirm free but I'll not let go. Then as his stiff body finally loosens, his head falls against my shoulder. Gently, I push him back. Then I lift his face up to see me.

"Jacob? Watch me talking. Can you read me, look at my lips? Let's go trek through the woods and get some fresh air?" I offer my handkerchief. He wipes his eyes and sniffs a few times. Next, he pats my hand before he grabs onto it with both hands to give it a good shake. Then I hear him taking a big, deep breath. He waits a bit before he slowly lets his breath out.

Outside, we stroll along at a good but slow pace and never stop as it's best to keep his mind off his worries. I keep hold of his arm, but lean in toward him so he can watch my lips move. He smiles, nods his head up and down and then signs with his free hand, "I will not run off. You can let go my arm, OK? Now, go ahead and sign to me."

"Jake, you know we cannot do without you. You are part of our family. Do not shake your head. Yes, you are. We all love you dearly. You cannot and should not be so ready to give up hope. You should never let another make you feel so bad." Does he take it in, am I using the right signs?

He looks at me, never smiling. But he is no longer in a trance, like when I first found him.

"Remember, Abigail treated you badly. She is at fault and not you. Get her off your mind or you'll not be able to think straight. You won't eat right and you'll just go downhill more and more.'

Jacob signs, "I know it is true. But cannot forget her."

"Well, you should be aware that Abigail takes advantage of people."

"Yes, she was not up to farm work, too dainty."

"Well, Jacob, dainty won't do. 'Dainty' should keep to home if she is so delicate. She should not mess with people and their feelings. She had no affliction and no reason not to work like any other farm woman."

He ambles along beside me, like a puppet, with no life to act like his usual playful self. I try again, repeating what I last said and adding more.

"Abigail is not the woman we all thought she was and surely you have guessed that by now?" He gives no reply, just turns away.

At last he looks at me, but then his mouth quivers and he turns away again. I'm ready to turn back and take him home with me. Then, of all things, we enter a clearing and I see we've come to our Pastor's land. This must be a good omen.

I grab his head and turn him to look at me, "Look, Jake, it's Elder Billings home, our Pastor. Let's ask for a good drink of water."

Maybe his counseling could do some good? Lord knows, mine doesn't. Somehow we got guided here in the nick of time.

Pastor Billings still works in the fields, despite his advancing years. He walks briskly from his pathway to greet us.

I ask, "We just happen to be passing by, might we drop in to visit?" The Pastor looks back and forth at each of us while stroking his beard.

Then, he says, "Come in, Joshua and Jacob."

He says, "Jake, would you like some fresh baked blueberry pie and a big slug of cold milk?" Jake's appearance, unlike his usual neat attire, must influence this offer of pie. He does look a bit emaciated.

He speaks slow enough so Jake cannot miss the invitation, but Jacob pulls on my sleeve, and then signs. "Joshua, thank him, say, OK, but I first need washing up."

I sign, "It's OK Jacob, you go wash up, take your time, while I talk to the Pastor."

The Pastor and I have a private talk on Jake's plight, his living alone—and needing company.

I ask, "Can you find someone to check on him now and again? I must make a trip soon and I would feel beholden if you could promise me that."

He agrees and says, "Would Jacob request someone for spiritual counseling?"

"I'll have to ask Jacob."

Just then Bethany, one of his daughters, walks or rather glides into the room, gently swaying a bit, like a windblown leaf. Do her feet even touch the floor, I wonder? She is quite a nice looking young lady. I wonder if Jacob has met her?

"Father, one of the heifers got loose but I was able to catch and return him to the barn." Then she turns to me, and says, "Morning, Mr. Haskell, was that brother Jacob I saw going to the well?"

"Yes it was, and Good Morning to you Bethany."

The Pastor looks intently at his daughter, and strokes his beard. "Joshua, you may consider if one is willing, to have one of my daughters return with you and Jacob. Well, Bethany, what do you say? You could receive something in return, am I right, Joshua?"

"I dare say he would be glad of it. Perhaps Bethany could make a selection from one of Jacob's fine carvings? He's glad to offer any choice, when favors are done."

"Yes, Father. I would be willing. Mr. Haskell, I could do cooking for Jacob and would expect nothing in return. He's given so much to our parishioners and most times he refuses any compensation. No I cannot accept any gift. Are we not taught to give without thought of receiving? Am I not right, Father?"

My, but her smile is so fetching. Those big greenish colored eyes, how they light up when saying Jakes' name. Does her father sense as I do, that her interest in him is so telling? She has no inkling of how she shows it.

Yet, something bothers me. Why has she not been taken in marriage by this time? She has everything a good man might want in a wife and as a mother for his children.

"Are you sure, Miss Bethany that you do not consider this to be an unusual request. Could you actually be pleased, not just being polite, at having to spend time at Jacob's? You must have other friends or chores to do? What time would be left for you?"

"Mr. Haskell, I've known Jacob since very young. We attended class at Meeting House on Sundays. He was a kind lad back then, and grew to be such a gentle soul. It would be my pleasure to befriend him, while I help with chores."

I said, "I thank you, it's kind of you to say that."

"He never acted like other boys, pestering us girls to no end. Father, what if I can start in right away? If it's all settled, just give me chance to pack a few garments."

When Jacob joined us, he learned of the plans. Though he did not object, he still showed no sign of a smile. I thank the Pastor and we leave.

Jake walks a bit quicker to keep in step with Bethany. She has so much energy. I hope it wears off on him. I follow behind, keeping up as best I can.

Lest I forget, I must discuss with the Reverend, what were the rumors going around about Bethany? Something about a 'funny uncle' having impure thoughts and possible acts, touching her when she was but five years old. I will have to walk lightly on that path and must discuss it with Helen. She always knows of most happenings and better ways to save the peace. Maybe it's best to 'let sleeping dogs lie.'

* * *

Helen, must know about Jacob, straight away. I am thankful how it's come about, yet when earlier, well I shudder to think on it now.

Dear Helen,

As I sit here with quill in hand, I see the sun is about to set once again, behind the ridgeline of Quaker Hill. Its glow fades and darkens the front room.

Yet, just now, chills creep over me and I shiver—but not from the absence of the sun. No, I just miss the warmth that emanates from your presence. My darling, my dear, how I wish you were here.

In response to your missive, I went, post haste, to see Jacob—and was quite shocked to see the troubled state he was in. I can give you details when I visit but as for now he is in good spirits. Thank heaven for your dream. Time will tell, but it's a blessing that you had that uneasy feeling about Jacob. If I'd arrived there one day later, I fear we would have lost him.

One of the Elder's daughters, Bethany, has agreed to stay with him. Although somewhat plain, when she is around Jacob she smiles and her eyes sparkle. She does seem quite nice and is sincerely interested in Jacob. Therefore, you must be relieved to hear he is alive and well. We must keep our fingers crossed that this new friend of his will surely be a good stroke of luck and might keep him out of the doldrums.

Bethany is well trained in woman's work and loves children. Her father said she can be of help to Jacob.

As to your concern about Betsey and Sally. Caspar brought them by after you had left. I gave them your jars of vegetables. Betsey is in good spirits and has made many friends in that hillside community in Hinesburgh. Needless to say, they were all quite shocked to learn that you had been taken away and could not understand the rhyme or reason for it all. Of course, I could not answer Betsey's questions. Sally is now fourteen and is turning into a fine looking young lady. But as to her socializing? No, not as yet. she still is so silent most of the time. Yet, she brought a gift for you. It is a nice box of lavender soap.

Elisha and Caleb send you hugs and kisses. Jacob gave a sign to me, to send to you. He said, "Tell Helen I miss her, and hope she comes home soon."

With all my love, Joshua

Chapter Twenty-four

INDICTMENT
THE COMMONWEALTH
vs
<u>HELEN NESBITT HASKELL</u>
MURDER.
Commonwealth of Massachusetts

BRISTOL SS. At the Superior Court in New Bedford within and for said County of Bristol, on the first Monday of February, in the year of our Lord one thousand eight hundred and fifty-three.

The Jurors for the said Commonwealth, on their oath present, -- That Helen Nesbitt Haskell of Randolph, Vermont, at Fairhaven in the County of Bristol, on the ninth day of April in the year eighteen hundred and fifty one, in and upon one Antonio SanAngelo and one Michael Fitzgerald, feloniously, willfully and of her malice afore thought, an assault did make, with a certain weapon, to wit, a Colt six cylinder Revolving Shotgun of the make Patent Arms of Paterson New Jersey, with serial number 219, causing massive injuries to both the before said, whereupon the said Antonio SanAngelo and the said Michael Fitzgerald then and there instantly died.

Therefore, the Jurors before said, bring forth, against Helen Nesbitt Haskell, an indictment of murder in the first degree of both the before said Antonio SanAngelo and Michael Fitzgerald; against the peace of said Commonwealth and contrary to the form of the statute in such case as is now made and provided.

TILTON J. CARLSEN,
Foreman of the Grand Jury

VERGILIO M. DESOTO,
District Attorney

Bristol ss. On this second day of March, in the year eighteen hundred and fifty-three, this indictment was returned and presented to said Superior Court by the Grand Jury, ordered to be filed, and was filed: and it was further ordered by the Court that notice be given to the said Helen Nesbitt Haskell that said indictment will be entered forthwith upon the docket of the Superior Court in said County.

Attest :- CARMEN DESOTO Asst. Clerk

Jack visits and reads the charges the Grand Jury gave to the Court. He places his hat in his hand. But he hems and haws.

Then, he says, "Helen, I shall represent you and not charge a copper penny in return." I know not what to say.

He says, "Do not worry, as this official paper called an Indictment, is only what the State has to give to the Court before the actual trial. You've not yet been found guilty, and you still have a very good chance to show innocence."

He sounds like a big lawyer talking to members of the court. And, what's this he hands to me?

"Helen, look I secured this from a reporter on the Daily Evening Standard. It's a photo of the Court House here in New Bedford. You may want to send it off to Joshua in your next letter. Would you agree, this is a grand place to hold the trial?"

"Yes, it is a fine-looking court." Does he think that because this is a grand building, it will comfort me as I go on trial for murder?

"Helen, you'll be glad to know, they dropped the charge of violating the Fugitive Slave Act. The commonwealth is opposed to this federal law."

"Well, I can't say that brings me much peace of mind. Now, Jack, hear me out on this. First, we must understand each other. You must know how hard put I am to forgive you and to let bygones be bygones. Lily was failing and not a word did she hear from you.' He glares at me, but shakes his head. Then closes his eyes.

"If only you had given her something to comfort her and help her peace of mind. How pitiful to see her losing the will to live each day. It went on right up towards the end. I'd catch her looking all around. Who was it she looked for? Not me nor Joshua. We were always there. Any smile she could muster was soon gone with only a sigh left in its stead. Do you know why? It's because not a sign of her Jack was to be had."

"Wait, now let me give explanation to that . . . you must let me tell—."

"No, you wait. My own husband, such a good man as he is . . . well, he helped give Lily some peace."

"I know not what you speak of. I was ill myself and needed to spend some time in a rest home in Hartford, Connecticut. It was a sort of getting away from all my duties. I had too many overwhelming responsibilities."

"Then how can you help me now when you did not, or could not help even your own wife?"

"But, you knew she left me and wanted nothing more to do with me. What could I have done? I could not leave. And what of that . . . wanting a divorce? Was that your doing? You took her away to Vermont."

"What? No, it was not my fault. You could've done a bit more than doing nothing at all. What possessed you to keep silent especially when you profess that you loved her. Good Lord, Jack, you should've known she was ill, did you not?"

"I sensed the change in her but she would not speak of it. I was thinking it was still all the grieving for our twins and their dying so early. And I was occupied settling my mother's estate."

"Oh, is that what it's called, being occupied? Occupied with what? Drinking till all hours and carousing down to the wharves?" His eyes won't stay still. They flash back and forth, up and down. He pops another mint in his mouth. That smell, yes, he did have a drink before coming here.

"You know that before she died she only could think of 'her Jack.' What have you to say to that?"

"My actions were not to be commended, I know. When Lily needed me at home, I admit I was in error to let business and my other family affairs take precedence over her needs. For that I am sorry and will be until my dying day."

We don't have money for a lawyer. I cannot refuse his offer.

"If that be the case and if you truly want to represent me, then I say yes. You can be at my table and I do thank you."

"Fine, Helen, then it's settled?"

"Yes, but Joshua will help if decisions are to be made. Above all, the actual happenings, the killings will not be told to anyone, no one at all. Give me your word on that."

"Of course, I agree and will swear as an officer of the court."

"Alright, when this is done with, I will thank you in all sincerity."

Time to tell him what happened. I close my eyes and tell him all that went on. I let him see, just as I did—the awful events as they unfurled.

"Now, when she heard the noise, Lily grabbed that gun and—." He stands up, and turns from me. Rings his hands . . . then, turns and glares at me.

"What are you saying . . . it was Lily? How could she—no, she could not."

"She had to do . . . those awful, like animals they were . . . think how ghastly it was."

He stares at me, then leans over the table, as his hands reach out. I grab his arms, and help him sit. He wipes his brow with his sleeve. I offer a glass of water. He gulps it down, then holds his head in his hands. I cannot just stand here. I pat him on his back.

"Ah, yes, yes . . . I see. But, Helen, oh dear. How? She actually used that shotgun?" I nod. He stands and paces back and forth while I tidy up my grand room. I hold up his jacket. He puts it on.

He holds onto his hat. "Helen, forgive me for doubting. I thank you for not letting Lily's name get dragged through the mud." His hand runs through his hair before placing his Derby square on his head.

I realize one other true fact. We cannot have his own reputation besmirched either—now can we? I pray for the day when Joshua is here. I need someone I can trust.

February 9th 1853:

Today is my birthday, but no one to celebrate it with. Joshua's last letter said he would be arriving with the children either today or tomorrow. He must have been delayed.

I hear footsteps in the hall. Matron jangles her keys, opens the cell door and who should walk in?

"Joshua! You made it. Thank Heaven."

"Did you think I would miss your birthday?"

"I was getting worried. Where are the boys?"

"Didn't Matron tell you? They can't visit here. But, they stay at a Quaker family home here in New Bedford. Take this, I brought you a present."

"What is it? A book, oh, I see. It's 'The Narrative of Sojourner Truth, a Northern Slave."[36.b.]

"Do you remember her? She joined the abolitionist cause. Then, was on the lecture circuit with William Lloyd Garrison and Frederick Douglass."

"Yes, I recall hearing of her. She worked for freed slaves and championed for women's rights all over New England."

"Here's a picture of her, take a look."[36.c.]

Matron opens my cell door. "Time to leave, Mr. Haskell. You'll have more time with your wife on subsequent visits."

I hug him fast. "Thank you, Josh. I'll get to work on my reading and it will help fill my day. Give my love to our boys."

Trial Day 1. Jury selection:

Joshua visits nearly every day. He thought I could look through the window to see Eli and Cal if he waited with them out on the street. But the window is too high up. Matron says we will think on it and manage somehow.

I now see him in the Court House. He sits two rows behind me. I feel I have the strength to now face this. My husband, my friend, is here. I catch his eye. He smiles at me and all is right once again. Well, aside from my having to sit in this court room.

Will it be all day that I must watch Jack and this District Attorney? They strut around and try to pick jury members. Some questions are insulting. Whose business is it if a man's religion is not the same as others? Or if they have a family member living on a farm.

Then, I hear the worst one, "Are you willing to find for the death penalty by hanging, if it's required?" I am so relieved that this first day is over and done with. But not quite, as Jack comes back with me to my cell to discuss our case.

I ask him, "Why are there no women to be picked?"

"Helen, women cannot vote, let alone be on a jury."

"Oh, but they can be sent to jail and hanged if found guilty? That is hardly fair. How many have they hanged in Massachusetts?"

"There were many women that were hanged in the late 1600s during the Salem Witch trials. Before that, a Mary Dyer was hanged, not only because she was a Quaker, but because she openly opposed the anti-Quaker laws in Massachusetts." [38.a]

That is not comforting at all. Now I am more worried than ever.

Jack now says, "Here's our strategy to set you free."

"How will you do that?"

"It won't be easy; DeSoto is one of the best District Attorney's in the Commonwealth. He's a hard man to beat."

"Are you giving up already?"

"No, I just want you to know what we're up against. Our best advantage is that he will not have any eye witnesses to the murder."

"I'm a witness and there were two others."

"Yes, but you cannot be forced to testify and no one knows the whereabouts of the other two."

"That's good, I would not want Jedediah and Belinda being arrested and caught up in all this."

I am so relieved that this first day is over and done with. As I write in my journal, Joshua agrees that my own rights don't seem to be served as well as if I were a man. But, he agrees with Jack's take on it and lets it go for now.

Trial Day 2. Opening arguments:

DeSoto: "Gentlemen of the jury, you see before you today a woman from Vermont, looking to be a kind and gentle soul. But do not be deceived. I will prove to you that this woman is evil to the core and it was her, and her alone, that caused the premeditated deaths of two of our finest young men – Antonio SanAngelo and Michael Fitzgerald.'

"To wit, in Fairhaven at the Wallingford farm on April 9th 1851, she did shoot and kill both lads with a Colt revolving shotgun. Said gun was found in the Wallingford's barn, hidden under hay with two shots fired. Also found in said barn, was Tony SanAngelo's knife with his carved initials 'TS' on the handle.'

"And to that damaging evidence, I will bring before you proof of 'Who did this dastardly deed?' Let it be known, that the knife was wrapped in an apron bearing the initials 'HH' sewn on the pocket.' What more proof do you need?"

"Some of you may question, "Could she have shot those men in self-defense?' The answer to that becomes apparent when I present Helen Haskell's motive. It is clear now, that the Wallingford farm was used as a "safe house" for runaway slaves – there being a Secret room in the house that was discovered by the new owners after buying the farm from Mr. Wallingford."

"Tony and Mike were known Bounty Hunters in New Bedford and Fairhaven, dutifully carrying out the provisions of the Fugitive Slave Act to capture and return runaway slaves to their rightful owners. If not Helen, then certainly her sister Lily knew why these men would be visiting the Wallingford farm on that fateful day. It was also known that Lily's health had been failing, so we can draw the following conclusions;'

"One, that Helen, the strong farm woman from Vermont did the killing and Two, she was protecting runaways in hiding at the farm, and Three, she killed so as not to be found in violation of the Fugitive Slave Act, the Federal law that makes it a crime to harbor runaway slaves."

Wallingford: "Gentlemen, you'll discover during the course of the trial that the prosecution's case is based solely on circumstantial evidence. Mr. DeSoto has no eye witnesses, no direct evidence, and a motivation that will not stand up under scrutiny. My client, Mrs. Helen Haskell is not guilty of this crime. She is a God-fearing woman who would not harm a hair on anyone's head.

I will ask you to find in your hearts the real truth during the course of this trial. Thank you."

Then, Jack leans over and whispers to me, "Helen, don't get your hopes up. The evidence pointing at you, and with other proofs of the crime—well it shows your involvement. No, it's not looking good for us, not good, at all."

The Prosecutor, Mr. DeSoto is now ready to be calling witnesses.

DeSoto: "Gentlemen of the Jury let me now address the victims in this trial, Mr. Antonio SanAngelo, known as Tony and Michael Fitzgerald, also known as Red.'

"Witnesses can and shall be brought forth to give testimony towards both men being good family members, good workers in their job establishments, and always the most regular churchgoers since they were just young lads. Both having good records of attendance and also as Choir boys.'

"Later, when still only young men, the same two were anxious to be helping Father Kerrigan as Altar boys. That in itself is a great honor, given only to the best of boys coming from good families.'

"Both Tony and Red were not known for being trouble makers. All through their school years they had good records as will be shown here in this court. Tony's mother and sister are here and are now ready to be called upon. I ask that Mrs. Carlotta SanAngelo, mother of the deceased Antonio be called upon to describe the whereabouts of her son on that fateful night."

Judge: "Let the first witness be called."

DeSoto: "Mrs. SanAngelo, please if you might be feeling up to it at this time, describe to the court the events leading up to the night of the unfortunate happenings to your son."

This poor mother weeps. But now tries to speak. First it is so low, I cannot hear. Jack coughs, and stands. DeSoto holds up his hand to us. Then he smiles, first at us and then at this mother.

DeSoto: "Yes, this is difficult for you. We shall wait while you give your best efforts."

Mrs. SanAngelo: "My son . . . my poor boy. My youngest."

DeSoto: "Please Mrs. SanAngelo, take your time and have a glass of water. We can be patient, knowing of your great loss and are quite willing to let you have time to compose yourself. When ready, please describe events of that night."

Mrs. SanAngelo: "Thank you. I needed the water and it will help I am sure. My throat is aching from all the crying I've done. Please forgive me. Well, my son Tony and best friend Red were just getting off from work down to the docks. Hard working men, they were, and just starting to have a time to be relaxin'. Another friend, one with more in his pocket to spend, dropped by asking if a party could be had."

DeSoto: "Ah, yes and from that time on the three were spending a night of quiet companionship. Am I right?"

Mrs. SanAngelo: "They went down to the wharves and met some other friends in the Ole Whaler's Tavern. Then Tony came home and told me where they would next be heading out. He said something about making a lot of money if working for the local constable, or some such official."

DeSoto: "And where was it they were heading? If you have that knowledge, please state it now."

Mrs. SanAngelo: "Over to Fairhaven to see about some fugitives needing to be caught. Could I have another glass of water?" DeSoto rushes to give her a glass.

Jack looks at me, and shakes his head, yet he smiles now. Men were at a Tavern downing a few . . . or more than a few. Then, after getting tanked up they decide to go catch some criminals. And, to make money.

Michael's sister is called to the stand. She is crying up a storm . . . same as Tony's mother. Can anyone blame them?

She says, "I heard tell how some had catched sight of that one at the farm."

Wallingford: "Objection. Might I ask that the court instruct the witness to identify the person she says is 'that one'?" DeSoto nods before the judge has to rule. He tells the sister how to answer.

Michael's sister looks at me, and points.

She says, 'Mrs. Haskell was over to the farm in Fairhaven. And, I know about all the bits of bone and blood that got found. Oh, Lord. Let me forget and see him as he was. Not stuck in cracks in that kitchen floor. So, yes, Michael . . . my brother . . . God rest his soul, he had red hair."

I can't listen to any more. I want to run back to my cot, and sleep the day away. I can't be thinking of it all. But Jack makes me look up and listen.

The one from the coroner's office says "Hairs matched the red hairs found out in the woods, that is near what was left of the remains of one body."

Jack keeps jumping up and objecting. Sometimes he makes the judge listen, and most times he does not.

Then the police tell how they found the knife, my apron, and the gun in the barn.

Jack leans over and whispers, "Helen, why would you put that apron with your initials in the barn?"

"I didn't, Jack. I had worn that same apron that evening while cleaning up, but I never took it out to the barn."

"Then, can you remember what you did with it?"

"It was so bloody, I wrapped it in newspaper and threw it in the rubbish barrel. Later, after I rested—yes, I would burn it. But, I must have fallen asleep . . . oh, no . . . they have it?"

Jack says, "It appears it was found. This still does not look good for you. No, not good at all."

Trial, Day 3.

Another day with more people talking about poor Tony and Red. By now everyone thinks they must be Angels, especially SanAngelo, floating around in Heaven. I don't rightly think so.

Now, Mr. DeSoto calls on a Dentist to give testimony.

DeSoto: "State your name and your profession please."

Dentist: "I'm Dr. Winslow Rampart, a Dentist with an office on Purchase Street in New Bedford."

DeSoto: "Did you examine the skull and teeth of one of the victims? If so would you tell the court what you found."

Dentist: "Yes, I'd be glad to. The teeth I examined matched one of my patients very precisely. An upper right side molar and a lower left side molar had been extracted. Also, there were two gold fillings and a gold cap. The fillings were in lower molars and the cap was on the right front tooth."

DeSoto: "Very good. Now can you tell me what patient of yours had the identical dental work done in your office?"

Dentist: "I am 100% certain that the dental work I examined belonged to a Mr. Antonio SanAngelo. There's no doubt in my mind."

DeSoto: "Thank you."

Wallingford: "I have no questions, your Honor."
Jack then called Joshua to be witness.

Wallingford: "Mr. Haskell what religion do you and your wife profess?"

Joshua: "My wife Helen and I are members of the Religious Society of Friends. Many people call us Quakers."

Wallingford: "And what do Quakers believe in?"

Joshua: "We believe in many Christian things. We believe most of all, that there is some of God in everyone. We believe strongly in the Christian commandment of thou shalt not kill and we try with all our might not to kill or hurt our fellow people."

Wallingford: "Then do I understand that Quakers have non-violence as a central part of their religion and that you are committed not to take up arms against fellow human beings?"

Joshua: "Yes sir. That's right. In fact, there would be no excuse to kill any man or woman. No, we must always exercise patience and understanding in all our dealings. We never want to reach a moment of grave ill will towards any human being."

Wallingford: "Very commendable. With that, there shall be no more questions regarding the religion that you and your wife Helen Haskell, follow. Your Honor, I am through with this witness."

Jack sits down as DeSoto, with a smile on his face, strides over to Joshua.

DeSoto: "Do you own a gun?"

Joshua: "Yes, sir."

DeSoto: "Has your wife ever hunted with that gun?"

Joshua: "No, sir. She has no need. We are farmers not hunters and if needing meat for the table I do the hunting in my family, not my wife."

DeSoto: "What has your wife, relayed to you about what happened at the Wallingford farm on April 9th 1851 when she . . ."

Wallingford: "Objection your Honor, Mr. Haskell is a character witness. He invokes the spousal testimonial privilege and cannot be compelled to be a witness against his wife. Anything that Mrs. Haskell may have relayed to Mr. Haskell is privileged information between them and the two of them only."

Judge: "Objection sustained. Counsel for the prosecution should refrain from this line of questioning."

DeSoto: "No more questions.

The Police Sgt. after being duly sworn, takes the stand.

Wallingford: I hold before you a knife. Is this the knife you found in the Wallingford's barn?"

Sgt. Perry: "Yes, Sir."

Wallingford: "Now I ask you, could the initials 'TS' on the knife stand for someone other than Antonio 'Tony' San Angelo?"

Sgt. Perry: "Well perhaps, but I doubt it."

Wallingford: "Of course it could. How about Ted Sylvia, Tim Swanson and another 200 people within the New Bedford area with the same initials?"

Sgt. Perry: "Yes, I suppose."

Wallingford: "Now, Sgt. if I turn the knife 180 degrees I want you to tell me what the rough carving of those initials looks like to you now?"

Sgt. Perry: "The first one looks like an S, the second could be an L."

Wallingford: "Exactly. The 'TS' could just as easily be read as 'SL' with the knife in this position. Now is it still highly probable that this knife belonged to Antonio San Angelo? I doubt it, and you, gentlemen of the jury should also place some reasonable doubt on this evidence. No more questions your honor."

Being that this was Friday, the Judge told us it was time to take a recess until Monday morning. I had time to wave goodbye to Joshua as we left.

* * *

There's time to catch up on my Diary. Joshua brought this new one for me. He just left to buy me some fish and chips and a stuffed quahog for my dinner. I also asked if he would bring me some pickled pigs feet from one of the local taverns. Anything is a good change from the stew or porridge that's delivered here.

My day gets brighter when Joshua is here. I mope about in this dreary cell, till hearing his footsteps echoing down the hall. He and our boys now stay in New Bedford. They board with a Quaker family but only Joshua is allowed to visit me here.

He brought Robert Browning's poem book earlier. Perhaps he's hoping it will lighten my mood. I'm so frazzled and at my wit's end. I just hope I've hidden my dismay from him. Ah, I hear his footsteps coming closer out in the hall so I'll put this Diary away.

"I've brought you fish n' chips, and your stuffed quahog but the tavern was all out of pickled pigs' feet so I thought you might like to try this Portuguese sausage called linguica. You recall how we had a taste of it at the carnival?"

"Thank you, Josh., Every so often I've thought of that time spent with Sal and Maria and the good food always comes to mind. This will be a special treat. Have some with me?"

I am proud of my Joshua, now more than ever. At all times, he's loyal, never complaining and not giving me any worries. He could not be better at standing by me.

He says, "We need you out of here and home where you belong. Let's pray for a quick ending of this farce and that the judge is smarter than the others in this court."

"It was good of you to come but this could be a long trial so I would not complain if you went back to Vermont."

"Don't worry. I'll make myself busy making friends and attending local Quaker meetings here in New Bedford. The boys and I have free room and board with Quakers in the community. In return, I give whatever services I can perform."

"That's a load off my mind. I'm glad you decided to bring the boys with you. I miss them so much. Are they making friends and fitting in?"

"Yes, yes, of course. You have no need to worry over them. The people here work in the same movements, righting wrongs against innocents and any that need help. Also, there's a good printing shop I've found and I may be able to work there while learning the trade."

"Is that right? Where is it?"

"One of the Friends has it and is willing to have me learn what I can in return for helping him out a few hours a day. When we have more time, I'll bring some of the newsprint to show some of the stories published in it. One in particular is about Frederick Douglass."

"You mean the ex-slave and abolitionist?"

"Yes, that's him. Well, he lived for four years, right here in this city. In fact, three of his children were born in New Bedford."

"I did not know that, but please bring me some of that newsprint. I need more to read but first let me check with the Matron to be sure it's OK. If not, she has ways of getting around the rules. She might help to get it in to me somehow."

Jack's coming down to my cell to visit. As soon as the Matron opens the cell door and allows him to enter he starts telling us about a good plan he believes might save me. He said the trial was going against me.

"We have no hope, Joshua, of her being let off." Jack walks back and forth in my cell. My room is so tiny that the last stride he cuts short and ends up almost in circles. Puffing up for his next important announcement he stops to gaze at the high ceiling but does not look at me.

"Joshua, can you give consent and ask Helen to go along with this. It may be our only chance. We must think of what's best for her."

Hmm, I wonder what that is, aside from getting free and out of here?

"I want Helen to have me plead, which is to ask the Judge, for a directed verdict based on insanity."

"Joshua opens his eyes so wide that he looks a bit comical but his mouth stays shut. Then Jack continues.

"Ah yes, this can be shown through her past actions and her state of hysteria. Then also there's another condition women often fall prey to, especially for Helen, after her sister's death."

How dare he suggest I might be tetched in the head. And worse, ask anyone else, like Joshua to decide for me? I will choose who and what to decide, to determine my fate.

"Joshua, forgive me please and Jack remember, I am here and you can speak to me. Now look at me. What is your plan?"

"It will be one of long standing, that is your prolonged melancholia. Then, we can see if this fits in, you possibly also are having dementia? We cannot leave any stones unturned. We must convince the jury of your being so unbalanced you could not possibly have known right from wrong."

"Come now Jack, you can't be serious about this new defense. What of my behavior up to this time? Was I having periods of being not so insane?"

"Well, we can prove you are sometimes in normal conditions and sometimes when least expecting it, you will go off on a tangent."

"'Hmm, and how will I do that, please tell me."

"Your periods of forgetfulness are apparent, so much so, you're unable to recall the murders. We'll have a doctor in to record the proof, since he'll observe your fragile condition and of course you'll be getting far worse by the minute."

"Jack, you think so? Joshua, you think I am fragile? That's a hoot. Go on."

Joshua stands up but I shake my head and warn him not to say a word. He shoves his shoulders straight back, then sighs and sits back down. He has use of the one lone chair in the corner, while Jack and I stand not more than three feet away.

No words are said by anyone. The quiet is only broken by my fast breathing. I must be the one to decide and Jack waits with a proud smile. He is so smug, just beaming at his grand plan to save me.

I hear Joshua's jaw clamp down and he grits his teeth while staring my way. His hands clasp together and he is pushing one against the other. I am afraid he cannot contain himself much longer. Now Jack speaks and as he drones on he doesn't notice how Joshua is fidgeting, ready to more than say his piece.

I must listen to this legal wit, this learned scholar peering down at me, almost swatting me as he waves his arms back and forth. I must step back. Smelling peppermint from Jack's mouth makes my stomach go round.

He looks over at Joshua, "Now this is how we proceed. Are you with me Joshua, uh, and Helen?"

He turns his head to look at me but swivels his head right back to peer over to Joshua in the corner.

"Joshua, your wife Helen, gradually becomes more addled. What's called in the legal sense having a case of diminished means. Thus, Helen is not responsible to stand trial. Because she does not have full capacity to understand anything. Neither at the present time nor at any time in the past. That being the case, then we get doctors to prove our plea for this as well as another mental inadequacy defense. That one being one of extreme melancholy along with the usual melancholy a woman is prone to experience. Now that should be sufficient. Do you think so, Joshua?"

He must not think I understand all the big words but little does he know. Now his words are getting jumbled together. I believe his partaking of spirits will be his downfall. Please Lord, let him last out this trial before he has to go and recuperate again.

He continues, "Joshua, I mean Helen, and forgive me for ignoring you. It can be done. We'd just need a reputable doctor to see you. We'll need one with a big heart and who will come by without expecting a fee. Others enjoy the experience and some want the publicity."

"Well, Jack, you certainly must know of one or two in all your travels?"

"Yes, yes, of course. Joshua, can you assure her this effort would be better in the long run?"

Joshua is not moving one muscle now. He appears to be cast in stone.

Jack continues, "Ahem, now listen to this. There's a fine new asylum not more than half a day's ride into Taunton, built with all of the very best accommodations. It's a sight to see. This building has all modern features like central heat, running water and a good sewer system." [37]

I wonder how much he had to drink since first waking this morning. I will play this game but not to his liking.

"Well, what else does this new fancy place offer?"

"There's new indoor plumbing and it has a sunny big room where all can look out at the quiet hillside. Well, what's your take on this. Do you not agree?"

"Wonderful, and how utterly charming, Jack. Imagine not having the need to go outside to be using an outhouse."

"Well, then you won't mind?"

He's gone too far with this. "In a pig's eye, I won't mind. What on earth can you be thinking of?"

Now what's this he's showing me? A book of some sort. Showing me all the features to prove how good the new asylum will be for me.

"Helen and you too, Joshua, think upon this. See here what I'm showing you. The new place will have a chapel, dining rooms, parlors, and open-air verandas. Inmates shall now only be called patients, same as any other needing help. You may even be lucky enough to enjoy your own private room. It shall be a nice hospital and good care shall always be available to suit your needs."

He turns and looks directly at Joshua.

"Joshua, being as you have your two sons to raise, it might be worthwhile at this time to ask for a divorce. That will enable her to have her room and board paid by the state. That should be helpful, since she will be considered indigent without means of support."

Joshua is breathing easier now and says, "No, I'd never consider such a blasted lie. She is not guilty and what you are proposing is not to be told to anyone, anywhere, or in any other way. And whoever spoke of any divorce? She knows that I can't live endlessly without her."

"Joshua, do you not see the folly of your reasoning. What of the sacrifice you and your sons will have to make if she is found guilty? It will be a deep scar you'll never recover from if she ends up on the gallows."

"Yes, I understand and know full well how our sons need her. Still, this is so outrageous, this plan of yours. You've gone beyond your limits, here."

No one spoke for a time, not even Jack. Then, Joshua drew me closer to his side. His voice was clear as he spoke to Jack.

"She is innocent and we will not say otherwise. My wife does not belong in such a place or in any prison. She cannot and will not act the lunatic. Jack, if you take nothing else from what's gone on here, remember this—I will not allow her to be treated with such disrespect. She is not unbalanced, for heaven's sake, man. Nor is she an imbecile and would never play that role."

Jack motions to Joshua asking to interrupt. But for once he cannot get a word in, as Josh continues, "No, it is my turn to have a say. I am not finished, just let me think. It's apparent that you've not done much work on her behalf. It's time we come to terms and figure out how to make payment to you."

Jack cannot keep still. "I told Helen beforehand that I would not charge a fee. I have other, more substantially well off clients to help my expenses getting paid."

"No, if you are to do the work, you must be paid. For now, we must help her stand her ground until truth rules the day. And why must we wait for the answers I've asked before of you. Where are they? Especially the witnesses she needs to prove the good woman she is?"

Jack has no answer and that must be answer enough for Joshua. My husband calls out to the Matron to ask for the door to open.

He says, "Thank you Ma'am, I just have need of some fresh air outside but I shall return shortly."

Jack takes this chance to see one of his men clients on the next floor. I sit here and wonder, what next?

When Joshua returns, he is silent until I get up to speak my own mind at last. But Joshua stops me.

"Wait, hear me out Helen, please let me handle this. I fear you might lose control and say or do something not in your best interests. Think on it, you cannot give proof of what Jack suggests you to do in court. I'll tell you more of what I believe is the right course from now on. But it'll be out of Jack's hearing."

Then we go over how the boys have been doing. I write some notes about the olden days, to have Joshua read to them at night. Just before Joshua gets ready to leave, here comes Jack, clicking his heels down to my cell again.

"Joshua, Jack said he'd be consulting with a paying client. If you detect a strong mint smell on his breath, it will tell you where he's really been off to."

The Matron let Jack in and I stand and say to him, "So Jack it's an Asylum, is it? That's the name of it now? It's not called what everyone around here knows it to be, the feeble-minded's lockup? Where most are chained to keep them from lashing out at the guards? How fortunate, that it has such glorious accommodations. Will I enjoy them, though? I do not think so, since I'll never be unchained, being the dangerous, deranged woman that I am."

Joshua holds my hands in his, "Helen, you must stop, this is not good for you."

"No, Joshua, I will not stop. Let me finish. If in time I behave better, I might be kept in the nice sunroom, to look through the bars, at the nice big green lawn. Jack, do you take me for a real halfwit? It's nothing but the same Hospital for Lunatics, the same old Looney Bin. Now, to gain entrance, let's see if I have this right."

I stand up straighter, fold my hands while their eyes focus on me. "Is this correct? I must act as if I'm in another world. With eyes going every which way. Perhaps my tongue will hang out to one side. Maybe I cannot remember my name. Then perhaps I should throw a conniption fit and, of course, spittle will drip from my mouth."

Poor Josh, is he as amazed as I am, that I went this far?

Jack recalls he has other business to attend. "After all, I need to service my paying clients."

I do not say what I must hold back. Yet, if I could, it would be, "Oh yes, my dear brother-in-law. Take your leave, be gone with you and be sure to have another stiff drink down to the Sailor's Inn."

No, it's just as well. As I do need a lawyer and cannot offend him now.

As soon as Jack leaves, I start in giggling without stop until I collapse on the cot. I hold my hands to my face. I try to stifle my laughing. Joshua is frowning at me and then holds me close.

My laughing gets louder and louder, and I must gasp for air. Then tears stream down my face. I shake, sobbing so loud till it hurts.

He says, "Talk to me, what's happening? You must get hold of yourself before the Matron comes running in here, thinking I've done something to upset or harm you."

"I can't help it. I've tried to be so brave for you and the boys. Josh, I'm so afraid. Hold me. I've trusted in God but I know the only way out, would be for me to testify that Lily was the one who did the killings. Jack does not want that done. I don't either."

He says, "We've had this discussion at the start and it was never an option, remember?"

"Yes, I know, because how would the jury believe me if I placed blame on my dead sister? Even if they were convinced, could they mete out justice to a dead woman? No, they could not and the families must be appeased in some way. That will only occur if they convict me."

Josh responds, "Of course, and we know Lily was without blame for what she did. You must take heed, we can do nothing to change the verdict, whatever it might be. Perhaps the jury will see that it is not clear that any good evidence was given to them. Whatever happens we must put our faith in the Lord and worrying will not help."

He strokes my hair and I am so worn down. I might just fall asleep.

* * *

My own worries crowd out concerns for our boys. Yet, Joshua is strong and he is so good, caring for them. He stops by of a morning to give reports on how they are faring. Here he comes, same time as usual. Today I shall see what he's needing to set his own fears to rest.

"Joshua, you've been such a help during this time. I am so lax in not asking about your days. Do you still pen your thoughts to paper, and have you written any new poems?"

"Yes, but, they are of no matter now."

"Why not? I've always enjoyed them. I keep them in my scrap book. If not writing, then what is it you do in your spare time?"

"There's plenty to busy me. The Friends' Meeting House has members in need of help."

"I've noticed you do much of Jack's leg work. He has taken too much of your spare time. How many nights at the library have you spent, fetching law books for him?"

"I have to help in any way I can."

"No, you need to put aside time for yourself. Though I love your visits, there's no need to come by here each day. Your own rest is most important and your health must be taken care of. You must help me by my knowing you are OK, as well as our sons."

"Of course we are OK. We do our best and no need to be worrying."

"Matron is trying to figure a way for me to see the boys by looking out a window. But she has not found one low enough as yet. Let us hope soon I'll have no need to be separated from them." He holds my hands in his and starts to speak. I interrupt.

"Wait, please listen: When you are not here, then your writings and the boy's notes help see me through any lonely times."

He says, "I'm keeping busy and do chores to help with our keep. Yet, I will find time to scout up witnesses myself, because Jack hasn't put himself out to find a good person to bear witness for you. Today, I had planned to visit Mrs. Tellatini, Lily's neighbor. She remembers meeting you during your stay at Lily's house. She'll be a good character witness."

He fishes through his trouser pockets.

"If my writings help bring solace to you, then here's what I worked on only last evening. Can you have a look? It's about us."

Early Morning
by Joshua Haskell [17]

The stillness of early morning
Is broken
By the sound of birds
Welcoming the sun.

As I awake
I find you in my arms.
Looking peaceful
Lying there
In repose.
I suppose
I'm fortunate
To know a woman like you.

Careful not to wake you
I place a kiss on your brow.
But one eye opens
And a smile appears
As you look at me now.

I wonder...
If there's anyone
Under the sun,
Beyond the blue,
And throughout all time,
Whose heart knows
More love than mine,
When I look at you?
Is there anyone?
I wonder...

With words unspoken...
A soft kiss to the lips...
Just a token
Of love's moment to come.
Just a reminder
As two hearts beat as one.

My cheeks grow warm and there's a lump in my throat. I have to swallow before I can say, "Thank you, my love. That was beautiful."

"Now, the boys, what about Eli and Cal? They must be OK, but I've not heard from them."

Joshua, holds my hand. He says, "Yes, yes of course. Both are growing good, eating so much and both are so smart. Look here—each gave me a poem, just for their Ma. Of course, I fixed up their grammar a bit. Here, take a look. This is one that Eli wrote as he remembers a time at Lily's farm."

Frogs

by Elisha Haskell for Ma [17]

I can remember happy days at Auntie Lily's farm
when I would bask in the warm sun
lying on my back watching cotton clouds pass
through a field of deep blue.
Then I be running down to the pond
Going slow as I near
So as not to disturb those Turtles,
Sunning themselves on the rocks.
Whoops, they hear me and off they go into the water.
That's OK I'll catch some Frogs today
Look at those guys – slimy green and hard to hold
Nearly got the bucket half full
Listen to them croak.
Back up the hill to the farm,
Gotta put these beauties down the Well
Where the water's much cleaner.
Can't understand why Uncle Jack was swearing
When he had to ketch those Frogs
And take them
From their new home.

"Here's one from little Caleb to his Ma".

Geese

by Caleb Haskell for Ma [17]

Ma, we ate Goose Eggs this Morn
But I hates to fetch those eggs.

I always tiptoes to the nests
Hoping the Geese won't see me
But they came charging
As soon as they saw me.
Spinning 'round with my eggs
I be running for the gate
But too late
Those Geese bite hard
And it really hurts.
But the eggs were good for Breakfast.

"Oh, Josh, I shall treasure these. When you come back tomorrow, I hope I can have something written for you and the boys. Goodnight my love."

* * *

"Joshua, so glad you came back. It's past supper time, but my Matron is a sweet lady, is she not—to let you in a coupla-three times, all in one day. I've hurried, and written a poem for the boys. It's on the next page, but here's what I have for you."

I Remember that Boy. [16]

Do you remember, on our very first day,
when sitting in school,
I caught a grin from a silly fool,
who would not turn his gaze away?
The teacher told you, "Stop, or you'll get a whack,
a rap on the knuckles 'if you don't turn back"
She then scolded me, "Now, Missy,
you'd better not smile at me,
or I'll send you packing, and
homeward bound you both shall be."
Still, you took to fancying me and I never
could figure out just why.
But I know it's true, with what I've
now been going through.
Yes, long ago you said, "I care for you.
And, it's just the way it is,
so I'll never, ever say,
a final or lasting, Good bye."
And now? Neither can I.

Your loving wife,
Now and Always,
Helen

"That was beautiful. I shall treasure it."

"Please give the other poems to Eli and Cal. If I am found guilty, you can tell them I am innocent, no matter what others say."

"No, Helen, you can't be losing faith, thinking that way. God will make the jury see reason."

"Still, if it turns out the other way, then you must tell them—I will always love them no matter where I might be. And, will continue to pray for His blessing for all of us."

Quick, turn my head. He can't see how I bite my lip. My teeth dig deeper and tears start to fall. Keep turned away, and wash my hands in the basin, and splash water on my face. Dry with my apron.

"I'm sorry, I must have had something caught in my eye." He sits back in the chair, folds his hands, and just nods.

"Josh, please read the poem for the boys. See if it's fitting or not."

Elisha and Caleb[16]

My land, what nice poems
You wrote for me!
We'll be together, you'll see.
And, it won't be long
when singing that song,
"Home Sweet Home."
You'll both get a hug,
when we tuck the two
of you in at night,
snug as a bug in a rug.
So, Eli and Cal ~ till then,
be good. Just tell Pa of your cares,
as he knows what's wrong and right.
Now, God bless, and say your prayers,
same as always, each and every night.
With love, Ma.

It's past time for Josh to leave. Matron waits with the door open. My cell echoes as the door shuts. Moonlight slips in the window, casting shadows of tree branches on the wall. That Jury, I wonder if they sleep well at night?

Chapter Twenty-five

The End is Near

Trial, Day 4.

This day's come round at last. Jack's strutting about, pacing the close quarters of my cell.

"Please let me declare your innocence once and for all. You must testify and tell all, to have a chance at being saved. Lily would not want you to suffer on her account and where she is, we're sure she is at peace."

Whatever happened to his insisting that the truth never come out?

"I can't. I must protect Lily, let her name not be damaged in any way. After all, we vowed silence on this score, did we not?"

Joshua nods his head at us. He stands with me on this, though we half way agree with Jack.

"Jack, do we believe the Jury to be simpletons? How would anyone believe a word I say if I cast blame on a dead sister who's unable to defend herself?"

* * *

Back in the court room, with Jack, I crane my neck, wondering where Joshua found a place. I try to becalm myself. I will not give way how scared, and how rattled I am. Yet, the crowd outside, they yell louder, till my ears need covering over. Jack takes my hands away to hear.

It's my name and they're clapping. Are they for me or against me"?

Now terrible things, awful names. Cannot be from any church, not these marchers. Shouting, "Should be ashamed?" Who? I did nothing to shame anyone. Why the booing from that crowd outside?

We wait the longest time. We still sit, but now Jack looks around.

He says, "Our Judge is nowhere to be seen."

Now I hear the clickety clacking of footsteps. I have heard them every day, and know who it is. He walks swiftly for once, but turns, to duck into his chambers.

Jack gets up and leaves the table. Who caught his attention? Is it someone in the back? It's too crowded. I can't tell.

The bailiff finally shouts out, "Hear ye, hear ye! All rise, the Honorable Judge, John W. Holmes is present."

Then he reminds us, "No talking, no moving round, no leaving, no spitting—except in spittoons out in the hallway."

It's hard to recall the rest of what 'not to be doing', though I should, as I've heard it many times. Yet, why do they not keep those big brass spittoons in here, as well as in the hallways. My shoe bottoms need scraping each time I return to my cell.

Jack is here, back to the table, with no explanation why he left.

The Judge bangs his gavel, then announces to all, "This court is now in session. I will remind the defendant and the plaintiff that all prior testimony and anything having been heard during this trial is still to be kept confidential.'

"Now the trial of defendant, Helen Nesbitt Haskell—accused of first degree murder, two counts and with malice aforethought, will under the rules of our land and with our God as our guide, *ahem* . . . well this trial will now continue.'

"Are counsels for the defense and prosecution prepared to give their closing arguments to the Jury?"

Jack stands up, asks the Judge, "Your Honor, if it pleases the court, I have one final witness I would like to call at this time."

What? I tug on his sleeve. "Who is that?" He ignores me.

Judge: "So be it, bring the witness forward."

Wallingford: "The defense brings to the stand, Jedediah Beaumont."

No, can't be. Not Jed. I look up and see he makes his way from the back, through this crowd. And, it's Joshua who leads him down the aisle. He has him sit in the witness chair, and then Jack comes to me.

I whisper, "Jack, no. You did not ask, you cannot let him be seen or talking, not in here—he's a runaway. Can't chance it, getting caught. He'd get taken back to his owner, and worse."

Jack, says, "No need to worry, Jedediah wants to speak. It will be OK. Joshua's the one who found him."

I can do nothing, but sit back and take a deep breath.

Jed's wearing those same clothes that David fixed for him two years ago. His swearing in is almost done with. Now he sits.

His eyes cannot be seen. He looks down at the floor. Jack moves closer.

He says, "Please tell the court your name, and where you live, and what is your present occupation?" My Lord, Jack, too many questions to answer all at once.

Beaumont: "Name be Jedediah Beaumont, livin on Davis Street, in New Bedford. I be's fishing man on Cappen Souza's boat, de *Gloria Donna.* Been fishin long days for most a two years."

He does sound a bit better. I almost understand every word. Still, he should slow down, and Jack should tell him, to talk louder.

Wallingford: "Do you know the lady at that table?"

Beaumont: "Yassuh, she be's Missus Helen. She be's Missus Lily's sister."

Wallingford: "Let the record show that the witness has identified, Helen Nesbitt Haskell, the sister to Lily Wallingford, now deceased. Now, Mr. Beaumont, describe what happened over two years ago, on the 9th day of April in the year 1851. In your own words, tell us exactly what you were witness to, and as you saw the events unfold, while at Miss Lily's farm located in Fairhaven."

Beaumont: "Yassuh, Belinda—she my wife, we get wed in church in New Bedford."

DeSoto: "Your honor! I ask that the witness stick to what happened that night and it is not necessary to bring us up to date on present circumstances."

Judge: "It's not necessary to instruct the witness, I assure you Mr. DeSoto. It's good he can state what the facts are. Now, proceed with the witness' testimony, Mr. Wallingford."

Wallingford: "Go on Mr. Beaumont, continue with your statement. What happened that evening in question?"

Beaumont: "We's all washing up inna Missus Lily's kitchen. Missus Helen done gon' out inna barn, fetchin eggs'n milk. I hear bangin onna door. One man, yellin, 'Open up.' But door, it been not lockin anyways, an both come runnin in t' kitchen. Nex, a man holdin knife on my neck, right heeyuh. He tyin rope round bout me, an so tight, an I'se stuck onna chair."

DeSoto: "Your honor! I strenuously object to the Defense's tactics in summoning this witness whose rambling, ungrammatical recitation, I'm sure is giving the Jurors difficulty in deciphering what is being said."

Judge: "Would you like a short recess, to compose yourself, Mr. DeSoto? Or can we continue? Now, Mr. Wallingford, what do you have to say?"

I must keep this smile off my face. But, I'm wondering if the jury can understand the Judge and the lawyers with all their own fancy words. For me, it was easy listening to Jed. Just need to listen close. Some Jurors smile, and nod to each other. It's Jack's turn, now.

Wallingford: "Your Honor, all witnesses must give sworn testimony in their own words, and not be coached by their lawyer or other persons present. However, if it pleases the court and the Prosecutor, I shall be glad to ask that the clerk provide a written, duplicated transcription in what the people, as represented by the Prosecutor, might call better English usage."

Judge: "Defense is correct in interpreting the law as presented, regarding witness's deliverance of testimony. We cannot, indeed, put words in his mouth. Everyone must pay attention, and Jurors should have no trouble discerning this witness' testimony. Objection overruled. Move on, gentlemen. Defense, continue with your witness."

Wallingford: "Mr. Beaumont, you may continue, from the time after the man first was accosting you, and then tied you up to sit in a chair."

Beaumont: "Wal, suh—lessee now. Dis mans shovin dish rag into my mouf, an nex man, he been grabbin towel offa Belinda—pushin her down on a floor. Nex, dat mans layin onto Belinda. Man wif knife sayin' 'Gal, if you been screamin, den yer nigga gets his neck slit.' An Missus Lily be's comin from Livin Room totin a big gun. Man holdin knife runs to Missus Lily.' An Missus Lily shoots gun into man's haid. Other man gets up, an grabs his own pistol. Missus Lily, she gon' shoot dat man in heeyuh . . ."

Wallingford: "Let the record show the witness points to his chest. Now, Mr. Beaumont, please continue."

Beaumont: "Missus Helen come in door an Missus Lily fall onna floor. She uh, Missus Helen, pullin man offa Belinda, an grab knife an cut my ropes. I den pull rag outta my mouf an I runs t' Belinda."

Wallingford: "Tell us what happened next, Mr. Beaumont."

Beaumont: "I'se tryin t' wipe blood offa Belinda, an she cryin crazy-like. I sees Missus Helen takin Missus Lily back t' bed. Missus Helen gets back an she say, "Stop cryin, Belinda." She say, grab clothes an go back inna hidin' place. An we did. An ats true, alla happenins."

Wallingford: "Thank you, Mister Beaumont. No further questions, your Honor."

Jed wipes his brow with his shirt cuff, maybe to catch sweat from falling in his eyes. Next, he looks at me and his head is held high. His chin juts out making his scar more prominent. Perhaps it's the first time someone's calling him 'Mister.' Next, it's Mr. DeSoto's turn to ask him questions.

DeSoto: "Did you help Miss Helen and Miss Lily, dispose of the bodies?"

Beaumont: "Dis-pose? Dunno."

DeSoto: "Yes, I mean to say, did you help drag the bodies outside?"

Beaumont: "No suh."

DeSoto: "Then who dragged the bodies outside?"

Beaumont: "I dunno. Me an Belinda, we inna hidin place."

DeSoto: "I find that very hard to believe. You like Miss Helen don't you?"

Beaumont: "Yassuh, Missus Helen an Missus Lily—treatin me and Belinda like own kin."

DeSoto: "First, let me remind you to only answer the question, as asked. I did not enquire about anything except for what you can give a yes or no answer in response. And certainly do not give your feelings towards the defendant or Miss Lily.'

"However, let the record show that since Lily's name has been brought in, I am now including both ladies in the previous question. Now, isn't it true that you liked them because you and Belinda are runaway slaves and they were helping you escape? And, isn't it also true you would now do anything to repay Helen Haskell—even to the point of lying to this court?"

Wallingford: "Objection! Your Honor, the Prosecutor is attempting to put words in this witness' mouth. He is also trying to discredit this witness by getting him to admit he is a runaway slave. The witness and the defendant are not on trial here for violations of the Fugitive Slave Act. Further, by forcing the witness to answer; denies him protection against self-incrimination under the U.S. Constitution's fifth amendment, as well as the Commonwealth's Constitution."

DeSoto: "Your Honor, it is quite obvious that the witness is a runaway slave when he mentions being sent back to his 'hiding place!' I'm merely trying to establish a possible motivation for the outrageous testimony this witness is giving."

Judge: "I'm going to sustain the objection. Witness cannot be forced to incriminate himself. He is not on trial here today. This is a murder trial, not a witch hunt for violators of the Fugitive Slave Act. That is for another day. Witness does not have to answer any but direct questions, with a yay or nay reply. Jurors will disregard prosecution's question."

DeSoto: "No further questions, your Honor. Witness can be excused, and if it pleases the court and if acceptable to the defense, I would like to proceed with my closing argument."

I catch Jack's sleeve, and ask, "Why does he want to proceed so soon?"

Jack says, "I believe he will try to discount Jed's testimony while it is still fresh in the jurors' minds, so they don't have time to think on it."

Judge: "If counsel for the defense is also ready and poses no objection to prosecution's request to proceed; then counsel for the prosecution may begin with his closing statement."

DeSoto: "Gentlemen, I have presented to you, over these past several days, clear evidence that the defendant Helen Haskell did murder with prejudice and in cold blood one Antonio SanAngelo and one Michael Fitzgerald, two citizens of the commonwealth who were merely attempting to enforce violations of the Fugitive Slave Act.'

"Let me summarize the key facts in this case.'

"The victims of this crime have been clearly identified. Most positively, in the case of Antonio SanAngelo, whereas two gold fillings and a gold cap were located in the jaw of the skull recovered from the skeletal remains found on property, formerly owned by Lily and Jack Wallingford.'

"Dr. Rampart, the Dentist, as well as the family of the deceased have confirmed that Antonio also called 'Tony', did, in fact, have two gold fillings in his lower jaw and a gold cap in his upper jaw.'

"In the case of Michael Fitzgerald, red hair was scattered among the bones discovered by the hunters. While Michael, known as "Red," Fitzgerald did in fact have red hair.'

"The prosecution has also established the time and place of these murders as the Wallingford farm on or about the ninth day of April in the year 1851. For the date and time, families and friends of the deceased last saw them alive that evening.'

"As to place, although blood evidence was found in Wallingford's barn, it is with certainty that the murders took place in the farm house, and specifically in the kitchen. Investigators found beneath a braided rug in this kitchen, substantial amounts of dried blood between the floorboards. But, most damaging—tiny pieces of human skull fragments were also located.'

"The victims have been identified. The time and place of the murders are established, but now—the question, 'who did it and why?'"

"Lily Wallingford and her sister, the accused Helen Haskell, were occupants of the farm at the time of the murders. Lily's husband Jack Wallingford, the gentleman currently serving as lawyer for the defense, was in Boston at the time. However, neighbors reported seeing Helen Haskell arrive at the Wallingford farm in that time frame.'

"Neighbors also reported Lily as being frail and in ill health, therefore it is very unlikely that Lily could even lift a gun as heavy as the Colt Revolving Shot Gun with its long steel barrel. But, no problem for Helen, a strong farm woman from Vermont, and probably accustomed to hunting with a gun just as heavy.'

"But, all that aside, Gentlemen of the jury, you cannot overlook the most damaging piece of evidence that ties Helen Haskell directly to these murders. That is the knife with the carved initials 'TS' wrapped in the apron bearing the embroidered initials 'HH' . . . Tony SanAngelo and Helen Haskell. What more proof do you need?'

"Now let's review the motive. Prosecution has established that the Wallingford farmhouse contained a secret room—most likely a 'hiding place' for runaway slaves. I contend that, at the time of the murders, fugitive slaves were being kept at Lily's farmhouse; a fact just confirmed by Defense's own witness! When Helen Haskell realized that the two visitors to the farm that day were bounty hunters and realizing that harboring slaves was a federal offense, she decided to kill both of them in cold blood. Then she disposed of their bodies in the woods and hid the murder weapon and other evidence under hay in the Wallingford's barn.'

"Counsel for the defense has just now dramatized and prejudiced this whole trial by bringing forward a highly questionable defense witness, unbeknownst to prosecution until this morning, and most likely rehearsed to place blame on a dead woman.'

"Gentlemen, I am deeply disturbed by this turn of events, as well you should be. Just who is this witness, Jedediah Beaumont? He's certainly not a citizen. He's a Negro slave. Slaves are in the habit of doing their Master's bidding. Would he think nothing of lying, if asked to do so by a person in authority? And what of his character? Look at that long scar on his face. Is he some sort of street hoodlum? Did the attorney for Mrs. Haskell dress him up in fine clothes to sway your opinion of him?'

"He swore on the Bible to tell the truth, but is he even a Christian? Don't let this witnesses' testimony influence you one iota. The defense has introduced a time worn excuse used by many accused murderers. Blame the dead, as they can't answer to the charge.'

"The one person, in this courtroom, who could have answered the question of "Who did it?" is the person who could have exonerated herself, if she were truly innocent—and that is Helen Haskell. She, who now sits before you, is mute, refusing to speak. The same as she has done for the past three days. Yes, she is the same and only person who has refused to testify in her own defense.'

"Gentlemen of the Jury I ask that justice be done so that the families of Tony San Angelo and Red Fitzgerald may finally find closure. Let's bring a close to this sad event. Let's ease their suffering and not add more grief to the memories of their sons, the two innocent victims. I ask you to bring back a verdict of murder in the first degree."

Wallingford: "Gentlemen of the Jury. You have just heard counsel for the prosecution present the Commonwealth's case against my client. Mr. DeSoto is an accomplished lawyer and has an enviable reputation as District Attorney for the city of New Bedford.'

"However, I will prove to you this morning that the strength of his case is based largely on circumstantial evidence. He has no direct evidence. He has presented no eye witnesses to the murders. The motive he puts forward is highly suspect. And, he has tried to influence you good gentlemen by discrediting the trial's most important witness—the only eye witness giving sworn testimony here in this court.'

"First let me discuss his inference that because my client has refused to testify, that alone, in and of itself, proves guilt. Gentlemen, under the Constitution of this Commonwealth, no person shall be compelled to accuse or furnish evidence against themselves. The same holds true, under our U.S. Constitution, that no person shall be compelled in any criminal case to be a witness against themselves.'

"Helen Haskell has chosen, for whatever reason, not to testify in her defense and therefore, she may not be called upon to provide a reason for her decision. That right is inviolate and cannot be challenged under law.'

"Gentlemen, you might wish to presume that her refusal to testify has tilted the balance of guilt or innocence against my client. Under law, that is a presumption that you are not allowed to make.'

"The only presumption, one that you must maintain during your deliberations, is that Helen Haskell remains innocent, unless proven guilty beyond reasonable doubt. That burden of proof is a task for the prosecution. The defense does not have to prove innocence, as the presumption of innocence has already been granted to Helen Haskell.'

"The accused, and only the accused, has the right to decide either to testify or not to testify. If the accused decides to testify, then she is subject to all that that entails—especially the rigid and unrelenting cross examination by the prosecution. Some accused, even though innocent, may fear that they will wither under courtroom pressure and unwittingly give answers that the prosecution would like to hear.'

"There are ones who will bow to persons of authority and entangle themselves into a downward spiral of 'acceptable' answers that they cannot escape from. So, Gentlemen, despite what has been inferred by the prosecution, keep uppermost in your mind that Helen's constitutional right not to bear witness against herself cannot be used, nor even questioned as a factor in her guilt or innocence.'

"Prosecution has claimed that Mrs. Haskell's motivation was two-fold. She did not want to be arrested for violating the Fugitive Slave Act and for a more altruistic reason, she just wanted to ensure the freedom of Jedediah and Belinda Beaumont. But motivation is one thing and acting on that motivation is another.'

"To prove murder with malicious intent one must also be convinced that the perpetrator of the crime was capable of doing the deed. I contend that it would be highly improbable for Mrs. Haskell to have taken the life of any human being.'

"Mrs. Haskell is a God-fearing woman. She lives each day according to what she believes to be God's Will. Her religion is not just going to meetings on Sunday but she lives it day in and day out. It is at the very core of her own personal beliefs, from her Methodist family when just a small child, and later joining her husband's Quaker beliefs.'

"One tenet above all that she subscribes to and is at the very core of Quaker beliefs—is that God is present in every person. Therefore, even if under a situation of self-defense, she would not be able to take another person's life.'

"Now let's review the long thread of circumstantial evidence presented by the prosecution and I shall show you Gentlemen of the jury, how quickly that thread becomes unraveled when held up to scrutiny. First, let us be clear in our minds of the difference between direct evidence and circumstantial evidence.'

"Direct evidence relates directly to the crime in question. It may come from eye witness testimony to the actual crime or it may be a piece of evidence directly related to the crime.'

"However, circumstantial evidence, although not directly linked to the crime, may have some probability of truth depending on the circumstance. Cases based largely on circumstantial evidence must be proven by presenting a preponderance of this type of evidence.'

"That means there must be strong and continuous, albeit indirect, linkage to the crime. Nevertheless, I must caution the jury, that some men have been found guilty and hanged based only on circumstantial evidence, when subsequently the real perpetrator of the crime has been found out.'

"For a case based on circumstantial evidence, each link, or thread of that evidence must be proven, that is 'shown to be reasonable with very little doubt'. If one or more of these threads cannot stand up to scrutiny, then the entire length of the thread becomes weakened and can unravel very quickly.'

"Now let us look more closely at some of the circumstantial evidence presented by the Prosecution:

"First, there is the knife and the apron. The prosecution has presented as his strongest piece of evidence the assertion that—because there was a knife with initials 'TS' wrapped in an apron with initials 'HH' there can be no other conclusion drawn than that the knife belonged to Antonio, known as 'Tony' San Angelo' and, that the apron obviously belonged to none other than Helen Haskell. Prosecution claims that this is direct irrefutable evidence that links my client to the murder scene of that evening.'

"They were so sure of this linkage that they did not even bother to call friends or family of Antonio to testify that the knife was indeed his—perhaps they wanted you Gentlemen to come to the same obvious conclusion, without having to give the defense the opportunity to cross examine and place doubt on this piece of evidence.'

"Well, in questioning Police Sgt. Perry, the defense clearly showed that those carved initials on the knife could have been anyone's initials other than Tony SanAngelo's initials."

"But even if we cast doubt aside for a moment, has the prosecution proved that it was Mrs. Haskell who wrapped that knife in that apron and placed it under the hay in the barn? No, they have not. They have presented no eye witnesses to confirm this assertion, nor have they even brought forth a witness that might have said "Helen told me she hid those items in the barn."

"Therefore, anyone could have placed those items in the barn, even well after the crime took place.'

"How convenient—HH and TS linked together. Surely the prosecution wants you to consider that to be irrefutable proof that Helen Haskell was guilty of this crime. But anyone could have framed Mrs. Haskell by wrapping that knife in the initialed apron. Now who would have thought of that.'

Jack slowly turns and looks directly at the prosecution's table. Then, turns back to the jury.

He continues, "Gentlemen of the jury, the Prosecution is asking you to believe, without any doubt, that Mrs. Haskell intentionally wrapped that damning evidence together and placed it where it would one day be found. You must ask yourself if that is a reasonable supposition? Why would any reasonable person even consider doing that?'

"Why would anyone want to link two pieces of evidence together, instead of wanting to burn or bury that evidence so it would never be found.'

"Gentlemen, do you believe this farm woman would be so careless, have so little sense to leave evidence in a barn where hay can easily be disturbed? A farmer's normal working day would have uncovered it in due time. A farm woman would have known a much better way to discard evidence if she had reason to get rid of any, that is. She could have buried it or just tossed it down the hole in the outhouse along with a few ladles full of lye. And never would it be found by anyone.'

"Again, Gentlemen, do you see how this thread of circumstantial evidence is beginning to unwind? Have I placed at least some reasonable doubt in your minds about the credibility of prosecution's claims against my client?'

"Prosecution has not presented any eye witnesses to this crime, yet when the defense brought one forward—Mr. Jedediah Beaumont, they tried vigorously to discredit him. One may ask why?'

"I'll tell you why. It's because one piece of direct evidence can outweigh many myriad pieces of circumstantial evidence. In this instance this eyewitness to this crime—this one piece of direct evidence has caused the prosecution's case, based on circumstantial evidence to fall like a house of cards.'

"Now Gentlemen of the jury, let me prove to you why Jedediah Beaumont is a credible witness: If Helen Haskell were guilty of this crime, one may ask, 'Why in God's name would someone, especially a fugitive slave, choose to risk his freedom and his family's freedom by coming forward to testify and lie, mind you, in open court? He would be subjecting himself, not only to perjury, but risking arrest and return to his former slave master.'

"No, Gentlemen, Jedediah told the truth today because he saw an injustice against this good lady, Helen Haskell. He told the truth because he knew not what else to do. He was willing to risk his freedom, just as he had heard after returning from a long fishing trip, that Helen was willing to risk her own freedom for him. That shows a man of conscience.'

"Jedediah Beaumont came to us of his own free will. Moreover, he was not coached, nor was he asked to lie, as prosecution has inferred.'

"Prosecution wants you to believe that because the witness was a Negro slave that he may have a greater propensity to lie than perhaps a White person. That is blatantly preposterous. The color of a man's skin has nothing to do with what's in his heart and soul.'

"Jedediah has lived as a free man for two years. He is not beholden to any Master or person in authority. He spoke the truth today even though the truth may have jeopardized his freedom. That convinces me, as I hope it will convince you good Gentlemen of the Jury, that Jedediah Beaumont has a somewhat higher moral conscience than many of us in this courtroom today.'

"And for what purpose did Helen Haskell choose to remain mute, and not speak in her own defense—as the Prosecutor clearly spelled out so all could hear—seemingly being a foolish act on her part? The answer to his question, after hearing Jedediah Beaumont's testimony is clear for all to now understand.'

"The answer? She, of course, desired not to cast blame on her deceased sister, but more importantly she wanted to ensure that Jedediah Beaumont and his wife, Belinda could continue their journey to ultimate freedom. Helen Haskell had no other choice, but to remain silent. This choice was made according to her understanding of God's Will, and her own conscience.'

"I fault the prosecution for not honoring Helen's right to remain silent and his blatant disregard for the law that says one cannot infer guilt because a person chooses not to testify.'

"Finally, I want to clear the fine name of Elizabeth 'Lily' Wallingford, now deceased, of any crime associated with this case. There were certainly crimes committed and laws broken on the ninth of April at the Wallingford farm, but Mrs. Wallingford was not intentionally responsible for any of them.'

DeSoto: "Objection, your honor, Mrs. Wallingford is not on trial here. It's known that she was the wife of Attorney Wallingford. This is an obvious ploy by the defense to gain sympathy from the jury."

Judge: "Both Prosecution and Defense have wide latitude to present their closing arguments without interruption as long as they stay within the bounds of propriety. Objection overruled. Defense may proceed with closing arguments."

Wallingford: "Thank you, your Honor. I will continue. Article XIV of the Massachusetts Declaration of Rights, guarantees that every subject has a right to be secure from all unreasonable searches, and seizures of his person and his house. If there is a requirement to make a search in suspected places, or to arrest one or more suspected persons, or to seize their property, then a warrant to do so must be issued with the formalities, prescribed by the laws.'

"The decedents, Antonio SanAngelo and Michael Fitzgerald first broke the law by breaking into the Wallingford household without a warrant. They further broke the law by forcibly constraining Mr. Beaumont against his will, while Michael Fitzgerald attempted to forcibly rape Mrs. Beaumont. Mrs. Wallingford shot both men in self-defense while under attack herself when trying to protect the two persons in her charge.'

"Some would argue that the two deceased were not entirely responsible for their actions because they were inebriated on the day of the incident. Drunkenness is not a defense for breaking the law.'

"I know my words fall heavily on the parents of Mr. SanAngelo and Mr. Fitzgerald and only add to the grieving they have already suffered. For this I apologize. But the record has to be set straight for the benefit of Mrs. Wallingford so she may now rest in peace.'

"Gentlemen of the Jury, I ask that you bring back a verdict of 'Not Guilty.'"

Jack sits down, pats my hand; and I am without words, for once.

Judge John W. Holmes: "I shall now give Instructions to the Jury.'

"The indictment in this case is in itself a mere accusation or charge against the Defendant and is not itself any evidence of guilt. No juror in this case should permit himself to be influenced against the Defendant because of, or on account of, the fact that an indictment by the Grand Jury has been returned against her.'

"This is a criminal prosecution, and the rule as to the amount of proof in this case is different from that in civil cases. A mere preponderance of the evidence does not warrant the jury in finding the Defendant guilty. Before the Defendant can be convicted, you must be satisfied of his or her guilt beyond a reasonable doubt.'

"The law presumes a Defendant to be innocent of a crime. Thus, a Defendant, although accused, begins the trial with a 'clean slate', with no evidence against them. This presumption of innocence stays with the Defendant through every stage of the trial, unless and until the State proves his or her guilt beyond a reasonable doubt. The Defendant is never required to prove that he or she is not guilty.'

"The presumption of innocence alone is sufficient to acquit a Defendant, unless the jurors are satisfied—beyond a reasonable doubt—of the Defendant's guilt. A guilty verdict can be given, but only after careful and impartial consideration of all of the evidence in the case. And the verdict must be unanimous among all jurors."

"I now charge the Jury to retire to the Jury room for deliberation and to arrive at a just verdict. Everyone is excused and court will re-convene after the Jury has reached its verdict"

* * *

This is the third day and no verdict yet. The matron lets Joshua in, and then relocks my cell door. I must tell him the bad news.

"Jack said I'd probably get a guilty verdict."

"Why? What's wrong with him? Of course, the jury will know better."

"I must prepare for the worse if it happens. Eli and Cal . . . tell them I am innocent. Say, that their Ma wants them to close their ears and not listen to any others."

"Do not worry so. You are going to get free. You must keep your spirits up." He draws me close, but I can hear those dratted lock keys jangling as small but hurried footsteps are getting closer. Matron must be coming to take me to the Court House for the verdict.

"She unlocks the cell door and says, "You'll have to leave now, Mr. Haskell." Josh gives me a kiss and leaves. He knows it's time.

I'm scared. She shackles me and we start down the hall. But before reaching the next locked door we hear a commotion outside.

Cannot fathom what's happening. The closest window is up too high to see out. Then Matron pushes a bench to the wall. She looks quickly around to see if anyone is near and then scrambling for the right key, she loosens my shackles. We grab hold of the iron grate that bars the thick and dirty window pane. My sleeve helps to give a quick rub over the layers of dirt.

I'm astonished! Such a crowd! Look at those signs out there, all bobbing up and down. I listen as they yell out my name.

"Who are they?"

The Matron smiles, pointing out, "Some must be day workers with sympathetic bosses allowing them to come here. Yet, it is not too far for outsiders to travel, since we are near New Bedford's wharves and many boats dock here."

I murmur to myself, "Perhaps I have a bit of a chance after all?" What a commotion going on. One board with plain scribbling reads, "*Give Em HELL, Helen.*"

Now I see a bigger sign, painted with red letters and blue stars for borders—it shouts out, "*WOMEN'S RIGHTS, NOW!*"

I wonder, who is that lady down in the street? I recall her pictures in newspapers. She is fanning herself while under her Parasol. She looks so regal standing there.

Matron whispers, "Down here, close to the wall, there's a brave one. He has dark skin and is coming onto the sidewalk." One sign is so big; I can see it from afar. Large red, white and blue letters scream out ~ *"AMERICA's BROTHERS AND SISTERS ~ FIGHTING FOR YOU, HELEN."* Over there, see, a smaller one, and it tells for all to see, *"JUDGE*, go *SET HELEN FREE!"*

I hear a cough, and turn round. Oh no, two guards stand behind us. But they smile as they try to peer out the windows, too.

"Listen Matron, are we hearing something different. Those faint, but high voices?"

"Yes, and the sounds get louder and I see small children marching in step, and singing what is on their signs."

The crowd, bless their souls, has made way for the children to come to the front. They too, have dark skins and start singing.

'Listen to us, singing our song.[16]
Mrs. Haskell done no wrong.
Oh Lordy! Hear our plea,
Set her free, set her free!'

"She done no crime,
as You must know.
Time to tell them, let her go!
Please, Lordy! Hear our Plea!
Set her free, set her free!'

"Could not kill those evil men.
Make Po-lice go look again.
Open eyes so they may see,
and tell the Judge to set her free!
'Please, Lordy! Hear our Plea!
Set her free, set her free!'

So much clapping, hooting and hollering is going on. But, we must hurry and get on with our walk. Ah, yes, it's good the guards have moved on. I stick the few wispy hairs back in my bun, and then tuck in my shirtwaist.

"Oh, oh, Look Matron, my sleeve from cleaning the window?" She helps me get down off the bench. Then, gathers the sleeve into a crease, right over the big long streak.

Then she whispers, "We cannot tarry any longer. It's time to get on to the court."

We drag the bench back against the far wall and then she binds my wrists in chains once more. She gives me a quick hug then bustles off ahead of me. I do a double step to keep up with her.

Can't help but see Joshua seated three rows from the back. He smiles and sends me a salute. Now the chains rattle on the table since I cannot keep my hands from shaking. So, I'd best keep them folded. There are footsteps hurrying along. But not too many. Oh, it's the Bailiff with the Court reporter. The visitors and balcony seats are filled and we wait and wait.

At long last each Juror strolls in as if going for a Sunday walk. If I could, I would go prod the end one to hurry on in. They've been hashing everything over for three days and still just poking along. Don't they know they leave me at my wit's end?

The Jurors finally nod to each other and then, the head one refolds a paper ever so carefully to hand to the Bailiff. He passes it to Judge Holmes.

Then His Honor lays it down—and, pauses to clean his spectacles along with a few clearings of his throat—then he reads it, but only to himself, not out loud. And I wait.

Judge: "Now, I ask the foreman, is this your true verdict, and have each of you agreed unanimously with the same?"

Foreman: "Aye, we have Your Honor."

Judge: "How say ye, guilty or innocent?"

Foreman: "We the jury find the defendant, Helen Haskell, innocent of all charges."

I am in such a state, my head spins.

Judge: "Say you one and say you all?"

Foreman: "Yes, sir." And the Jury, in turn, repeat their "Ayes."

The Judge asks me if I have any final words to be saying?

I nod "Yes" but wish I had not, since I can barely stand on my own.

"I did not know I was going to speak. I hope I can say what is in my heart and give truth to what made me silent.'

"You see, I was not an eye witness to the actual shootings. So, I could not let anyone else be the focus of the blame—especially my dear departed sister, Lily."

With no warning my knees start to buckle and I start to fall back but Jack grabs my hand, steadies my chair and sets me down.

Judge: "Can you continue? Your attorney can help you up, if so. Bailiff, get this lady some water."

"Thank you your Honor. I need just a few sips. Now my head feels much better.'

"That is all I have to say—except I will pray for Mrs. SanAngelo and Mrs. Fitzgerald. Not only for the loss of their sons, but for their poor son's souls to find peace. Oh, and I am beholden to the Jury; they said I was innocent. Finally, I shan't forget the thoughtful acts done for me while in your jail." Then I made a point of looking at the Matron.

Judge: "Mrs. Haskell, the court thanks you for your generosity and your exemplary conduct while in confinement. They will be noted for the record. Now you may be seated. Attorney Wallingford, mind you, get hold of her arm, do not let her fall."

The Judge says, "For the record, also, I wish to make a statement:'

"In my 32 years on the bench I have not experienced a more brave and honest human being as I've witnessed with the testimony of Mr. Jedediah Beaumont.'

"Forsaking his own safety, he has come before this court to tell the truth. A truth that he knew full well could put both him and his wife in jeopardy. This man of honor was willing to be sent back to a life not one of us ever could dream of as being so wicked—a life of cruelty and inhumane treatment, under slavery with his former owner.'

"Owning another human being is an act, in and of itself, completely against God's will and this Commonwealth's Laws.'

"Forthwith, I will send a formal request to the Governor to declare Jedediah and Belinda Beaumont as free citizens of this Commonwealth.'

"We shall also inform the Governor of the state he was held captive in, that under no circumstances shall any illegal acts be allowed here, against either Mr. or Mrs. Beaumont in our Commonwealth.'

"Also, included in that letter will be my ruling that Mrs. Helen Haskell shall not be subsequently tried for any alleged prior violation of the Fugitive Slave Act.'

"There are certain truths that withstand the test of time, by being above any man-made laws. The principle truth in this matter was laid out very succinctly by our founding fathers in the Declaration of Independence 'that these truths be self-evident, that all men are created equal, that they are endowed by their Creator with certain unalienable Rights, that among these are Life, Liberty and the pursuit of Happiness'.

"The Fugitive Slave Act is an abomination that should be disregarded by any State wishing to protect the freedoms of its citizens. The Act is completely against our constitution and is illegal in every sense.'

"I may be challenged by this ruling but, by God, I will stand up before the highest court in this land and defend this right to the fullest. A right that if any of us had taken from us—we should be surely baying to the moon—not sitting by silently.'

"I quote the saying, all must have heard by now, and shall paraphrase accordingly. 'When seeing evil be done, if not one good man shall give objection but instead, stands beside other silent men; then surely evil shall flourish.'" [38]

"Ladies and gentleman of this court room, and the good gentlemen of the jury, this court rests. Court is now adjourned, with today being the formal and final ending to this trial."

* * *

On the courthouse steps, I lean against Joshua, and I'm not shaking. Must be this sun warming me up. This bright light makes me blink, and it's hard to see.

Josh says, "Look at the crowd. They're clapping, cheering and waving."

I see them. I wave back. They cheer louder.

"Joshua, is that Jed and Belinda coming down the steps?"

Jed shakes Joshua's hand. Then he hangs back, but I hug him.

He says, "Hello, Missus Helen, I'se glad seein y'all t' day, an lookin so fine. An I'se real surprised to see Mistuh Joshua lass week. Soon's I gets my door open—it been like seein a ghost. How long it been? Alla two year?"

What? Did Josh know he could speak this well?

Belinda says, "An I thank y'all for bein so nice, helpin us an all. An gettin us t' Middleborough. Jed an I got lots a books t' read in Mr. Hawthorne's library. He give us a lot. I jess can't talk as good as Jed."

Joshua says, "Jed, which school did you go to? The African one run by the Methodist church, or the Quaker school?"

"No suh, I read lots a books out t' sea. An sailor men be's talkin t' me, explainin big words. Same as Frederick Douglass did, when he learnt his letters. An I be's pest'rin everyone roun me . . . ats how I learnt all about alphabet. Did I say it right?"

I say, "You surely did. Couldn't have done better. But you took a big chance showing up here."

"I hadda come. Mistuh Joshua been tellin me about a trial goin on? An y' all needin me t' say all about it? I shudda got a post off t' y'all long afore now. But, I jess got in from whalin afta stayin t' sea near on t' two year."

"You must have been scared to testify?"

"You mean, y'all dint see me sweatin? Tryin t' be's talkin jess like afore, when I been livin at Missus Lily's house? But, it sure gets me some pity, dint it? Y' know, bein a poor slavin man." Belinda points to a horse and wagon in the street.

"Gotta go, but hadda stop, t' tell y'all about how bad we feelin for Missus

Lily. Hearin bout her goin t' her restin place. She been a good lady an we knows God is seein t' her now."

Belinda pulls at his sleeve, "Jed, say g' bye, we gotta go now, the wagon man is waiting. We hope we will be seein y'all again."

"I'll ask Jack for your address. Just don't miss your ride. Maybe we can write? Send a post?" They nod and run down the steps.

"Joshua, where is Jack? He was just here by my side."

"I see him, down by the sidewalk, walking away."

I call out, "Jack! Please stop. I want to thank you!"

When we meet up with him he says, "Mr. DeSoto took the loss very personally. He was so upset and so surprised at the people's reaction toward him that he decided not to bring a further charge against you, nor Jed and Belinda, for being accessories after the fact."

Joshua shakes Jack's hand and says, "Helen and I thank you for a job well done."

He doffs his hat at me, smiles, and then walks on.

Joshua says, "The Vermont train won't wait for us. We better get to the station." Joshua walks so fast I have to run to keep up.

This train, it's clickity clacking and rocking back and forth—. I watch the woods rushing by—. But I can't sleep. The trial, was it a dream? Heavens, no. It was a nightmare.

"Joshua? Open your eyes. Are you awake?' One eye half opens.

"I was lucky Jed showed up. But how on earth did you find him?"

He sits up straighter. "It's not so much a matter of luck."

"What do you mean?"

"I kept thinking we need an eye witness. I was thinking that Jed and Belinda would be in Canada. And, it might be impossible to find them."

"So, what did you do?"

"I took a trip to Middleborough to find Mr. Hawthorne. Remember when we left Jed and Belinda in his care, at his safe house? I was surprised to learn that he had taken them to New Bedford. They had been constantly pleading with him to take them there. He finally gave in."

"My goodness, Josh. That's what they had been planning all along. That night of the hurricane at David's house is when they first started hatching their plan. The independent nature of those two will take them far in this world. But how were you able to locate them in New Bedford?"

"James Hawthorne gave me the address of the family he left them with. From there it was easy to track them down. I went to the wharves and started asking for Jedediah by name until I found him."

"Why didn't you tell me what you were doing?"

"I did not want to get your hopes up in case I was unable to find him."

"Joshua, you never cease to amaze me. Thank you, my darling."

With that I went back to listening to the clickity clack of the wheels along the tracks until I fell off into a pleasant slumber in Joshua's arms.

Chapter Twenty-six

Home Life in Randolph

Here I sit, still keeping my journal up to date with letters, news clippings, and notes of remembrances. Maybe, as Josh says, I'll have enough to write a novel someday. But, pray tell, who would read it?

April 2nd 1855:

Joshua was asked to escort a colored man and woman from a safe house in Bethel to our home. They were travelling with a child who was not their own.

"I won't be gone long. One of the Elders has offered to drive me down this afternoon. I'll pick up this family and then wait for nightfall."

"How will you get back?"

"I'll stay alongside the railroad tracks. We have a half moon tonight and it's just an eight mile treck back to our place. Will you ask Caspar and Rufus if they can stay at their place, until we can make plans to move them further north?"

"Yes, I will. Be careful. We'll await your return."

Almost midnight and Josh returns from Bethel. Caspar and Rufus have been waiting with me.

"Helen, Caspar, and Rufus, this is Mr. and Mrs. Toby Danforth. The ten-year-old boy they brought with them, will be in shortly. He had to stop at the outhouse."

"Pleased to meet you. I've prepared tea and sugar cakes, and I'll fix a meal if you are hungry. What is the name of the boy?"

"We thankin you Ma'am, but not hungry. The boy's name is Jeremiah."

"I've heard that name before. Caspar, was your boy named Jeremiah?"

"Yes Ma'am. Many darkies got Jeremiah for name."

The door opens and the boy walks in. Caspar jumps up.

"No! Good God, no! It cain't be. Is that you, Jeremiah?"

The boy runs and jumps into Caspar's arms.

Rufus says, "Jeremiah, he only six-year-old when we lost him. We thanks the Lord, he still alive."

Toby says, "We find him all alone in woods. An it be, oh . . . long about four year gone by. He live wiv us eber since. Reason we comes t' Randolph, cuz folks we meet tell bout dis Caspar losing his son. Jeremiah, he allus be good boy . . . an we hates it, but we hafta find his real Pa."

Caspar, wiping tears from his eyes, hugs Mr. and Mrs. Danforth. And then shakes Joshua's hand and says, "You brought my boy home."

We now have another to add to the Haskell family.

June 4th 1855:

I must write all of this in my Journal.

Jacob is grateful to Bethany and her devotion as a friend, but keeps his distance from the start. Abigail scared him such that he cannot trust so lightly again. But Bethany's a fit young lady. I imagine her appeal creeps up on him.

Jacob signed to Josh, "Bethany visits sister Calista. Needs help with Calista's new baby. She's gone for five days."

Josh said, "Why are you telling me this? Are you OK?"

"I forget my chores. My new born calf got the colic. Something terrible must have gone wrong. Oh Joshua, she was the best, and I miss her."

"Who? The calf?"

"What? No. Bethany. My heart aches. I want her here, for good."

"Then take it up with her father, after you and Bethany agree on making a permanent bond."

When Bethany returned, Jacob got up the courage to ask Bethany to consider a more permanent relationship.

Bethany signed to him, "What do you mean? I am living in your cabin. Isn't that permanent?"

"No, Bethany. I mean we get hitched up."

"You silly goose, of course. I've just been waiting for you to ask."

Finally, Jacob signed to the Elder, to ask permission to wed his daughter. He agreed and notice was given.

The day has arrived and we are on our way to the Meeting. On this day, Jacob and Bethany carry out their intentions to marry.

"Josh, look, here they come. Look at the beautiful dress that Bethany's wearing. I hope no one says it is too fancy. Will they sit down front?"

"Yes, of course. And I'll need to go sit with them. When it's time to say their vows, I can give voice to Jacob's signing."

They enter together and sit facing friends, family and meeting members. Joshua moves forward and sits with them. We all begin our silent worship until Jacob and Bethany feel it is time to say their vows. They rise, hold hands, and Bethany begins by speaking and signing.

"In the presence of God and before our families and friends, I take thee, Jacob Haskell, to be my husband. I promise love and tenderness, and with Divine assistance, to be unto thee a loving and faithful wife so long as we both shall live."

Jacob signs to Bethany while Joshua voices Jacob's oath to all at the meeting. Jacob then pats his chest and gives out the OK sign. Turning to Bethany, he completes the ceremony with a final and sealing kiss—which needs no words, nor hand signals to explain. They both sign the Quaker marriage certificate and take their seats.

Joshua reads it aloud.

"On the Seventeenth Day of June in the Year One
Thousand, Eight Hundred and Fifty Five, in West
Randolph, Vermont,
Jacob Haskell
and
Bethany Billings
entered into a mutual covenant of holy matrimony before God.
On this joyous occasion, Bethany and Jacob did offer each to the other
love, tenderness and dedication, promising in the presence of those they
hold most dear to share a devoted life for all seasons to come.

And we set our names in witness of those vows and pledge to
celebrate and support this union."

Everyone at the meeting continues with their own silent worship—until one by one, congregants stand to voice their support and advice for the couple. The meeting ends and all those present step forward to sign the certificate as witnesses.

Bethany's father, the Elder, walks over to shake Joshua's hand.

He says, "Joshua, your family is now my family and mine is now yours."

"Thank you, Elder Billings, we welcome Bethany into our family."

"And Jacob into ours."

Jacob and Bethany approach.

I sign, "Look at you both. I'm so proud of you, Jacob. And Bethany, you look beautiful in that dress." They both smile and Bethany gives me a hug.

Now at home, Joshua says, "None should complain of this bride and groom's wedding not being in earnest. Not with Jacob standing there, proud as could be."

I say, "Bethany, too, showed pride and will have wonderful memories of her crowning day. I loved her delicate white lacy veil, over the beautiful old wedding dress her great grandma first wore.

July 4th 1856

We watch the 4th of July parade in Randolph. It's our 80th year of freedom from British rule. My ears ring from trombones blaring. Children do cartwheels on the lawn. Guess the boys imitate the clowns. Then, they lick on maple sugar ices. Such a grand time.

But Joshua tugs at my arm and points to the carriage. He rounds up our sons and Jacob and Bethany follow. Good, I'm ready to head home.

We just got here. What's this, a letter from Ellie Hutchins stuck in our postbox? I tear it open.

And, oh my, "Joshua, see what Ellie writes!"

Dear Helen and Joshua,

I received a post two days ago, from a woman named Solange Busque, living in Granby, Quebec, Canada. She informed me that she had hired a colored seamstress by the name of Daisy Corinda Carrington. She and her husband and five-year-old son, are living in a Guest House on her farm.

Helen, that's the same Daisy you took in some years ago. Back then, my husband James was able to transport her and her baby to a safe house in Montpelier owned by a relative of Rowland Robinson from Ferrisburgh. That relative planned to take them to Rokeby House in Ferrisburgh. It is obvious from the letter that Daisy and her family have now finally made it all the way to Canada.

Mrs. Busque writes how Daisy says 'thank you for food and shelter you provided. and the clothes for her and her baby. She sends this dollar in payment for your boots you insisted she wear. She hopes that sometime your family can come and visit her.

My best wishes to you both.

I remain, Ellie Hutchins.

"Joshua, I am just so glad for them. I thought I wouldn't hear of her again. But the Lord answered a prayer."

Joshua says, "Amen to that, and see this dollar? It was probably a week's wages for her."

December 26th 1856:

Joshua's oldest sister, Orinda, died early this morning from Consumption. She had such a time trying to breathe for many months before passing on. The doctor said it was probably due to the quality of air in the mills. Other girls said later, they were tempted to write home to complain about all the cotton dust floating around above the looms. But tattling would only get them fired.

She worked in the same Lowell mill for 19 years. She was known for her tireless efforts to establish a 10-hour workday for Factory Girls in Lowell and other New England towns. However, she never saw less than a 12-hour workday before her death. I will let Joshua finish this tribute with a fitting memoriam to his sister, since he knew her so much better than I.

Orinda rests upon the hill
Midst Primrose and Daffodil
Her grave so simple and clean
Made of granite, not of slate
Like the lady and her cause
The likes we've never seen[17]

* * *

March 5th 1857:

Good news! Mary, our youngest, was born today. Elisha, Caleb, and of course, Joshua were overjoyed at the arrival of this newest member to our family. Elisha is now eleven years of age and brother Caleb is nine.

May 3rd 1857:

It's our 12th wedding anniversary. Eli and Cal tend to Mary, while Joshua and I celebrate with a picnic by the swimming hole down at Ayer's brook. The air is nice and warm but the water too cold for bathing. In place of it, we just laze around. How peaceful. He starts plucking up blades of grass, and clovers. I look close, hoping for one with four leaves.

Joshua starts humming, then pulls out his harmonica. He plays a quick run and puts it back in his pocket. He says something about ridding his mind of dark, troubling thoughts.

He says, "I must confess. "I cannot keep it any longer to myself. There is a secret you should know of—these past seven years."

All of seven years he has had a . . . no . . . "What secret?"

"It's, well . . . I deceived you, and if your love changes for me, I will understand. All I can do is to ask for your forgiveness."

No, Lord, he's not telling me about another woman? Could it be that — that Lucretia? No, too old. Or worse, could it be . . . no, not Abigail? I don't want him to say another word, I cannot bear it.

He stands silent, but coughs a bit. Maybe it's some loose trollop in a Windsor tavern?

"Remember when I said the Elders had the idea for me to leave."

Is he daft? The Elders would never advise him to seek out another woman if married.

"What? The Elders? They would never have anything to do with—." He places two fingers against my lips. His hand grabs my wrist, but I pull free. He does not make sense. What does he confess?

"Hold on, I am not done. I truly believed it was our Lord speaking to me during silent times at Meeting House. I had to do what He asked."

"Your Lord told you? That gave the permission I suspect? What else is there to tell? How can you blame our Lord? Who else—what name is there to tell?"

"Nothing. It was my idea to go help the runaways. Not the Elders. I have never lied nor deceived you before nor since. I hope you can forgive me."

We pack up and walk home, awkwardly. I am so angry. Yet, not at him. What a waste, all those nights worrying. Wondering if he found another to love. So, now he confesses to something I never suspected.

Yet, between the two, a lie and another woman? There is no comparison. But, he did leave me with too much work, running this farm. No, I'm not ready, cannot give in, not yet.

This evening while readying for bed, the darkness is upon me. Perhaps without light I can speak my mind to him. Yet, I long for the way we always were so close, especially at night.

Gently I lift myself into our ready warmed bed. We lay, not touching but near enough. I hear his even breathing. I scoot over inch by inch. I reach out my hand, it touches his shoulder. I cough. Then cough again. He turns towards me.

Next morning, I join him as he chops wood out by the shed. He stops work and lays down the axe. Then on one bended knee he stretches out his hand, and here's a four-leaf clover.

A simple offering, it is, and I carefully tuck it into my apron pocket.

Joshua looks up at me but my smile leaves. I must replace it with this stern look I have practiced so well.

"Joshua, your words yesterday caused me much anguish. Although I believe you did not plan to tell a lie and that you did have a special calling. A powerful holding one at that. So, there is nothing for me to forgive. Except I am still angry at your leaving us, and we should never have been parted—not for one night."

He lets out a long, deep breath.

"Joshua, if you ever do that again—tell a lie of any sort, I might just drop my iron skillet, right smack on your head." He raises his eyebrows, but then starts to smile, which then turns into a big grin.

"Do you suppose, Helen my love, that we might be going back to the brook today to continue where we left off . . . that is before I opened my dumb mouth?" He stands with hands in his pockets, his head at a tilt as he looks down. Now he goes side to side from one foot to the other. So patient he is. Then, I hurry into his arms.

I say, "In answer to your question, about continuing our picnic, it might be a possibility later. But now, I shall need a hand to get all my chores done—gathering eggs, milking cows, tidying up, tending to the boys. What is your answer?"

"Ah, Helen, of course yes. Here take my hand. We've work to do."

* * *

Mary tries to walk. I must follow behind her. Now she sits, doesn't crawl but scoots right along for Joshua's feet. He sits reading his paper at the kitchen table. Mary is ten months old and much too quick for me. Joshua reaches under the cupboard, and puts some pots and pans on the floor. She bangs a cover on Joshua's boot—and pulls on his boot laces. I pick her up.

We sit quiet, until she reaches for his paper. Joshua puts it down.

"Hello Mary, almost time for bed, is it?" She laughs, and claps her hands. And reaches for me.

She sleeps before I get her covers up to her chin.

"Helen, do you remember Alexander Twilight?

"Was he the one that went to Randolph Academy and later built that large stone school somewhere in northern Vermont?"

"Yes. I just read that he died last year on June 19th 1857 and has been buried in Brownington, Vermont. He was 61 years old."

"Sorry to hear that." Josh continues reading.

He asks, "Do you recall the Dred Scott case."

"Was he the slave who sued in the courts, that he was a free man because he had lived in free States."

"Yes, he started his case in the courts more than ten years ago, and it finally went all the way up to the Supreme Court. That was when the Court ruled that people of African descent could never be citizens of the United States and, therefore, could not expect any protection from the Federal Government or the courts." [39]

"I remember the date. It was in March of last year,"

"Yes, Helen, and do you remember the outrage it caused among the abolitionists in Vermont. We had outlawed slavery in our State, going all the way back to 1777. Now we were being told by the highest court in the land that Negroes in Vermont could no longer be citizens."

"Yes, but why do you bring this up?"

"Well, yesterday our State legislature decided to tell the Supreme Court that Vermont was going to disregard their decision—."

"Wait Josh, let me fix a tray with a pot of tea and biscuits and fixings. When I come back, I'd like to hear more about that."

I put the tray on the table beside Josh and then pull up another chair.

"OK, now what did our State do and how did you find out about it?"

"It's right here in this morning's paper. In regards to the Dred Scott case, it says, in October, our legislature had passed a resolution saying, 'these extra-judicial opinions of the Supreme Court of the United States are a dangerous usurpation of power, and have no binding authority upon Vermont, or the people of the United States.'" [40]

"That was in October. You said something happened yesterday."

"They decided to put some teeth into that resolution and yesterday our legislature passed Act 37, which said that '. . . the Supreme Court had no binding authority upon Vermont and that no person could be considered property of another person. And, every slave who entered the state would be set free.'" [41]

"My goodness, Joshua--what a bold move for any state to take against the federal government."

"Yes, and Act 37 also said that 'every person who violated Vermont's anti-slavery laws could be imprisoned for up to fifteen years, and fined up to two thousand dollars.'" [41]

"But, didn't we do the same in 1850, when Vermont went against the Fugitive Slave Act?"

"Helen, the 'Habeas Corpus' act which said no slave could be removed from Vermont without having the opportunity for a Jury trial, was one of the reasons I became committed to helping runaways. If our own State was that committed to helping slaves, then I certainly wanted to be part of that movement."

"I'm proud of our State and I'm proud of you, Joshua."

Chapter Twenty-seven

Thanksgiving with the Beaumonts

November 18th 1859:
Received a post from David.

I show Joshua. "Oh? So David's had correspondence with Jed and Belinda. What have we here? Can this be real? The Beaumont's have issued a grand invitation for us to visit."

"Yes and could Jed have written it? You'd think he was addressing royalty."

Joshua reads it aloud.

"To please join the Beaumont's this Holiday season.
Come join us for Thanksgiving."

"Can we go, Josh? It would be so nice to see them again?"

"Of course. We shall certainly go. I'm sure Jacob will tend the animals while we are gone."

"Good, I shall bring some of my preserves for a gift."

November 25th 1859:

I love this sun, but it blinds me, trying to see the trees out there, and the hills go by too fast.

What's this? "Mary, be careful, my boot must be in your way. You almost tripped over it. Just sit still."

Joshua, says, "No need looking out each window. Time won't go by any sooner, so wait till we get there." Joshua puts her on his lap.

Eli and Cal sit back with eyes closed. They only move their heads when the train rounds a curve and they get tossed about for a bit. I wish Mary would try to nap, too.

We arrive at their home on Davis Street. Jed greets us and straight away calls out, "Belinda, come see, they're here."

The smell of cooking comes from the kitchen.

Jed beams down at us. "Please come in. Give me your wraps and your coats. What a grand day we will have. Welcome Joshua and Helen. It's so good to see y'all. Caleb, you are the youngest boy? Elisha, the eldest? Welcome, and Missus Helen, who might this young lady be?"

"I forgot to tell you ahead of time this is our Mary, the youngest."

"Hello, Miss Mary. Pleased to meet you."

"Jed, you've taken me aback, talking like white folks. Where did you get all this polite talk?"

Before he could answer, Belinda comes in, and throws herself into my arms, "Misssus Helen and Mister Joshua, we're so glad to see y'all. Jedediah was at our window all mornin and prayin no harm be comin' to y'all. And I heard Jed, just now. He's tryin' to sound so uppity. He's gone to school, much as he can, and I get to read his books, too. Both of us finally learnin proper English an all."

"That's good, Belinda. You knew some reading and writing before you left the plantation, didn't you?"

"Yes, I did. Round here our friends are like us and we don't have to sound like a 'Yassuh, no suh, is at all, suh? Like a plantation darky. So please come in to our Living Room and make yourselves comfortable."

Then, she went back to the kitchen.

Jed then introduced his children and I was surprised hearing their names. Twin girls named Helen and Lily and their youngest, a boy named David.

Eli and Cal wander around the Library. Jed points out recent good books he's read. He tells them to help themselves, and they do.

Mary went off to the girls' room to sing songs. We hear squealing at the end of "Ring around a rosy . . . all fall down." They must love the falling songs. Now it's "London Bridges falling down, falling down."

A dinner bell rings, and Jed leads us to the dining room. My goodness, what a fine-looking spread. Belinda presents a to-be-proud-of feast including Turkey and many vittles from her South Carolina 'heritage.'

Our Holiday spread had plenty of fish from Jed's recent return from the Sea. The cranberry sauce, Belinda said, came from cranberries grown in bogs over by Cape Cod.

I ask, "Jed, tell us how you've been faring in New Bedford.?"

"When Belinda and I came to New Bedford we joined the Zion Methodist Church. Those folk told me about Frederick Douglass, a Negro and a good preacher. He spoke as if he always knew the English language. He knew so much, 'specially about the Constitution and how it is against slavery."

Joshua said, "I heard him speak one time and also read his book. A fine man he is."

Jed says, "Anyway, they read me his newspapers. They were called the 'Frederick Douglass Papers.' I know then, I must learn how to talk better and to read and write. And, to learn more about this fine Gentleman."

Joshua asks, "Who taught you to read and write your letters? How did you manage to get the speller you needed?"

"Church folks helped until I worked on Captain Souza's fishing boat. He teaches me during the long times we spend at sea. I next went to a Quaker school to learn my grammar."

Jed continues, "Captain also says I must read more every day. I am almost done with 'A Narrative of the Life of Frederick Douglass, an American Slave.'

Joshua says, "I've read his book. He was an excellent writer."

Would you like me to read some of Mr. Douglass' writing?"

I say, "Yes, Jedediah. Please do."

"Mr. Douglass wrote, '*I have often been utterly astonished, since I came to the north, to find persons who could speak of the singing, among slaves, as evidence of their contentment and happiness. It is impossible to conceive of a greater mistake. Slaves sing most when they are most unhappy. The songs of the slave represent the sorrows of his heart; and he is relieved by them, only as an aching heart is relieved by its tears.*'" [42]

I say, "Jed, that's a fine picture of Mr. Douglass you have there. And, what a difference. I mean, the way you can read. I'm glad you like books. Since first learning about what books can teach me, I've not gone long without one."

"I'm knowin that feeling, Missus Helen. How would me and Belinda get anywhere without reading good books. How about y'all, Belinda?" She smiles, and nods at me.

"Jed, at times, while I was reading by the fireplace at Lily's, I heard you both singing. It was so faint, coming from behind the wall to your room. I could not catch it all, but the sadness came through. Is that what Mr. Douglass meant?"

Jed says, "Yes, Missus Helen, those were sad songs from aching hearts. Like we use to sing on the plantation."

"I see. Do you have other heroes, beside Mr. Douglass?"

"Have y'all heard about Harriet Tubman? Arminta was her slave name, and Tubman was her marryin name. She escaped and took her Momma's name of Harriet. Anyway, listen to what she writes.'

"I had reasoned this out in my mind; there was one of two things I had a right to, liberty, or death; if I could not have one, I would have the other; for no man should take me alive; I should fight for my liberty as long as my strength lasted . . ."[43]

Jed continues, "Harriet's nickname is Moses. She ran away, and then went back many times, helping colored folks using the underground railroad. She's also been telling slaves the best ways to run away, and she gets others to help.'

"She said, *'Quakers are almost as good as colored. They call themselves friends and you can trust them every time.'*"

"I drew a picture of Moses. Do you like it.?"[43.a]

Joshua says, "Well done. She looks very determined. I do believe that she knew some religious men were not as trustworthy. They spoke of being a helper in church, but when it came down to it, they oft times fell short."

I say, "Joshua gave me a book about Sojourner Truth while I awaited trial. She's another strong woman, and despite all the dangers presented—she is quite amazing." Jed draws Belinda closer to him.

"I have her book, too. Belinda likes to read it. Wait, I'll fetch it."

"Y'all see how Jed is takin t' readin."

Jed says, "Here it is. It's called 'The Narrative of Sojourner Truth, a Northern Slave."[36.b.]

"Thanks, Jed. Here's the passage, yes it shows how strong her character is where she would never give up when on a quest. She never learned to read or write, but a marvelous memory helped her along the way."

"See where she preached quite extensively. Yes, as Minister of the Gospel, religion was the answer and she would follow what God told her. Same as her mother from early on said 'she had a mission to fulfill.' But never knew what it was, still she kept on looking."

Belinda says, "The best part is right here. She took white people to court an sued, can y'all think on it? I cain't imagine how—."

Jed says, "But, Lindy Bell, a lawyer did alla work. An it was to get her son back from Alabama, from an owner who broke alla laws."

I say, "Nevertheless, she dared, as a colored woman, to take a white person to court. And there were two other times when she would not sit back and let the unjust laws walk all over her."

Belinda says, "I been lovin where she suing a white conductor who did not stop. Coloreds never got rides afore, but she wanted t' get on. He jest kep' on going and dragging her on his ride. And she gets her shoulder hurt, real bad."

Jed says, "But, that was in Washington where lawmen work."

I laugh. "I did read about it. And, again she won in court. Maybe it helped wake those good men up, the ones making the laws in our Capital. Probably not, but good for her."

Belinda nods in appreciation.

Joshua says, "Jed, I'm glad to hear your plans for wanting to learn more. But you don't have to hope to be like someone else. You did Helen a great service at the trial. You have in you the capability to enlarge that greatness. Being a man of honor, that's what really counts."

* * *

Now on the train, the boys are so quiet, except for mentioning the books they are reading. Each had borrowed one to read. I don't like borrowing anything, but it will give us a reason to return them for a visit at another time.

I gaze out the window, watching the trees and fields going by so fast.

Josh says, "We're almost home."

I say, "Wasn't it a good day? No more worrying over those two."

"Yes, I'm glad they've settled into such a good life. And think of it, Jed and Belinda both have so many good books to read."

"How did you know I was thinking of that? Jed is ahead of me. Even with the Frederick Douglass' book—I haven't even started that one yet."

Chapter Twenty-eight

Garrison Speaks at Meeting House

"Helen, see this headline in our newsprint. It's today, 19 October 1862. It's plastered all over the front page, showing Garrison will speak at the Meeting House. And you can't miss this picture."

"I see, but I've no time now to read it. Mary needs her bonnet tied. But give it here. I'll look at it in the carriage on the way."

"Hurry Helen or we'll be late. I've hitched the wagon and Eli and Cal are dressed and ready to go."

"Someone carry out the picnic basket. Oh, and grab a jug of apple cider from the buttery. What will Mr. Garrison be talking about today?"

"I'm sure he'll mention President Lincoln's recent announcement. The Emancipation Proclamation—can you imagine? It's what we've all been waiting for."

"What will that do? C'mon Mary sit up there with Eli and Cal."

"Well, it declared that on 1 January 1863 all slaves in States that are in rebellion against the Union shall be forever free."

"What good is that, if Southern States refuse to let them go?"

"It also directed our Army and Naval forces to protect slaves as they escape to freedom."

"Josh, give me a hand so I can sit up front with you."

Josh says, "Giddy up,' and asks, 'Are you boys familiar with William Lloyd Garrison and his efforts to free the slaves?"

Eli says, "Yes Pa, everyone in town is talking about him."

"What are they saying?"

"They want to know why he's not speaking at one of the churches in town?"

I say, "He and his friend Oliver Johnson, editor of the Antislavery Standard, are staying at the Hutchinson homestead.[44] When efforts were made for him to speak at a church in West Randolph, none would allow it. Josh, do you know why he was denied?"

"Well, he is known as the great abolitionist, and can be quite outspoken and controversial in his remarks. So I reckon that's why the Churches in town did not want to get involved. We can thank Reverend Nichols for inviting Mr. Garrison to speak at the Quaker Hill meeting house."[44]

Cal asks, "Pa, which way are we going?"

"Well we could take the Quaker Hill road, but today we'll go by way of Pethville Road."

Mary asks, "Why can't Rufus and Caspar come with us?"

"It's better and safer if we don't have them seen too much in public. Don't worry, we'll tell them all about Mr. Garrison's talk when we get back."

"Helen, take a look at these skies, such a deep blue, and those white clouds, growing bigger. Tis a wonderful day we're having."

Approaching Quaker Hill, I see wagons and carriages already there awaiting Mr. Garrison's arrival.

"Josh, have you ever seen such a large gathering at the Meeting House?"

"No, I never have. Some have come all the way from Montpelier, and beyond."

Elisha points to the road up ahead and, says, "Is that him, Pa? A fine carriage, not from these parts . . . look, it's getting near."

"Yes, indeed, Mr. William Lloyd Garrison, himself."

We find a seat in the meeting house. People are standing in back and along the sides. The crowd outside has to listen by the open windows.

Mr. Garrison gave a fine rousing speech, and the audience was most appreciative. Cookies and tea were offered after his talk.

On our way back to the cabin, I ask, "What did you think of his speech, Josh?"

"I thought his appeal for the slave was earnest and effective."

"I liked the way he expressed admiration for the 'beautiful panorama of hills and mountains around here.'"

"Remember him saying that 'such a country could be peopled only by those who love liberty. And, since us Vermonters insist on freedom for ourselves, we should also insist on freedom for all others.'"[44]

It' so good to get back home. Can't wait to get my shoes unbuckled and sit back a bit and rest. But can't be taking it too easy. Time to start setting the table. Hope the lamb's been cooking long enough.

Cal asks, "Pa, why did you say churches in town did not want Mr. Garrison to speak?"

Well, son, "Sometime back, he and Frederick Douglass the former slave, and some other men burned the American Flag and a copy of the U.S. Constitution. He also started to preach that maybe it was a good idea to follow the ones who believed in violence."

Eli asks, "Why did they do that?"

"They said the Constitution allowed slavery even though our Declaration of Independence said that 'all men are created equal.' They were very angry with our government in Washington."

"But Pa, Mr. Garrison praised President Lincoln during his talk."

"Yes, he did, and that was because our President Lincoln issued the preliminary proclamation that he would order the emancipation of all slaves in any state. I do not condone violence in any form, but some believe it is the only way to bring change."

"Did other people feel the same way?"

"Yes, there was a man named John Brown. Helen, do you remember him.?"

"I remember him well. He was in all the papers about three years ago."

Eli asks, "What did he do, Pa?"

"He took some very violent action. He led 21 men, 5 blacks and 16 whites on a raid of the federal arsenal at Harpers Ferry, Virginia. His plan was to arm slaves with the weapons." [44a]

"What happened to him?"

"Helen, can you find that last paper we saved?"

I get it from the tin box, and hand it over. He rifles through it to the page he needs.

"See here. It says, 'Local farmers, militiamen, and Marines led by Robert E. Lee, killed or captured most of Brown's men. And, they included two of his sons who were killed. Brown was badly wounded and captured. He was tried and then convicted of treason by the Commonwealth of Virginia, and was later hanged."

"And here's his picture. It's showing not such a violent minded man, wouldn't you say?"

Caleb asks, "Pa, was he a bad man?"

"That depends, son. He was always kind and helpful to run-away slaves."

Eli asks, "How was he helpful?"

"Well, he gave land to fugitive slaves. And, he and his wife agreed to raise a black youth as one of their own. He also participated in the Underground Railroad, and worked to protect escaped slaves from slave catchers. When he first met Frederick Douglass, he told him about his plan to lead a war to free the slaves." [44a]

Eli nodded his head and the rest of us kept quiet. I pondered what Josh had just said, as I passed the potatoes and lamb for our dinner.

It's a glad day, today. No more worries, not big ones at any rate. So, Joshua and I sit in our Parlor with the draperies pinned back to enjoy this nice sunny day. I'm thinking of all that's good in our lives now.

Jacob and Bethany are doing well. Jacob works long hours in his Wood Shop and it is a good source of cash. Bethany is also doing good, selling canned goods and is paid well for the fine tailoring work she takes on.

They both really dote on their child, Anna-Marie, especially Jacob. Bethany learned signing early on and steadily teaches their daughter how to talk to her Pa.

Jacob is over his fascination with Abigail. We've heard that Abigail is now supporting the war effort by folding bandages and putting together medical supplies for soldiers in the field.

"Josh, something bothers me, and it concerns our Mary. Could be worrying when none is needed but she doesn't have the same companionship now that Elisha and Caleb are grown and hang out with their own friends."

"She doesn't seem to mind."

Just then Mary enters the room, walks over to the window and just stares outside. Joshua nudges me and whispers, "What's wrong with her? Look at her, she came in here not saying anything to either one of us and now she's just standing there staring out the window. Is she day-dreaming, again? Look at her face. She seems as if in a trance."

"Not too loud, Josh, or she'll hear us. Do you remember I wanted to have her checked out when she was a baby, when she was slow in walking? She was content to just sit by the window and watch birds fly around."

"Ah, that's so, but other than that she seemed quite normal."

"Yes, I know. She loved looking at books with big pictures and never asked for much. She always seemed to be in her own world. Quite content, she was."

"But, what concerns her today?"

"Joshua, lower your voice, she might stare off into space, but she can hear OK. I hadn't thought of this before, but could her hearing not be up to par?"

"Perhaps she can see ahead, Helen, same as you?"

"I just hope she isn't the same in that way and has not been given that gift. It makes life too hard, at times."

"Alright, and never mind whispering, I'll mouth these words as if talking to Jake, OK? Read my lips, can you understand me now?"

"Stop your nonsense." I pinch his arm, just a little bit.

"Mary has some Indian blood in her after your real Pa."

"I suppose, but she certainly does not behave like me, not at all. She would rather not get herself worked up about anything, just blends into the woodwork most times."

"Of course, Helen, that's it; she is her own person."

Mary walks over saying, "Hi Ma, Hi Pa. Why are you both whispering?"

Joshua answers, "Oh, oh. We've been caught. Come here child and sit with us."

She climbs up on Joshua's lap, looks into his eyes.

"Pa, if all men are created equal why are there slaves?"

"Look at you now, almost six years old and you're already thinking about the world's problems. Goodness, were you remembering what Mr. Garrison was saying at the meeting house?"

"Well, I suppose so. I was just watching Rufus and Caspar tending the crops. They used to be slaves, but why? I like them. Did they do anything wrong? Who made them get owned by anyone? And, why'd they have to run away?"

Joshua says, "Let's just say, there are some bad men and some good men in the world. President Lincoln is a good man and he's trying to free all the slaves."

Mary says, "I like President Lincoln."

Now she's headed out doors, on her way to talk to Caspar and Rufus.

That's our Mary, somewhat different than other children, but in a good way.

"Josh, did I mention that her teacher has been very surprised at her performance in class. She said she broke all the past Spelling Bee competition records. There were even a few words the teacher found difficult to spell. She's getting high marks in all her lessons, and she's an avid reader of books."

"She'll be a great woman, someday. She will probably work for equal rights for everyone. Maybe persuade the men in our legislature to go ahead and let women vote."

Chapter Twenty-nine

Difficult Decision

I must write this now, about the Civil War. It has us all in such a state, with all that needless killing.

May 2nd 1863:

The Civil War is now two years in the making. Nothing could calm the unrest in either the north or south. Young men eagerly still rush to fight for their own side.

Elisha won't let me be and begs, "Ma, please tell Pa I have to go. I can't be a coward, and hang back. All my friends have left by now."

"No, son, I will not interfere. Your Pa had his say and I'll have none of it. You know I don't want you to leave and like it or not, we must respect his wishes. Now, hush up, and that's the last word from me. It's not my place to persuade your Pa, or you—at your age for that matter."

At that moment, Joshua walked in for dinner, "What's this all about? You said, his age? Did you forget, woman? He's only seventeen! And he's still objecting to what I told him?"

"Pa, talk to me, look at me. I'm right here."

"Elisha, did nothing sink into that thick head of yours?"

"Pa, can't you understand why I need to go. Weren't the Quakers the very first to denounce slavery? Shouldn't we now be supporting President Lincoln in his attempt to free the slaves, forever? I'm not a coward and my friends, even Ashton and Adam went in. I can't hang back."

"Eli, you do not have to go off to any war. Your faith, your beliefs are against killing, remember?"

"Yes, but times are different. I would go to help make sure slaves are free for good, same as you do, in your way."

"It is nowhere near the same. How can you go join up without carrying a gun?"

"I cannot just stay here and do nothing. How about Cassius Peck from Brookfield? You heard how brave he was? He was a Union soldier in action against Confederate forces at Blackburn's Ford, Virginia. He was only a Private but took command of such soldiers as he could get and attacked and captured a Confederate battery of four guns.' [45]

"Yes, it was a brave thing that Cassius did. But remember, your friends Ashton and Adam are not Quakers. And you are. Do you think you can just cast aside the most important of the Ten Commandments, 'Thou shalt not kill?' Do you believe in that commandment, Elisha?"

"I do, Pa. I really do. I would not intentionally kill anyone."

"Then what will happen on the battlefield if someone is about to run a bayonet through you."

"Well, I would, uh . . . I would . . . maybe try to wrest the bayonet from him?"

"My son, you are foolish. I fear that I'll lose you in the first battle you become engaged in. Don't do this to me and your mother. Stay home."

"I can't Pa, I've already signed up."

"What? You've already defied me?"

"Wait Pa, you should take some comfort in knowing that my duty with the Regiment will be as a Scout. We'll look for the enemy but not directly engage . . . and . . . maybe, uh. just help the others somehow. I can help with the sick and wounded, they said."

"Well, son, I've no more to say to you. Do as you will and don't speak of it again. Not to me."

With that, Joshua left, slamming the door on his way out.

"You've upset your Pa."

"I know Ma, but please talk to him. I need his blessing as I will need yours."

Joshua returned later that evening, "Sorry, didn't mean to act like a sore head, but I had to do some walking and some thinking. Maybe he's right. Am I wrong, Helen?"

"Whatever you decide, it must be right. For now, please just get some rest. Tomorrow you can speak of it."

"Helen, we can't lose him, and it's too big of a chance that we will, in this war. Yet if he stays, he might never be the same . . . the son we raised to be just as he is. A good lad and now a good and unselfish man. But it will pain me to no end if he is killed in battle."

"Ah, yes, I knew that was it, not so much his killing someone else but your fear of him being killed. That's also my fear. Get some sleep Josh."

* * *

This morning while Josh and Eli are out gathering wood for our fire, I see they are actually talking to each other. Not with his father saying most of it and Eli just answering yes or no.

Then Elisha_crashes into the kitchen. A big grin is plastered on his face. He grabs me. Takes the wind out of me as he crushes me in a big bear hug.

"Ma! It's all OK now. I can go with Pa's blessing!"

"Don't have to yell in my ear; I can hear you. Well that's good. Then, it's settled."

But, it is not good and my heart feels as if it is made of stone.

* * *

May 16th 1863:

Eli leaves Randolph to join Company D. of the 1st Vermont Cavalry Regiment.[46]

I said, "Go, and God bless, we'll be thinking of you, and praying for you to get back soon." I gave him a quick hug.

Joshua shook his hand and grabbed hold of Elisha's shoulder.

He said, "Do not forget your home, where your roots will always be. Our love, through God's hands will surround and follow you. Makes no matter where you are. If ever you have any doubts, just look to the sky above. At night that same big sky, filled with stars, extends all the way from our hills in Vermont to wherever you might be. So, you'll see what we see."

"Ah, Joshua, you and your fancy talking, Elisha knows you well by now."

Elisha mounts his horse. So very proud he is this morning, waving to us with one hand and carrying that heavy musket in his other hand. Sitting straight up astride Lightning, his black Morgan stallion.

Joshua snaps his head, looking right at me with tears in his eyes. Then he turns his head quick and keeps looking at who knows what.

I blow a last kiss as Eli rides off. "God, he's in your hands now. Please bring him back whole, same as he is now leaving."

My son gallops away. He is soon out of sight.

I close my eyes to picture our Elisha from long ago. He runs through the fields, never walking. My head is full of that small boy, my Elisha seeing him so clear, reaching out hands cupped together yelling for Caleb.

"Hurry, Cal, come see! This frog won't wait, it's really big! We have to hurry to show Pa!"

Joshua is so proud of his first born. Eli, since early on, was forever tagging after him. My heart would go out to this young one, eagerly following his Pa before the crack of dawn. Even on stark winter days Elisha would be dressed; waiting to join his Pa. No matter if the sun was still sleeping or if I told him, "No, son, stay here and cover up. It's cold out there."

He never listened too well. Running as fast as his little legs could carry him, he'd lumber along, even across winter snow, managing to keep up with Joshua.

OK time to put a smile on. I shall not worry, not now. Just keep remembering that God will take care of our son and he will be back. But Caleb has me worried.

June 1st 1863:

Caspar and Rufus joined the Union Army. Joshua and Jacob have promised to tend the crops they've just planted. They were proud to know they would be joining an all-Negro outfit in Massachusetts.

At the Train Station, they tell why they must go.

"If Elisha fight fo' us, then we needs be fightin fo' Elisha."

They walk proud in their Army uniforms and wave as they board the train.

No word yet from Elisha.

Joshua just came in from the fields. In the nick of time, as I'm near to exploding.

"Joshua, can you take some time to listen to me? I'm boiling up inside, and I need to let it out. Don't just eat and leave again. Wait."

"What is it? Are you sick?"

"No, but I will be if . . . I need to talk. How sad, how utterly wasteful!"

"What are you talking about?"

"So many young lives used up, to be lost or maimed in this useless war. Every woman and child of both sides will be bothered by this war, with their men off fighting one another."

"I know, Helen. Also, what of relatives living on the other side? Will they be shot by a brother, a nephew or a grandson?"

"And what of our son. Why haven't we heard from him. For all we know, he could be lying in a ditch somewhere. Josh, why did we let him go?"

"When the President signed the Civil War Military Draft Act in March it encouraged a lot of young men to join up. I guess Elisha got caught up in that patriotic movement. There was nothing we could do to stop him."

"But Josh, why so many young men, many still in their teens?"

Joshua thought for a while and then said, "You know, that draft act allows well-to-do men the option of providing a substitute to go in their place or pay $300.00 to avoid the draft altogether."

"So, are you telling me that poor men and boys are fighting the war for the rich?"

"You could put it that way. I've often wondered if the rules were changed so that the well to do, and the sons of our congressional leaders had to be the first drafted—if that would lessen the urge for our nation to engage in warfare. If that were so, can you imagine how many more wars we would have. I would venture a grand total of none.'

"Come Helen, go with me? We'll walk down to the pond to see if the minnows are growing yet."

"Yes, it sounds like a nice time."

"That sun promises to shine bright all day. Perhaps your butterflies have returned. The ones you and Lily looked for in warmer days. We'll think on better, more positive happenings, like what nature unfolds before us. I'll check on the sheep, first. Call when you're ready."

"I will."

I try not to be a worry wart, a weepy mess . . . though my heart is aching for Elisha. Yet, what of Caleb? Cannot let him spend so much time alone. He needs to get out more. See friends his age. Do not allow him too much time to wonder about Elisha. I must show a good front for his sake, at least.

I grab my bonnet, but need to shove loose strands of hair back in the bun. Now I plop the cap on my head. All set to clear this nasty war talk from my mind.

Tidy up the kitchen. Look through the window pane and I see Joshua's heading back for me. Our sheep must be penned in by now. Quicken my step, show him I'm ready to go. Jump off the last few steps on the porch.

Hmm, it is a nice warm day, and the sweet smell of honeysuckle is telling the bees where to go.

Take a deep breath, stop . . . slow down a bit. Good, now I can hurry along, keeping in step with Joshua. I hang onto Joshua's hand, look up and give him a nod along with a great big smile.

Letters

Elisha's letters finally start arriving. Sometimes they arrive in groups of four or five. I've been keeping Elisha's letters in my scrap book. He's doing well in the Cavalry, but mentioned some of the hardships other soldiers are having to endure. I'm wondering is that all that he has to tell? There must be more he cannot write about. He's not yet seen battle but camp sickness is taking its toll as seen from this letter:

June 5th 1863:

Dear Ma and Pa.

I am watching over a Corporal Abraham Sanborn, who is sick with a fever. He has not been able to do anything, being troubled with lung complaints and lately he has grown worse. 5 or 6 days ago he was taken with a sort of Dysentery and Fever.

Justin Morrell, another of my tent mates and I have watched by him, a night each for the past 5 nights. There is not much to do only to give him tea and lemonade and get him up 2 or 3 times in the night. He is going to be taken to the Hospital sometime this A.M. He will probably be discharged as steps are being taken to that effect. [47]

Lightning is doing fine. I groom him every day and his coat is black and shiny.

Give my best to Cal and Mary.

Your son, Private Elisha Haskell

After opening this letter, Joshua says, "Elisha tells how they are battling the weather."

June 11th 1863:

Virginia has seen a lot of rain, and the Infantry soldiers are making slow progress tromping through the mud. They have mules and oxen to pull their heavy artillery pieces, but needed extra help over these last two days. That's when our commander detailed twenty-four of us to ride our Morgan horses over to help pull some of the cannon up a fairly steep ridgeline.

You should have seen Lightning at work. Almost a foot deep in mud he took to the task, as if enjoying it. He needed no whip cracking. I just walked alongside him and spoke in a soft voice. Just like we were pulling logs back home. All of the Morgans did themselves proud on that detail.

Excerpts from Elisha's other letters.

June 30th 1863: *This month our Vermont Regiment joined the Army of the Potomac and we proceeded to Gettysburg.*

July 2nd 1863: *Our General Farnsworth was killed today on the fields of Gettysburg as he led us into battle. Penetrating the enemy's lines for nearly a mile, we encountered the fire of five regiments of infantry and two batteries. He was a brave leader and our men, those of us who survived, will miss him.* [46]

July 18th 1863: Joshua reads in the paper that riots have broken out in New York because of Lincoln's imposition of the federal draft.

"Helen, they are up in arms over the clause that allows exemptions for those who can provide a substitute or pay three hundred dollars. That would be a year's wages for many working men." [47.a]

"Was there any damage done."

"Quite a bit. They've been looting and burning buildings. It's been going on for four days and over one hundred are dead." [47.a]

"That's terrible. It's enough that blood is being shed in the war. Now we have this."

* * *

Days pile into weeks and no letter from Elisha. Until I almost stop waiting, but cannot give up. Months go by. It's too much to think about what might have happened. It's also been five months since Caspar and Rufus joined the Union Army and we've not heard anything about their whereabouts. For all we know . . . and I hate to think on it, but all three could be dead and left on some field of battle."

December 23rd 1863:

Joshua comes in from outside stomping his boots in the mud room.

"Joshua, it's been months, why can't Eli write?"

"He did. The Post rider handed me this as I was about to come in. Let me open it and we'll hear what he has to say."

December 16th 1863: *This Virginia winter has been very cold. Yesterday we participated in a raid on Richmond. We attempted to enter the city and release Union prisoners confined in Libby Prison and on Bell Isle. I was with a portion of the Regiment that rode with Colonel Dahlgren when we made a dash within the fortifications around the city.*

Colonel Dahlgren and many of our men were killed in this raid which was unsuccessful. Lightning was shot from under me and I crashed badly to the ground. Timothy Green from Chelsea rode by and I was able to swing up behind him on his steed. We both escaped. We were among the lucky ones. [48 49]

"His colonel was killed? Eli's horse got killed? And it's so cold there? No, Josh, we should've kept him here." Joshua puts his arms round me until I stop sobbing. Then, sets me down at the table, and fixes some tea.

The war is getting worse. Elisha writes.

May 3rd 1864: *At midnight, we will leave Culpepper, Virginia, under command of Lt. Col. Preston, as part of a major Union Army offensive against General Lee and the Confederates. We plan to cross the Rapidan at Germanna Ford at daylight on the morning of May 4th.*[46,49,50] *Our Cavalry will clear and hold the bridges ahead of the Infantry. Of more details, I am not privileged to provide.*

I now have a Morgan named "Gantry." His rider was shot and killed in the last battle. He's a good steed.

I pray all is well at home and if God be willing, this war will be over soon and I will be back with you and Pa and Caleb and Mary. Say hello for me to Uncle Jake and Aunt Bethany. I hope their Anna is as smart as our Mary, but knowing my family, she probably is.

God bless all.

Your loving son, Elisha

"Joshua, where are you? On the porch? I am reading this again. I could not fathom it before. Too much, I did not want to understand. But, see this. They are going after General Lee, and what is Eli to do as the others shoot their way in? Is he just to stand there and be shot at? He cannot tell us more?"

Joshua says, "Let me have the letter."

I say, "Is he not supposed to keep back of the line? This does not bode well." Joshua's not speaking. He goes into the living room and sits by the Fireplace, staring into the fire. The letter is still in his hand.

Please, Lord, keep my Elisha safe.

May 12th 1864: Here comes the post man. I run outside, and grab that post. But, why is it not the same? No string to secure it, but a stamp in wax on the back.

"Joshua, come quick, look at this. This isn't from Elisha. It looks very official. Here, you open it."

Joshua removes the letter. Reads it, but he stops. Then, I can barely hear him read the last parts.

'The War Department, Washington, D.C.

Dear Mr. and Mrs. Haskell, this letter is to inform you that your son, Corporal Elisha Haskell was missing in action on May 5th 1864, in the vicinity of Craig's Meeting House, Virginia. If he is still alive, we have no news of his whereabouts. It is with deep regret, that we must inform you of this tragic event. May God be with you and your family.

Signed: Colonel Paul Tiverton"

What's that . . . if still alive? No, it does not say . . . Joshua must be mistaken. I catch onto the porch chair, then stumble along the railing; must grip it with both hands. I will myself to stay upright. Mary will be home from school soon, I must not, cannot get sick. Joshua takes my hand. We walk indoors together.

"We must not fall apart." He murmurs, and keeps walking.

Back and forth we wander, from one room to the other and landing up in Eli's bedroom. I step in, and pitch forward, but he catches me as I fall. Then, hands me pictures and keepsakes. I sit on this bed and rock back and forth. Joshua wraps his arms round me . . . then rubs my hands, but I feel no warmth, none at all.

* * *

June 1st 1864:

Writing in my journal, it's not the same as before. Too hard, now to keep my wits about me to think, to wonder what next. We wait for the post, and all the long days in betwixt each mail stop, but no news yet. Not even from Colonel Tiverton. Did they all get done away with?

I cry this afternoon and not just in my room. I do not stop, nor do I care who can see. It keeps coming back—Eli and our sleigh, poor Jim, Caleb—how'd he get so far away? That accident and Eli, he trudged through deep snow that day. Probably the light from Jake's cabin caught his eye. Though how he found it I'll never know. What a terrible time for him, with the banging about, and not knowing what happened to me. Was he trying to find Caleb? No, he could not even speak, as Jake said later.

Now, I fear of hearing that he was not lost, and I will get a post saying, "Sorry, he was k—."

No, I will not think of it. He is my son, and I need to keep up hope till he comes home. Is he alive? He cannot be gone for good. I won't have it. Lord, if he is lost, then please find him. Where did he end up? I must know. I need answers. Tell me—and I will go bring him home.

Chapter Thirty
The Newspaper

January 15th, 1865:
Joshua says, "A Mr. Ripley wants to publish a newspaper here in Randolph. It's called the Orange County Eagle.[51] He invited me to join up and be part of that endeavor."

"What could he want you to do?"

"He suggested an editorial about our Vermont women. The ones sent to work in the textile factories in Massachusetts. Can you help with this?"

"Me? How would I or . . . how could we know? We've never been in a textile mill."

"Lily's letters told a lot, remember? Would it bother you to go over them again? Also, my sister, Orinda's letters—she worked in one mill much longer than Lily."

This would occupy him, instead of always wondering what happened to Eli. Of course, I need to get my head off all this worrying, too.

"Maybe . . . I can think on it. Wait, yes, I believe it could be done. But, we don't need to give names for the girls, do we?"

"No, never. They can rest in peace on that count. I want to show how slave labor in the south produces cotton. And, in turn, it's shipped to our 'factory girls' who slave to turn it into cloth."

"That would be interesting. I wonder how readers would accept that, especially the owners of both places making money on the system. Do you have anything I can read as yet?"

"Here's the start of a draft I've been working on."

> *The free slave labor in the South, makes cotton king of the exports. As a result of cotton shipped North, female mill workers, work long hours for barely subsistence wages. Both types of labor make plantation owners as well as mill owners wealthy beyond their dreams.*
>
> *The 'Masters' down south argue that they are providing free room and board for their slaves and their 'workers' are doing the work that even poor whites refuse to do.*

While up North, the mill owners 'have no regrets.' They are paying wages 'unheard of for farm workers' and they also provide room and board for their female workers.

"That's a good start, Josh, but how many times did you rewrite that. Look at the mess you're making. Papers all over the table and some on the floor. Never mind, I sound like a shrew, but actually this does sound like a good way to bring light to the problem."

"Can you make us some tea? Then put your thinking cap on, you need to give me ideas on this, too."

"What is it you'll want your readers to learn from this editorial?"

"Cheap labor does give more profits, but at the workers' expense."

"How could you show that?"

"The owners of southern slaves and factory owners in the north only have one purpose. They each attempt to maximize profits on the backs of their laborers."

"Aha, that's a good comparison. However, slaves have no freedom at all, but why do the factory girls keep working when they can leave, whenever they want?"

"Found it. Look at this paper . . . go ahead and read it. There's proof of Negroes suffering tremendous cruelty. It was heaped on them by their masters with little or no consequence to pay. Even the right to kill a slave is protected by law in some southern states."

"What? They've gone that far to justify their greed and hateful ways? Oh, I see in this part . . . yes, you do write about how the south sweeps it all away under the guise of saying, 'They get free room and board.'"

"How about the mill owners? What is their reasoning?"

"They tend to say, 'We treat our workers so good, they don't want to leave us.' But there's an important difference. When textile mills in New England started hiring farm girls, their wages were fairly good, although much lower than men's wages. Then, as time passed, the mills started cutting their costs to increase profits."

I need to get Lily's letters. We can go over them. Here they are, altogether in the same box.

"Yes, and as Lily wrote in this letter, the factory girls bore the brunt of these cost cutting measures. Her pay was docked more and more for the bed and board she received. Nothing much was left to send home."

Josh says, "I've got one here from Orinda. She sometimes worked more than 72 hours a week. She told my Mother she knew her work was getting worse, and not worth it. Yet if she left she would be immediately blacklisted, and unable to get a factory job anywhere else."

I say, "See this? Lily sent home a paper the girls wrote, but was kept secret in her mill. The owner didn't know about it. All that cotton dust floating around in the air and the windows staying closed . . . some of the girls were continually coughing and some even started coughing up traces of blood."

"We agree, then. It's the point I'm making. That is, slave labor in the south can be compared to 'semi-servitude' labor in the north."

"I don't know, Josh, you'll have to work more on that to convince me. I can't see how anything can compare to slavery in the south. What else will you put in your editorial?"

"There is a lot of hypocrisy going on during the war. Did you know the Confederate Congress prohibits the sale of cotton to the North? Yet an illicit trade across military lines still flourishes between Southern cotton farmers and Northern traders.[52] So the mills continue to produce cotton cloth during the war. Look at this accounting, see how profits are soaring, both north and south." I read it, and can't argue.

"You've done a good job. It's all there, the proof's in the pudding. Yes, it is a disgrace. Why does our Congress let it go on? Is that what's called war profiteering?"

"Yes, of course. But at this time the nation is split apart so Congress has a time trying to make sense of it all. Look here, how about this for an ending?"

> *Lincoln started the movement to free the slaves. Our next great endeavor as a nation should be to set free the young girls in the textile mills. They must be given work under healthier conditions and be allowed to come and go as they please after work hours. And to be paid a wage comparable to a man's wage for the same work.*
>
> *Byline: Joshua Haskell*

"What will you have for a title?"

"I thought factory girls are not actually slaves, but they, like the Negroes, suffer under bad conditions. How does this sound for a title? 'Slavery and Servitude—the Difference.'"

"I'd like to read it, but only when it's all finished. Cal's been picking up on your part of the chores. So, you should thank him, when he comes in.'

"Here comes Mary, home from school. I need to get busy and start fixing our supper."

Chapter Thirty-one

Letter from Daisy

January 25th 1865:

"Josh, look at this . . . a letter from Daisy. I couldn't wait to open it. Seems they still live in Granby, Canada. Tom Junior is now almost 14 years old. He's enrolled in Grammar school. She says he speaks good English. And hear this. They have a new baby called Corinda Lee."

"She writes, 'We live in a good place. Tom been farming on our own spread. Not too big, but nice.'"

"What else does she have to say?"

"She writes, 'So much time gone by when I run to Tom as he was coming up the hill at Rokeby house. And I saw the sky covering all over us. I enclose a photograph. The beautiful sunset reminds me of that day.'"

"See Josh, here's the photograph."

"Daisy says, 'I told Tom to stop and look up. He told me been 'jess like a big warm comforter, all soft and with mebbe cotton inside for filling. Then he told me he wanted to crawl under a real cover, instead of laying on hay.'"

"Very nice. I see how it looks like a nice blanket to get under."

"She says, 'After we get home to Rokeby house, he forgets about his ole shack, till one night he wakes me, shaking, and asking, 'Daisy, is it you?' He was sweating so bad, I gave him a towel to wipe his face. Next day, he nare talks about it. But the awful dreaming at night always come back. And scars on his back, they don't go away."

"Here she writes, 'After Church on Sundays, we gather on the green here in Granby for music time. Tom always gets asked to tell his story. His English is good but he tells his story in that same old plantation talk. He sounds different, but says 'I won't change it now, as my story must get told same as how it happened.'"

"She wishes we could be there for a visit to hear Tom, Jr. He beats on drums while Tom sings. She's enclosed Tom's song. I wonder if Tom Junior wrote it down?"

The Story of Tom [16]

"Run, run, runnin' I say—
T' day I'se gon' an run away."
But dogs sniffin my track.

"C'mon Boy, git down, outta yer tree!"
"Wait, I'se jumpin down, an flat onna ground."

"Good! Now gotta git back t' yer shack.
Uh, uh! Boy . . . aint no mo' hesitatin—
See? My cat-o-nine tail, it bin waitin
t' learn yer dumb head
t' pay heed t' me. Yah, instead
a jess runnin away.
So take yer shirt offen yer back."

"Agh! . . . Eee, ah!"
"Hey, it jess good ole vin-e-gar,
An it gon' stop yer runnin afar.
Yah, it gon' sting, but workin fine.
Same's yer fav'rit, ole turpentine.
Now take yer pick, but make it quick.
Wal, how bout half a foot?
Atsa real hoot—only needin a haffa boot!"

Boss, he bringin now, a big iron collar?
An—big spokes is stickin out?
"Oh, no . . . Ow!"

"Hey, Boy, why y' gotta holler?"
Still he clampin it on, an cain't move about.
An it achin so bad, I gotta shout,
"Cancha git it offa me?
It aint fittin, it be so tight.
How I gon' be sleepin t'night?"

"Please, Boss cancha hear?
Ise takin my pick . . . say, jess an ear?
I gits two, an one'll do.
An, gotta keep a foot t' go
an plow alla yer lands.
Same fer needin two a my hands."

"OK, Boy, now how's it feelin?
It's off yer neck, but keep on kneelin.
An bess ye be watchin yer Nana, too.
Or she gon' feel lashin, jess lak you."

"Why y'all pickin on Nana?
She hurtin, an lookin so sorrafull.
She done no wrong, an alla day long
her ole bones, feelin so awful."

Boss bin drinkin, an rum near gone.
So he ain't payin no mind t' me.
An, maybe he sleepin til early morn.
Look, sun's gone low, an time t' go.

Oh, Lord, looka my Nana,
she nice an high sittin inna sack—
hangin on my back, all safe an dry.
"But, Lordy, cancha see, she gittin so heavy."

Huh? What bin happenin?
I'se flyin like a wind pushin my back.
An, we ain't even leavin no track.
"Whats at, Lordy? It bin jess You?
An, totin my Nana, too?"

"Hole on, Nana, here we go—

but lissin, gotta stop, an keep still.
Whozat slidin, tumblin down a hill?"
"C' mon, looka me, Daisy! Grab my hand,
we's almose home in Gloryland."

"Look Josh. She's included a picture."

"This picture was given to us by a friend. A larger one hangs in our living room. Who could the woman be? Only one answer is right. And, yes, the man is my Tom."

"She signs the letter with--wait, just look at her name, will you?"
Joshua takes it and reads on.

"*We've reached our Gloryland.*
With love. Yours truly,
Mr. and Mrs. Thomas Carrington (Daisy and Big Tom)"

"Josh, think of it. They've got their farm and their children. And they live in a good community. If only the scars on Tom's back might disappear some day? Perhaps, we can visit them soon?"

Chapter Thirty-two

Caleb - What happened?

April 2nd 1865:

Could not help but hear Caleb talking. He and his friend are behind the Meeting House. They are outside the window where I pour cocoa for our members. I hear his friend Reggie.

He says, "Let's go down the line this evening?"

"Huh? Now Reggie, that ain't right. My Pa, sure as the sun shining down tomorrow, would give me a stern talking to."

"Shucks, my Pa would take away my walking legs with a strapping."

"Nah! C'mon Reggie, your Pa would do that? My Pa would never do that, he being a Quaker and all."

"Yeah, My Pa would do it and it would hurt so bad, I couldn't walk for a fortnight. But that don't matter none, c'mon let's find us some excitement this evening. No one will know and I sure ain't gonna tell on you."

"You must be . . . you mean you want to . . . well? Hmm, if you do plan to, well all I can say is bully for you!"

"Sure do! Cal we need learning on it sometime and doncha know we might get into that war sooner or later."

"I'll think on it. But only if no one can know."

"Don't be a Jonah. We don't need no worrying and nothing to bring bad luck."

"Don't you know any, uh, the kind that might—."

"You mean, like Mary Lou? No, not a fast trick like her!"

"Hey Reg, take a swig of this but real fast so no one sees."

"Y' know, I got a good buddy, older and wiser. He says we gotta stick with the fancy girls 'cause they take care of what they need to do."

"Nope, we best leave them alone. Should not go walking to other side of the tracks. Never know what's liable to catch onto us, since never know what's crawling around on them."

Good Lord! Is that my son? Should I tell Joshua what I've heard? No. I'll just have to think on it. Dear Lord, don't let me lose two sons.

* * *

Caleb's tying up his horse outside and is about to come in. Must dry my eyes. Can't let him see I've been crying.

"Hi Ma. You been writing in your journal again?"

"Yes, son, where have you been? You didn't come home last night, and your Pa and I have been worried. What's happening?"

"Nothing, Ma."

"Why are you chewing on that sprig? Is that mint from my garden? You never liked mint."

"Dunno, guess I like it now. Just been hanging around with my friends; you know, Reggie and the others."

"I certainly know Reginald Hawkins and his reputation. Is that the kind of friend you like to hang out with? Does he help himself to drinks like hard cider, wine, or whatever?"

"C'mon, Ma, take it easy."

"No I won't take it easy. Your Pa and I have seen you straying from your Quaker teachings and word around town is that you've been seen with certain ladies of the evening. You're turning out worse than Reggie."

"Why are you shouting at me? I've just been trying to have a good time. I've gotta leave now, my pals are waiting.'

"Oh! Hi Pa . . . didn't see you come in."

Joshua hangs up his jacket, pulls off his boots, and accepts a hot cider mug from me.

"So Joshua, here's our son. He's back but says he'll be off again. You talk to him. I cannot."

"OK, I will. Hold on Cal, we need to talk. Been rounding up the sheep. I could've used your help."

"Do I have to, Pa? I gotta go." He wraps his knuckles on the table, fidgeting. Cal makes me so nervous. I must leave and let Joshua handle him. I wave to both, and head back to my room. Joshua gives me a salute just as I close the door.

"Yes, Cal, and no back talk now. Try folding your hands. Now, what's all the shouting about and what's this about having a good time? Your brother's missing in the war and all you can think about is having a good time? That's not the Quaker way."

"Well Pa, was it the Quaker way when you let Elisha go off to war? For all we know he's dead and lying in a ditch someplace."

"You stop that talk."

"No, I won't. Elisha's dead. I just know it. You let him go off to be killed—and you and Ma, did nothing to stop it. I'm going to my room."

Mary yells as he passes her room, "Caleb, can we play. I have my doll, you can get your tops?" But he keeps going and shuts his door. Shall I make him come back or just wait? He is grieving, same as us. Best to not rake up dead leaves. We need to let him get through it in his own good time. After all he is a young man, almost. He's old enough to want to 'sow his wild oats'—even if not knowing how to go about it. It's best to wait. I'll tell Helen I'll have a talk with him in the morning, before we start our chores."

* * *

Helen is still sleeping. Good, and I won't disturb her.

"Good morning, Cal. Come sit with me in the kitchen."

"Morning Pa. Sorry, I sounded off to you and talked awful about Ma last night."

"Your Ma is resting for a bit. How about the two of us having a talk now, OK? You're worried about Eli. Well you have a right to be worried. But your Ma is upset. She's at her wit's end. Don't look away, look at me. Please, Cal, don't add to her dark days. Her spirit is near to breaking. It's like a twig with one more cold snap to make it fall. Can't you see? It would kill us if we lost not only your brother but you along with him."

"What do you mean? I'm not going off to war!"

"I know son, but there's a war raging within you. Am I right? If you keep on like you're doing, then nothing good will come of it. Wait, don't get up, stay put—don't pretend nothing's wrong. I've seen you change. Open up to me. What's bothering you?"

"I don't want to talk about it. I gotta go soon, gotta meet someone."

"Why? Stay and talk to me. You know that your Ma and I love you and we want to do all we can to help."

"Yeah, just like you helped Eli. You loved him so much you sent him off to war to be killed. I knew you loved him more than me, but you sent him off to war anyhow. So, what's left for me? Watching you mope around, wondering about him all the time?"

"Cal, I can't believe what I'm hearing. First of all, Eli could not be persuaded to stay home. But he promised he would not carry a gun, and would only help out in other ways."

"Oh? Why wasn't I told that? Don't I live here; don't I get to know what goes on? Maybe it's time I went some place where people will talk to me."

"I am sorry we didn't tell you more. We wanted to protect you and spare you from our own sad feelings. Now I see how wrong that was."

"Really, you mean that? Kinda late, can't go back and change it—can we? Ah shucks, I gotta get outta here."

"No Cal, set yourself down. Leave when I say it's time. You hear?"

"Well, will it take long?"

"No, just listen. Can you remember when you were about ten years old—when I scolded you and sent you to bed early? It was because of that dead grasshopper you pushed into Eli's biscuit when he wasn't looking?"

"Yeah I know. That was a mean trick. But, he taught me some good ones, too. Still it was wrong what I did."

"After I sent you to bed, you got up later that evening and came to the living room and said 'Pa, I can't sleep.' I asked you to come in and lie on the couch. I knew you needed to be comforted."

"Yes, I did. I felt bad, getting crosswise with you."

"I put your head on my lap and stroked your hair until you fell asleep. Then as I looked down at my hand on your brow, the thought struck me that someday you might comfort your son in the same way. Just as my father did when I was growing up and no doubt, his father before him.'

"You know, Cal, I've thought back on that moment many times. I've pondered how humans seem to sense without speaking what is needed. It is more powerful than any word spoken aloud. Yes, and family members and loved ones know exactly what it means." I wish Cal would look at me, and not stare at the table.

"The peaceful look on your face as you slept, it showed me what we share with each other. Without a word leaving my lips, I felt such love pouring out for you that evening."

"Yah, I guess what you say is . . . but I gotta go soon. No? OK, but if it ain't gonna be too long . . . go on, Pa."

"Cal, I believe that life is glorious. It's grand and beautiful. Despite its trials and tribulations, it is one great adventure."

"Pa, I don't understand any of it. Before, you said you had love pouring out. Did it come our way? What love did we get, when you went to help colored people?"

"Don't son, don't speak of things you are not privy to." Cal stands up and pounds the table.

"Yeah, did you know how we fared when you left? Who did you think did the work around here? Uncle Jake? Sometimes. But he had his own chores. Me and Eli? Nope, Ma did it all. She kept at it, till after supper. And, she'd fall asleep in her rocker. Eli had to shake her, make her go to bed. We never heard any grumbling from her, either.'

"Pa, it made me think you cared more for them coloreds, than us. And, giving land to Caspar and Rufus? They aren't your sons."

"Son, there's a difference. Love for my own blood kin is a bond that never breaks. Remember, God is within all of us. The coloreds also have the same God inside, since our Father made us all."

"You believe it, sure, if you say it but for me, can it be proved? Pa, you sound like everything is hunky dory. You been acting sometimes, as if your head is so much at peace. Nothing nags at you. Nothing about Eli? Nothing about me?"

Caleb's elbows lean on the table and his head drops down into his hands. Sobs come out. It's breaking my heart to hear this boy cry, my youngest.

Then, he says, "Can't take it anymore, Pa. I feel so alone. Where is the love for me? Is there any left? Even a few drops? Sometimes I just want to end—." How could I have not seen how alone he's been, with Eli gone? And, poor Cal, he must have thought we didn't care enough about him to let him in to share our grief.

"Cal, stop that. Come here my son. Put your head on my shoulder. Cry if you like. Don't worry and don't be ashamed. I am the one to be ashamed. I failed to fathom what was tearing at your heart. Such talk about wanting to end it all. I won't have it. And your Ma, it would surely kill her. Never, ever think that way again. And what of Mary? She's always wanting to be by your side. How heartbroken she'd be if losing her big brother. Believe me when I say this—we love you with all our hearts. Now it's time for you to love who you are and plan for the glorious life ahead of you."

"Tell me Pa, what's so glorious about it? What can fill this big hole I've got inside me? I hate to say it but this is not a glorious life, not for me. I should go to be with Elisha, go find him and just do anything but stay here."

"What's so glorious? Well, for example, just the miracle of life—as we've seen our babies born and take their first breath." Why is he looking away?

"Cal, please look at me. Here's something you never heard of. Like you, I had many dark days when I felt so hollow inside. I remember how terrible it was for me when my own Pa had his accident, when a tree fell on him—one he was taking down, but it took him instead. I could not save him, could not pull him out from under that blasted tree."

"Pa, I never heard of that before. Why didn't you tell me?"

"Cal, it was such a terrible time, it was. I'd be sad for days on end whenever it got dredged up, even years later. Even now.'

"My hands were bleeding from scratching at the dirt, trying to dig him out when I couldn't lift that tree off him. My mother explained to me later why he never was what I expected of him . . . never putting his arms around me like my pals had their fathers do. He never would rough house with me, hold me up in his arms. I thought he didn't really care. Yet, I'd see him holding brother Jacob."

"Huh? Is that right, Pa? You and your Pa weren't that close? He never held you--not even for a bedtime story?"

"My father left the stories for my Ma to tell. He never expressed or showed any outward signs of emotion. When I think back on it, the few times when he would put his hand on my brow or stroke my hair or pat me on his shoulder, I always felt a surge of good feelings. He was passing on his love for me through this silent form of communication I mentioned earlier. His actions were much stronger than his words."

"Your grandma reminded me later of one fact I had not realized. Your uncle Jacob was always the one who ran to our Pa when he got home. I would hold back waiting for him to make the first move."

"Pa, I'm thinking on it now. Maybe I can understand. Would you tell me more about your ideas of our glorious life? I want to hear it now. I do."

"I'll go on if you like. How about blazing sunsets? The smell of honeysuckle and lilacs wafting on a summer breeze. Cotton clouds floating in a sky of blue. The bright red and yellow maple leaves in autumn. Ice crystals on trees, glistening like diamonds in the sunlight. A hand-in-hand walk with you when you were a boy." Cal's eyelids start to shut. They stay closed.

"I remember, now, Pa. Yah, they were warm feelings. They made me so relaxed."

"Yes, it's a start, but first understand yourself. You need to love who you are, a good person bound to do good things in life. And it will be a glorious life.'

"Build your life around those memories and remember that good hard labor will also bring good times to enjoy and think back on. You'll get satisfied each time the job is done and you see the fruits of your labor. So, look to the future, when you will have children of your own and the joy they will bring you. But to get all of it, you have to be the best you can be so you can meet, and then wed the best girl for you."

He leans closer, and whispers, "Look Pa, who's that creeping up on us. It must be a little elf?" Mary slides along the wall, but then stops short. She rubs her eyes, and yawns.

Then sweet, innocent Mary sneaks up behind Cal and yells, "Boo!" Cal makes his legs jump all over as if he is going to fall out of his chair. At the last moment, he rights himself.

"Hi Caleb, where you been? Can I hug you? Why not? Bring me anything? Gee, I kinda missed you. I wanted my story, doncha remember?"

Mary is just in time. Cal bends down, pats her head. How can anyone resist our Mary? Caleb hugs her. Then tickles her till she pushes his arms down.

"Stop!" she yells. Then tries to tickle him, but he pulls away.

I say, "Come here Mary, sit on my lap. Cal, you come here, too. Let us now join hands and feel blessed we can enjoy life while we are here."

"I gotta go now. My pals are waiting. OK with you Pa?" He heads for his jacket. Puts it half on and looks out the window.

Mary stomps her foot. She says, "No Cal, you can't go."

Just before the door, he stops—and turns around.

He grabs the nearest chair, and sits. "OK, Pa, tell me . . . what else?"

I finish with, "OK, ready? Now let's endeavor to leave our mark on this path through life to make it just that much more wondrous and grand for those who will follow us. And when our task is done and we depart this world let us take solace in knowing this: We did our best and our Father will be there to place His hand on our brow and comfort us on our final journey. Now, God bless everyone and and you too, Elisha, wherever you may be."

"OK Caleb, you may leave now if you like" He doesn't move.

"No Pa, I think I'll stay for a while. Mary bring me your story books and I'll read to you."

"No Cal. I'll get my books, but I will read to you."

That's our Mary.

Chapter Thirty-three

Bells Ringing

April 10th, 1865:
It is mid-morning and church bells are ringing in the distance—ringing and ringing and not stopping. Joshua hitches up the wagon to take us to town.

As we pass across the bridge onto Main Street the bells get louder. What on earth? Why are these bells clanging so much, so loud? Then, the bells from the old Congregational Church start in—they become louder.

"Look Joshua, what's going on? The crowd's running amok. What news could do that?"

"I can see—but do my eyes deceive me? Are those a few of our Friends and an Elder, dancing in the street?"

"Joshua, look at that man, grabbing his crutch, limping along. What is he yelling?"

"I'm not sure. 'You there, what's all the commotion? Is that a telegraph you're holding?'"

The man screams, "General Lee surrendered yesterday! Yes, don't shake your head, man! Yes! It's true! He surrendered to General Grant at Appomattox, Virginia! The war, are ye deef? It's bloody well over! Too late for my boy, but . . . it's over, hooray, it's over!"

Oh, wonderful—but how sad for him. There's a black band on his coat sleeve. His eyes are glazed over, and tears stream down his face. He turns and limps away, repeating, "It's done with, we won, we won, we won."

"Joshua, that's such good news. Think on this. I recall you telling me before—wasn't Randolph's own Al Chandler one of President Lincoln's special telegraphers?"

"Yes, it was Albert Chandler, and he could have been the one to send the good word all the way from our Capital in Washington."

* * *

April 15th, 1865:
Our joy over the past five days, knowing we won the war, has now turned to grief.

How utterly shocking, and tears still keep falling whenever I think on it. President Lincoln was shot in the head yesterday by a man named Booth at

Ford's Theater. How horrible, who could think to do something like that? The Devil must be lurking in that man. Many folks in Randolph walk the streets in silence. Many wipe tears from their eyes.

The news looks to be painful for Joshua. He wanders aimlessly. I say nothing and go about my cleaning chores. I tidy the Parlor, straighten the top of the desk. He picks up his ink well—holds onto it, as I offer his quill—but he places both back on the desk.

I follow as he circles around our Front Room, and touches pictures of Elisha and Caleb. Now he grabs onto his rocker in front of the hearth.

He sits. Stares at our President's portrait hanging over the fireplace.

But not for long. He gets up and heads out the door. Soon, he totes back a load of wood for a fire that we don't need on this warm spring day.

Caleb went for a carriage ride early this morn and has not returned. Mary hangs around near me. Not saying much, but then asks, "Where are my brothers?" Josh and I have nothing much to say. Without a word, she heads to her room. Before she shuts her door, she says, "Hope they come home soon. Hope no one shoots them."

I don't just hope, I pray for their safety. If either one ends up dead, then my mind will surely shut down.

I pray for poor President Lincoln. May God bless and rest his soul.

* * *

I'm reading in my Ladies magazine that, *"Time goes on no matter how sudden the nation was pitched into mourning our President. We find that bad news can leave us so sad. But our daily lives must go on."* Yes, I must leave this on the table for Joshua. Our farm has needs and we cannot just mope around. No, a rooster will give the wake up call and our cows won't wait long. I know all of that. Time for Joshua to carry his main part of the farm chores again. And our sons need to pitch in, too.

"Helen, what is this . . . do you mind if I take a look?" Of course, that's why it's there for you to accidentally have it staring you in the face. He sits and reads, and then sees the questioning look on my face.

"Helen, what's the matter. I feel that something is bothering you." Ah, now's the time to start having good discussions again.

"Well, it never bothered me before my trial, but was it not strange that no women were on that jury?"

"At that time, no, I worried more about getting you home. Finding someone to help. Not who was judging you."

"I had time to look and wonder about them. How could they judge me? Why is it that men are the only ones who know what I, or any woman, could or could not do? Was I less than a man? And why is it, that women do not have the right to vote? Frederick Douglass, the ex-slave, said it would not be fair for him to vote as a Black man if women were not also provided the same right." [53]

"Well, it looks like you have given this a lot of thought."

0"Yes, I have. I also wonder about the white men who founded our nation? Why did they believe a woman was not equal to them? Are women any less a being than a man?"

"You have a good point. As Quakers, we do believe women are equal. And I believe you are much more equal than any man I know. Men cannot produce children, can they?"

"Do not patronize me, Joshua. I did not suddenly become intelligent overnight nor did any other woman. We've waited much too long. We must gain the same privileges and the same rights as men."

Joshua does not try to interrupt.

"Here's another bother—and you mentioned it in your editorial—why do men get paid more at a work place? Lily told of how one lad, the sweeper, got more pay than her. That is unfair, so it cannot be equal, can it?"

"No, it is not. Perhaps at next Meeting time, we could discuss it. Yet, for now, I am wondering about . . . well, just look at you!"

"What do you mean?"

"You've changed."

"Why would you say such a thing. Am I getting old, with wrinkles to prove it?"

"No, not in that way, but you did need convincing about the evils of slavery, and ways we could help the slaves. Yet, you would not be easily persuaded, not back then."

"I had no idea who they were, and they did not look and behave like us. My concern was for my children, and you were leaving. Going off, letting us fend for ourselves. Then, too, I had never met one, until Daisy showed up at my door."

"Looking back, I can agree with all your objections. But, now? You never spoke of wanting a job outside of our home. Will you be joining the Suffragettes, the ones wearing bloomers, marching for women's rights?"

"Hmm, that is a thought. Maybe, yes . . . but, I suppose I have changed. You have, too. You do not just do a farmer's work now. Think on this; I could help more in your printing shop, yet I would expect from the owner, my own worth to be paid equal to a man's wages. Is that not a fair bargain?"

"Whoa, slow down. Did I just get bamboozled into something? We aren't making much as it is."

"No, of course not. I would not ever try to hoodwink you. Yet, we are equal, are we not? Is it not possible for me to at least work in a print shop?"

"I have no quarrel with that and I will stop now--before I hear of you pestering them at the Capital, to start changing laws. Or worse, to see you running about smashing kegs of spirits in the General Store." Then, he grabs my hand, kisses it, and gets down on one knee.

He says, "M' Lady, I bid you allow me to grant your pleasure, whatever that may be, and so on and so forth." From one of his treasured books, I am sure, and then a big grin plasters his face.

Chapter Thirty-four

Waiting at the Station

Joshua and I stand at the train station awaiting the first special Army train to arrive. It's bringing back soldiers from the war. We're hoping against all hope that Elisha might be among them. But if not Elisha, we may see Rufus and Caspar step off the train.

"Here it comes, Helen. Look at that head of steam! What a sight. Be careful, step back." The train slows to a stop, and not more than ten soldiers step onto the platform.

"Joshua, is Elisha among them? I can't tell."

"No, he's not but I recognize Bill Hollinger from Braintree. I see he's a Lieutenant now and he's with a young colored soldier who can't be more than thirteen or fourteen years of age. They are coming our way."

"You go talk to them, Josh. I'm not in the mood for socializing" I wish I had not come this morning. I know it's useless, yet he won't give up. He insists, just in the event Eli steps off the next train.

Josh says, "Hi Bill, were you with the Cavalry—thought you might have come in contact with our son, Elisha?"

"Hello Josh. No, I was in the Infantry with the 9th Vermont Regiment."

"Who's this you brought with you?"

"I'd like you to meet Ben Roberts. Ben was a slave who joined us as we were marching through Newbern, South Carolina. He was working a cornfield with a mule when we called out to him to join us. What was it you said to us Ben?"

"I sez to soldiers 'No, gotta go ask my Massa.'"

Bill says, "Ah yes, but we convinced him otherwise and he joined our unit and now he's come to live with us." [54]

"Pleased to meet you Ben. Tell me, if you don't mind. Was your Master mean to you on that plantation?"

"He be OK but sometime mean. Not like Massa Roberts, my other Massa. Massa Roberts was a kind man and he always fed us good. Not like most Massa's, I been tole bout."

"Then, thank heaven not all slave owners were mean to their charges."

"But I sure been missin my Momma."

"Why is that?"

"Me and my Momma, we first live in North Carolina. But Momma left me when I war three-year-old, cuz she been sold to a Massa in New Orleans. I never seed her agin. Later when I war eight or nine, I been sold to Massa James Farnum."

"Was he a kind Master?"

"No. Cause on my way to Massa Farnum's plantation I see my Papa working in Massa Robert's field. I say to Massa Farnum's driver, 'Please let me say goodbye to my Papa.'

"But Massa Farnum's wagon man say 'No.' An I never seed my Papa agin. I been called Ben Farnum but I change name to Ben Roberts after my old Massa." [54]

"That's sad, Ben, but you're a fine-looking soldier. Yes, he is, Bill, and welcome home to both of you."

"Thank you kindly. Well we must be off, as I see my father just arrived with the horse and wagon."

As Josh takes my hand, I am glad my having to smile is over with for now. We walk slowly to our wagon. We don't speak. I start sniffing and wipe tears from my eyes.

Josh says, "Bittersweet, yes, I know it is. A letdown since Elisha is not here, but at least one young lad made it through to a new life. Don't worry, Helen. We'll come back tomorrow."

* * *

Joshua and I stand at the train station again. Two hours came and just as slow they went. We wait and wait, craning our necks hoping to catch sight of the special Army train to arrive. We were told, this will be the last troop train, bringing soldiers back from the war. We will not concede that our son is gone or as some say 'passed on' thinking that makes it easier to bear. And no one dares utter that dreaded final word such as 'dead.'

"Joshua, I just hope to heaven we're not waiting in vain. Remember, no word came from the Army after that letter telling of his missing. None of the letters we wrote ever came back or were answered."

"I know but all we can do is hope. The same as other neighbors are doing."

Joshua nudges me and grabs hold of my hand, "Hear it? That same whistle screeching through the valley. Soon the train will be here."

"Now I can see it." Everyone claps and cheering starts up, louder and louder. Children run, jump and hoot up a storm.

"Look', Josh points out, 'some cannot wait."

Soldiers jump off ahead of the last jolt of the final braking. I grab onto Joshua's hand squeezing it hard. He gives me a quick hug, and a smile.

"Look Josh, some need help, some have crutches. Oh dear, some have got patches over their eyes or slings on their arms."

Others are taken away in rolling carts. Oh, no, there's one poor soldier, laughing, and will not stop. Over and over, though he covers his mouth with an arm that's bandaged halfway to his elbow. The other arm? There's none in that empty sleeve. Eli is not on any of the carts. Thank heavens. But where is he? I jump up and down, try to see over the heads of those on the platform. Oh, oh. I lose my footing and Joshua grabs me from falling.

The long wooden boxes are moved out last. The men remove their hats. I look away.

"Come along Helen, time to go."

As we turn to go, Joshua shouts, "Good God Almighty, there's Caspar and Rufus holding someone up between them. By Jove! Is it, no, can't be. The fellow has a beard. His uniform hangs on him—he's thin as a bean pole, kind of scraggly and not husky as our boy. And he's limping."

He holds me up to see, "Oh, Josh, you silly goose. It's our Elisha!"

"Ma, Pa! Here I am! It's me."

Joshua yells, "Come here my son." I rush to meet him. His arms hold me tight. How skinny he is. He needs my good cooking in him.

Joshua asks "How you been doing? Everything OK?" Eli nods, but stares at the ground.

"What happened to your leg?"

"I'll explain later. But, except for my leg, I'm alright, can't you see?"

"Son, you look just fine. Say, look at who you brought . . . or rather, was it Caspar and Rufus who brought you home? Welcome back Soldiers. What outfit were you with?"

We been in Mass-chuset 54th Infantry Reg'ment, a Negro reg'ment."

Joshua says, "Is that the all black outfit?"

"Yassuh. Did y' all know, it be same reg'ment two of Frederick Douglass' sons belongin to." [55]

"Mr. Douglass? The speaker for antislavery? I heard their father talk in New Bedford, when I . . . but that's for later on. You all must be tired after that train ride, so let's not tarry. More can be told when we get home."

Eli says, "Wait Pa. I have to tell something now. I know as you taught me, don't let things simmer inside."

"What is it, son? Can't it wait till we get home? There's no hurry."

"No, I'd best get it off my chest now. I spent most of a year in the Confederate's Libby prison."

I can't believe what Eli's saying, "We never knew. No one sent word. Oh, never mind, I'm just glad you're here. You must be tired. Let's go to that bench over there."

Joshua grabs Eli around his shoulders and leads him to sit down.

Eli says, "I could not send word from prison. You must be wondering why I look so thin—there wasn't much food there to go around. Mostly we got grits and beans and some pork rinds. Barely enough to keep us going. But, lucky for me, I had help from a Southern guard. He knew some medicine, enough to tend to my leg."

Josh asks, "What happened to your leg?"

"I cracked it when falling from my horse, Gantry. He was shot from under me. That prison guard was not so bad. At least not for me, the enemy. He told how he had cousins in the north, and hated having to fight at all. But the men in his family were expected to do their duty. Yes, he ended up in prison hospitals tending their wounds. So, we were a lot the same."

I said, "Eli, how fortunate when you met up with the likes of him."

"Yes Ma, he knew to keep my leg from festering too much. That guard said, 'I've tended to people living on my father's plantation. A doctor taught me, right good, how to set bones.'"

Joshua says, "Son, enough for now. We need to get you to Doc Chambers and have him take a look at you."

"No. That's not the whole story. When I fell from my horse, I landed about ten feet from a wounded Confederate soldier. He was moaning and blood was pouring out of him. After moving his shirt away, I could see his stomach was ripped open, and sorry Ma, but his guts were spilling out. I took out a roll of bandages from my back pack and quick taped them over his wound. Had to stop the bleeding. It was so bad, I gave him a shot of whiskey we carried for the pain.'

"Just then a Confederate Colonel walked over and pointed a pistol at my forehead. He must've thought I was robbing this soldier or harming him worse than ever. I know it's hard to believe, but at that moment I wasn't afraid. I had this sort of a calm feeling come over me. I waited but nothing happened. The Colonel, he lowered his pistol after the wounded man shook his head, saying 'No, no.'"

"That's when the Colonel took me prisoner. I found out later, that wounded soldier had died." Eli goes to stand, and his cane falls to the ground. Joshua jumps to pick it up and hands it to him.

Joshua says, "Come here, my son." Eli walks to him, then hooks his cane over one arm, while Josh gives him a big embrace.

I say "Thank you, Caspar and Rufus. Come here, let me give you both a big hug." Caspar steps back—and stumbles away from me.

"Missus Helen, please—cain't be doin, uh, touchin. What folks gonna say when seeing you huggin us colored men?"

"I don't give a . . . well, two hoots and a holler, what people say. Who cares? C'mere Caspar and you too, Rufus. Don't shrink away. I'm gonna hug you as I please. Welcome home Soldiers."

Joshua heads to the hitching rail and readies the horses. Then by hand signaling and shouting he hails us, "Come hurry, times a wasting!"

Joshua asks Rufus and Caspar to help Elisha step up and into the back of our wagon.

After calling out "Giddy up!" Joshua yells back to Eli, "Oh, what a turn to this day! Cannot wait until we get back home! Jacob and Caleb will be so surprised to see what we found at the station."

"Don't forget our little Mary. She'll be running circles round Eli. Do you hear me, Eli?"

Elisha does not reply. He makes no sound at all. His cap covers his face and his head leans down on one shoulder. He's sleeping. I do not ask again. Just tilt my bonnet back and gaze up to the big clear blue sky. Time to give up a silent word of thanks that's long overdue.

"Thank you, Lord for bringing my son home."

"Look Joshua, more over there, and how pretty. They light on the Milkweed along the road, then fly away as we draw near."

That one almost hit my bonnet . . . a butterfly, my favorite. We were so young, when trying to catch a few. They are monarchs. What is going on to bring them here, and so many? Here's one—it landed next to my boot. It's orange on top and lighter under its wings. So striking, it is, with black around each part.

I grab Joshua's arm so he won't swat this one. It flew near his face. Now it's next to my boot. Is it the same? This one does not move, not even its wings. So lovely, so delicate reminding me of Lily, and her last days down by the brook, watching butterflies and birds circling. This one . . . when will it fly off?

Wonder how Lily is doing up there, in her special heaven? Does she know what's happening down here? If these butterflies can carry a tale, flying all around, and perhaps way up to—well, maybe Lily knows.

Now I worry over Caleb, though I try not to, but I'm still troubled by the way he's been acting. Hope we don't lose him. I still puzzle about the sleigh accident, and where Jake found him. He had deerskins wrapped around him, too.

"Josh, help me understand this, will you? I wondered, when our sleigh overturned on the way to Jacob's—just how did Caleb land so far away from us? He was covered, too."

"What exactly do you mean?"

"Someone had to help him. I had no deer skins with us, so where did they come from? Don't give me that look. I am not telling of a dream, either. My Pa had a brother. Ma told me in her letter. He was to keep an eye out for us, but Pa said, 'he would not intrude, would not show his face.'"

"If he cannot make himself known, then just be thankful. Keep him in your prayers."

Yes, it's all falling into place now. He probably ran off when he heard Jake's horse. Now, fill my mind with . . . look, pretty flowers, birds flying, and white fluffy clouds.

"Helen, are you day dreaming? Look who's running up the road to meet us. Ah yes, yelling and hooting, as usual."

"It's Caleb? Stop the wagon Josh. Let him climb aboard."

"Jump up on back, Cal. We brought your brother home."

As he scrambles on board, he yells, "Yahoo, it's Elisha! Is he OK? Why are his eyes closed? He didn't get blinded, did he? Nah, can't be. C'mon, Elisha wake up, it's me! Hi there, Rufus and Caspar. Welcome home!"

"He's OK,' Joshua says, 'just sleeping but his leg is hurt. So be careful."

Caleb takes off his jacket, folds it, puts it in his lap and pulls Eli over so he's resting his head on the jacket. Cal pushes back the hair from his brother's eyes. Elisha looks up at Cal and smiles.

I am blessed, dear Lord. Looks like You've brought both my boys home. If only Lily was here, but I know You are taking care of her.

Now, where are those butterflies—that special one.

The End.

Historical Note 1: Notable African Americans from Randolph, VT.

Ben Robinson was the former slave who was brought to Randolph by Union soldiers after the Civil war. He rests in South View Cemetery, in Randolph, Vermont. Buried in 1910, he received full Veteran honors by the Grand Army of the Republic. His Epitaph reads: "Ben Robinson, Of African Descent, Born a Slave in North Carolina, Escaped to freedom by the aid of, Co. G 9th VT. Reg in 1863, And Brought to Vermont by, Lieut. Wm. C. Holman in 1865, Died in Randolph, VT. May 31, 1910, Aged 60 years. Down at the bottom and just barely readable is the inscription, ***"Under God and the Strong Arm of our American Republic, The Negro Slave is Free."***

Ben received a school education in Randolph and had been heard to say, "he didn't believe there was another place in the world where, in spite of his dark skin, he would have been treated so white." [54] He appears in the story as "Ben Roberts" and Holman appears as "Hollinger."

Another notable African American from Randolph was Alexander Twilight. Alexander's father, Ichabod, fought in the Revolutionary War. Alexander is noted as the first African American to graduate from a U.S. college (1823) and the first black American to win election to public office, joining the Vermont Legislature in 1836.

Alexander labored for a neighboring farmer in Corinth, Vermont when he was only eight years old. For the next twelve years, he learned reading, writing and math skills while performing various farming duties. At age 20, he took a six-year accelerated course of study at the Orange County Grammar School in Randolph Center. This is where the Vermont Technical college is now located. He completed not only secondary school courses but also the first two years of a college level curriculum. He went on to Middlebury college as a third-year student for his Bachelor's degree. He's buried in Brownington Vermont with his wife, Mercy Ladd Merrill Twilight.[12]

George "Sonny" Holt, Randolph, Vermont, December 1st 2016

Historical Note 2: Manjiro and the Old Stone School House.

In 1841, Captain William H. Whitfield on the whaleship *John Howland* rescued fourteen-year-old Japanese youth Manjiro Nakahama from a small island in the Pacific Ocean, on which Manjiro and four other fishermen had been stranded for nearly six months. Manjiro (or John Mung as he was known at the time) returned to Capt. Whitfield's Fairhaven home, becoming the first Japanese person to live in America. He attended classes in 1843 at the Old Stone Schoolhouse, which was built in 1828.

The school desks were originally long planks set on empty flour barrels and the seats were boards setting on crates or wood blocks. Existing photographs from about 1895 show the later use of wide double desks on cast iron frames, as shown in the photo below.

After learning American customs and studying **advanced mathematics, surveying and** navigation in Fairhaven, Manjiro eventually returned to Japan. He became a prominent figure during the opening of Japan to western trade. Manjiro became a professor of navigation and ship engineering at the Naval Training School in Tokyo. He also compiled *A Short Cut to English Conversation*, which became a standard book on practical English. Twice Manjiro returned to America on diplomatic missions for the Japanese government. Japan's Emperor Akihito visited Fairhaven when he was Crown Prince in 1987, the same year a Sister City agreement was signed between Fairhaven-New Bedford and Tosashimizu, Japan, where Manjiro grew up.[56]

Historical Note 3: Early Black Settlers on Lincoln Hill, Vermont.

In "Run Away to Glory" the fictional characters Sally and Betsey settle in a hill-side community in Hinesburg, Vermont. The road leading to this once all-black community was renamed after the Civil War to Lincoln Hill Road, to honor President Lincoln's freeing of the slaves.

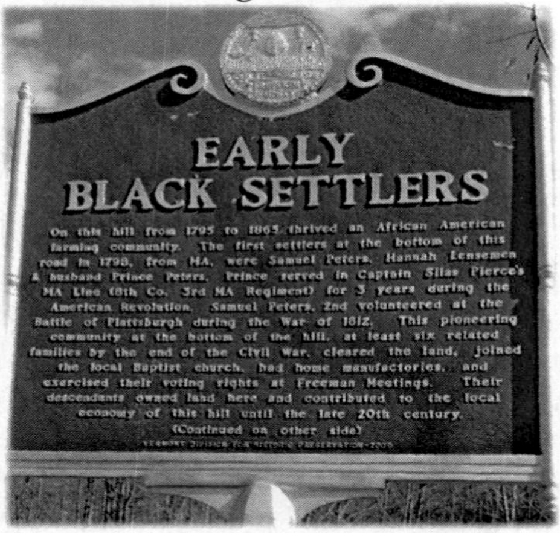

It reads, "On this hill from 1795 to 1865 thrived an African American farming community. The first settlers at the bottom of this road in 1798, from MA, were Samuel Peters, Hannah Lensemen & husband Prince Peters. Prince served in Captain Silas Pierce's MA Line (8th Co, 3rd MA Regiment) for 3 years during the American Revolution. Samuel Peters, 2nd volunteered at the Battle of Plattsburgh during the War of 1812. This pioneering community at the bottom of the hill, at least six related families by the end of the Civil War, cleared the land, joined the local Baptist church, had home manufactories, and exercised their voting rights at Freeman Meetings. Their descendants owned land here and contributed to the local economy of this hill until the late 20th century." *Continuiing on the back it reads,*

"Violet and Shubael Clark, from CT, arrived at the top of this hill in 1795. Their farm grew to 175 acres spilling over into Huntington, and one son owned 100 acres nearby. During the 1850s-60s, the home of their daughter, Almira and William Langley, became a place of refuge for those escaping slavery. Three Langley brothers and a cousin fought in the MA 54th Regiment and the SC 33rd during the Civil War. Loudon Langley, born here about 1836, stayed in SC after the war and represented Beaufort at the 1868 Constitutional Convention. He and his brother Lewis are buried there in the National Cemetery. The original Clark settlers expanded to 5 related families just before the Civil War, and many are buried in an abandoned cemetery at the top of this hill."

About the Authors:

Elizabeth Palm and George Holt Jr. are sister and brother. They grew up in Fairhaven, Massachusetts. George, known as Sonny, is living in Vermont. Both have a passion for writing. Elizabeth, known as Betty, was associated with the medical profession. She wrote the poem, "Tom's Story" about a slave's escape and run to freedom. Sonny has published a number of books. His most recent, "The B-58 Blunder – How the U.S. Abandoned its Best Strategic Bomber."

Scenes and characters in the book depict historical events and, in some cases, real life experiences of the authors. For examples: Two runaway slaves are found in a hidden room, almost identical to the one in their Grandmother's old farm house. Also, Ginny-town, where two runaways hid, is where Gypsies encamped during summer months. The place is well known to the authors.

Reference Notes

1. Map of Orange County, Vermont, 1853, Library of Congress.
https://www.loc.gov/resource/g3753o.la001188/

2. Excerpts from the Liberator, Author: William Lloyd Garrison, Published: 1831.

3. Exhibits from the Rokeby Museum, Ferrisburgh, VT.

4. Nat Turner's Uprising (1831).In Southampton County, Virginia, Turner and a group of slaves killed more than fifty whites over a two day period. The Oxford Companion to United States History.

5. Elizabeth and Sonny's Uncle, Joe Warburton was noted for his almost superhuman strength as a young man. Brought up on a farm, he lifted a cow on his shoulders like Joshua did. Also, he and a friend were attacked in New Bedford by four other men and he threw two of them over an automobile and they landed in the street.

6. The Underground Railroad: An Encyclopedia of People, Places, and Operations by Mary Ellen Snodgrass.

7. Fairhaven, MA, History by Christopher J. Richard.
http://fairhavenhistory.blogspot.com/2011/11/fairhaven-chronology-1800-1849.html

8. "The Underground Railroad from Slavery to Freedom", Wilbur Henry Siebert (Randolph mentioned on page 131, as part of underground railroad route to Montpelier.)

9. Abolition and the Underground Railroad in Vermont by Michelle Arnosky Sherburne.

10. Model 1839 Shotgun: 16 gauge smoothbore caliber, 6 shots single action. Serial numbers from 1 to about 225. Manufactured in 1839 to 1841. Weight = 9 pounds, 4 ounces. Markings on barrel = Patent Arms M'g. Co. Paterson, N. J. - Colt's Pt. –

11. Vermont's Constitution of 1777, CHAPTER I, A DECLARATION OF THE RIGHTS OF THE INHABITANTS OF THE STATE OF VERMONT: I., THAT all men are born equally free and independent, and have certain natural, inherent and unalienable rights, amongst which are the enjoying and defending life and liberty; acquiring, possessing and protecting property, and pursuing and obtaining happiness and safety. Therefore, no male person, born in this country, or brought from over sea, ought to be holden by law, to serve any person, as a servant, slave or apprentice, after he arrives to the age of twenty-one Years, nor female, in like manner, after she arrives to the age of eighteen years, unless they are bound by their own consent, after they arrive to such age, or bound by law, for the payment of debts, damages, fines, costs, or the like.

12. Orleans County Historical Society. http://oldstonehousemuseum.org/twilight-bio/ and Wikipedia https://en.wikipedia.org/wiki/Alexander_Twilight

12a. This is a photo of Justin Morgan's original gravestone. It is located in the Randolph Historical Society Museum.

12b. The Morgan horse (Figure) is buried on the former Marilyn Childs' farm in Chelsea, Vermont.

13. Vermont Women, Native Americans & African Americans by Cynthia D. Bittinger.

14. "Bound For the Promised Land: Harriet Tubman, Portrait of an American Hero" by Kate Clifford Larson, Ph.D. http://www.harriettubmanbiography.com/harriet-tubman-myths-and-facts.html

15. Ginny-town was a place at the north end of Sycamore St. in Fairhaven, MA, where Gypsies (or Romani people) made their encampment during Summer months. Sonny has memories of the Gypsies but the best recollections are from his eldest sister Doris who now lives in Alaska. She remembers them driving their wagons past our house on Sycamore St., decked out in their gaily colored costumes, selling their wares. Further research in this area concludes that the original spelling for this place was more likely "Jenny-town." Records show that a man named Jenny, deeded acreage to the town of Fairhaven in this area.

16. Poems attributed to Helen Haskell, Elizabeth Hatcher, and other poems like "Tom's Story", "Captain's Log", and pieces like Fortune Teller, and Side Show, were written by Elizabeth Palm.

17. Poems attributed to Joshua Haskell (or Elisha and Caleb Haskell) were written by George "Sonny" Holt.

18. Fairhaven, MA, History – Chronology 1800-1849.

19. The authors, grew up in Fairhaven, MA from the 1930s to the 1950s and became familiar with the story about John Manjiro (or John Mung as he was known in the 1840s) by visits to the Millicent Library, seeing the displays and reading the account of the rescue by Captain Whitfield. However, further research and reading, especially the following references have broadened their knowledge. Whitfield's first residence was at 11 Cherry St. which was renovated in 2009 and dedicated as the Whitfield-Manjiro Friendship House.

20. "Drifting Toward the Southeast," a translation of John Manjiro's autobiography by Junji KiDavidai and Junya Nagakuni, published 2003 by Spinner Publications. Also appeared as a story on page C3 of The Standard-Times on May 25, 2003.

21. "The Life and Times of John Manjiro" by Donald R. Bernard, published 1992 by McGraw Hill.

22. Poverty Point (Old Oxford Village – part of Fairhaven). Oxford Village was the business and shipbuilding center as early as 1710. At least 15 great ships were built in the yards at the point and whalers set out directly from Oxford. With the construction of the New Bedford Bridge in 1790, transport to the open sea was cut off plunging the area into economic collapse, thus the name Poverty Point was associated with the area. Most of the commerce moved south to the growing Fair-Haven Village.
http://www.fairhaven-ma.gov/Pages/FairhavenMA_Visitor/Poverty%20Point%20Brochure%202013.pdf

23. Extensive research was done on the Amistad story to portray as accurate an account as possible of the facts surrounding this landmark case. The most factual material came from transcripts of the proceedings at the Supreme Court as well as Circuit and District courts. Newspaper accounts of the time were read and many excellent Internet sources provided a wealth of material, for examples; "Exploring Amistad at Mystic Seaport" http://www.mysticseaport.org/search/?q=amistad and "Famous American Trials, Amistad Trials, 1839 – 1840, by Douglas Linder." http://www.law.umkc.edu/faculty/projects/ftrials/amistad/AMISTD.HTM"

24. A good description of the slave ship Tecora was found in the "Maritime Digital Encyclopedia Project" founded and maintained by Frederic Logghe. It is interesting to note that Logghe, in turn, references "Wikipedia" but he makes no mention of the following text contained in the current version of Wikipedia, i.e., "At times when supplies ran low, the crew would chain 30-40 slaves and attach a heavy weight at the end, then throw it over board, forcing the chained Africans into the water to drown." (Author's note: This incident, although shown in the movie version of Amistad, has been disputed by some authorities. Slave ship Captains ensured that they had more than enough food to last the voyage. However, there were instances when a slave ship did this to all the slaves on board to destroy the "evidence" if they were about to be captured by a British ship---still a horrific happening.)

25. "The Captured Slaves," New York Morning Herald, 2 September, 1839.

26. From a collection of Charlotte Cowles letters at the Connecticut Historical Society. Letter cited is March 24th 1841.

27. Riverside Cemetery, 274 Main St., Fairhaven. Created in 1850 by Warren Delano II, the grandfather of President Franklin Delano Roosevelt.

27.a http://www.livescience.com/44512-gypsy-culture.html

28. In this same way, Sonny and his teenage friends brought fish back to Fairhaven in their Dory, from the New Bedford fishing piers.

29. Sonny's father taught him how to catch crabs using this method.

30. Sonny and Elizabeth's mother and grandmother prepared dandelion greens this way. Their grandmother also made dandelion wine which was bright yellow in color.

31. Sonny, Elizabeth and their siblings, as children, ate periwinkles this same way.

32. Carnivals nineteenth century: http://en.wikipedia.org/wiki/Freak_show.

32.a Library of Congress photo collection. Slaves of the rebel Genl. Thomas F. Drayton, Hilton Head, S.C.

33. "The Factory Girls" A collection of writings on life and struggles in the New England factories of the 1840s by the Factory Girls themselves, and the story in their own words, of the first trade unions of women workers in the United States. Edited by Philip S. Foner, Published 1977 by the University of Illinois Press. An approximation of working conditions, wages, boarding house life, etc. (as represented in Lily's letters) were gained from this publication.

33.a While Sonny was in High School, he worked the night shift in a mill, running two quilting machines at one time. Work was hard and pay was minimal.

34. Feeney: Christmas And Vermont. Interview by Vince Feeny, Vermont Public Radio 12/21/2010. http://www.vpr.net/episode/50136/feeney-christmas-vermont/
Also see ref: http://www.history.com/topics/christmas/santa-claus

35. The Journal of George Fox, first published in 1694, after editing by Thomas Ellwood—with a preface by William Penn.

36. Discovering Black Vermont - African American Farmers in Hinesburgh, 1790-1890 by Elise A. Guyette, Publication Year: 2010.

36.a See **Historical Note 3: Early Black Settlers on Lincoln Hill, Vermont.**

36.b. Narrative of Sojourner Truth a Northern Slave, Emancipated from Bodily Servitude by the State of New York, in 1828. With a Portrait. Boston: Printed for the Author. 1850.

36.c Library of Congress. Sojourner Truth, three-quarter length portrait, standing, wearing spectacles, shawl, and peaked cap, right hand resting on cane. (cropped)

37. Taunton Lunatic Asylum. https://en.wikipedia.org/wiki/Taunton_State_Hospital Taunton, MA.

38. Edmund Burke, 18th Century statesman, England.

38.a http://www.quakersintheworld.org/quakers-in-action/15

39. Dred Scott Case: In this ruling, the U.S. Supreme Court stated that slaves were not citizens of the United States and, therefore, could not expect any protection from the Federal Government or the courts. The opinion also stated that Congress had no authority to ban slavery from a Federal territory. https://www.ourdocuments.gov/doc.php?doc=29

40. Acts and Resolves passed by the General Assembly of the State of Vermont, at the October Session, 1858, Bradford: Joseph D. Clark, Printer 1858, pages 67-68. "Resolved further, by the Senate and House of Representatives, That the doctrine maintained by a majority of the judges of the Supreme Court, in the case of Dred Scott, that slavery now exists, by virtue of the Constitution of the United States . . . has no warrant in the Constitution, or in the legislative or judicial history of this country. Resolved, that these extra-judicial opinions of the Supreme Court of the United States are a dangerous usurpation of power, and have no binding authority upon Vermont, or the people of the United States."

41. Vermont Act 37, passed in 1858 "An Act to secure freedom to all persons within this State." Sec. 5. Neither descent, near or remote, from an African, whether such African is or may have been a slave or not, nor color of skin or complexion, shall disqualify any person from being, or prevent any person from becoming, a citizen of this State, nor deprive such person of the rights and privileges thereof. Sec. 6. Every person who may have been held as a slave, who shall come or be brought or be in this State, with or without the consent of his or her master or mistress, or who shall come to be brought, or be involuntarily, or in any way, in this State, shall be free. Sec. 7 Every person who shall hold, or attempt to hold, in this State, in slavery, or as a slave, any person mentioned as a slave in the sixth section of this act, or any free person, in any form, or for any time, however short, under the pretense that such person is or has been a slave, shall, on conviction thereof, be imprisoned in the State prison for a term not less than on year nor more than fifteen years, and be fined not exceeding two thousand dollars. https://www.sec.state.vt.us/media/64796/Act37_1858.pdf

42. "Narrative of the Life of Frederick Douglass, an American Slave," Written by Frederick Douglass, 1845.

43. "Harriet, The Moses of Her People, 1886" by Sarah Bradford.

43.a Pencil enhanced digital photo, by Sonny.

44. The history of Braintree, Vermont: By Henry Royce Bass – Garrison's Visit. pages 46-47. This visit occurred one month after President Lincoln issued the preliminary Emancipation Proclamation.

44.a Africans in America, Narative, Part 4. http://www.pbs.org/wgbh/aia/part4/4p1550.html

45. Medal of Honor Recipient - Peck, Cassius, Private, Company F, 1st U.S. Sharpshooters. Place and date: Near Blackburn's Ford, Va., 19 September 1862. Date of issue: 12 October 1892. Citation: Took command of such soldiers as he could get and attacked and captured a Confederate battery of 4 guns. Also, while on a reconnaissance, overtook and captured a Confederate soldier. Entered Service in the US Army from West Randolph, VT. Died: July 12, 1913 at the age of 71. Buried in Brookfield Cemetery.

46. 1st Vermont Cavalry Regimental History by William L. Greenleaf. Although Elisha Haskell is a fictitious character the companies and cavalry regiments and their battles were real events as described by Greenleaf. http://vermontcivilwar.org/units/ca/

47. Excerpts, with names changed, from a Civil War letter written by Charles F. Bancroft to Clarissa Bancroft, dated January 11, 1862. http://cdi.uvm.edu/collections/item/cwvhsBancroftCharles07

47.a The Devil's Own Work: The Civil War Draft Riots and the Fight to Reconstruct America. by Barnet Schecter.

48. Libby Prison, Richmond, Virginia, Official Publication #12, Richmond Civil War Centennial Committee, 1961- 1965, no copyright claimed, but the original was compiled by R. W. Wiatt, Jr. http://www.censusdiggins.com/prison_libby.html

49. Bio. of Gen. Kilpatrick, by Dr. Jay Schroeder. http://www.tennessee-scv.org/camp72/biographies.html

50. Some battle events taken from Journal of Maj. Gen. Gouverneur K. Warren, U. S. Army, Commanding Fifth Army Corps. MAY 4---JUNE 12, 1864---Campaign from the Rapidan to the James River, Va http://www.civilwarhome.com/warrenwilderness.htm

51. The Orange County Eagle was started in Randolph in 1865 and its name was changed to the Green Mountain Herald in 1873.

52. "The Confederacy" A Macmillan Information Now Encyclopedia, article by Orville Vernon Burton and Patricia Dora Bonnin.

53. In 1848, Frederick Douglass attended the Seneca Falls Convention in New York, the only Black person attending. When a motion was made by Elizabeth Cady Stanton to pass a resolution to ask for women's suffrage, Douglass announced that he was in favor of such a resolution, stating that it would not be fair for him to vote as a Black man if women were not also provided the same right.

54. Randolph, Vermont, Herald and News, Thursday, 2 June 1910, p. 1. Randolph: Death of Ben Robinson, once a Slave, He is buried in South View Cemetery in Randolph. He appears in the story as "Ben Roberts." and Bill Holman, the Lieutenant who brought him home appears as "Bill Hollinger."

55. Joseph R. Laplante, a staff writer for the New Bedford MA, Standard Times wrote about the 54th Regiment and their heroics during the Civil War (October 2009) – although Caspar and Rufus are fictional characters, Frederick Douglass's two sons were actually members of the 54th Regiment.

56. A great deal of credit goes to the oldstoneschool.blogspot.com, as well as the Manjiro-Whitfield Society, Inc., the Fairhaven, MA Office of Tourism and previous reference notes 19, 20, and 21.

Added note 1. William Wilburforce along with Thomas Clarkson were two English abolitionists that led the fight against the British slave trade for twenty-six years until the passage of the Slave Trade Act of 1807. In later years, Wilberforce supported the campaign for the complete abolition of slavery. That campaign led to the British Slavery Abolition Act of 1833. English Quakers and Evangelicals were also strong advocates against slavery during this same time period.

Added note 2. To be as faithful as possible to actual slave dialects of the 1800s, the authors studied recordings contained in "Voices From the Days of Slavery" at the Library of Congress and other sources such as "Army Life in a Black Regiment," by Thomas Wentworth Higginson. Higginson's work is valuable because he wrote down the speech patterns of black soldiers as close as possible, according to the conversations he had with those soldiers (former slaves) at the time they were speaking. The latter reference also has numerous songs sung by these soldiers during the civil war.

Added note 3. "African Americans in Addison County, Charlotte, and Hinesburgh, Vermont, 1790–1860." This is a very detailed and well researched paper by Jane Williamson, the Director of the Rokeby Museum in Ferrisburgh, Vermont.

Added note 4. Although the locales in "Run Away to Glory" are set primarily in New England and in the towns of Randolph, VT and Fairhaven/New Bedford MA, the reader is encouraged to read "Bound for Canaan" by Fergus M. Bordewich. His novel provides a comprehensive look at the Underground Railroad from a national perspective and has been exhaustively researched.

Bibliography

Narrative of Sojourner Truth a Northern Slave, Emancipated from Bodily Servitude by the State of New York, in 1828. With a Portrait. Boston: Printed for the Author. 1850.

Bound for Canaan, The Epic Story of the Underground Railroad, America's First Civil Rights Movement, by Fergus M. Bordewich. 2005.

Narrative of the Life of Frederick Douglass: An American Slave, by Frederick Douglass. 1845.

To be a Slave, by Julius Lester. 1968.

The Underground Railroad: An Encyclopedia of People, Places, and Operations, by Mary Ellen Snodgrass. 2008.

The Underground Railroad from Slavery to Freedom, A Comprehensive History, by Wilbur Henry Siebert. 1898.

The Life and Times of John Manjiro, by Donald R. Bernard. 1992.

Abolition and the Underground Railroad in Vermont, by Michelle Arnosky Sherburne. 2013.

Vermont Women, Native Americans & African Americans: Out of the Shadows of History, by Cynthia D. Bittinger. 2012.

Slaves in the Family, by Edward Ball. 1998.

Drifting Toward the Southeast, a translation of John Manjiro's autobiography, by Junji KiDavidai and Junya Nagakuni. 2003.

Bound For the Promised Land: Harriet Tubman, Portrait of an American Hero, by Kate Clifford Larson. 2004.

The Factory Girls, A collection of writings on life and struggles in the New England factories of the 1840s by, the Factory Girls themselves, Edited by Philip S. Foner. 1977.

The Journal of George Fox, edited by Thomas Ellwood. First published in London, 1694.

Discovering Black Vermont: African American Farmers in Hinesburgh, 1790–1890, by Elise A. Guyette. 2010.

Harriet, The Moses of Her People, by Sarah Bradford, 1886.

The Devil's Own Work: The Civil War Draft Riots and the Fight to Reconstruct America. By, Barnet Schecter. 2007.

The history of Braintree, Vermont, including a memorial of families that have resided in town, by Henry Royce Bass. 1883.

CPSIA information can be obtained
at www.ICGtesting.com
Printed in the USA
LVOW07s0154200617
538694LV00001B/140/P

9 781503 136175